AFTERSHOCK

Also by Philip Donlay

The Donovan Nash Novels

Deadly Echoes

Zero Separation

Code Black

Category Five

AFTERSHOCK

A Novel

PHILIP DONLAY

Longboat Key, Florida

ISBN: 978-1-60809-139-3

Published in the United States of America by Oceanview Publishing
Longboat Key, Florida

www.oceanviewpub.com
10 9 8 7 6 5 4 3 2 1

PRINTED IN THE UNITED STATES OF AMERICA

For Rebecca "Bex" Norgaard Peterson

There's not a single scenario where I get to where I am today without you in my life. You have my eternal thanks.

ACKNOWLEDGMENTS

A heartfelt thanks goes to the gracious people I met during my time in Guatemala. You and your country are beautiful, and I couldn't have written this book without your hospitality.

For their patience, friendship, and insight, I offer my deepest thanks to Scott Erickson, Bo Lewis, Gary Kaelson, Pamela Sue Martin, Richard Drury, Nancy Gilson, Mary Clare Sullivan, Kerry Leep, and Brian Bellmont. You've played a bigger part in all of this than you'll ever know.

For always giving me the unvarnished truth as only family can, I want to thank my brother, Chris; my parents, Cliff and Janet; and especially my son, Patrick. You're an indispensable group of gifted people.

A very special thanks goes out to Dr. Philip Sidell and Dr. D. P. Lyle, for their remarkable medical expertise. As always, I'm most appreciative on many levels. Thanks also goes to my agent, Kimberley Cameron, and her team of talented professionals. You all do amazing work.

I'd also like to thank the experts, the people who shed light on a myriad of subjects. Shanna Schmitt, for educating me on all things volcanic, which I promise was an arduous job, and you did it superbly. Samantha Fischer, Al Iverson, Vicki Harlander, and Maddee James, you're all amazing, and I'm the first to admit that I couldn't do what I do without your efforts.

Finally, to Oceanview Publishing, the people who turn my words into books. Utmost praise goes to Patricia and Bob Gussin, Frank Troncale, David Ivester, and Emily Baar. I know there isn't a better team anywhere. Thank you all.

Last but not least, to Susan Hayes, you will be missed.

AFTERSHOCK

PROLOGUE

The mist swirled in the treetops and the steep trail rose into the opaque sky, then vanished altogether. Stephanie VanGelder felt both wary and excited. Towering above her, unseen in the fog, were three volcanoes; one of them, named Atitlán, was showing signs of life after lying dormant for nearly one hundred sixty years. The sounds of the forest were muted and soft in the damp air. In the gray, overcast Guatemalan morning, each unidentifiable noise made her hesitate and wonder, at least on some primal level, if the sound was coming from the volcano. She was thrilled to once again be heading to a photo shoot, and a little apprehensive that the assignment was an active volcano.

Stephanie felt the burn in her lungs and her legs. She was breathing hard in the thin air and tried to convince herself that she wasn't out of shape, that it was only a combination of the steep path and the ever-present camera equipment she carried. They'd been climbing for nearly two hours. She continued to put one foot in front of the other as she trudged up the damp trail, determined to keep pace with Rick Mathews, who was a dozen paces in front of her.

Rick was a volcanologist with the United States Geological Survey. He was tall and muscular, with seemingly endless energy. His intelligent eyes dominated his angular face—and he seemed on the verge of a perpetual smile. His head was topped with a mass of curly black hair badly in need of a trim. In fact, he needed both a haircut and a shave. His attitude was casual and carefree, reminding her of an overgrown puppy. She joined up with this group because the USGS was keenly interested in the recent signs of life from Atitlán, one of the three peaks that made up the southern shore of the lake, and one of five active volcanoes in Guatemala. The job this morning was to hike up the mountain and place a seismometer in a predetermined spot to better follow the volcano. Stephanie registered satisfaction at the sight of sweat beginning to soak the collar of Rick's shirt. He was in his mid-thirties, a good ten years younger than she.

Behind her was Oliver Pelletier, an aspiring volcanologist who had eagerly volunteered to accompany Rick on this journey. In his mid-twenties, Oliver was short and very fair-skinned. His rounded face was smooth and his cheeks flushed easily. From what little Stephanie had gathered, he'd recently joined the USGS as an intern. Stephanie didn't know much beyond the fact that he was from Canada, and that he was working on his PhD in geophysics. Oliver seemed quiet and reserved, but he whistled softly as they climbed—she wondered if it was because he was musically inclined, or just nervous.

A young armed guard brought up the rear of their small group. Quiet, with a quick smile, he dressed in civilian clothes and toted a rifle, but, as they climbed higher into the foothills and left the town of Santiago Atitlán behind, she decided she didn't mind the idea of protection. The State Department reports of the general lawlessness in the country had been disturbing. This part of Guatemala was fairly remote and the USGS staff in Guatemala City had assured her that their small group would be safe.

"We're almost there," Rick called over his shoulder. He held up the small GPS unit in his hand to confirm. "It's just beyond the next rise."

Stephanie felt a little deflated—she hoped they would climb above the cloud layer or that the cloud deck would show some signs of burning off. She wanted a mix of sunshine and clouds to shoot. Rick warned her it was the rainy season and that the sun was somewhat elusive this time of year. Still, even with the subdued light, observing these two scientists installing a seismic monitor in the rugged terrain would go a long way in her photo essay documenting the efforts of volcano researchers.

Atitlán had been considered dormant until a week ago. There had been a series of earthquake swarms detected by the USGS lab in Guatemala City, followed by a cloud of steam and ash released from a vent at the summit of the mountain. The nearest seismic arrays were focused on Mt. Fuego and Mt. Pacaya, the active volcanoes located just outside Guatemala City. In a race to get a more accurate pulse of the mountain, to try to discover what may or may not be happening deep underground, Rick and Oliver were "wiring the mountain," as they called it, and Stephanie had been granted the opportunity to photograph the process.

Stephanie had been a professional photographer for twenty-five of her forty-eight years, and she frowned as she studied the light coming through the swirling mist at the tops of the trees. As happened so often in her line of work, the site and Mother Nature would dictate how she approached the subjects.

"This is the place!" Rick stopped and spread his arms as if he were giving the clearing his own personal blessing. "Perfect."

Stephanie joined Rick at the edge of what amounted to a small cornfield carved out of the surrounding vegetation. She turned and looked north, toward the lake. Through the trees she could just make out the water far below, and she felt a slight twinge of vertigo as she saw how far they'd climbed. Above her she caught sight of a sliver of blue sky through the drifting clouds. They might have sunshine yet.

"Oliver," Rick said, as the two scientists stood together on the narrow path and surveyed the immediate terrain, "I think if we set up the equipment over there, at the edge of this field next to those trees, it'll be fairly unobtrusive."

"I agree," Oliver replied.

"Which way is it—the volcano?" Stephanie asked.

Rick pulled himself up to his full six-foot-three height, spun his baseball cap smartly until the bill was pointed backward, and pivoted on one heel to his left. He put out his arm and raised his thumb as if making a precision measurement. "Up above us we have the tallest of the three volcanoes, Atitlán, the object of our immediate concern. It rises to nearly eleven thousand, six hundred feet above sea level. Slightly to the north we have Tolimán, its cone is a shade over ten thousand, three hundred feet in height, and behind us, across the bay from Santiago, is San Pedro, another ten-thousand foot volcano. These three volcanoes form the southern edge of Lake Atitlán, which is actually a huge volcanic crater that filled up with water. The noted author Aldous Huxley once called this place the most beautiful on earth."

"I might agree with him—this is amazing." Stephanie shrugged herself free of her backpack and lowered it gently to the ground. "You do what you need to do, and I'll maneuver around and see where I can get the best shot."

"No problem," Rick replied. "We'll be over here where it's fairly level, just before the path starts back up the mountain."

Stephanie guessed that the clearing was a little less than an acre. It gave her enough room to maneuver and capture a variety of angles. While Rick and Oliver began to shed their gear, she slung two cameras over her shoulder and moved up the incline to shoot down the hill toward the lake. The air was perfectly still, and as she moved away from the two scientists and their conversation, she could hear the sounds of birds high in the trees. It took her several minutes to find exactly where she wanted to start, carefully eyeing the light and her subjects. Satisfied, she checked her beloved Nikon digital camera, removed the lens cover, and began to frame her shot. Slightly below her, Rick was leaning over, hands on his knees as he discussed something with Oliver. Beyond, shafts of light were penetrating the clouds, creating small irregular shapes of sunlight on the distant water. It was a beautiful sight.

Stephanie began shooting; first she zoomed in on the men, and then adjusted the lens to take in more of the surrounding area. Without taking her eye from the camera, she moved more to her right, then forward, seeing the results through the lens and firing off several exposures. Stephanie focused in for a tight shot of Rick, who was holding up a GPS receiver, a serious expression on his boyish face. She was still adjusting her framing when she saw him jerk his head downhill toward the path, a look of confusion in his eyes. Out of habit, she swung the camera to her left in one fluid motion and found a young girl running up the path. It took Stephanie a moment to understand the girl wasn't running for fun; her youthful features radiated stark fear—she looked like she was fleeing for her life. Stephanie zoomed in on her face, could see the terror in her large brown eyes. The girl was barefoot, wearing a bright red dress and loose-fitting white top. Her long brown hair flew back from her dirty face. Stephanie guessed she was no more than ten years old. Instinctively, her actions honed by years of covering war-torn locations around the world, Stephanie fired off a string of exposures.

Through her lens, Stephanie watched as the girl flung herself at Rick, who had moved to intercept her. She heard shouts, but the voices came outside her framed shot and she was forced to swing her camera back along the trail where the girl had appeared. She found three men charging up the path; they wore makeshift military uniforms. Each of the men moved quickly, rifles at the ready. Stephanie squeezed off three more shots, then swung back smoothly to Rick and the girl as the shouts grew louder.

As if she were completely separate from events, but only thirty yards away, Stephanie crouched to make herself smaller and continued to shoot. She focused on their security guard who had now raised his weapon. He was yelling in Spanish when a bright plume of red erupted from his chest. Stephanie caught the image as the single shot echoed through the clearing. In her viewfinder, Rick was pushing the girl behind him as the gunmen moved closer. Two more gunshots reached her ears, and she saw Rick's knees buckle, two crimson stains spreading out from the center of his USGS sweatshirt. The force of the bullets staggered him backward and he fell to the ground.

Oliver moved sideways, reaching for the girl, when a small

round hole appeared on his forehead followed by a plume of red mist from the back of his head. Wordlessly, he crumpled to the ground, landing face first in the dirt. Fighting her horror, Stephanie tried to make herself invisible behind the vegetation. Afraid to move, she watched as one of the gunmen grabbed the young girl around the waist and held her there as she flailed helplessly in midair.

Stephanie knew she hadn't been seen. Carefully, she began to inch backward toward the trees. If she could make it to the heavier foliage, she could disappear into the forest. If she panicked, she knew she'd be killed along with the others. She tried to visualize how far she would have to circle around to make her way back down the mountain for help. She stayed low, backpedaling in the soft dirt toward the trees. She never took her eyes off the armed men as she inched her way toward safety. Stephanie hesitated as she sensed something behind her, more of a feeling than a sound, then she felt cold steel pressing into the tender skin just behind her left ear. She wanted to scream, but no sound came from her throat—it was as if in her final moments she'd been robbed of the ability to speak. She silently pleaded with the gods to let her live—but all she heard was the dry metallic click of a gun being cocked.

CHAPTER ONE

Donovan heard the helicopter long before he could see it; the sound echoing off the granite cliffs told him the chopper was coming low and fast. Probably the forest service. Several fires had been touched off by lightning a few days ago and aerial activity had picked up in the valley.

The morning sun had just peeked above the mountain tops in southwest Montana. Donovan was thigh deep in the cold water of the Bitterroot River, working his casts upstream toward an eddy and the big cutthroat trout he'd seen feeding on the surface. He made two false casts and then set the dry fly perfectly so as to drift naturally within striking range of the cutthroat. The fish inhaled the fly and Donovan set the hook and began stripping line to keep the tension. The fish powered downstream, using the current to take back the line that Donovan had fought to win. Forced to move downstream to stay with the fish, he maneuvered past a fallen log when the unmarked helicopter burst from behind the cottonwoods and made a tight turn overhead.

Donovan forgot about the fish, dropped his fly rod, and reached under his left arm for his holstered .40-caliber Sig Sauer. There was no need to jack a shell into the chamber. The gun was always ready. Slowed by his chest waders, Donovan ran up the path toward the cabin. He caught another glance of the helicopter through the treetops. It slowed to nearly a hover, and Donovan was convinced they were landing in the clearing next to his cabin, effectively cutting him off from communications and the remain-

der of his arsenal. There was no cell phone reception this far up
the West Fork River valley and, in a rare lapse, he'd left his satellite
phone in its charger.

The whine from the helicopter's turbine engine eased back to
idle, telling Donovan it was on the ground. From the size of the
helicopter there wouldn't be more than five on board, including
the pilot. The Sig held fourteen rounds. Donovan slowed his pace,
his rubber-soled wading boots moving him silently toward the
intruders. He watched as a solitary man stepped out of the helicopter, seemingly unafraid. He was tall and solid, dressed in jeans
and a leather jacket. His dark glasses made recognition impossible.
Donovan guessed he was in his early thirties, both of his hands
were empty, but he could easily be carrying a concealed pistol. In
Montana, he would be the exception if he wasn't. The pilot sat behind the controls and made no move to exit the machine as the
engine idled.

"Mr. Nash!" The man called out in the direction of the river.
"We saw you as we flew over. I'm a friend of your wife, Dr. Lauren
McKenna. She sent me to find you. It's urgent we talk."

Donovan surveyed the scene, two men against his fourteen
rounds. He'd spent months practicing with the Sig, and was confident that if the interlopers caused any problems, the advantage
was his. He lowered the Sig to his side and walked into the clearing. For Lauren to enlist someone to track him down from his
self-imposed exile was more than worrisome.

"Who are you?" Donovan called out as he neared, mindful
of the spinning rotor blades.

"I'm Special Agent Gregory Charles, Federal Bureau of Investigation. I understand I'm intruding, but please holster your
weapon."

"As soon as I see some ID," Donovan said, as he closed the
distance between them while holding a position that allowed him
to keep an eye on both men.

Agent Charles slowly reached inside his jacket pocket and
pulled out his FBI credentials. He handed them to Donovan. "Dr.

McKenna told me to expect this kind of greeting. I know what you've been through and, actually, I don't blame you, but we're losing valuable time. Can I brief you in the air?"

Donovan handed Agent Charles his ID and slid the Sig back into its holster. "I'm not going anywhere until you tell me what this is about. Start by telling me how you know my wife."

"I once did liaison work with the Defense Intelligence Agency. I met Lauren while working with her department on some classified matters. Since then, she's needed a few favors from inside the Bureau, as you both have. This is another of those favors."

"What's her boss' name?"

"Deputy Director Calvin Reynolds."

"Okay, why are you here?" Donovan felt his mistrust of the man diminish. He at least knew the right names.

"First of all, I need you to understand I'm not here in any official capacity. Today's my day off. Lauren called me early this morning. She said she'd chartered a helicopter and asked me to come get you."

"How did you know where to find me?" Donovan couldn't drop his suspicions. In the last year he'd almost been killed by a terrorist, and most recently, an enemy from his past had nearly destroyed everything Donovan held dear. People he cared about had died. That's why he was out here in the wilderness of Montana—he'd needed some perspective.

"Three months ago she alerted me to the fact that you'd rented this place. As a favor, she asked me to keep a general watch on the activity down here in the valley."

"Sounds like her," Donovan replied, not knowing whether to be touched by the gesture or pissed off that she was having him watched. "Now, what does my estranged wife think is so important that she's sent you out here to get me?"

"A Stephanie VanGelder is in Guatemala on a photo shoot. She's missing. It's a suspected kidnapping."

The words sent a sick icy chill straight to the pit of Donovan's stomach. He resisted the urge to lean over and put his hands on his knees for support. Stephanie was one of Donovan's closest friends—she was like family, a younger sister—they'd practically grown up together. She was the niece of William VanGelder, the man who Donovan thought of as his father.

"What can I do to help?" Agent Charles asked. "Do you need assistance to close up the house? We're flying from here to Missoula. A chartered jet will be waiting to take you to Washington. Your wife has made all the arrangements. She told me to tell you William needs you, but that he doesn't know you're coming."

"Give me five minutes to grab a few things and we'll be out of here," Donovan said as he turned and ran for the house. The moment he was inside, he shed his fishing vest followed by his waders. He ran to his bedroom, slipped on a pair of khakis, a clean shirt, a pair of loafers, grabbed the go-bag he kept packed for emergencies and tossed it on the bed. He slid in the framed picture of his daughter Abigail he kept on his nightstand, his Sig, and two extra clips of ammo. He caught a glimpse of himself in the mirror and stopped. He was lean and hard from a summer of chopping wood, fishing, and hiking the Bitterroot Mountains. He was toned and strengthened, and in better shape now than he was at thirty. His full beard was peppered with gray, as was his hair that easily fell past his ears, a by-product of cutting himself off from civilization. A few weeks earlier he'd turned fifty, but the reflection was that of a younger man. He'd shave and get a haircut when he could. He made a mental note to call the real estate agent and have her come and close up the house. He zipped the leather bag, snatched his briefcase, wallet, phone, and keys, then ran for the helicopter.

When the pilot spotted him, the turbine engine immediately began to spool toward full power. The moment the door was closed and he was strapped in his seat, the helicopter lifted off, pivoted smartly, and began to accelerate down the valley.

Donovan wore a headset against the noise of the helicopter. He stared at the shadow of the helicopter as it raced across the trees, rivers, and hay fields of Southwestern Montana. Lost in the maelstrom of his thoughts, he inevitably spun back in time to when he'd last seen Stephanie. It had been a little over three months ago. They'd been together in the San Juan Islands in Washington State. He'd been there to pay his final respects to a friend, and Stephanie had shown up unannounced and helped him through a difficult time. She ended up staying with him a week. She'd traveled with him to Montana and helped him set up the leased cabin. They'd talked at length about death and transition, his separation from Lauren and the state of his marriage.

They also spent hours discussing her return to professional photography. He'd urged her to pick up her camera again and to get back out in the world. She was a brilliant artist. A decade ago, her photo reporting from Africa, chronicling child soldiers, had put her in the running for a Pulitzer. The fact that she'd been shooting pictures in Guatemala made him feel even worse, as if his nudging had led to her disappearance.

He couldn't imagine what his longtime friend William must be going through. Stephanie was all that was left of his family and the two were close. He doted on her, as would any uncle.

Donovan thought back to when he first met Stephanie. They were just kids, brought together because his family was close to her Uncle William. She grew up in London, but spent almost all of her summers with William—Donovan remembered her natural grace and athleticism were trumped only by her keen artistic talents. From the time she was ten, she always carried a camera that her Uncle William had bought for her, taking pictures of everything except other people. Her habit of waving him out of her field of view was maddening, and he could remember trying to peek into her shots, only to receive a verbal tongue lashing. In the end, what Donovan most liked about Stephanie was that she could mix and float in and out of any different social setting. A proper upper-crust debutante one moment; the next, yelling and cursing at him as they chased each other through the trees and meadows on his family's country estate in Northern Virginia.

When he was fourteen, Donovan had lost his parents at sea. He'd been the only survivor as their private yacht, caught in a storm, began to break up and take on water. It had been William who'd flown halfway around the world to be at his side after he'd been thought lost, and, not long after that, Stephanie had made it clear that she was there for him as well. In those dark days, she once described to him that she felt like they were cousins, and then later revised her position and pronounced that they were more like brother and sister. She was one of the few bright spots in a very difficult time in his life. Donovan loved her and would do anything for her.

She'd been instrumental in getting him to talk about the loss of his parents. William tried, as did many others, but it was Stephanie who got through to him, helped him honor his grief, yet keep pushing forward. Two years later, her own family was killed in an automobile accident on the M4 outside London. It was July, and Stephanie had been with him and William in Virginia when they received the news. The three of them boarded the Concorde, and Donovan remembered the depths of her sorrow and loss as they flew to England faster than the speed of sound.

They each had seen how quickly the universe could snuff out the life of a loved one, and the specter of that violence created an even tighter bond. As time had passed, the one element they always had in common was the fact that they were both identically wounded.

Donovan noticed the change in the sound and speed of the helicopter. The Missoula airport was straight ahead. After Donovan said his good-bye to Agent Charles, he walked across the ramp toward what looked to be a brand new Falcon 900, the airplane that would have him in Northern Virginia in three hours.

He settled into his seat and his thoughts drifted not to Stephanie, but to Meredith Barnes. A woman he'd loved and lost twenty years ago in Costa Rica. Instead of suppressing the inevitable memories of Meredith, he allowed his guilt, anguish, and rage to wash over him. It was a volatile mixture that threatened to undo him, but it also provided an almost divine focus and clarity of purpose. Meredith was dead and Stephanie was alive. Despite what William, or Lauren, or anyone else thought of his current emotional state—Donovan promised himself that nothing on earth was going to stop him from going to Guatemala. Regardless of the cost, he'd do everything in his power to save her. The clock was ticking, and rescuing Stephanie became as important as if he were trying to save his own life. He'd do whatever it took—even if he died trying.

CHAPTER TWO

Donovan deplaned in front of the Eco-Watch hangar at Washington Dulles International Airport. He'd spent his time on the chartered flight on the computer, pulling up everything he could find about Guatemala. He'd found it odd that Stephanie's disappearance wasn't mentioned in the news. He'd debated calling Lauren to announce his arrival, but since she was the one who set it up, she knew damn well when he'd land. He decided to wait and talk with her in person.

He let himself into the hangar. On Sunday, no one would be around, which suited Donovan. The hangar was home to Eco-Watch's two highly modified Gulfstream jets. The *Spirit of da Vinci* was out of the country on a research mission in Africa, and the *Spirit of Galileo* was flight-testing a new instrumentation platform in California. Donovan operated under the title of Director of Flight Operations for Eco-Watch. Very few people knew that he'd not only founded the company, but that his hidden fortune also funded parts of the private research organization. Besides the two Gulfstream jets, Eco-Watch operated two ocean-going research ships, and the keel had been laid for a third. One was based in Hawaii and served the Pacific Ocean arena; the other called Norfolk, Virginia, its home port and sailed the Atlantic. Both the Eco-Watch Aviation and the Eco-Watch Marine divisions were booked months and sometimes years in advance.

Donovan walked into his office and found it exactly as he'd

left it all those months ago. Michael had taken over the day-to-day operations, and all that waited on Donovan's desk were several pieces of personal correspondence. He turned to go, but hesitated at the sight of a picture taken the day Eco-Watch had begun. Twelve years earlier, he and Michael had arrived on the ramp outside with the very first Eco-Watch Gulfstream. Standing in front of the jet was the first handful of employees, but the person truly responsible—was missing. Donovan's thoughts once again spun back in time to Meredith Barnes, the woman he couldn't ever seem to bury.

It seemed a lifetime ago they'd met, but in ways it felt like yesterday. In all that time she'd remained the same—the dead earn that privilege. She was still twenty-eight years old, an intelligent, fiery redhead with emerald-green eyes and freckles. A brilliant woman who'd changed the world. First, by her environmentalist-themed bestseller, *One Earth*, then, by her wildly popular television show and string of documentaries about saving this planet we live on—our one earth. She became larger than her accomplishments. She became the face of an exploding environmental movement. Part celebrity, part television star, part global emissary, Meredith flew into the face of any and all opposition to accomplish her goals. Her followers, fueled by a media that loved her, ensured that her message was received by nearly everyone on the planet.

Robert Huntington at the time was a rich, brash young man who'd been elevated to CEO of his family's oil company. He was smart and driven, a shrewd businessman, as was his late father. Robert was also smart enough to surround himself with the best and brightest men in the business. He was a playboy, a high visibility partygoer in Hollywood. It wasn't unusual for his picture to be on the cover of a business magazine the same week he was on the cover of the gossip tabloids. He always seemed to have yet another beautiful A-list actress on his arm, while his wheeling and dealing propelled Huntington Oil into a major powerhouse in the global energy business.

When Robert Huntington met Meredith Barnes, sparks flew. She very publicly tore up a three-million-dollar check he'd written toward her environmental causes and threw the pieces in his face. The media went wild, and Robert Huntington felt as if he'd met his match.

Their relationship progressed slowly and steadily, until they both acknowledged their feelings for one another on a romantic night in New Orleans. Robert had been at a conference dealing with offshore oil platform safety reforms. Despite heavy opposition to his costly recommendations, Robert had promised that Huntington Oil would proceed without a consensus to help create a zero-tolerance attitude toward any type of oil spill.

They were an unlikely power couple—the environmentalist and the oil tycoon. Members of both camps loudly denounced the relationship. There were constant murmurs that he was using her and vice-versa. They didn't care and made future plans for themselves as a couple, as well as their common vision for a better planet. Their entire future came to an abrupt halt when Meredith was kidnapped and murdered at an environmental summit in Costa Rica. Robert Huntington was never a suspect in terms of the authorities, but in the public eye he may as well have pulled the trigger. Robert Huntington murdered the world's beloved Meredith Barnes, and no amount of evidence would ever change the public's mind.

The fallout was massive. Crowds threatened Huntington Oil, there were bomb threats, violence against employees, sabotaged equipment in the field. Shareholders demanded Robert's resignation. Almost overnight, Robert Huntington had become the most hated man on earth. The threats became deadly, so much so that Robert wasn't able to attend his fiancée's funeral. Meredith was buried in Monterey, California, and he hadn't been there to mourn or even say good-bye to the woman he loved.

What the public didn't know was that Robert had asked Meredith to marry him. They were waiting to make their announcement until after the Costa Rica meeting. Then, as he tried to grieve the loss of the woman he had planned to spend the rest of his life with, a reporter released a series of photographs depicting him romping on some remote beach with an unidentified blonde, instead of mourning his loss. The images were from years earlier, but the collective shriek of public outrage reached new and more dangerous levels.

Robert withdrew deeper into an alcohol-and-pill-infused depression. His best friend and guardian, William VanGelder, asked him candidly one night if he'd thought about ending his life. Robert admitted that he had. William's response was: "When do you want to get started?" That night marked the beginning of the end of Robert Huntington's life and the beginning of Donovan Nash. Barely three months later, Robert Huntington was killed when the plane he was piloting crashed at sea. A vengeful public cheered, funeral parties were thrown worldwide, the media spread the message that the universe had delivered Robert Huntington the violent ending he deserved.

Donovan tried to shake off the thoughts of Robert and Meredith, but, as always, found it difficult. He still missed Meredith, and he thought about her every day. He didn't miss Robert Huntington. When Robert died, he became a new man, a blank slate, and Donovan had become twice the man that Robert was ever going to be. He'd built Eco-Watch, the preeminent nonprofit, private scientific research organization in the world. He provided funding for university projects, expeditions both on earth and in space. He maintained a fleet of state-of-the-art platforms, be it Gulfstream jets, helicopters, or ocean-going ships, all for the single purpose of furthering scientific research. Money was never an issue when it came to understanding the planet. He liked to think that Meredith would be proud of him. Eco-Watch was the monument he built to honor Meredith's memory.

He fished out his keys and began the drive home, not exactly sure what he'd find. Would Lauren and Abigail be there, or would she have maintained her distance and gone somewhere else? Their marital stalemate was an ongoing process that defied predictability. He swung onto Pleasant Valley Road, drove past the golf course, and Cox Farms. Up ahead was Virginia Run Elementary School, where he turned left and headed the final few blocks home. As he rounded the gentle curve of their street, he saw a familiar car in the driveway. The vintage green Jaguar belonged to William.

Donovan shut off the car, let himself in the front door, and called out to whoever was inside. He heard the familiar shriek of his four-year-old daughter followed by urgent footfalls as she raced toward the sound of his voice. She rounded the corner, all smiles, her curly reddish-blonde hair flying in the wind when she abruptly stopped, her smile replaced by confusion.

Donovan knelt, he understood his beard and long hair wasn't what she'd expected. "It's okay, Kitten, it's Daddy."

With the reassurance she needed, Abigail flung herself into his arms. Donovan felt the tears well up in his eyes as her little arms clamped fiercely around his neck. He drank in the smell of her shampoo and marveled at how much she'd grown since he'd last seen her. All of the things Skype doesn't allow. Through the separation she'd seemed fine, she'd rolled with the travel, and if what she told Donovan was true, she thought of it all as a grand adventure. His daughter was a dreamer like he was, less analytical than her mother.

Abigail pulled away and gave him a big smooch on the cheek, then touched her skin where the whiskers had rubbed and made a face. She took his hand and began to lead him down the hallway. "Daddy, Mommy and Grandpa are in here. They won't know who you are at first, either. Then I want to show you my room. I'm not a baby anymore, and I have a big bed and a desk. I drew some pictures for you. They're of airplanes. The *da Vinci* and the *Galileo*."

Donovan rounded the corner and found Lauren. She looked like she'd lost weight, and her auburn hair was longer. She looked good, as if being on her own suited her. They hugged, and Donovan kissed her on the cheek. It was then he noticed that her eyes were red. Lauren was not only one of the smartest people he knew; she was also one of the strongest. She was a doctor, a scientist who for the most part looked at the world with a calm sense of methodical reasoning—one of the many things he loved about her.

"I'm glad you're here," she said, as she hesitated a moment and studied his beard and long hair. She reached out and stroked his whiskers, then brushed some of the hair away from his ear. "I like it. Go talk to William. He needs you. He's in the study. I've already heard most of what he thinks might have happened, but you need to hear it as well."

Donovan nodded, though the tone of her voice unsettled him.

"Come, Abigail," Lauren said to her daughter. "Daddy has to talk to Grandpa for a little bit, and then he's all yours. Remember what we're going to do now?"

"Yeah!" Abigail said as she jumped up and down with excitement. "We're going to make Daddy a chocolate cake for his birthday!"

"I'll meet you in the kitchen," Lauren said as she followed Abigail.

Donovan let himself into the study. William was seated on the sofa. As usual, he was wearing one of his trademark tailored suits, complete with vest and carefully knotted tie. Donovan knew he purchased his wardrobe from a small, but exclusive, shop in London. Tall and wiry, William had a head full of shock-white hair and piercing dark eyes that were surrounded by the lines of age. He was seventy-six years old, but as tough and hard-charging as men half his age. Donovan often joked to William that he would outlive them all. In the Washington, DC, inner political sanctum, William was revered by many and outright feared by others. He'd been a special envoy to the State Department for the better part of three decades. William had amassed a huge fortune, first as Donovan's father's right-hand-man at Huntington Oil, then as Robert's.

They'd been inseparable in life and business since Donovan was a boy. William had raised him from the age of fourteen when he'd become his legal guardian. Guided by William's vast experience and expansive view of the world, Donovan knew that nearly everything he'd accomplished was either directly, or indirectly, the result of his relationship with William. He was one of six people in the world who knew the truth—that he was once Robert Huntington.

"Lauren finally admitted she'd contacted you," William stood to meet Donovan. The two men shook hands warmly, and then it quickly turned into a hug. "I had mixed feelings, but I'm glad you're here."

"I came as fast as I could." Donovan pulled back. Etched on William's lined face were dark circles and overall signs of stress, reconfirming Donovan's commitment to help in any way possible.

"How are you, son? Are you okay?" William asked as he looked him up and down.

"I'm fine," Donovan replied. "I took the time off. I needed it. But I'm here to talk about you and what's happened to Stephanie."

William lowered himself back to the sofa. He rubbed his eyes as if trying to compose himself in preparation for what he was about to say. Donovan waited. He knew William well enough to know the statesman was nothing if not deliberate.

"I've already given Lauren a quick version of events as I know them. I'll admit, I have serious reservations about telling you any of this, but in the end I know you'd never forgive me if I kept you in the dark. Four days ago, there was a minor eruption of a long-dormant volcano in Guatemala. As you may or may not know, Stephanie had recently decided to resume her career in photography. At the behest of a former editor, she immediately boarded a plane and flew to Guatemala City, where she joined up with a United States Geological Survey team that was en route to the volcano. That's the last anyone's seen or heard from her. That was twenty-seven hours ago."

"Then what?" Donovan asked, fearing the answer. He could see that William was trying to gauge his next words carefully.

"This morning, the Guatemalan police searched the mountain where the USGS team was headed. They found the bodies of the two scientists and the guard who was assigned to protect them. They'd all been shot and buried in shallow graves. There was no sign of Stephanie."

Donovan shifted uncomfortably, he knew what was coming and could feel the sudden heat as his face went flush. There was a ringing in his ears, and his shoulders slumped as if a great weight had been placed on top of him. His mind raced back and forth between Stephanie and the unavoidable memories of Meredith Barnes. The effect was quick and devastating. Donovan pressed his fingers to his temples as both guilt, sorrow, and anger all fought to consume him.

"We don't know anything for sure," William put his hand on Donovan's shoulder. "She may have escaped. She could simply be out of contact in some village. I can tell from the look on your face I was right in being hesitant to tell you about any of this."

Donovan straightened as if regaining his strength. "I'm fine."

"I understand how you feel, that on many levels this is probably harder on you than it is on me," William said the words quietly, as if he could sense that Donovan was poised between two worlds, fragile. "You've been through a great deal in the last few months, I'd understand if you needed to sit this one out."

"We all went through the same ordeal and survived. That's the last I care to hear about how damaged I might be." Donovan stood abruptly and went toward his desk. "It's already been twenty-seven hours. We can be in Guatemala City later tonight."

"Sit down," William motioned Donovan to come back and join him on the sofa. "I've already been in touch with the State Department. Stephanie and one of the murdered scientists are US citizens, so I've called in a few favors. There is a State Department jet flying us there first thing tomorrow morning."

"I can get us there faster." Donovan picked up the phone and prepared to dial.

"It's not about speed," William said. "It's about making correct, well-thought-out decisions. If we come screaming in on an Eco-Watch jet and start taking names, we've done nothing but draw unwanted attention to ourselves, and perhaps even panic the people who may have Stephanie. Now please, hang up and come sit; listen to what I have to say."

Donovan's impulse to act was at odds with William's calmer, more reasoned approach—a no man's land that Donovan had always hated.

"Put the phone down," William repeated. "If I thought rushing down there would solve anything, I'd already be on my way, and we'd be having this discussion via satellite phone. I've spoken at length with Michael. He has no idea you're here, by the way. I'll leave that for you to explain. Anyway, he informed me that an Eco-Watch mission to Alaska, centered on the volcanic eruption of Mt. Resolute, was scheduled to begin in a few days."

"Yeah," Donovan replied. He thought about the development of the new airborne drone that would aid scientists in observing volcanoes. Michael Ross, the man Donovan had left in charge, was doing exactly what he should be doing—solving problems.

"Michael is canceling the Alaska mission and bringing the entire test to Guatemala. Eco-Watch will have a presence there, but it will be due to the volcanic activity, not the disappearance of my niece. Michael is fully briefed and staffed for the mission. He's going to arrive in Guatemala City as soon as he can. You can fly with me tomorrow on the State Department jet, as an emissary between Eco-Watch and the Guatemalan scientific community. My plan is to work the official diplomatic channels—my position as a diplomat-at-large actually requires that approach. I'm guessing the kidnappers know who Stephanie is and her connection to me. My arrival in a government jet sends a message that I'm ready to do business. She's fine for the moment because everything is static. It's when the deliberations begin that considerations start to shift. It's understandable after your history with Meredith, that waiting is difficult. But together we can cover all the bases and make this happen in a way that works for Stephanie."

Donovan couldn't help but think that the bureaucratic delays and red tape over trying to secure Meredith's release twenty-two years ago were beginning to play themselves out again. If Stephanie were indeed kidnapped, only the name of the country had changed, Guatemala instead of Costa Rica. One set of third-world politics and politicians for another. He had failed before, and Meredith had paid for it with her life.

"I think we should bring Buck into the loop," Donovan said, cell phone still in his hand. "We may need his particular skill set."

"I've already spoken to him. The injuries he received in Alaska are healed. The doctors have cleared him to return to work. He's joining us on tomorrow's flight," William answered. "I'm not taking you down there without a chaperone. Who'd be better at that than Buck?"

Donovan nodded. Howard Buckley, former Navy SEAL, had joined Eco-Watch less than a year ago. Donovan hadn't hesitated for a moment to hire Buck, as he was affectionately called, to head up security for Eco-Watch. He'd become an indispensable member of the Eco-Watch team. They'd need every advantage in Guatemala.

"We'll handle this differently than we did Costa Rica. I promise, which brings me to my next concern. I know I can't talk you out of going with me. I won't even try. Promise me if you come, you'll act within the parameters we decide are best."

Donovan nodded his agreement. He knew his impulsiveness, while at times effective, perhaps wasn't the best play this time around. "You have cash, for a ransom?"

"I've arranged for four million dollars. We'll take it with us under the umbrella of diplomatic immunity. If they want more, we'll have to adjust. I'm expecting more information on the situation from the embassy this evening," William said. "I think we'll have a better picture in the morning."

"What time does the flight leave?" Donovan asked.

"I'll have the driver swing by and pick you up at five-thirty. We're leaving out of Dulles, which saves us the drive across town to Andrews Air Force Base."

"Okay," Donovan nodded. "I'll be ready."

"You're sure you're good to go?" William asked.

"Yes," Donovan said, though all he could imagine were the problems, everything that could go wrong, as well as the consequences.

CHAPTER THREE

Lauren woke from an uneasy sleep. A quick glance at the clock told her it was three o'clock in the morning. She was a little surprised she'd managed any sleep at all. She threw back the light bedspread and pulled on her robe. She peeked in on Abigail and found her sleeping soundly.

Her thoughts turned to Donovan. He'd been so wound up, she knew there was no way he'd sleep. They'd tried to talk earlier in the evening, but Lauren recognized that he'd already left her, his thoughts and concerns focused on Stephanie and Guatemala. She'd seen it before; his mind started the journey long before his body. But that had been hours ago, and now she wondered how he was doing, and she was worried.

She padded silently down the steps and made her way toward the study. A thin strip of light coming from under the door told her she'd found him. In the hallway was his bag, packed and ready to go. She let herself in and discovered Donovan sitting at his desk. Lauren could see his expression, something between pain and torment. On the desk was his pistol, the clip was missing. He was honoring her request to not have a loaded gun in the house with Abigail around, though she knew the clip was probably in his pocket, and the gun could be fired in seconds if needed. The weapon represented one of the ways in which their relationship had changed. She, too, carried a loaded weapon when she left the house. Protecting themselves was the result of their experience when a terrorist had nearly killed Michael and Donovan as well as

Lauren. That event changed a great many aspects of their life and was one of the many stressors in their marriage.

He glanced up as she joined him. Looking over his shoulder, she saw the image of Meredith Barnes on the screen. The whole world knew the Meredith Barnes story, her murder, a death blamed on billionaire oilman Robert Huntington, who had died only a few months after her.

Meredith had been young and attractive. Her charisma, intelligence, and her in-your-face environmental activism won the hearts of the world—and Robert Huntington. Lauren knew he'd been devastated by her kidnapping and subsequent murder. He'd been with her when she was taken. He was injured in the abduction, their driver killed, but it was the immediate aftermath that no one could have predicted. The standing government policy of not giving in to the ransom demands had doomed Meredith. In the end, he'd ignored the maneuvering bureaucrats and managed to bring in the money to pay the ransom himself, but it was too late. Within hours, her body was discovered in a muddy field outside San José.

Lauren remembered what a tremendous shock it had been to learn Donovan's secret. She'd been among the Meredith supporters who believed in the conspiracy and she'd quietly rejoiced, along with the rest of the world, when Robert had died. She and Donovan had been at sea when he shared all the details of his life—and the intricate reasons why he'd done what he'd done. As she'd listened, she slowly grasped the enormity of his decision, and the complexities of his subsequent actions. Instead of anger at being lied to and misled, everything came together, every loose end and inconsistency she'd felt made perfect sense. She found in him a measure of courage and honesty that made her love him even more. Six months later they married.

"I could make us some coffee," Lauren suggested, wanting him to know that she would sit up with him if he wanted.

Donovan shook his head.

"What are you looking for?" Lauren asked.

"It's Meredith's eulogy. I was just looking, thinking." Donovan clicked to another link. "I don't know, looking for closure, or anything I could do differently this time. I know this isn't what you want to see your husband grappling with. I'm sorry."

"You don't have to apologize." Lauren was a little taken aback at his admission and his concern as to how it might affect her. "We all have our pasts. I don't care what it is you're struggling with as long as you tell me and let me go through it with you."

"I'm trying," Donovan said as he looked up at her, a sad smile on his face.

She leaned down and kissed him. "What did you find?" Lauren wanted more than anything to keep him talking. If they stopped, the sorrow and tragedy that filled the room would be all they had.

"The same things I've seen for over twenty years. I failed to protect her. I should have been far more careful. I should never have dealt with the government—they didn't care about her. They were only concerned about sending the right message to the next group of kidnappers. Because of the bureaucratic posturing, there was a delay assembling the cash. I think the kidnappers panicked and killed her."

"This time will be different—it's you, Buck, and William. Plus, with one of the Eco-Watch jets there, you'll have Michael as well. The past doesn't repeat for those who are aware of history."

Donovan nodded weakly. "I hope you're right—for all our sakes. I keep thinking about Stephanie, and our past. She's always been one of the voices of reason in my life. William did a great job raising me after my parents died, but it was Stephanie that brought a softer, more feminine perspective to my life when I needed it most. She's done so much for me. I can't fail her."

"I love her too." Lauren replied, feeling her own sorrow and pain. "You know, she and I talk about you a lot, and do you know what she said that I've always treasured the most?"

"What?"

"She said that for a while at least, when you and I were

together, you were happier, less tormented, and more at peace than she's ever seen you. Despite all our subsequent problems, she thanked me for giving you that respite from your pain."

"I spent time with her three months ago." Donovan looked up at Lauren. "We were in the San Juan Islands, right before I went to Montana. She told me that the reason you and I were separated, was that I was afraid of you getting too close, of you seeing how broken parts of me were. She explained that after years of hiding my past, I was so compartmentalized, and guarded, that no one ever got the full sense of who I am. That people either happily accepted what they get from me, or they didn't, and felt excluded. In three sentences she summed up why you and I aren't working—was she right?"

Lauren was momentarily startled by his openness, but she also knew Stephanie wouldn't have limited her comments to Donovan. "There could be an element of truth to Stephanie's view. But we both know there's more than just your part. What did she say was my culpability in all of this?"

"She said that you're too analytical, you sometimes get in your own way. Instead of being emotional and speaking or acting, you withdraw and analyze, then get angry. Who wouldn't? I'm not an easy man to be around, I understand, and I want to apologize."

Instead of bristling at the assessment, Lauren recognized that Stephanie had spoken from the vantage point of being outside the conflict. Lauren knew how poorly her internal process meshed with her husband's at times. It was the epicenter of their conflict. "She's not wrong."

"I don't want us to fight," Donovan said. "I only wanted to say that I haven't given up on us, and that for the moment, all of my energy is focused on Stephanie. I'll never be able to change that part of me—it's who I am."

"I know," Lauren said. "You once parachuted into the middle of a hurricane to save me."

"And I'd do it again tomorrow," Donovan said, then turned and looked at the image of Meredith glowing on the computer.

"You'll find her," Lauren urged, trying to comfort him.

"I'm afraid the same thing will happen to Stephanie that happened to Meredith. I failed her, and then I couldn't even go to her funeral. Her family didn't want me there because they thought I was responsible. All I saw was what was televised. I never did get to say good-bye."

Lauren studied her husband. She watched as his eyes left the screen and went up to a framed picture in the bookcase. It was a picture of Stephanie, lean, tan, her blonde hair blown by the wind. She was sitting on a motorcycle, a camera in her hands. She'd been touring somewhere in the Italian Alps. Her wide beautiful smile lit up her face. Lauren watched helplessly as Donovan's blue eyes grew moist. Lauren felt her own tears finally push through the surface and trickle down her face. Unsure where the boundaries of their relationship were at the moment, she leaned over, kissed the top of his head, and stroked his hair. She held her husband for a long time as he silently battled his demons.

CHAPTER FOUR

Donovan looked up from the stack of State Department documents they'd been handed the moment they'd stepped aboard the gleaming Boeing. Painted in the same scheme as Air Force One, the specially equipped 737 was used almost exclusively by the diplomatic corps. "Guatemala has been declared a 'failed state' due to an inability to provide security for its citizens. It says here that with nearly six thousand murders last year, Guatemala is one of the most dangerous countries on earth."

"It's a fact of life," Buck replied. "I spoke with a friend who works security at the embassy. He says whatever we read about the crime and violence, in reality, it's twice as bad. We're going to have to deal with the added risk, and I can't stress enough how careful we're going to have to be while we're on the ground."

"There was a young girl kidnapped six days ago," William said. "She was taken in broad daylight, her armed escort gunned down. According to this, the police say there have been no ransom demands. Could there be any correlation to Stephanie's abduction?"

"Does this girl have a name? Is she Guatemalan?" Donovan asked.

"It doesn't say."

"It would be rare for kidnappers to grab more than one victim at a time," Buck replied. "And just because no ransom was made public, doesn't mean there isn't one. The fact that she had an armed escort tells me that she was already at some risk. Considering where we're headed, she could be the leverage for a drug deal, illegal weapons, or, as bad as it sounds, she could already be part of the illegal sex trade."

"I agree." William quickly scanned the report in his hand and put the sheet on top of the small stack of things he'd already read; he didn't say another word until he finished the last of the documents. He took off his reading glasses, then glanced up at the others. "Gentlemen, I think we should reconstruct events as best we can, take a detailed look at current conditions—political, criminal, as well as seismic. Here's an update of the volcano activity, which I'm afraid could create some problems for us. Then we prioritize our immediate objectives."

Buck unfolded and then smoothed out a map on the table. He'd spent the last three months rehabbing cracked ribs and pulled muscles in his lower back. Not a large man, Buck was solid, always in shape, without an ounce of fat anywhere on his frame, though now it seemed he'd added a layer of muscle. Buck's clean-shaven face appeared neutral and unthreatening, but as Donovan had seen firsthand, when his face tightened, his eyes filled with a quiet, vigilant determination that left no doubt as to his lethality. Donovan knew Eco-Watch was lucky to have him. The former SEAL represented a calm presence in the face of any situation. Though quite deadly, Buck would resort to violence only if needed. While William and Donovan moved in to get a closer look, Buck spun the map around so they wouldn't have to read it upside down.

Buck softly cleared his throat and then began. "Ms. Van-Gelder—Stephanie, if I may—had been photographing the volcanoes on the big island of Hawaii when she was made aware of the sudden eruption of Atitlán in Guatemala, at which point, she immediately departed Hawaii for Guatemala City. She changed planes at LAX, then flew into Guatemala City. She was met by Dr. Malcolm Lane, the senior USGS man there. He arranged transportation for her out to the small town of Panajachel, located here on the north side of Lake Atitlán. According to Dr. Lane, she was scheduled to arrive late, and the plan was for her to meet the two scientists Saturday morning for their trip up to the volcano."

"When was the last time anyone saw her?" Donovan asked.

"That's where the intelligence gets a little iffy." Buck looked up from his notes. "The volcano has been fairly restless in the last thirty-six hours. Nothing big has happened, but there has been steam and ash venting from the mountain, as well as minor earthquakes. Almost all the population in that region is situated around the lake, and I read that the 'at risk' population is somewhere between fifty thousand to one hundred thousand people. Volcanoes are a part of life in Guatemala, but the proximity of this eruption to the lake has spooked the locals enough that there's been a large exodus from the area. Anyone in the area who might have seen Stephanie could be anywhere by now."

"Once we land in Guatemala City, how soon are we going to be able to get to that area?" Donovan glanced down at his watch. In his mind it was the logical first step. He looked at Buck for the answer, but the former SEAL seemed to be waiting for William to speak.

"We're going to have to tread a little softly, I think," William said. "Like we discussed last night, stealth is going to be our biggest tool. You and Buck need to move behind the scenes, try not to draw attention to yourselves. Once you meet the USGS team, I'm sure opportunities to venture out to the volcano will present themselves. As far as anyone on the ground knows, you're both members of Eco-Watch, not part of the cavalry riding in to rescue my niece."

"Understood, sir," Buck replied in his clipped military manner.

Donovan exhaled heavily, frustrated with all the posturing and diplomacy. His lack of patience wasn't doing him any favors. "Show me where they found the bodies."

Buck quickly pointed to a spot on the map. "It's a small clearing on the side of the mountain right about here."

"How did they get there?" Donovan continued. "What was their route?"

"She and the USGS team went by boat from Panajachel to Santiago Atitlán, located here." Buck slid his finger along the map.

"From there, they rode by truck to the trail head and trekked in a generally southeastern direction to the coordinates they'd chosen to install a seismograph. When the equipment didn't come online, the USGS notified the Guatemalan authorities, who then sent out a search party."

"Who got there first and what exactly did they find?"

"The Guatemalan police," Buck quickly riffled through his notes. "The Guatemalan army was forced out of that area years ago due to atrocities committed by their troops. I have a report of those specific events for you to read if you're interested. As to what they found I have the following: They recovered the destroyed equipment that the USGS team was going to install, it was strewn in the forest. They also found four spent shell casings, 7.62 millimeter. They found some blood, which led them to the shallow graves of the three victims. The bodies were then brought back to Guatemala City."

"Four bullets fired, three bodies," Donovan said. "Either they were very good marksmen, or they opened fire at close range. Do the police have any theories at all?"

"I thought about that too," Buck said. "The shell casings are a common caliber, easy to get, usually found in automatic weapons, which could make the enemy some sort of paramilitary operation, or drug smugglers. The police haven't offered up any suspects, but I don't think we're dealing with a random act here. I think whoever did this are professionals and the act was premeditated."

"Does that make this situation better or worse?" William asked.

"In my mind, better," Buck said without hesitation. "If Stephanie has been captured by professionals, then they'll keep her alive and follow one of several scenarios to get money for her safe return. I'd rather be up against a somewhat predictable enemy than rank amateurs."

"But, if it was premeditated," William interjected, "how did they know Stephanie was coming? Her arrival was rather spontaneous."

"That's a part of this puzzle that I find troubling." Buck

rubbed his chin as he considered the question. "If the group is organized, they might have connections inside the airlines, or even Guatemalan immigration. It wouldn't take them very long to run a check on all prospective visitors, see if there was a target of interest on the manifest. Unfortunately, Ms. VanGelder's reputation may have preceded her."

"Because she's my niece?" William replied, his voice faltering momentarily. "You think they singled her out because she's related to me and my assets?"

"It's highly possible," Buck replied. "She's also a noted photo-journalist in her own right, so her name alone may have sparked a closer look. It didn't take me very long online to discover she was related to you and connected to considerable wealth. We have to assume that they could have easily accomplished the same thing."

"So, we can't trust anyone?" Donovan asked. He could tell from the grim expression on William's face that he needed a moment to collect himself.

"Until proven otherwise," Buck said. "Everyone should be viewed as a potential threat."

"Even the USGS?" Donovan asked, knowing that everyone connected with Eco-Watch would be in close contact with the scientists on scene.

"Everyone," Buck said without emotion.

"We know William's arrival will be news, but what about the two of us?" Donovan asked. "If we're followed the minute we hit the ground, then what good are we going to be?"

"My guess is they're hoping William will show up," Buck answered calmly. "In fact, if he didn't, they might lose interest. His presence gives them incentive to keep playing the game. As for you and me, I'm hoping they take a look and decide we are what we say we are, members of Eco-Watch. When Michael shows up with the *Galileo*, that will further cement our cover."

"I trust William will be well protected." Donovan needed to hear that his closest friend wasn't in any danger from the people they were seeking.

"Of course," Buck replied. "Embassy security is always tightened when someone of Mr. VanGelder's stature arrives. He'll have a twenty-four-hour armed detachment guarding him. I'm confident that he'll be well protected."

"What about the rest of the Eco-Watch personnel?" Donovan thought of Michael and the other crew.

"They'll have armed drivers taking them to and from the airport. As far as the hotel goes, we're all staying at the Camino Real. It's close to the airport, and we've reserved a block of rooms that are set aside for visiting VIPs. Again, security will be provided by the embassy, and everyone we've just spoken about will have rooms within the designated perimeter. I have full confidence in the plan to protect our people." Buck's eyes narrowed and he looked squarely at Donovan. "Everyone except you."

"What about me?" Donovan recoiled slightly.

"I want to be straight up about this. I know how you operate, I've seen it firsthand. You're smart, resourceful, brave, and impulsive. The problem is that you dive in headfirst and make it up as you go. We're in the equivalent of a shooting war; my area of expertise, not yours. I can already tell you're chomping at the bit to kick ass and take names. Wrong approach. I want to make perfectly clear that when a situation goes fluid and we need a measured response, you follow me—not the other way around."

Everything Buck had just said was true and made perfect sense, but Donovan knew he wasn't going to operate differently. Buck knew that as well. "I'll do my best."

"I'd appreciate that, and when you disregard everything I've just said, I hope you at least consider that you were warned. I can't keep you alive if I'm bringing up the rear."

CHAPTER FIVE

They began their descent into Guatemala City. The last hour of the flight passed in silence, all three engrossed in their thoughts. Donovan couldn't help but be struck by the criminal climate in Guatemala. It reminded him of 1930s Chicago—gangs, robberies, and running machine-gun battles. The tone of the report had a special emphasis on the number of kidnappings, and spoke of sophisticated weaponry and massive amounts of force used to extort, kidnap, and kill. Despite ransom demands being met, the victims were often killed. Many of the victims were foreigners, though the report was careful not to point at a trend toward targeting Americans, only that the appearance of wealth might be enough to trigger abduction. Donovan thought of the section that dealt with sexual assaults. The number of attacks was disturbing, and he knew that a huge percentage of sexual assaults go unreported, so the number was even higher. The fact that Stephanie was being held against her will in the hands of a nameless, lawless group generated nausea, followed by unbridled frustration and anger. Nothing in his world was more difficult that being unable to use all of his resources to help someone he cared about.

Donovan looked out the window and saw small cumulus clouds floating in the distance. Later in the day the heat would create lift, and they'd grow into large thunderstorms. Every day, from noon well into the evening, held the chance of a localized downpour—it was the rainy season in Central America. Far to the west, just peeking up above the layer of haze, were three distinct volcanic peaks. One of them was throwing up a plume of steam and ash that rose far up into the atmosphere. His first glimpse of Atitlán.

The Boeing descended into the clouds, and Donovan couldn't see anything outside the small window. Turbulence nibbled at the plane, and Donovan paid close attention to the sounds that spoke to him as a pilot. The whine of the flaps being set, the distinctive thump of the landing gear as all three struts swung into position. Donovan understood they were less than four minutes from touchdown.

Glimpses of green and brown were visible through the ragged bases of the clouds. Donovan found small shacks and buildings, tiny houses clinging precariously to hillsides. A low-hanging smudge of black smoke covered the city. As they descended, he could actually smell the city, a faint, yet pungent, odor. What came to mind was part landfill mixed with auto exhaust. Donovan felt a hollow pit in his stomach as they touched down and turned off the runway at La Aurora International Airport. This place had the same feel and smell of Costa Rica.

Donovan barely noticed the plane had come to a stop and the pilots had shut down the engines. Buck was up and out of his seat, scanning the perimeter outside the airplane. Donovan saw a Mercedes and two dark Suburbans pull up to the left side of the 737. Six men in suits jumped out and took defensive positions around the vehicles.

"Looks good. I recognize their faces from the advance report. They're embassy staff." Buck picked up his bag and slung it over his shoulder, then gestured for both William and Donovan to go ahead of him.

"I'll see you later at the hotel," Donovan spoke over William's shoulder as they neared the door. "Stay in touch, maybe we'll have a chance to have a late dinner or at least a drink."

William nodded, seemingly distracted by all the fanfare.

At the foot of the steps there was a flurry of handshakes as introductions were made. Donovan hung back from the bulk of

the activity, letting William and Buck both speak with Ambassador Richardson. Donovan breathed deeply, noting the thinness of
the air. Guatemala City sat almost a mile above sea level. Due to
the altitude, it was surprisingly cool, so he didn't feel overly warm
in his sports coat. Even though it was overcast, Donovan slid on
his sunglasses and watched closely as their luggage was trans-
ferred from the plane to the SUVs. He paid particular attention
to the two metal cases containing the four million dollars.

William slid into the Mercedes with the ambassador, and it
sped away being tailed by one of the SUVs. Above the noise of
a departing airplane, Buck introduced a slender, almost elegant
man. "Donovan, this is Dr. Malcolm Lane. He's the lead man
down here with the USGS. Dr. Lane, this is Donovan Nash."

Donovan shook Lane's hand, surprised that such a firm
grip would come from the rail-thin scientist. Donovan had read
in one of William's dossiers that Malcolm Lane was a noted volcanologist, who'd spent nearly his entire professional life studying the volcanoes that ranged from Mexico all the way south to
the tip of Argentina. Lane was nearly bald, half-moon glasses
were perched midway down his smallish nose, a measured smile
seemed frozen on his face. The volcanologist wore creased khaki
slacks and a denim shirt with USGS emblazoned across the left
pocket.

"Dr. Lane. Nice to meet you, I just wish it were under better
circumstances."

"Please, call me Malcolm. Yes, it's been a very difficult time.
We've lost people before. When you study volcanoes for a living,
something's bound to happen eventually. But we've never lost
people as senselessly as this. There will be plenty of time to discuss that later. Right now, I'd like to say what a pleasure it is to
finally meet you. Your reputation among scientific circles is well
deserved. I can't thank you and Eco-Watch enough for bringing
in your equipment and expertise at the last minute. You're a god-
send."

"No thanks necessary, we're all on the same team," Donovan

replied, trying to shrug off the kind words. From long-established patterns, Donovan always tried to avoid being singled out or put in the spotlight. "So, where are we with *Scimitar*? Has it arrived yet from California?"

"It arrived yesterday," Malcolm replied with unconcealed enthusiasm. "A private cargo jet flew in the *Scimitar*, as well as Professor Murakami and his staff. They also brought in equipment we weren't expecting. We've set up our entire operations center in the hangar over there. Would you like to take a look now?"

Donovan was more than curious what extra equipment had been added to the manifest. He'd been privy to the specs on *Scimitar* for nearly two years. The project's funding had come in large part from an Eco-Watch grant given to the University of Hawaii, which, in conjunction with NOAA and the USGS, had developed the remarkable aircraft.

"I'd love to see the *Scimitar*." Donovan couldn't help but be impressed with Lane's enthusiasm. Donovan was also curious about Professor Benjamin Murakami, the brains behind *Scimitar*. A tenured professor at the University of Hawaii, Murakami had delved into the problems of gathering data from active volcanoes using a highly modified Predator UAV, or unmanned aerial vehicle. Donovan had been skeptical at first, as a pilot with over 12,000 hours of flight experience, he knew he probably harbored a built-in bias about planes without pilots, but the technology was very real and had a proven record. After learning more about what Murakami was trying to do, Donovan had approved the funding for the project. Murakami had been ingenious, blending off-the-shelf technologies to create a revolutionary aircraft that could withstand not only the heat, but also the extremely corrosive properties of the volcanic ash cloud. This represented the first actual trial for the *Scimitar* involving an active volcano.

"I trust all the modifications on the Eco-Watch Gulfstream went smoothly?" Malcolm asked. "We're really in a bind as far as observing Mt. Atitlán, and right now the *Scimitar* is our best bet to understand what might be happening."

"I'm not sure I fully understand." Donovan said.

"Rick and Oliver were trying to install seismic monitoring equipment directly on the mountain when the attack took place. The USGS has banned all personnel from the area. With the weather what it is this time of year, we usually only get a small window of opportunity in the morning to actually observe the mountain itself, before the clouds and rain make visual assessment impossible. There are satellite resources, but they make a limited appearance overhead, and the time delay for analysis is less than ideal. We have seismic arrays in place at two other volcanoes, but they're quite a distance, so the readings for Atitlán aren't as precise as we'd like. If we can get the *Scimitar* in the air, it would give us a great deal of information we simply don't have right now. Of course, the helicopter you've provided will go a long way in helping us monitor the situation as well."

Donovan stopped and turned toward Malcolm. "A helicopter?"

"Come, it's in the hangar with the *Scimitar*. I'll show you." Malcolm gestured to one of the doors on the side of the hangar. "We'll go in this one, all the rest are locked."

Donovan followed Malcolm inside and stopped just inside the hangar to give his eyes a moment to adjust. When they finally did, he could see the ominous black shape of the *Scimitar*. Next to it sat what looked like a brand new Bell 412 helicopter. It lacked any paint except for a base coat of white. The only markings were on the tail, a United States registration number: N819EW, the EW he knew stood for Eco-Watch. It was a replacement for the Bell 407 that had been lost in Alaska. After some deliberations, he and Michael had decided to go with the twin-engine 412 for operations out at sea. As far as he knew, this machine, which was destined to be based aboard the Eco-Watch ship *Pacific Titan*, wasn't being delivered for two more months, and should still be at the Bell helicopter factory in Fort Worth, Texas.

"Mr. Nash? Buck!" A woman, more cute than beautiful, called out as she stepped from behind the helicopter. She wasn't tall, no more than five feet five, she'd lost some weight, and was less pear-shaped than when the two men had last seen her. She wore overalls and her wavy brown hair was pulled back in a ponytail, but her fully charged smile was just as infectious as always.

"Janie Kinkaid, I can't believe it's you!" Buck put his arms around her, the two hugged intensely, he lifting her off the ground and then returning her gently to earth. The two had grown close after serving together on an Eco-Watch mission in Alaska.

Janie turned to Donovan, cocked her head, and studied his long hair and beard. "Mr. Nash, I assume you're in there somewhere?"

Donovan reached out and gave her a hug. Janie had shown them all, firsthand, that she was one of the best helicopter pilots around. He and Michael had first met her years ago in Australia. They learned she'd grown up with four older brothers, and had developed a wicked sense of humor as well as a rough-and-tumble attitude toward life. One night in Perth, Michael and Donovan learned firsthand that they couldn't out-drink her—it hadn't even been close.

Janie was typically based aboard the Eco-Watch ship *Pacific Titan*. Three months ago she'd been injured in a helicopter crash, the same crash that had injured Lauren and Buck. Thanks to Janie's remarkable flying and Buck's quick thinking, they all escaped with recoverable injuries. As far as Donovan knew, Janie was supposed to be recuperating from a broken elbow at home in Australia. To find her in Guatemala was a complete surprise.

"It's good to see you," Donovan said as they disengaged. "How are you? How's the elbow doing? Why are you here?"

"I'm fine," Janie nodded. "Since I was cleared to return to flight status ahead of schedule, Michael, Mr. Ross, was able to arrange with Bell to take an early delivery of our 412 last week. Eric and I finished our training, and yesterday we loaded it on the cargo plane with the *Scimitar* and flew down here. When we're finished, it'll go back to Fort Worth for paint and a final inspection before we take her out to the *Pacific Titan* and her sea trials. She's a beaut, isn't she?"

"Eric Mitchell is with you?" Donovan asked. Eric was the helicopter pilot on the other Eco-Watch ship, the *Atlantic Titan*.

"Yeah," Janie replied. "Michael thought it would be smart to train us both at the same time so we could standardize the new machines within Eco-Watch operational specifications. Eric's off talking to another Bell operator based here. He should be back shortly."

"Is it flyable?" Donovan asked.

"You bet. I'm just fussing with my new baby. You want to go up right now?"

"Yes," Donovan replied immediately. "Can you get us out to the volcano?"

"No problem," Janie smiled. "Eric and I will have her ready to fly in an hour. That'll give you and Buck a chance to check out the *Scimitar*."

"Perfect," Donovan said, ignoring the annoyed expression on Buck's face.

Donovan turned from the helicopter and took in the *Scimitar*. His first impression was that the drone was far larger than he'd expected. The basic airframe came straight from the latest version of the Predator. The MQ-9 Reaper was bigger, faster, and more powerful than its older cousin. Buck let out a low whistle as they both approached the nose.

"What do you think?" Malcolm asked.

"I've seen the military version of this thing." Buck put out his hand and touched the black surface. "But this looks completely different, the skin feels more solid. What is it?"

"A ceramic resin," a deep, resonant voice said from the other side of the *Scimitar*. "It helps it deflect heat, like the ceramic tiles used on the space shuttle, only four generations more advanced."

Donovan discovered a short, rather rotund man walking their way. He had on white coveralls and was wiping his hands with a rag. A full head of black hair framed an oval face and bright smile. From five paces away Donovan could see the unmistakable intelligence in the eyes of Professor Benjamin Murakami. Donovan held out his hand in greeting. "Professor, I'm Donovan Nash. It's a pleasure to finally meet you—and the *Scimitar*."

"The pleasure is mine, Mr. Nash."

"This is my colleague, Howard Buckley." Donovan let his eyes travel down the sleek lines of the *Scimitar*. He felt the aeronautical enthusiast within him begin to formulate a dozen questions.

"Hello, Mr. Buckley." Murakami shook Buck's hand. "What is your position within Eco-Watch?"

"I'm in charge of logistics," Buck replied instantly. "I'm sort of Mr. Nash's go-to guy."

"Ah, I see. We should all have someone like that in our life." Murakami turned back and faced Donovan. "Well. What do you think?"

"I'm intrigued," Donovan said honestly. "Why don't you give us a walk-around, but first, I'm curious about the name."

"*Scimitar* was a name chosen by my graduate students at the university. They likened the project to cutting through the darkness, which is exactly what the *Scimitar* will do. A round-the-clock, scientific sword if you will."

"Perfect," Donovan said, as he touched the ceramic-based covering that protected *Scimitar*. The UAV was big; it was almost forty feet long with a wingspan of sixty-six feet. It had a nine-hundred horsepower turboprop engine mounted aft, which pushed the *Scimitar* through the air at speeds close to two hundred thirty miles per hour. Aerodynamically, the tail was V-shaped, a proven design with the benefits of less drag. The graceful wings were built like a glider's—long and straight, for high endurance and maneuverability. The one characteristic that Donovan couldn't get used to, no matter how many times his eyes swept across the carefully constructed airplane, was the fact that there were no windows, no cockpit. The *Scimitar* was going to be flown by a pilot who may have never actually flown a real plane.

The operator sat in a mobile control room and flew the *Scimitar* from miles away.

"This is, of course, the business end of the aircraft." Professor Murakami gave the *Scimitar* a gentle pat on the nose. "I won't bore you with all the technical specifications, but suffice it to say, we have a full-color nose camera that the pilot uses for navigation. There is also a variable aperture camera, which is not unlike a television camera that functions as *Scimitar*'s main set of 'eyes.' We also have low light or night viewing with the infrared camera, as well as SAR, or synthetic aperture radar, for seeing through smoke, clouds, or haze. Each one of the cameras can produce either video or still frames. As for the particle sensors, we carry a sophisticated mass spectrometer to sample gases directly from the plume. We can read the amount of carbon dioxide, sulfur dioxide, water vapor, and hydrogen sulfide. As we measure the gases, we also log the winds aloft to keep a running calculation of where the gases are headed."

"Impressive," Buck said. "Has any of this been done before?"

"No, not at the level we're about to attempt. *Scimitar* will actually be able to loiter in and out of the plume for hours, measuring changes and showing trends about what's happening deep within the mountain. We haven't yet installed the necessary satellite uplink capability. We're still working on that issue. Antennas don't react well with the caustic ash and gas from a volcano. That's where Eco-Watch comes into play. We need a set of eyes to help guide the *Scimitar* in real-time *and* maintain a line-of-sight data link. Our pilot will be in the back of the Eco-Watch Gulfstream controlling the *Scimitar*. We'll also have the advantage of the Gulfstream flight crew looking out the window, sort of like a mother ship."

"Well said," Malcolm nodded his approval. "The ability to monitor a volcano, day or night, without being hampered by clouds, or even steam and ash, is unprecedented."

"How did you solve the problems of keeping the engine free of ash, and protect it from the high temperatures?" Buck asked. "We all know volcanic ash is a deadly mixture of rock and glass fragments. I remember a Boeing 747 that flew into an ash cloud over Alaska, and all four of its engines shut down. They almost crashed before they could restart enough engines to make an emergency landing."

"That was the first of many problems we needed to address," Murakami said. "There are elaborate filters for the engine, but the heart of what protects the *Scimitar* is a liquid nitrogen heat exchanger. We circulate super-cooled jet fuel throughout the airframe. Everything that the heat of a volcanic plume could affect is protected by this system, including the air that is ingested into the engine."

"Amazing—what's the endurance on the *Scimitar*?" Donovan asked.

"Fourteen hours with a thirty-minute reserve."

Donovan thought how difficult it must have been to engineer all the complicated systems and still keep the aerodynamics intact. "How do you keep the corrosive aspects of the ash from destroying the optics? I wouldn't think it'd take very long for the ash to eat away at the lenses, and then all you'd have is one very expensive, but blind, airplane."

"Yes, you're correct. In laboratory tests, we discovered that the typical ash cloud renders the *Scimitar*'s optics unusable in about eight minutes. I devised a rotating lens cover system that continually slides a new protective film into position when needed. The optics system is unproven, and that's one of the necessities of flying the *Scimitar* from inside your airplane. In the event that the *Scimitar* is blinded, our pilot can guide the drone to a safe landing by actually looking out the window of the *Galileo* and visually controlling the flight."

"Professor, thank you for the tour. I'm looking forward to seeing the *Scimitar* in action."

"As am I," Professor Murakami replied, as he nodded a farewell and went to resume his work.

"Incredible," Buck said. "I've seen firsthand what these things can do out in the field, at least the militarized version."

"Here we are." Malcolm held open the door to a small office connected to the hangar itself. "We set up a makeshift office here at the airport to be closer to the *Scimitar* and the data we hope to recover from the test flights."

Donovan could see that the room was small and hastily put together. The air was filled with the acrid smell of over-cooked coffee. Donovan guessed that this place was manned twenty-four hours, and coffee was a by-product of that vigilance. Along one wall were several computers situated on old metal desks, the floor snaked with the wires of multiple connections going to printers and phone lines. On the facing wall was a row of seismographs, each contained white rollers with long metal pointers etching lines on the drums. Donovan knew enough to understand that each small variation of the ink reflected some unseen movement deep inside the earth. Seated at one of the terminals was a small-ish woman with straight, mostly gray hair tied in a ponytail. Her glasses were pushed up onto the top of her head.

"Honey," Malcolm called out. "We have company."

The woman turned, and Donovan saw that she was probably in her early sixties, similar in age to Malcolm. Her features were sharp, but the lines of time and obvious exposure to the elements were visible around her eyes. She struck Donovan as someone who spent a great deal of time in the outdoors, thin and tall, almost stately, she was the perfect match for Malcolm. She rose from her chair to greet them. As she neared, Donovan could see in her eyes what looked to him to be a great sadness. She didn't smile, but Donovan immediately felt a kinship with this woman.

"Gentlemen, this is my wife Lillian," Malcolm said. "Honey, I'd like you to meet Donovan Nash and Howard Buckley. They're with Eco-Watch."

"Nice to meet you," Lillian replied, then turned toward her husband. "There were a series of three small-scale earthquake swarms about twenty minutes ago."

"I'd like to see what that looks like," Donovan said, as he

turned and tried to figure out exactly which instrument in the room might show an earthquake swarm.

"It's right here," Lillian said, pointing to one of the seismograph drums. "See how we get a big spike and then it gradually goes back to normal?"

Donovan could clearly see what she was talking about. It looked like a drawing of pine tree, the lower, bigger branches indicated the start of the swarm, and it gradually got smaller like it would at the top of the tree.

"Where is this being detected?" Donovan asked. "It's my understanding that Atitlán doesn't have a seismograph."

"This one is located south of here on Mount Fuego," Lillian explained. "There are also other seismographs in other parts of Guatemala. It's not ideal, but it's all we have right now. The swarms are miles deep, but we've learned that earthquake swarms are one of the precursors to a major eruption."

"How many people do you have monitoring the situation?" Buck directed the question toward Malcolm. Buck had walked closer to the lone window in the room and pulled back the grimy blinds; he glanced outside, and his eyes swept the immediate area.

"There are only the two of us," Malcolm replied. "We try to split it up into ten-hour shifts and let the Guatemalan monitoring station take over the task when we're away. There are two other USGS people on their way; they should arrive here in the next several days."

Through the window, Donovan saw that the Boeing 737 was still on the ramp, though in the distance he could see a fuel truck pulling away from under the right wing. He hadn't thought to ask William if the Air Force crew and airplane were staying with them, or leaving. From all appearances it looked like they might be getting ready to depart. Donovan shrugged, it probably didn't matter. He and William weren't leaving anytime soon, plus, later today, they would have the *Galileo* at their disposal.

"Buck!" Janie yelled from the far side of the hangar. "Hurry!"

In an instant, Buck, gun drawn, was racing across the building. Donovan and Malcolm brought up the rear. As Donovan rounded the helicopter, he saw Janie holding a large envelope. In her other hand was a sheet of paper.

Buck holstered his pistol, and he and Donovan walked around behind Janie so they could see what was written. At the top of the page was a bloody fingerprint, below that were the words:

three million u.s. dollars
to see Stephanie alive again
you have three days

Buck turned to Malcolm. "I need you to call the control tower and stop the Air Force jet!"

"Where did you find this?" Donovan asked Janie.

"It was leaning against the rear door. I heard what sounded like the sliding door on a van open and close. Then someone pounded on the door. I opened it and there was no one there, but the envelope was, so I opened it."

Buck opened the door and looked up and down the access road that connected the private hangars, as if quietly assessing their vulnerability. "I want everyone inside. I also need something to handle this with besides my fingers. Can someone find me some gloves? Or better yet, tweezers, or forceps?"

"I've got some in my kit," Janie said, returning moments later with a small pair of forceps.

"Let's get this to the office." Buck carefully picked up the letter and the envelope with the forceps, careful not to contaminate the evidence any more than Janie already had.

"The tower said they'd relay your message to the Boeing," Malcolm said as he rejoined the group. "That was all they could promise. The 737 hasn't moved, so I think we reached them in time."

Buck hurried back to Malcolm's office. They quickly photographed the contents of the envelope as well as the envelope itself.

With Lillian's help, they carefully secured all the items in a large plastic bag, which Buck then sealed.

Malcolm eyed the plastic bag. "Are you sure we shouldn't call the police, or the embassy, first?"

"The Air Force jet we flew down here on is headed back to Washington, DC. In four hours this can be in the hands of the FBI. I'm hoping they can give us some clues. I also have to ask everyone to keep everything you've seen here to yourselves. As far as Eco-Watch goes, it's business as usual." Buck looked at Malcolm and Lillian. "I'm not sure why they delivered this here, but I'm going to request round-the-clock security for the two of you. I don't think you're in danger, but I'd like to err on the safe side."

"Thank you," Malcolm replied with genuine gratitude.

Donovan led the way as he and Buck headed out the door. As they burst from the hangar, Donovan saw that the Boeing was still on the tarmac. Buck took off running toward the jet. Standing helpless on the ramp, Donovan felt like he'd been punched. The ransom note pounded at him on different levels. Whatever small hope he held that she was in hiding had just vanished. Even if they gave in to the demands, there was every possibility she'd be killed anyway. Stephanie had been taken and the clock was ticking.

CHAPTER SIX

Lauren sat at the desk, moved the mouse, and the screen on the computer came to life. She deftly went through the steps until she found what she was looking for—in front of her was the Internet site history Donovan had looked at the night before. Lauren had no qualms about what she was doing; she'd been with him and was fully aware he was reflecting on his past. What made last night different from other nights was her presence as he battled his past. He obviously blamed himself for mistakes made, real or imagined, but what she had no idea was how wounded he'd been by the fact that the repercussions over Meredith's death had come so swiftly.

She clicked the mouse and flinched as the first image filled the screen. It was a full-screen image of Robert Huntington. It was probably taken when he was in his mid-twenties, already at the helm of Huntington Oil, a private company that Robert had inherited at the age of twenty-one—an inheritance that had made him one of the ten richest men in the world.

The photo was before all the surgery. Nothing about it reminded her of her husband, except the eyes—they remained the same. Robert had always been a good-looking man, Lauren mused. He was often referred to as the billionaire playboy, dating starlets and other high-visibility women. A cross between a young Howard Hughes and John F. Kennedy Jr. For many women it was an intoxicating combination of looks and power.

Lauren scrolled down to the biography. Robert Huntington had lived a privileged life accorded to the ultra-wealthy. His grandfather had founded Huntington Oil and two generations later, it was one of the largest private petrochemical conglomerates in America. Robert had been orphaned at the age of fourteen by a boating accident that took his parents' lives—while sparing his own. Robert Huntington attended both Dartmouth as well as Oxford universities. He'd been a collector of expensive automobiles, a three-handicap golfer, an avid fly fisherman, as well as an expert marksman in both skeet and wing shooting. Despite being gifted at many pursuits, his overriding passion had been flying, and he was recognized as an exceptional pilot. Upon graduating from Oxford with an advanced degree in international business strategies, he took his place at the helm of Huntington Oil.

A frown came over Lauren's face. Why was Donovan looking at this? It was ancient history. Another click brought up a later picture of Robert, one taken near the end. Though not even thirty, he'd aged appreciatively, his features hardened and strained. Lauren scrolled down to discover Robert's obituary. The article was from the *New York Times*. It detailed the known events leading to Robert Huntington's death. He'd been flying his own plane from Reno, Nevada, to Monterey, California, when air traffic controllers lost radio contact with the flight. They tracked the plane as it flew far out over the Pacific Ocean before running out of fuel and plunging into the ocean. The embattled Robert Huntington was dead at the age of twenty-eight.

Lauren skipped to another page and found a picture of Meredith Barnes. Under the photo were bold letters proclaiming her murder at the hands of Robert Huntington. Lauren winced as she read the article, one of thousands that had surfaced after her death. Each piece had soundly condemned Robert Huntington as the instrument of Meredith's murder. Her global message of environmental activism had been silenced at the hands of big oil. A horrific crime viewed as against not only Meredith—but the planet itself. The entire world mourned her, while at the same time convicted Robert in the court of public opinion. Lauren knew the rest by heart. Robert hadn't died in the plane crash—he'd engineered his death and fled to Europe, where he'd undergone plastic surgery. Lauren had met him years later, when he was firmly entrenched in his new identity as Donovan Nash running Eco-Watch.

Lauren wondered what had compelled Donovan to come downstairs in the middle of the night to relive his past? What had he been feeling when he saw the man he used to be? Did he regret the change?

Lauren needed to know more. Not just about Donovan, but what was happening in Guatemala. Technically, she worked for the Defense Intelligence Agency, though her current title was analyst consultant, which didn't allow her access to ongoing investigations. At one time, she was the lead climatologist with the DIA, her PhD in Earth Science from MIT had bolted her to the top of a special projects division. Her particular skills were in deciphering mass amounts of satellite data and forming weather models that could affect ongoing military operations. She'd resigned her full-time position, but she still put in ten to fifteen hours a week studying reports. Her DIA credentials would only get her so far into the government's intelligence network, and the FBI was certainly out of reach.

She tried to think of anyone she knew at the Bureau, someone high enough on the food chain to keep her in the loop about Stephanie's kidnapping. Her scientific mind began to process what little she knew. She drummed her fingers on the table as she processed the facts, and as she did, her frustration began to build. Her husband, Abigail's father, was, in her opinion, riding the crest of a wave toward oblivion. Donovan had suffered devastating losses in his life. He'd been unable to do anything to save his parents as they both drowned in a boating accident. His fiancée, Meredith Barnes, kidnapped from his side and later murdered. As if that hadn't been enough, there had been other people in his life he felt he should have been able to save. Lauren had heard most of their names over the years, in the dead of night, as her tormented husband murmured names in his sweat-drenched nightmares.

She glanced at the secure line that her boss, Calvin Reynolds, the deputy director at the Defense Intelligence Agency, had installed for her home use. It allowed her to freely discuss DIA business from home. She could easily picture Calvin sitting at his desk; even at this early hour he would already be working. She had the pull to be invited to the investigation, but with Donovan's current mindset, she was hesitant. The more high-level investigators brought into the mix, the harder it was to operate within the lies about his past that she and Donovan had told over the years. She debated a minute longer and then discarded the entire idea, electing to leave Calvin and the DIA out of the picture for now. Which left her with one lingering thought—what if she asked for help from someone who operated outside official channels, someone who already knew the truth about Donovan's past?

She glanced at the clock, surprised at how long she'd been sitting at the computer. Her coffee had grown cold. If she were going to make the phone call, she needed to do it quickly, before Abigail woke up and wanted breakfast. Lauren found the number and, without hesitation, dialed the phone. As it rang, she had no idea how the person on the other end was going to react. In fact, she wouldn't be surprised if who she were calling told her to go to hell.

"Hello." A woman answered the phone.

"Is this Ms. Montero?"

"Yes."

"This is Dr. Lauren McKenna. Are you free to talk?"

"What could you possibly want to talk to me about?"

"Donovan's in trouble."

"He's been in trouble since I've known him. Why call me? Why now?"

"I need someone who knows the truth about him, about

us, someone I don't have to tiptoe around like I'm working in a minefield. I promise it'll be worth your time. Money's no object."

"You don't have any reason to like me, or trust me. I blackmailed you and your husband, and nearly got all three of us killed."

"You're right, I didn't like you. I'm not sure I do now, but I do trust you. I know the depth of your commitment and your capabilities as a former FBI agent. They're the reasons I made this call. I'm willing to put everything aside and work with you, for Donovan's sake."

"I believe you, this couldn't have been an easy call to make. I don't know how much your husband told you about what happened to us, but he saved my life. I made him a promise I'd always be there if he needed me. Keep your money, Dr. McKenna, it's not what motivates me. I'm in—where do we start?"

"What do you know about Stephanie VanGelder?"

"She's William's niece, right? Other than that, I know very little."

"She's in Guatemala, and she's been kidnapped."

"Oh no. So, Donovan's there now? In Guatemala?"

"Yes. He and Stephanie are like brother and sister. Donovan showed up in Virginia all ready to rush to Guatemala, swoop in and rescue Stephanie. William, thank God, talked him down and managed to cool him off."

"Dr. McKenna, what is it you want me to do?"

"Please, call me Lauren. I know that one of the reasons you were able to uncover Donovan's secret is that you were, and still are, a great admirer of Meredith Barnes, and by default, you know a great deal about Robert Huntington. You're also a trained investigator, and one of six people in the world who know the truth about my husband. I want you to help me find the people who have Stephanie."

"There should be an entire FBI 'Fly Team' on the ground by now. FBI agents involved with the rapid deployment teams handle logistics, and have hostage negotiators, crisis managers, evidence response teams. They're very good at what they do. I ask you again, what is it you think I can do?"

"William, with his status in the State Department, waved off all help from the FBI. William, Buck, and Michael are all down there thinking they can do this alone. They're operating in a completely reactive mode, waiting for the exchange. As far as I can tell, William is treating this as a business transaction."

"I'm not sure that's the best approach. Does he have the ransom money? Have there been any demands? Does he have proof of life?"

"That's exactly why I need you," Lauren said. "Yes, there's money in Guatemala for the ransom. As far as your other questions, I have no idea."

"Are you still connected with the DIA?"

"Yes, but I'm hesitant to use them directly. I have some indirect access, but nothing high-level."

"You've got to be kidding," Montero said. "The two of us trying to find specific kidnappers, in a third-world country without federal help, is like trying to find the *Titanic* while standing in Kansas."

"I'm not saying we don't have some assets," Lauren replied. "We have an unlimited budget, and you still have connections in this town. You're a decorated former FBI agent, and I'm a research analyst. If we can get access to the right files, we can be more than reactive. We can be proactive."

"Where do we even start?"

"I'll get an update from Donovan and William later tonight. I think I can also get Buck to keep me in the loop."

"I'm a *former* FBI agent. Even when I was an active agent, the FBI didn't always like the way I played. What makes you think they'll even talk to me?"

"You brought down a terrorist cell bent on killing millions of Americans. You shot and killed the terrorist leader. The only person more famous than you in this town is the Navy SEAL who pulled the trigger on bin Laden. You need to embrace that celebrity."

"We both know I didn't pull that trigger," Montero said.

"We can discuss that detail another time, but for now, the rest of the world believes differently. We both know you're a master at getting what you want. Use whatever connections you have inside the FBI and learn what you can. I'll dig up everything I can find through my channels, and we'll sort it all out together."

"You think these people have kidnapped before?"

"I believe so," Lauren replied. "There are roughly three thousand kidnappings a year in Central America. Once we filter out the drug-related, the custody disputes, and the kidnappings of locals, the number drops precipitously. I think there's a chance we can identify the group, maybe even the individual responsible. It's what I do. I sift through mountains of data— it doesn't matter if it's meteorological or statistical, the methods are the same. We look for small anomalies, trends, repeating patterns, commonalities, and then make predictions on future behavior. Add to the equation your instincts as an investigator, and we can cover a great deal of ground. We just need better data."

"How's Donovan doing?" Montero asked. "Emotionally I mean, being in Central America and dealing with another kidnapping?"

"I don't really know, but if I had to guess, not very well. Last night I found him on the computer, reliving his past. He was looking at pictures of Meredith and Robert Huntington, reading both of their obituaries. We've been apart, so I have no real fix on the depth of his guilt these days or his state of mind. I'm worried."

"Worried enough to call me, I get it. I'm on my way. Once I arrive in Virginia, I'll need a hotel and a rental car."

"Where are you?"

"Boca Raton, Florida."

"I'll arrange a private jet, then text you the details. And, Veronica, I can't tell you how much this means to me."

"I made Donovan a promise, and that's something I don't do lightly. Though I do have one more request."

"Okay."

"Don't ever call me Veronica. It's Ronnie, or Montero."

CHAPTER SEVEN

The State Department Boeing lifted off and Donovan watched as it climbed and banked to the north, the ransom note safely aboard. Behind him, two vehicles, a Mercedes and an SUV, pulled across the ramp and eased into the hangar. William and his security detail had arrived.

William read the crude note Buck had photographed, and then closed his eyes as if saddened by some great weight.

"Where did you get this?" William asked, after he'd collected his thoughts.

"Janie found it outside the hangar," Buck said. "The airplane we flew in on was still on the ramp. I took the liberty of packaging the envelope together and sending it with them back to Washington. I just got off the phone, and the FBI has agreed to meet the airplane to collect the package. I was promised a preliminary report as soon as possible. I also spoke with the embassy here and managed to expand the security to cover all the USGS employees."

"I see. The FBI makes sense. That was quick thinking on your part," William said. "If we're going to get any leads, it'll most likely come from their laboratory, as opposed to here. Do we think the fingerprint is Stephanie's? And, if so, was it really her blood?"

"It could be anyone's. The bigger question was how the note was delivered—what made the kidnappers think the USGS is connected to you?" Donovan said. "And how did they know it was this hangar? There's no name on the door, nothing to differentiate this from the other dozen-or-so structures that line this side of the airport."

"Someone is watching the activity at the airport," Buck said. "That's the only explanation. We can't trust anyone. I go back to what I said earlier, these are most likely professionals, not amateurs, and we know that at least one of them is in Guatemala City."

"Do you think Stephanie is in Guatemala City as well?" William asked.

"To be honest, sir," Buck shook his head. "She could be anywhere."

"We've got less than three days to find her," William said softly.

"Did you learn anything at the embassy?" Donovan needed to know they were making progress, that their collective brain trust would come across something, *anything*, that would send them down the correct path.

"Nothing encouraging, I'm afraid." William shook his head. "I was briefed by the ambassador, who, along with his deputy chief of mission, explained that right now diplomatic relations with the Guatemalan government are far from ideal. The ongoing corruption, drug trafficking, and now all of this—hasn't helped mend any fences. This entire country is experiencing a sharp increase in the number of crimes committed against foreigners. It's an epidemic."

"How many of those crimes were kidnappings?" Donovan asked, trying to shift the focus back to Stephanie. Donovan knew enough about the third world, as well as William's sensibilities, to understand the elder statesmen's anguish.

"Did you sense anything when you were talking to them?" Buck asked. "Is there some kind of organized gang at work here?"

"No. Gangs are certainly a problem, but they're not well organized, though they tend to be well armed and extremely violent. In some of the cases, I was told the suspects wore partial police uniforms, which indicates certain elements of the police could be corrupt. In fact, it almost goes beyond simple corruption—into the realm of human rights violations. In Guatemala they have an abundance of weapons, governmental and judicial dysfunction, and an entrenched legacy of violence. The ambassador told me that there are more private police in Guatemala than actual police officers—because of the abuses."

"If we can't trust anyone local, are we going to be able to protect all of our people?" Donovan asked.

"Yes," Buck said without hesitation. "And if I need to bring in some more people, I will."

"Did you talk to *anyone* who might be able to help us?" Donovan asked William. If the entire country was corrupt, and they couldn't trust anyone, they were going to have major problems finding Stephanie. "Do we have any leads at all?"

"I'm afraid we don't," William said quietly, angrily. "All I heard today was the usual diplomatic rhetoric. We're outsiders, and whoever did this knows we're here and that they have the upper hand. I'm afraid for now, we can only wait until another note arrives. Then we react."

"What about the girl who was kidnapped several days ago, any more on her situation?" Buck asked.

"They said it's a local matter," William replied. "End of subject. What I was told is that we need to get the *Scimitar* into the air. The people studying this eruption have precious little information about the mountain and the people who may be in danger. I think our project may provide exactly what they need. Also, if the kidnappers are still in that area, and I believe they are, we may be able to spot something. I'm certain they haven't calculated a drone into their operation parameters."

"I agree," Buck said. "My feeling is Stephanie isn't far from where she was taken. I know in the Middle East, when we took hostages—I guess I should call them POWs—we never wanted to move them very far if we didn't have to."

"Sounds like we each have jobs to do," William said. "The

overriding message I walked away with today is that the people we're up against are brutal. We in turn shouldn't hesitate to play by their rules; do whatever we need to do and deal with the consequences later. And Buck, whatever you do, don't forget your primary job, which is to protect the people of Eco-Watch."

"Yes, sir," Buck replied. "I understand completely."

"Thank you," William replied. "Now, if you'd be kind enough to give me a moment to speak with Donovan privately."

Donovan waited patiently as Buck excused himself. Once he was gone, he looked at William expectantly.

"I can see it in your eyes," William said with a soft, yet authoritative tone.

"What is it you think you see?" Donovan asked. "And is it anything I don't see in yours?"

"I don't think you see bloodlust in my eyes," William replied. "In yours, I see a desperation that I haven't seen for over twenty years. I noticed it the second we stepped off the airplane. The feel of this place set you off, didn't it? It's something I'd hoped I'd never see you experience again. And now that you're here, I'm worried."

Donovan wished he had something to say to refute William's words, but every denial he gave would sound like the lie it was. William had known him his entire life and missed little.

"Good," William said. "At least you're not going to deny it. I've seen you grow from a boy into a man, a process that hasn't been easy. I've also seen you since you met Lauren and started a new life as a husband and father. Despite all the problems the two of you have, you're still as happy as I've ever seen you, but the changes in the last two days are—worrisome. You know I love you as if you were my own son, and right now I'd like nothing better than for you to go home. I can't stand the thought of losing either Stephanie or you. To lose both of you would be immeasurable."

"I'm not going anywhere," Donovan stated. "Since you know me so well, I'd like to remind you that the one thing I don't do—it's something you've instilled in me since I was a teenager—I don't run from something just because it's difficult. I'll get through this, and right now we both have bigger things to worry about than my mood."

"Go home," William urged, his voice barely a whisper.

"You, of all people, should understand why I'm not leaving. I can't believe you'd even ask."

"Go home to your wife," William insisted.

"Meredith understands!" Donovan responded with far more force than he intended, and the moment the words escaped his lips, he realized what he'd said. Thoughts about Meredith had somehow merged with Lauren's, and two women were blurred. His subconscious swirled with guilt and confusion, his emotions sparked by his anger.

"I rest my case," William said.

As William walked back out to his embassy-supplied Mercedes, Donovan watched and thought of all the valid reasons William wanted him out of Guatemala. There was only one reason to stay, which was Stephanie, and that was enough.

"Donovan! The chopper's ready," Buck called out from the ramp. "Let's go."

CHAPTER EIGHT

Donovan found Janie and Eric already in the cockpit. A short, muscular soldier wearing a beret smiled broadly as he waited for them at the door. Donovan thought the 412 looked like a minivan with rotors. It was far bigger than the helicopter it had replaced.

"Janie says the weather at the volcano is good right now, but thunderstorms will start building soon," Buck said as they neared the helicopter. "The man in uniform is Cesar. He's a flight mechanic with lots of experience operating the external hoist. A friend of mine recommended him from back when the CIA was down here running joint anti-drug operations with the Guatemalan army."

Donovan shook hands with Cesar as he stepped up onto the skid and into the cabin. He went forward, said hello to Eric and Janie, then took a minute to scan the instrument panel. The inside of the helicopter smelled like a new car, everything clean and pristine. As with any piece of Eco-Watch equipment, no expense had been spared. Both Janie and Eric looked and acted at home as they began starting engines.

Malcolm and Lillian boarded and chose their seats. Malcolm sat next to the door, his wife in a middle seat; Donovan settled into a seat by the opposite door. Malcolm and Lillian were instantly busy. From their duffel bag came an array of cameras, printouts, notepads, and markers. Malcolm handed Donovan a pair of expensive binoculars. He thanked him and looped the strap around his neck. Through a narrow gap between the front seats, Donovan had a partial view of the instrument panel. He watched Janie's deft movements as her hands moved swiftly from one task to another. Donovan recognized a comfortable pilot when he saw one, and, even though he disliked helicopters, he relaxed a little at the thought of Janie at the controls.

The main rotor sliced through the air above them, and then accelerated. Cesar stood out on the ramp, giving the helicopter one last look before flashing Janie a thumbs up and running and jumping aboard. He sat in a small chair facing Lillian, buckled in, and pointed up to the headsets hanging above them.

Donovan slid his headset on and swung the boom microphone into position. "Hello? Testing."

Moments later, everyone in the helicopter was plugged in and communicating free from the noise of the rotor. The 412 lifted off, hovered briefly, then Janie pivoted the helicopter smartly to the west, and they surged forward across the airfield.

Donovan automatically tightened his harness. This was the unnatural part about helicopters—the lack of a proper takeoff roll. Below him, Donovan was able to survey the airport. To his left, across the runway, was the main terminal, its assortment of familiar commercial jets clustered together. To his right, and of far more interest, were the other planes—some flyable, others, obvious derelicts. There were ancient DC-3s sitting abandoned in the long grass. A Boeing 727 and a DC-8 sat on a separate ramp, the equipment nearby told him he was looking at the air cargo facility. Scattered amongst the hangars were a slew of smaller wrecked planes. There was one section of the tarmac where the planes were parked in organized rows; these were the planes that might actually fly. There were the usual, small twin-engine Piper and Beechcraft models, plus a couple of older corporate jets, and some other single-engine propeller types. Off to the side were two high-winged Cessna 185 amphibians, the floats allowing them to land on water or land. Both were painted in the same yellow, orange, and red color scheme. Donovan tagged them as sightseeing planes.

The airport flashed beneath them, and then there was nothing below them but Guatemala City. As far as Donovan could see were houses and buildings stacked upon one another. Power lines crisscrossed from one block to the next. Smoke drifted from chimneys scattered between satellite dishes. Narrow, unorganized roads snaked through brightly painted concrete structures. The further they flew, the more the poverty became evident. Fragile, makeshift shacks perched on hillsides, livestock fed in the ditches, and smoke-belching buses inched though it all in the morning traffic. The thought that Stephanie could be down there terrified him, because if she were, he knew they'd never find her.

"Mr. Nash?" Lillian touched his arm.

Donovan glanced over, thankful that she'd drawn his attention to the inside of the helicopter. She handed him a clipboard; attached were sheets with numerous images of the volcano, and most looked like they were taken from a satellite.

"We just received these this morning," Lillian said as she leaned over.

Donovan nodded as if he understood what the complicated data meant.

Lillian used the tip of her pen as a pointer and began to explain. "As you can see, this first image is from NASA's Terra satellite. It uses a complicated algorithm to seek out high-temperature heat sources, or hot spots, if you will. These are usually an indication of lava working its way toward the surface. The interesting thing about this image is that the hot spot on Mt. Atitlán is growing in intensity at an alarming rate, actually. It's extraordinary."

Donovan glanced up to see if Buck was reacting to this information. He knew the former SEAL was listening and should be just as interested as he was in these new developments.

Buck turned. "How long before it could erupt?"

"Days, weeks, months, or maybe never." Lillian shrugged. She took the clipboard from Donovan, flipped through several pages, then handed it back to him. "This is also from the Terra satellite, only this format measures changes in the surface itself. It looks down at the ground from different angles, and then creates a digital 3-D image of the mountain. Any major surface deformation becomes obvious. Like this right here, tells us that there has been a meter increase in the bulge on the side of Atitlán in the last thirty-six hours."

"Is that a lot?" Donovan didn't doubt for a moment what Lillian was telling him, the evidence was clearly visible on the image, he just didn't have any point of reference.

"We volcanologists get excited about seeing a twenty-centimeter rise over the span of two years. For perspective, the bulge on the north flank of Mt. St. Helens was growing at a rate of five feet per day just before it exploded. So, to answer your question, Mr. Nash, yes, it's a lot."

Donovan felt his ears pop as the helicopter climbed. The terrain below had changed; the sprawling city had given way to scrub trees and mountains. He scanned the horizon. With the sun behind him, he was met with an incredible vista of the mountain range that traversed the southern third of Guatemala. To the south was Pacaya; a wisp of steam blew from the cone at the volcano's summit. Farther away he could pick out Agua and Fuego. They rose to over 11,000 feet above sea level and towered high above them. Donovan felt a chill not related to the dropping temperature. The volcanoes were a sharp reminder of the energy that lay beneath the earth. He couldn't ignore feeling small and insignificant against nature's fury.

The helicopter thudded along as Janie followed the main road that led the one hundred miles from Guatemala City to Lake Atitlán. The road gave her a constant reference and kept them clear of the hills; it would also be about the only suitable place to land if they had mechanical problems.

"There they are." Buck's voice filled Donovan's headset. Buck turned and pointed out the front windscreen.

Donovan stretched until he could finally see. Lying in a shadow of clouds were the distinct cones of all three volcanoes bordering the south side of Lake Atitlán. Mt. Tollimán, San Pedro and Atitlán. The lake's cobalt-blue water glistened in the morning light. As they sped closer, Donovan used the binoculars to make out some of the details. The clouds that shadowed the peaks weren't clouds at all, he discovered, but a plume of ash venting from Mt. Atitlán.

"Isn't it amazing!" Lillian said.

Donovan could see the exhilaration on her face and he began to understand what motivated these people.

"The lake is the remnant of a huge volcanic eruption, a gigantic crater that filled up with water," Malcolm said, looking up from adjusting his camera. "We're talking a mega eruption that would make Mt. St. Helens look like a polite after-dinner burp. St. Helens released two cubic kilometers of rock and ash. It's estimated that the explosion here, some eighty-five thousand years ago, released over one hundred eighty cubic kilometers of debris."

Donovan raised the binoculars. Despite the vibration from the helicopter, he was able to pick out the small white dots that represented the villages that lined the lakeshore. As he scanned south along the shore, the ground took on a different pallor, the vivid greens and whites faded and blended into sections obscured by sections of gray. Donovan studied the shift in colors and realized he was looking at the ashfall from the earlier eruptions.

Janie was flying low and fast as they passed over the eastern shore of the lake. Below, the shoreline was steep and rocky. At first glance, the placid water seemed devoid of any boats, but as Donovan's eyes swept the water he spotted the telltale wakes from two small vessels. The lake was virtually deserted.

"Where are we going first?" Donovan asked, not sure who might answer.

"We're going to where Stephanie was taken," Buck replied. "Janie will drop you and me off, and then Malcolm and Lillian can make their observations. When they're finished, they'll swing back and pick us up for the trip back."

Donovan straightened up in his seat and focused on the distant shore. The lake itself was probably eleven miles across at this angle. The closer they got to the far shore, the bigger and more ominous the volcano looked.

"I won't be able to land in the clearing you want to visit," Janie's voice filled Donovan's headphones. "It's too steep, but I will be able to hover close to the ground not far away, and you can jump."

"What about when you come back to get us?" Donovan asked.

"Several hundred yards downhill is another clearing that might allow me to hover just above the ground," Janie replied. "Otherwise, we'll use the hoist."

Cesar smiled and pointed to the harness that was coiled on the floor—it was attached to the thin cable of the rescue hoist.

Janie flew the helicopter in a wide circle and began to slow. Buck pointed out the left side and called out to Donovan. "That's the village of Santiago Atitlán. They came over on a boat from across the lake, and put to shore down there and started up the mountain."

Donovan watched as Janie slowed the helicopter and guided it closer to the trees. He was stunned by how sharply the terrain rose above them. The volcano dwarfed both man and machine. After what seemed like forever, there was a small break in the canopy of trees. Janie brought the craft smoothly into a hover and at the same time inched the 412 closer to the ground. The rotor wash whipped the trees bordering the clearing into a frenzy.

"Let's go!" Buck yelled back toward Donovan after he removed his headset.

Donovan unfastened his harness, handed his own headset to Cesar, and stepped closer to the door. He let Buck go first. Donovan guessed the distance at only four to five feet. Once Buck moved out of the way, Donovan too stepped free of the helicopter and hit the soft earth. The buffeting from the 412's main rotor was enormous. Overhead, Janie pulled away from them, electing to dive down the hillside and pick up speed as she headed out over the water. The whine of the engines and the drumbeat sound of the helicopter quickly vanished until the air was strangely still. Donovan was unprepared for the ominous feeling generated by standing on the side of an active volcano. Far above them, the steam and ash drifted away and posed no immediate threat, but the potential of what could happen made him uneasy.

"Follow me," Buck said as he moved quickly toward the nearest group of trees. "Stay down. I want to wait here for a moment and make sure our arrival hasn't drawn any unwanted visitors."

Donovan knelt next to Buck. "I can't believe it's so quiet, there's no noise from anything."

"I noticed," Buck whispered in return as he set his pack down and unzipped the main compartment. "That's what bothers me, it's unusual. We'll wait here and watch what happens. We have a portable radio, and Janie's monitoring the frequency. So stay close. If we need to get out in a hurry, she'll be here as fast as she can."

Donovan watched as Buck pulled a compact automatic weapon from the pack, quickly checked it over, then slung it over his shoulder. Donovan quietly jacked a shell into the chamber of his Sig.

Buck glanced at Donovan's weapon but said nothing. He slowly turned side to side as he listened intently for any sounds that might indicate they had company. "I think we're good. Let's have a look around. Stay where I can see you, and unless I tell you specifically to shoot, leave the gunplay to me."

Donovan stood up and joined Buck and they made their way through the cornfield. A fine coating of ash dusted most of the leaves, but the deposits here weren't nearly as severe as he'd seen earlier through the binoculars. It didn't take Buck long to find where the three men had been killed. The plants surrounding the area had been trampled flat by the boots of the searchers who'd discovered the bodies.

"This is the place." Buck turned and looked toward the west. "You can still see where the ground soaked up the blood. From what I understand, the bodies were found partially buried amongst the trees down below us. The spent 7.62mm shell casings were over there. The USGS team had just started digging this hole for their seismic equipment when the people who shot them arrived."

"They're scientists, so they wouldn't immediately run if they saw someone on the footpath. Plus, they had an armed guard."

"The initial investigation didn't find any other shell casings," Buck added. "They must have taken the guard completely by surprise because he didn't get off a single shot."

"But why would they come out of nowhere and just start shooting? It doesn't make any sense. Especially if they're kidnappers, they'd want to neutralize the guard, but keep the others alive." Donovan tried to stay focused, but the thoughts of Meredith came rushing at him with astonishing clarity. He tried to shut it out, but in his mind's eye, he was back in Costa Rica. Meredith was next to him in the back of their hired car. A vehicle blocked the road. The dark-clad figure had dashed out of the shadows, the windows of the car shattered, the doors flung open. Their driver died instantly in a hail of gunfire. A rifle butt was slammed into Donovan's face as Meredith was physically dragged from the car, screaming for help. The echo of her screams was all he could hear as his world faded and he lost consciousness—it was the last time he ever saw her alive.

"Donovan!" Buck jostled his arm. "Quit thinking so hard, you're going to hurt yourself."

Donovan's face felt flush. When he opened his eyes, the images started to recede, but the physical effects lingered. He looked to his left and found a puzzled expression fixed on Buck's face. "What? What did you say?"

"I think the bad guys walked into the clearing and started shooting. Any other scenario puts the shell casings closer to where the victims were killed. The question is, why?"

"The question is...where was Stephanie?" Donovan let his words drift off as a thought came to him. Here he was, standing in a clearing looking downhill at one of the most beautiful lakes he'd ever seen. Stephanie would have been shooting images like crazy. Donovan turned and studied the terrain up the mountain from where they stood. "I'll bet she was up there. If Rick and Oliver had just begun, then so had she. The first place she'd go would be to the high side of the clearing. She'd want to frame the pictures against the backdrop of the lake. I doubt if she was helping them dig. I'm going up there."

"Let's go look," Buck agreed. Gesturing for Donovan to lead the way, Buck brought up the rear, the machine gun balanced firmly in both hands.

Donovan moved carefully so that he didn't miss anything. If Stephanie had walked in this direction, there might still be tracks. He took a quick glance behind him and saw that Buck was doing the same thing, studying the ground as they walked. Silently, they made their way upward. Far in the distance, Donovan could just make out the faint sound of the helicopter, beating rotors reached his ears then just as quickly faded away. Donovan thought about how quiet it was, as if there was a complete absence of life around them. That's what's happening, Donovan thought, the birds and animals are gone, as if they somehow sense an impending eruption.

"Over here," Buck's voice broke the silence. "I found some tracks."

Looking down at the dirt, Donovan could see the impressions. It looked as if someone had stood in one place, and then moved from side to side. Exactly what a photographer would do to frame the shot. Beyond was a series of different marks in the soil.

Buck scanned the area, then pointed. "She squatted to get a different angle. See how the impressions are deeper at the balls of her feet? Different center of gravity. See these marks? They're hers, backing up while she tried to stay low. You were right, she was up here when the shooting started. Stephanie was trying to escape into the trees."

"She didn't get very far." Donovan could now clearly picture the events. "There's another set of boot prints coming out of the trees. Someone came up behind her."

"The bad guys rushed into the clearing and started shooting. Stephanie was up here, and I'm guessing she was trying to back out of the clearing into the trees. When they did spot her, they didn't kill her like the others, they took her. Seems she was the target all along."

Donovan slumped, deflated. He was standing in the very spot Stephanie had been taken. If Buck was correct, she'd watched the murder of three men and then been taken prisoner. Donovan tried to take a deep calming breath, but couldn't. He looked out over the lake, toward the towns he knew were located on the distant shore. Was she close? Had she heard the sound of the helicopter as they'd flown over earlier? Did she hope it was someone coming to rescue her—had her hopes been dashed when the helicopter didn't land, but, instead, droned on into the sky?

"Let's look around some more," Buck said. "We've got some time before Janie comes back for us."

Donovan turned toward Buck and then hesitated, not really understanding why. It was as if something was out of place. A momentary flash of color had registered, and his subconscious itched at him to stop and go back. Slowly, so as not to disturb the process, Donovan retraced his thoughts and actions, not at all sure what he'd noticed. His eyes darted from one footprint to another, seeing only the dirt and matted-down plants. He moved closer and knelt to get a different angle. He spotted a red object, hidden in the curl formed by the leaf of a plant as it grew out from the stalk. Donovan crouched and carefully reached out, as if it might vanish if he made one errant move.

"What are you doing?" Buck had stopped, turning toward Donovan. "Did you find something?"

Donovan pulled the memory card off the leaf and held it up for Buck to see. "This has got to be Stephanie's. She's clever, I'm guessing she somehow managed to leave it behind on purpose."

"We'll know soon enough." Buck slid his daypack from his shoulder and from a pocket pulled out a compact camera. He removed his memory card and slid in the one they'd just found. Donovan moved in close so they could both see.

The first exposures were of the lake, followed by shots of the boat. It had been a cloudy day so the volcanoes weren't visible. Casual shots of both Rick and Oliver as they set out to hike up the mountain, she standing between them, her hair pulled back, a green jacket and khaki field pants. A floppy hat with the bill turned up revealed a smile on her face. There was no fear in her eyes. Buck kept cycling through the images and then slowed as they both recognized the clearing. The next half-dozen pictures were of the two USGS men as they began to set up their equipment.

The next shot was taken through a fairly long lens, but the stark terror was plainly evident on the young girl's face pictured in the photo. Donovan cringed as the image sent involuntary chills down to the small of his back. The next image was of three armed men dressed as soldiers.

"They're not soldiers," Buck said. "The uniforms don't match, there are no insignias, and they're approaching the clearing all wrong. These men have never been in anyone's army."

"I see that, but we agree the men are chasing the girl?"

"Yeah," Buck replied and went through the next few images. There were three different pictures of the soldiers. Stephanie had gotten a clear shot of each man's face.

The next photos began with an explosion of blood as the USGS guard was shot and killed. The next one showed the taller of the USGS men standing in front of the girl, followed by him falling backward, two holes in his shirt where the bullets had penetrated his chest. By the time Stephanie captured an image of the remaining scientist, he had already been shot and was in a heap on the ground. The final image was of the girl standing alone, surrounded by the three bodies. Both of her hands covered her mouth in what must have been abject disbelief. Even on the camera's small screen, Donovan could see her expression of horror, mixed with all-encompassing fear. He wanted to look away, but didn't; he could feel the white-hot heat of revenge as it spread from the flush of his face and ran his entire body.

Buck lowered the camera. "I was wrong. The kidnapping hadn't been planned, it was a spontaneous accident."

Donovan felt an odd vibration through the soles of his feet that quickly turned into a distinct tremor as the ground moved beneath them. Buck snapped his head uphill as several sharp reports sounded from up the mountain. The shock waves ripped past them in seconds then echoed through the hills. The trees around them shook. Dislodged by the earthquake, a small avalanche of rocks, some the size of bowling balls, rolled out into the clearing—then it ended.

A moment later, Donovan smelled the strong odor of sulfur.

"Run!" Buck yelled as he put his hand over his nose and mouth.

Donovan took off down the hill. Each breath he took seemed to sear his throat and lungs. His eyes watered and he had trouble seeing the path.

"Janie!" Buck yelled into the radio. "An earthquake opened a vent, there's poison gas. We're moving downhill as fast as we can. Hurry!"

Donovan was light-headed and felt like he was going to be sick to his stomach. Another earthquake shook the ground. He lost his balance and was about to go down when a strong hand gripped him under the arm and steadied him.

"Keep moving!" Buck yelled as they pounded down the dirt trail.

Donovan wanted to reply, but each breath of toxic air burned and hurt. The light-headedness was getting worse. His head was spinning. He blinked wildly to try to clear the tears so he could see. He had no idea how long he could keep running. The earth rumbled beneath him and seemed to be getting louder. Donovan felt disoriented, oddly detached from the events going on around him. With Buck urging him on, he kept putting one foot in front of the other, his entire field of vision was focused three feet in front of him, trying not to fall.

They burst into a small clearing, and Buck tackled Donovan from behind, bringing him to the ground. Donovan hit hard, gasping for air. He rolled onto his back as the big Bell 412 roared into the clearing only inches above them. Janie locked the helicopter into a motionless hover. Through tear-filled eyes, Donovan could see Cesar motion them into the open door.

Donovan swayed as he tried to stand. Buck once again clutched him under the arm and pushed him up to where Cesar could use both hands to pull him into the cabin. Buck was next and, once they were aboard, Janie pivoted the helicopter and accelerated away from the mountain.

"Lie still," Lillian ordered as she knelt over him. "Open your eyes if you can."

Donovan did as he was told. The feeling of fresh air going into his lungs was the sweetest thing he'd ever experienced. He relished the feeling of cool water hitting his face, flushing out his tortured eyes. He could finally see well enough to take in the fact that Malcolm was doing the same to Buck. He felt his head clear and the dizziness ebb.

"You'll be fine in a few hours," Lillian said.

"What happened?" Donovan asked, his voice dry and raspy.

"An earthquake opened a large vent in the crust and released a toxic mixture of gases. I can still smell the sulfur on your clothes, so we know there was sulfur dioxide. There was probably hydrogen sulfide, carbon dioxide, and any number of other elements. Most of them are extremely toxic in high concentrations. You were lucky we were close."

Donovan nodded and closed his eyes. He thought of the little girl. The lost expression on her face as she'd witnessed the savagery of the men who'd captured her. They were the same men who'd taken Stephanie.

CHAPTER NINE

Lauren sat in her Land Rover outside Signature Flight Support at Dulles airport. The late summer sun was low on the horizon and cast an orange glow on the buildings. A text message had alerted Lauren to the fact that the chartered jet she was waiting for had landed. Up ahead, the glass doors opened, and a dark-headed, attractive, athletic-looking woman in dark glasses strode out into the sunlight. Veronica Montero, former FBI special agent, had arrived.

Lauren knew a great deal about Montero from reading confidential files. Montero was a natural blonde, looked thirty, but was in reality pushing forty. She'd never married, and until recently, had been a career FBI agent. Highly decorated for her work bringing down a terrorist cell, she'd retired, partly because of her injuries at the hands of one of the terrorists, but mostly because her public exposure had ended her days as a field agent. Through benefactors, she'd been given the money to expand a series of women's shelters in Southern Florida where she could work outside the public eye. She was an expert shot and a martial arts instructor, and unless some miraculous transformation had occurred in the last eighteen months, Montero had an attitude, a temper, and could be trusted to resort to violence if provoked.

Montero also knew Donovan's secret. She'd uncovered the truth during an investigation she'd led in Florida. Upon learning about his past, her first instinct had been to blackmail him, but her subsequent actions had been to save his life and help bury his secret. If nothing else, former FBI Special Agent Montero was an intelligent, complex woman, with resources and a moral compass that, for the most part, pointed north. Lauren steered the SUV to intercept her guest, wondering if she were even remotely doing the right thing.

As Lauren pulled to the curb, Montero removed her sunglasses, slid them on top of her head, leaned down, and the two women locked eyes. They were well aware of each other, and though they'd only met in person once, briefly, they'd significantly altered each other's life. Montero opened the backseat passenger door, placed her roller bag on the floor, and then closed the door. Without a word, she looked up and down the line of cars around them and then slid into the front seat of the SUV.

"Did you have a good flight?" Lauren asked, not at all certain what Montero's mood would be.

"Yes, it was good, thank you for that. I was able to work and we've already received some information from a friend of mine at FBI headquarters." Montero slid her sunglasses back into place. "I was able to get an update from Guatemala, as well as some archived files. I think you might be right about a reoccurring pattern."

"I've done some digging as well." Lauren put the SUV in gear, checked her mirrors and swung out from the curb. "We need to sit down and talk in private where we can compare notes."

"Any place in mind?" Montero asked as she put on her seat belt.

"My house," Lauren said, before she'd really thought it through. Technically, it was their house, and even though she'd been gone a year, these last three months with him gone made it feel more like her place than Donovan's. "I'm assuming you know that Donovan and I are separated?"

"I knew that—Donovan and I do stay in touch—though I haven't talked to him since he went to Montana. I guess that makes it three months or more since we last spoke."

Lauren hadn't known the two of them had stayed in touch and hesitated, then reminded herself this was the exact reason she'd called Montero, so she didn't have to filter each and every action and comment. As she drove, she caught Montero looking at her, assessing her.

"You're what I expected—for the most part you look like a suburban housewife," Montero said. "I know you've read a file or two on me, and that you know a great deal about who I am. Since I was asking for files from the FBI, I asked for yours."

Lauren smiled at the fact that Montero was on her game. Lauren had expected no less. "And?"

"You're far from a suburban anything. You're part scientist, part vigilante, on any given day you're without a doubt the smartest person in the room, and you carry a Glock. You attract men, yet intimidate them with your looks *and* your brain, and for the very same reasons, you don't have many women friends. You've authored the solutions to national emergencies, and yet you deflect the credit elsewhere. I was particularly interested in a recent report, the one about France and Alaska. It was heavily redacted, but thanks to already having heard most of the story from Donovan, I was able to read between the lines. You and Eco-Watch pulled off some amazing things, yet you broke the law and were in considerable trouble with both the FBI and the CIA, weren't you? If you're separated from Donovan, and I'm not here to judge, why do you keep working on his behalf?"

"Being separated doesn't mean I don't love him."

"What *does* it mean?" Montero asked.

"Do we have a conflict of interest? Do you have an agenda I need to know about?" Lauren asked, acting on impulse. "Have you slept with him?"

"You are direct, aren't you? The simple answer is 'no.' Look, I know without a doubt why I'm here. I made Donovan a promise. Your motivation seems a little less clear. I'm just trying to understand your level of commitment and where it comes from."

"I'm trying to help my husband and save Stephanie. The by-product of those two actions might save my marriage. So, yes, I'm pretty committed."

"Are you prepared to use your weapon?"

Lauren glanced down at her purse wedged into the console between them. Her Glock was within easy reach. Montero was pushing buttons, the former FBI agent's way to try to gain an advantage. She'd seen this behavior before in highly aggressive people. If nothing else, Montero was straight to the point. She understood a little more about why her husband trusted this woman. "I think we both know the answer to that question."

"I'm not trying to create barriers," Montero said. "I know all you think we're doing is research, but history says it's never that simple with you. If this turns into a fight, can I rely on you?"

Lauren swung into the driveway, opened the garage door, pulled in, and then made no move to exit the Range Rover. "Yes, you can count on me to answer force with force. Now, I have a question for you. You've been talking with my husband more than I have. What's your assessment of his mental state?"

"This is just my opinion, but I'll tell you what I told him. When his past intrudes, it pulls him back and he relives his perceived mistakes. He's caught in some kind of loop, and, in my opinion, until he gets some kind of absolution for those perceived sins, they'll eventually unravel him, and he won't make it back."

"I couldn't agree more." Lauren opened the door and led the way into the house. She called out to let Aimee, the babysitter, know she was home. The sound of running feet told her Abigail was coming at full steam. The four-year-old blew around the corner, curly hair streaming behind her. She was clutching a sheet of paper.

"Mommy! Aimee and I drew pictures!"

"Slow down, young lady." Lauren leaned down and caught her excited daughter around the waist and swung her up into her arms. "I thought we talked about running inside the house?"

"But, Mommy, I needed to show you my picture."

"We have company." Lauren stepped to the side so Abigail could see Montero. "This is Ms. Montero. She's helping me with some things from work."

"Hello, Abigail," Montero said.

"Hello," Abigail said politely, and then quickly turned back to her mother. "I drew a picture of me and Daddy and you. See, we're all together, just like when we made him a chocolate birthday cake."

"Very nice," Lauren said. She set her daughter down just as Aimee came down the hallway. "We'll put this one up in your room. Can you and Aimee draw another one while Ms. Montero and I get started in the study? After your bath, Aimee's going to go home, and I'll read you a story and tuck you in to bed."

"Nighttime snack?" Abigail asked.

"There might still be some cake. Only have a small piece, and then brush your teeth." The moment the words left Lauren's mouth, Abigail took off and ran toward the kitchen with Aimee in pursuit.

"Why did she draw Donovan with long hair and a beard?" Montero asked.

"When he showed up here, he hadn't shaved or gotten a haircut the entire time he'd been in Montana."

"Abigail looks like you, but she has Donovan's eyes," Montero said.

"If she looked like her father, we'd hardly know, would we?" Lauren replied with a well-intended shot to Donovan's appearance-altering surgeries. "What we do know is she inherited his impulsive, stubborn streak, and disregard for rules."

"Good for her. I'm a big fan of rebellion."

"That's what Donovan says," Lauren replied. Abigail was Daddy's girl, and one day she'd learn the truth about her father. Either from her parents, or God forbid, a resentful public. Lauren hoped that either way, that particular discussion was years from now. "Let's get started."

They settled in the study and Lauren unloaded her pistol but kept the clip in her pocket and the pistol in a drawer.

"I'd prefer to keep my weapon loaded," Montero said.

"Then it goes in the safe," Lauren said. "I have a four-year-old. No exceptions. I'm assuming you can load your weapon quickly if needed?"

Montero nodded as she pulled out her gun, dropped the magazine, slipped open the chamber and removed the bullet. She placed the now-empty pistol into her bag.

Lauren sat at the table and pulled out her laptop, motioning for Montero to take the seat across from her. Lauren then retrieved two bottles of water from the wet bar and, as computers booted up and papers were organized, Montero took her seat.

"Okay," Montero began. "The latest update I received from Guatemala is that a ransom note was delivered this morning. It was flown back to Andrews Air Force Base and taken directly to the FBI lab for analysis. The kidnappers asked for three million dollars and specified they'd only wait three days. There was also a bloody fingerprint on the note. As it turns out, it's fish blood, and it's not Stephanie's fingerprint, or anyone else's in the system for that matter. My contact says the move was more than likely meant to shock. It's a tactic the FBI behavioral psychologists suggest is an act of simple intimidation. The symbol of a bloody fingerprint is fairly common in relatively lawless regions such as Guatemala."

"Maybe it's where we start," Lauren said as she opened her laptop. "Kidnappings with a bloody fingerprint on the ransom note."

"In Central America, over the last twenty-five years, there have been three hundred eighty-one kidnappings with some variation on the theme. The FBI ran the parameters through the computers for similarities and nothing connected them together."

"Of those, how many were in Guatemala?"

"Eighty-four," Montero said as she handed Lauren a printout.

As Lauren scanned the numbers listed beside each country, her phone pinged, alerting her to an e-mail. She picked it up: a message from Buck. There were attachments and she elected to access his e-mail via her laptop:

Lauren–
Found these pictures on a memory card at crime scene.
We assume they're from Stephanie's camera.
See what you make of them, but show them to no one.
William is still adamant about no outside help.
–Buck

"What is it?" Montero asked. "What's wrong?"

"You need to see this."

Lauren and Montero huddled over the laptop and wordlessly clicked through each of the pictures.

"Go back," Montero said. "Go through them again."

Lauren and Montero went through the images a dozen times until Lauren finally stood and began to pace. "Okay, let's review what we think so far."

"The men are definitely chasing the girl."

"That makes the girl the primary target, not Stephanie," Lauren said. "Stephanie was at the wrong place at the wrong time."

"Which is good," Montero said. "It eliminates a vendetta against Stephanie or William. The kidnappers, who we know aren't soldiers, are in it for the money. William may have made the right call. Three million and his niece is returned."

"Except she's seen her kidnappers. She knows what they look like. Hell, we've seen them. We also have no idea if they've figured out a memory card is missing."

"I say we go back to the primary victim," Montero said. "We need to look for a motive in her abduction."

"There was a girl missing from Antigua." Lauren sat back down at the computer.

"How long ago? What's her deal? Where are her parents?"

"Here it is. A girl was abducted in Antigua six days ago by multiple men who shot and killed her armed escort."

"Okay, let's start with the girl and see what we can find out. I'm thinking not every grade-school girl in Guatemala has an armed escort. We need to know what's up with that. Maybe we can find a motive, and, from there, perhaps a suspect."

"Where do we start?"

"I work with six women's shelters in Florida. Most of the women I see are there because of a husband or a boyfriend. The fights are often due to children, custody battles, child support, and the like. There's a global network that lists missing children. We'll start there."

"I almost forgot about your work with at-risk women and girls," Lauren replied offhand as Montero typed.

"I find that odd, since you donated five million dollars to the shelter. Money we desperately needed to expand."

"That was supposed to be a secret," Lauren said, without so much as blinking.

"You said it yourself. I'm a detective. And thank you for the donation. You helped a great many people."

"It was a way to say thank you for all that you did for my husband," Lauren replied. "I'm glad it worked out."

"You're not going to believe this. I just found her." Montero shook her head in disbelief and then looked up from her laptop.

"What?" Lauren got up to look for herself. Pictured on the screen was, without a doubt, the girl from Stephanie's pictures.

"She was taken eighteen months ago in Los Angeles. Kidnapped from the house she shared with her mother. The girl's name is Marie Vargas; she's eight years old and an American citizen. Her mother, Alicia Vargas, claims her daughter was taken by her late husband's family, after the murder of Marie's father, Miguel."

"So, if what we're reading is true, Marie was kidnapped by her father's family after the death of her father." Lauren moved around the table and quickly began typing into her laptop. Moments later, Lauren was skimming an exposé that came out six months ago in the *Los Angeles Times*. The in-depth report was about children taken from the custodial parent and whisked from the country where they vanish. Even if they're located, the situation often turns into a bureaucratic nightmare. Marie Vargas was showcased as one of the examples. "Listen to this. Marie's grandfather, the man widely believed to have abducted his granddaughter, is not only a Mexican national, but he's also a rich, well-placed politician."

"What kind of politician?"

"He's listed as the Mexican emissary to Guatemala."

"This just got way more complicated," Montero said as she pressed her fingers to her temples. "And far more dangerous."

CHAPTER TEN

Donovan was sitting with Janie at a corner table in the hotel bar. The place was half-full, the Monday evening business travelers had begun to trickle in, and the low murmurs of surrounding conversations eclipsed the Latin music playing through the overhead speakers. Donovan had a clear field of view, wanting to spot Michael when he arrived. The *Galileo* had landed earlier, and work on the *Scimitar* interface had pushed past dinner. Michael was on his way to join them for a drink. The only news was the FBI had relayed to Buck that they'd found no solid fingerprints on the ransom note or the packaging. The next move still belonged to the kidnappers.

A slight headache and a sore throat were all that lingered from his earlier encounter with the volcano. That Janie had reacted so quickly made all the difference. When Donovan spotted Michael, he raised his hand to get his friend's attention.

Michael walked closer, a quizzical expression crossing his face as he studied Donovan's hair and beard. Donovan rose to greet his friend. Michael hugged Janie first, then turned to Donovan.

"Happy birthday, old man. What's with the hippie look? It's a little late for a midlife crisis, isn't it?" Michael said as they gave each other a handshake and then a hug.

"I was thinking about a tattoo next," Donovan replied, genuinely happy Michael had arrived. Their twelve-year friendship had been forged in the high-stress environment of flying Eco-Watch jets. Donovan would, and had, trusted Michael with his life.

"You could get a tattoo of your actual birth date, you know, to remind yourself you're fifty!" Michael replied. "All kidding aside, it's good to see you. How are you doing?"

"I'm good." Donovan didn't want to talk about himself, he wanted to talk about Eco-Watch. He knew very little of what had been happening for the last three months. "Who are you flying with?"

"I'm with Craig. He had to call home, said he'd join us shortly."

"What was the delay this evening with the *Galileo*?" Donovan asked, as the waitress arrived and took Michael's order.

"Something kept popping a breaker on the symbol generator for the *Scimitar* control board. They finally found a defective relay. It's complicated. All I know is the *Scimitar* is fixed, and we're all set to go in the morning." Michael thanked the waitress as she brought him his drink, then raised his glass. "It's good to see you both."

Donovan raised his glass in return. "Thank you for taking care of Eco-Watch. You made my sabbatical a little easier."

"We were all shocked to hear about Stephanie. Who went to Montana to get you?"

"I didn't think anyone knew where I was until a friend of Lauren's arrived."

"We all knew where you were," Michael allowed himself a crooked smile. "We respected your wish to be left alone, we just kept tabs on you."

"So much for a man's privacy," Donovan said, as he spotted a woman come in and sit by herself at the bar. Though Donovan was easily thirty paces away, his first impression was that she was beautiful, elegant, in a very refined way. She sat at the end of the bar and placed her jacket and purse on the empty barstool next to her, presumably to dissuade anyone from joining her. She had thick black hair that hung down past her shoulders. Her bangs ended right above large expressive eyes. She wore dark slacks and a sleeveless top, a silver necklace hung from her neck and teased the cleavage revealed by her low-cut blouse. Lean and slender, she was about five-foot six, but even at this distance he could see the graceful, sculpted muscles in her arms. Her bronze skin seemed flawless. Donovan watched as she tossed back her hair and ordered a drink. She glanced at him, turned away, and then slowly came back to him. She tilted her face and smiled coyly before turning her attention to the arrival of her drink. In that briefest of moments, he couldn't help but notice that the flash of her smile was framed by perfectly formed lips.

Donovan decided offhandedly that she was easily one of the more beautiful women he'd ever seen. He blinked away his thoughts and refocused on Michael.

"We're excited by the *Scimitar*'s possibilities," Michael said. "According to the USGS, the seismic activity comes and goes, which isn't unusual. What *is* unusual is that the intensity and endurance of the earthquake swarms is growing. We'll have a far better picture tomorrow."

The conversation centered on work, as Janie started asking Michael questions about the *Scimitar,* and he began inquiring about the new helicopter. Donovan was only half-listening, and he couldn't help but once again glance past Michael and Janie toward the woman. She sat with a wine glass in front of her. She turned unexpectedly and caught Donovan watching, her demure smile turned mildly suggestive. This time she held his eyes with hers a little longer before turning away. Donovan was slightly amused by her behavior. He watched as she languidly shifted positions, using a finger to slide her long hair behind her ear. It briefly occurred to him that she might be a prostitute; he'd spent enough time in hotel bars to know that it was the typical haunt of working girls. He watched as several men stopped and spoke with her, but she deflected each of them with practiced ease, and they moved on. Donovan decided she wasn't working. His thoughts were interrupted at the sound of Michael loudly clearing his throat.

"She must be attractive," Michael said. "And if you don't

quit looking at her, I'm going to have to turn around and look for myself."

"She's worth a look," Donovan said, smiling.

Michael slowly turned, then snapped his head back, eyes wide. "Wow."

"You blokes are terrible." Janie rolled her eyes, but then she, too, turned to take a look. "She's top-shelf, that one."

Donovan could see that the woman had positioned herself at the bar and was using the mirror behind the bar to keep an eye on the door. A distinguished-looking man walked into the bar and stopped as if to survey the room. When the woman noticed him, her expression went from recognition to fear, and then a mask of panic clouded her delicate features. She didn't move, but she quickly averted her gaze and signaled for her check. Donovan's eyes darted to the door. The man had walked to a table and was shaking hands with the men seated there.

Donovan watched as another man entered, furiously searching the semi-crowded room. The moment he spotted the woman at the bar, he reached inside his jacket and pulled out a pistol.

Before Donovan could say or do anything, the man opened fire. The varnished wood of the bar next to the woman exploded, throwing splinters into the air. The roar of the pistol was deafening, followed by screams and shouts as patrons began to panic.

Donovan was immediately out of his chair, gun drawn as he dropped to the floor and pulled Janie down as well. He heard another shot reverberate through the room, followed by the sound of breaking glass as the bullet just missed the woman's head and slammed into the bottles behind the bar. Michael hit the deck and shielded Janie's body with his own. More shots were fired from across the room. Through the smoke and chaos, Donovan saw the gunman go down. Moving in behind the fallen man, guns drawn, were two embassy security men assigned to protect Eco-Watch. The customers were making a mad rush for the door, an onslaught that quickly overran security.

Donovan looked for the woman, hoping she hadn't been

shot. He scanned the bar and both her jacket and purse were gone. He holstered his weapon and went to the fallen gunman. Donovan took one look at the man's face and recognized him as one of the men from Stephanie's pictures. He hurried toward the lobby, but the woman wasn't there either. Outside, it was pouring down rain. Donovan pushed through the doors; despite the weather, the street was full of cars, buses, even motorcycles, their riders soaked from the downpour. The sound of sirens in the distance rose above the general roar of engines and honking horns. A block away, he saw a woman walking fast, her jacket pulled up to shield her from the rain.

He lost sight of her and began to run. Comforted by the weight of his pistol, he raced along the sidewalk, eyes scanning both sides of the street. He came to the first intersection and stopped. He looked as far as he could in each direction, desperately trying to catch sight of her again. He studied the people inside a bus that roared by, wondering if she'd made her escape via public transportation. As soon as traffic allowed, he bolted across the street.

Breathing heavily, Donovan stopped at the next corner. The pedestrian traffic was lighter, and he studied each person on both sides of the street, confident he'd be able to spot her if she were close. He turned around and looked the way he'd just come. Then he took advantage of a gap in the traffic, crossed the street, and continued moving away from the hotel. The sound of sirens filled his ears as the first of two police cars raced past, no doubt heading toward the hotel. In his peripheral vision, about three doors down, he spotted a flash of something bright, but it was gone as fast as he'd seen it. Donovan slid closer to the wall, and as quietly as he could, began moving closer to what was a recessed doorway of a building.

Donovan kept his pistol low against his leg. As he drew closer in he could hear a woman's voice as she talked on a phone. The flash he'd seen was from the screen of a phone. She was speaking fast, obviously agitated. Without hesitation, Donovan rounded the corner and faced her.

She was even more beautiful than he'd thought. Her hair was wet and fell across the side of her face. Her chest was moving rhythmically from what was probably a mixture of both fear and exertion. Her dark eyes flared wide at the sudden surprise of being found. With a trembling hand she lowered the phone, her eyes darting back and forth like a wild animal.

"I won't hurt you," Donovan said as she looked up at him, as if measuring the man and the words. "Do you recognize me? I was in the bar—I saw what happened. I can help you."

"You're an American?" She replied in English with a heavy Spanish accent.

"Yes. The man who tried to shoot you, who is he? Do you know him?"

"They will kill me," she said quietly, renewed panic in her eyes. She searched the street behind him. "I must go. They are trying to kill me."

"Who's trying to kill you?" Donovan asked, though she seemed suddenly distracted, as if her fear was getting the best of her. She was preparing to bolt. "Please, listen to me. My name is Donovan Nash. I'm staying at the hotel and I can protect you."

"I am not safe." She shook her head. "I need to hide—I have seen too much."

"What did you see?" Donovan raised his voice, hoping to break through her panicked state. "I have to know what you saw!"

"I fled the lake. The volcano was getting bad, and we had to leave." She leaned forward, placing the palms of her hands on Donovan's chest. She found his eyes with hers. "They know who I am. I saw them."

Startled by her closeness, Donovan could smell the wine on her breath and the subtle aroma of lavender. She was trembling. "Who did you see? Who did you see at the lake?"

Behind him, Donovan heard the urgent screech of brakes. As he turned, he found a small blue Toyota at the curb, rusted and dented. He never saw her deliver the sudden blow to his throat. Donovan doubled over, gagging as tears clouded his vision. He tried to stand up straight but couldn't. He struggled for a full breath, but nothing happened. He felt her hands steady him as he dropped his pistol and went down on all fours to the wet sidewalk. Donovan reached out and grabbed her by the wrist, using all his strength to keep her from running. He lost his grip as he fought to get air back into his lungs.

She bent down and whispered, "I'm sorry. I can't get you involved." She patted him on the back as if to comfort him.

Donovan gurgled, unable to answer. Furious, both at her, and himself; he could do nothing. He heard her run away. The door to the car opened, then slammed shut, and the car sped away into the rainy Guatemalan night. It took him a few minutes before he was able to breathe well enough to pull himself to his feet. He reclaimed his pistol and walked back to the hotel in the rain.

The lobby was humming with police. Donovan could see that the body of the gunman had been covered. Buck was waiting, obviously furious. Together they took the elevator up to their floor. The only conversation was Buck confirming that Michael and Janie were okay. Once inside his room, Donovan toweled off as they waited for William and Michael to join them. Once everyone had gathered, Donovan explained what had happened when he left the hotel.

"You're convinced this woman knows who the kidnappers are?" William asked.

Donovan nodded. "The gunman downstairs was one of the guys in the pictures. The woman claims she saw something, and now there are people who want to kill her."

"I'd say she's right," Michael said. "I mean, the guy just walked in, pulled a gun, and opened up on her. She'd be dead if the embassy guards hadn't reacted so quickly."

"She wasn't sitting there for more than ten minutes," Donovan added. "Our only hope is that the Guatemalan police might be able to identify the gunman's body."

"What now?" Michael asked.

"I'll follow up with the Guatemalan police," William said.

"But there won't be any news until tomorrow. Gentlemen, I'd like to talk to Donovan privately. Buck, why don't you go downstairs, lend a hand if need be. If you discover anything I need to know, please call me."

"I'm flying *Galileo* on the *Scimitar* test flight in the morning. We should land by early afternoon," Michael said to Donovan as he stood. "Where are you going to be?"

"He'll be going with you," William said, as if the matter had already been decided. The stern look in his eyes left little room for argument.

"What time shall we meet?" Donovan asked as he gave in. He knew William was angry with him for chasing the woman and wanted him aboard the *Galileo* so he'd be out of harm's way. It wouldn't be worth the energy to try to change his mind.

"Lobby at seven, wheels up at nine," Michael replied as he joined Buck at the door. "See you then. Good-night."

"You didn't argue. That's unlike you," William said as Michael and Buck departed, closing the door quietly behind them.

Donovan got up and walked to the bar. He grabbed a beer, opened the bottle, and then sat next to William. "I'm sorry about tonight."

William sat quietly, as if searching for the right words. "What you did was beyond reckless. Did you stop to think about anything before you ran after this woman? The answer is no— you didn't think—you reacted blindly, irresponsibly."

There was no defense. Donovan also knew it wasn't so much about him, as about everything else that was happening. "You're right."

"I can't afford to lose you. I'd never be able to look Lauren or Abigail in the eyes again. Do you ever think about those of us who love you when you jump into the line of fire?"

"I was fine," Donovan replied, trying to get William to calm down. "It's why I went after her. I want the three of us—you, me, and Stephanie—to get on a plane and leave this place together. Finding the woman from the bar was a link to who we're after."

"We're not after anyone!" William squeezed his eyes shut as if to control his emotions. "We're here to pay the ransom and go home. Do you have any idea how many strings I had to pull to keep this from becoming an all-out manhunt? The State Department wanted to send people, the FBI would normally have dozens of agents down here, as well as the CIA, and God knows who else. It would be a goddamned three-ring circus, and all we'd be able to do is stand around and wring our hands while those people bickered and got in each other's way. You know the scenarios as well as I do!"

Donovan nodded. It was exactly what had taken place when Meredith was kidnapped—and more than likely one of the reasons she was killed. "I understand, but if we could find them first—we could turn a ransom exchange into a rescue. I'm not willing to rule out that option."

"I'm terrified of that prospect," William whispered. He shook his head and looked down at his hands and his lower lip began to quiver. He collected himself and turned toward Donovan. "So many things can go wrong. I just want Stephanie alive."

William's tears caught Donovan off guard. Ever since he was a little boy, Donovan had always looked up to William as a pillar of strength. It seemed as if William could do anything in the world, and, more times than not, he had. Right this moment, all Donovan saw was a fragile, frightened man, and it broke his heart. Donovan leaned over and put a protective arm around the man he loved, just as the phone on the nightstand rang.

"Hello." Donovan expected it to be either Buck or Michael.

"Mr. Nash?"

Donovan recognized her voice immediately and felt the hair on his arms stand at attention. It was the woman from the bar. "This is Donovan. What can I do for you Ms...?"

"My name is not important," she said. "I'm very sorry I hit you. But it was for your own good."

"What do you want?"

"The reason I came to the hotel," she began, haltingly, "was to find Mr. VanGelder."

"Go on."

"I need to meet with him," she continued. "I have information about his niece."

"Are you trying to sell this information?" Donovan was growing even angrier with himself for letting her get away in the first place. Now, here he was, listening to her trying to make some kind of deal. If he'd managed to get her back to the hotel, they would probably already know everything by now.

"No," she snapped defensively. "But it is information that will get me killed if I am not careful. I want to trade."

"What kind of trade?"

"Get me out of the country. They want to kill me. I know these men, and they will never give up. I must leave Guatemala."

"Come over and we'll talk," Donovan replied, knowing that it probably wouldn't be as easy at that. "You'll be safe here."

"Not when the police are there. They cannot be trusted."

As Donovan listened intently, it sounded as if she put her hand over the phone to speak with someone.

"I have to go," she whispered, suddenly sounding frightened. "I will call tomorrow evening."

"Was it Stephanie you saw at the lake? We have to find her!" Donovan practically yelled into the phone. His pleas were met with silence—she'd already gone.

"Well?" William pressed.

"That was her. She wants to make a deal," Donovan replied. "What she knows in return for a way out of the country. She saw something, otherwise there wouldn't be people trying to kill her. I think we need to listen to what she has to say."

"How do we tell her she has a deal?" William went to the wet bar.

"We don't," Donovan said and watched the glimmer of hope

fade from William's eyes. "She said she'd call us back tomorrow evening. In the meantime, all we can do is wait."

William poured three fingers of Scotch and then without joy took a measured sip. "Then let's pray she can survive the next twenty-four hours."

CHAPTER ELEVEN

"I say we just call them," Lauren remarked as she sipped from her cup of coffee. It was a little past six in the morning. She and Montero were both up and had already been working for an hour. "You're Special Agent Ronnie Montero. You don't have to ask them—tell them what you want. We want the file on Marie Vargas, her father, mother, and grandfather. See where it goes from there."

"I get that part. I'm just trying to figure out who at the Bureau to call these days. I didn't make any friends when I up and resigned."

"What about Deputy Director Norman Graham? I'll bet he'll take your call."

"Oh, I know he will," Montero said. "I'm just not sure how receptive he'll be when he finds out I'm working with you on the kidnapping of Stephanie VanGelder."

"He can't still be mad at me, can he?" Lauren replied.

"The story I heard was you belittled him, outmaneuvered him, and then threatened him in front of a room full of his subordinates. He didn't appreciate all that, but, between you and me, nice work."

"I was having a bad day." Lauren clearly recalled each distinct moment of that morning. "Graham was being a monumental jerk and got what he deserved, but he loves you. Give it a shot, what have you got to lose?"

Montero nodded, stood, and stretched, then picked up her phone and dialed a number from memory that was answered immediately. "This is Ronnie Montero for Deputy Director Graham. Yes, I'll hold."

"Put it on speaker," Lauren said, but Montero's response was to turn her back.

"Good morning to you too, Norman," Montero said. "I hope I'm not disturbing you."

Lauren quietly poured herself another cup of coffee while the two of them exchanged pleasantries.

"The reason I called is to ask a favor." Montero went to her computer screen. "I'm looking for information on a young girl who was kidnapped eighteen months ago in Los Angeles. Her name is Marie Vargas."

Lauren was unprepared for the sight of a sudden look of surprise flash across Montero's face. An instant later, Montero's eyes narrowed and a subtle smile crept across her face.

"Yes, she's here. I'm putting you on speaker."

"Good morning, Dr. McKenna."

"Good morning, Director Graham, or may I call you Norman?"

"Director Graham works just fine. Now, I can only deduce from Ronnie's request that the two of you are working on the VanGelder kidnapping in Guatemala? Is that correct?"

"Yes, we decided to take a look into some cold cases to see if we could contribute to the investigation," Montero offered. "Marie Vargas popped up on the network of missing and exploited children with connections to Central America and Mexico. We were looking for more information."

"Veronica, that's the biggest load of crap I've ever heard you try to peddle. There must be thousands of missing children with ties south of the border. Level with me, what new information do you have about Marie?"

Lauren saw Montero's nostrils flare as she placed both hands palm down on the table and leaned in toward the phone. "We've talked about that, and you know my name. Now, I asked you a favor, will you help us find this girl?"

"I know both of you think you're pretty clever, but did it occur to you that despite William VanGelder's considerable influence, the FBI did not in fact just wave good-bye to him and stop working the case? I have an off-site location with my top analysts looking at Marie, her murdered father, and her very corrupt grandfather. Why should I share?"

"Off-site?" Lauren asked. "What are you hiding?"

"A hunch," Graham replied.

"Maybe we can help?" Montero asked. "We're not exactly forced to hole up in a safe house. What's your hunch?"

"Dr. McKenna, with your connections at the Defense Intelligence Agency, I'm surprised you haven't already gotten a phone call."

"What does that mean?" Lauren felt the rush of blood that signaled impending bad news.

"The moment the embassy in Guatemala was notified about Ms. VanGelder's disappearance, the director of the FBI himself was ready to throw every available asset into her safe release. William VanGelder quashed all of that with one call to the attorney general. The working theory here, as well as at Langley, is that Stephanie VanGelder's kidnapping is payback, aimed directly at William VanGelder for his transgressions in Central America that stretch back over thirty years. An FBI task force is being formed to take a long, hard look into William VanGelder's business and political dealings."

Lauren felt as if she might be sick. That William was in any way dirty was beyond her comprehension—that the FBI was digging, threatening to expose everything, including the fact that Donovan Nash wasn't who he said he was.

"I find that hard to believe," Montero said, looking at Lauren as if waiting for a reaction.

"I've heard speculation mixed with rumor on the subject," Lauren said as she carefully calculated her words. "I haven't known Mr. VanGelder all that long, but I get the impression that you could be correct about his niece."

"Coming from you, Dr. McKenna, that's a valuable piece of insight," Graham said. "Ronnie, I'll send you some files, but they come with a price tag."

"What are we talking about?"

"I do have a use for the two of you, but you answer only to me. Is that understood?"

"I'm still waiting to hear the price," Montero replied.

"It involves another hunch," Graham said. "I'll send you the files, but then I want you to make a call to the Central American desk, ask for Special Agent Curtis Nelson. Ask him for the file regarding kidnappings and oil companies. I'll approve the action. I'm curious what he sends you or what else might come out of the woodwork."

"I've met Nelson, he seemed like an okay guy. Do you think he's dirty?" Montero asked.

"Maybe not dirty, but there are some flags that say he might be helping some old secrets stay hidden."

"I see," Montero replied. "Is that all?"

"For now. Is the e-mail we've used in the past still good?" Graham asked.

"Yes."

"Keep your eyes open and stay out of trouble, both of you," Graham said. "Again, it's important to report only to me. I'll include my private direct number along with the files. I hope all of this turns out to be nothing, but as we all know, rumors sometimes have an origin in the truth."

Montero reached for her phone; Graham had disconnected the call. She turned to Lauren. "What the hell was that? William is like a father to Donovan."

"Exactly. I lied so we could be on the inside of this thing," Lauren said. "We're going to get a look at what they have, and for the moment, Graham trusts us with his office politics. The second those files arrive, call Nelson and see what he'll do for us."

"Are you sure? We send the pictures to Graham and it becomes obvious that William's niece being kidnapped was a completely random act."

"And the men who have Stephanie kill her and vanish," Lauren replied. "William's reputation can withstand a few more days of FBI analysts digging around. Hopefully, by then, we'll have Stephanie back safe and sound."

"Graham's e-mail is here," Montero said as she checked her inbox. "Is there a printer?"

Lauren checked on Abigail while Montero printed out the pages Graham sent. Her daughter would sleep for at least another hour. She returned to the study and Montero wordlessly handed her a sheet of paper. It was a list of kidnappings. The FBI was focused on a group of crimes that they suspected may implicate William. The first victims were a family from Brazil. With a determination she hadn't felt in a long time, Lauren found a pencil and notepad, then settled in and began reading.

Montero looked up from her pages, glanced at the time, and then made the call to the Bureau and asked for Special Agent Curtis Nelson. She put the conversation on speaker, and, of course, Nelson remembered Montero. He said he'd have to get approval to gather the files, but that he'd get started right away.

Twenty minutes later, Lauren looked up from what she'd been reading. "I think I found what the FBI used as a common thread. All of these kidnappings resulted in either property, drilling, or mineral rights changing hands. Assets went to various companies over the years, but, ultimately, they all ended up as a part of Huntington Oil."

"Which takes us back to William VanGelder. How long was William a part of Huntington Oil?" Montero asked.

"He resigned his seat on the board roughly fifteen years ago," Lauren said.

"Of all the criminal files the FBI sent us, when did the last entity finally become a part of Huntington Oil?"

Lauren sifted through the papers until she found the one she wanted. "Right here, Sun West Petroleum became a part of Huntington Oil the year before William stepped down."

"So, conceivably, he could have been involved in all these crimes."

"In theory, though some of them go back to when Robert was CEO of Huntington Oil, before Meredith was killed. So, Donovan could also be complicit in these crimes. Speaking of Meredith, I wonder why her file wasn't included?"

"You said it earlier—no land, leases, or drilling rights were involved."

"I guess that makes sense, though the oil industry had to have taken a collective sigh of relief when she was gone."

"Another reason they didn't send that file is that it's listed as a solved case."

"We both know that's bullshit," Lauren snapped, surprised at how quickly she came to Meredith's defense. "The authorities botched the whole thing from beginning to end. They no doubt buried the file to try and stave off further embarrassment."

"You're pretty close to the truth," Montero replied.

"That's too bad; I'd have liked to have a look."

"I just got an e-mail from Curtis Nelson." Montero pulled her laptop closer and opened the message. She quickly scanned the attachments. "They're all here. He sent every case that the task force handled."

"That leaves us with a stack of reports that, if you squint hard enough, makes William look like some sort of master criminal. I don't believe it, and I don't think you do either. We need more data."

"We need different data. Files are only going to tell us what someone wanted the after-action report to say. Trust me, field reports can be slanted to a certain bias without too much problem. I saw a name on some of the files. I think he's the guy we want to talk with, a former FBI agent by the name of Gordon Butterfield."

"Why him?" Lauren asked.

"Butterfield was in and out of Central America for most of

his career. He might be able to shed some light on these kidnap-pings as well as some of the other players. Hector Vargas is in his sixties, which means he could have been around when Butterfield was down there as well. Butterfield is worth tracking down, if he's still alive. But it might take a while to find him." Montero fished under the pile of papers on the table for her phone. "Oh, and about what we talked about a little while ago, about Meredith's file? You called it earlier. I've been interested in her life and sub-sequent death since I met her in college. I've had the file for years. Let me know if you want to read the thing."

"Has Donovan?"

"He has his own copy," Montero replied, then dialed her phone. "I need to report to Deputy Director Graham, he needs to know that Nelson sent the files."

Lauren grabbed both their coffee cups and went back into the kitchen for one more refill. Abigail would be waking up any minute. She poured the last of the coffee, rinsed out the carafe, and carried both cups back to the study.

"Graham did us a favor," Montero announced as she took the fresh cup from Lauren's hand. "He gave us Butterfield."

"Where is he?" Lauren asked, as she sat down her cup and reached for her phone.

"He's retired. He lives in Johnson City, Tennessee. Graham says the man lives and breathes golf. Who are you calling?"

"We have an airplane on twenty-four hour standby and we need them to fly us to Johnson City. I'll see if Aimee can come over and watch Abigail. Grab what you need for the day, I want to be out of here inside thirty minutes."

"You know, you're just like him," Montero said as she began gathering the reports.

"Who?"

"Donovan."

"Hardly," Lauren said dismissively.

"Really? In the last twenty-four hours, you've collaborated with me, lied to the FBI, and now we're chartering a jet to interrogate a former FBI agent. Oh, yeah, you also carry a gun and aren't afraid to use the thing. And right this moment, heaven save anyone who gets in your way."

Lauren started to argue and then clenched her jaw shut at the realization that Montero was more than a little right.

CHAPTER TWELVE

Seated in the back of the *Galileo*, Donovan leaned forward to take in the view. Outside, flying just off the right wing was the *Scimitar*. Donovan was at one of the empty science stations away from the activity near the front of the cabin. Professor Murakami, as well as Malcolm and Lillian Lane, were hovering over the large console installed specifically for *Scimitar*. Wearing a headset, his hands firmly on the controls, was John Dorsey. John was with the USGS and was the program pilot of the *Scimitar* team. Tall and lanky with an easygoing smile and a crew cut, John had explained he'd been in the Air Force and had flown the military version of the *Scimitar*. Introduced earlier, Donovan had immediately liked the young man.

Donovan watched as John moved a small control stick, not much different from the type used for video games, and saw outside that the *Scimitar* responded immediately. There were two primary computer screens positioned in front of John. One was the real-time view using the nose-mounted camera; the other was used for either the synthetic aperture radar, or the infrared imaging system, or split to observe both at the same time. As they flew westward, John switched back and forth, checking out the various systems of the *Scimitar*.

William and Buck had stayed behind at the hotel. The Guatemalan police were trying to identify the gunman who'd been killed in the bar, and Buck had been concerned with the delicate task of trying to balance what they knew with what they could expect from a corrupt police force. In the end, they'd decided that they wouldn't share any of their findings with the local authorities.

"Mr. Nash," Professor Murakami called back to Donovan. "You might want to come take a look at this. It's rather breathtaking."

Donovan stepped behind Lillian and studied the images on *Scimitar*'s flight display screens.

"We can see the volcano from here," Malcolm said excitedly. "There looks to be more ash being expelled than yesterday. Once we get closer, we'll set up a grid and get as many baseline measurements as we can. Then we'll fly the *Scimitar* through the ash cloud itself and, using the mass spectrometer, sample the gases. Primarily, we expect to find carbon dioxide, sulfur dioxide, and hydrogen sulfide. It's amazing to think we used to go up on the side of a volcano and manually test for the chemical compounds by hand. If this goes as planned, we could be seeing a new era of volcano research."

Donovan nodded. He could hear John talking to Michael through the headset, advising him to begin his on-station orbit. The Gulfstream would fly a large holding pattern that would keep them safely out of reach of the ash, while John guided *Scimitar* on its first circuit around the volcano. Seated at a station next to John, Professor Murakami controlled the sensors that would collect the much-needed data from the volcano.

Donovan glanced toward the cockpit as Craig emerged and motioned for him to come forward. Then he worked his way past John and the others and negotiated the narrow aisle that led to the flight deck. "What's up?"

"Michael wanted me to go back and take a look at the *Scimitar* operation," Craig said. "He said something about if you wanted to come up where the real pilots sit, he wouldn't mind the company."

"Thanks." Donovan nodded and grinned at Craig. The young man had been with Eco-Watch a little over a year now and had blended in nicely with the tight-knit group. Craig was a good, solid pilot, and Michael, as always, had played a big part in smoothing Craig's transition.

"Coming up." With practiced ease, Donovan slid himself into the right seat of the Gulfstream. In one smooth motion he brought the seat forward, buckled himself in, and quickly scanned the instruments before taking in the view out the window. The mountain itself lay perhaps five miles away and nearly four miles below them, but the gray boiling ash reached upwards straight for them before shearing off at the top by the high altitude winds—not unlike the anvil top of a thunderstorm.

"Pretty impressive, isn't it?" Michael asked. "I don't think I've ever flown this close to an active volcano."

"Amazing," Donovan agreed, and then listened as a stream of Spanish came over the overhead speaker. "Who are we listening to?"

"Right now we're in contact with Guatemala air traffic control, such as it is. We're the only aircraft in this part of the sky, so we can do pretty much anything we want. The commercial traffic is being routed around the ash cloud. As near as I can tell, we're the only ones flying an airplane this close to a known airborne hazard. All the other pilots seem to have enough common sense to fly someplace else."

Donovan nodded in agreement. Michael's comment held an element of truth.

"We didn't really get a chance to talk much last night," Michael said. "You seem a little off. Are you feeling okay?"

"Thanks—I'm good. I'm not sleeping well, is all." Donovan felt both troubled and touched at Michael's observation, though there was no way to describe how he felt. Michael had no clue about Donovan's past, which was exactly the way he wanted it to remain. He and Michael were close, closer than anyone he'd had as a friend when he was Robert Huntington. If Michael ever found out, the dynamic of their relationship would change overnight. So right this moment, there was no way to explain to Michael that his world was coming unraveled, that the distant past had somehow leapfrogged into the present, and managed to blur everything in between. Meredith Barnes seemed to be calling to him, and, at times, hers was the loudest voice of all.

"Okay," Michael replied. "But if memory serves me correctly, you never sleep well."

"You're right, it's not just the sleep. I'm worried about William." Donovan hesitated. He knew he was touching on dicey territory. "I've known him, as well as Stephanie, since the formation of Eco-Watch. It's why all this is so hard."

Michael studied his friend. "I completely understand. William is one of a kind; we all love the guy, but try to remember you've been on a well-deserved sabbatical. Now you're trying to go from zero to full speed virtually overnight. I can't help but wonder if you should be here in Guatemala. I don't want anything to happen to you, and I know Lauren and William don't either. It's obvious to me your head isn't in the game. It might be a sign to sit this one out."

"Can't do it," Donovan answered, not bothering to dispute anything Michael had just said. "Sometimes you've got to play hurt. I can't go home until this is finished."

"Good enough. Then at least be smart enough to let your team take some of the load. We're not all here just because of our good looks." Michael shot Donovan a crooked grin. "Well, in my case, that might be partly true. We're all good at what we do. If you need us, don't hesitate to ask."

Donovan nodded and turned to look out the side window. It pained him to not be able to tell Michael the real reasons about why this was affecting him to the extent that it was. He'd resolved long ago never to tell Michael, or Buck, or anyone else who worked at Eco-Watch, the truth about who he was. It was the price he paid for his actions in the past. He allowed himself to wonder what Meredith would say about his predicament. She'd been the catalyst for so much of who he was today. It had been twenty-two years ago, but he was nearly overcome with the feeling that it had been only yesterday. He looked off in the distance to the southeast—where the sky met the earth was Costa Rica. It was where she'd left him. Right this moment, Donovan could almost feel her, as if the years had melted away and she'd be there when they landed.

Donovan caught sight of the lake and the volcano as they wheeled in the sky and his reality crashed down around him. Meredith was dead. He'd lost her. He'd lost everything he'd had with her and everything he was *ever* going to have with her. There was something incomprehensible about losing the promise of tomorrow that made it worse than anything else a human could experience. He'd been helpless to stop her death, and as he looked down at the ground below him, he knew Stephanie was down there somewhere, and he felt as if she too were going to die unless he did something.

"Guys," Craig called out from just outside the cockpit. "We need to head back now. Professor Murakami has discovered that the *Scimitar* has a coolant leak. John says we should return to base before more problems develop."

Michael picked up the microphone to relay the request to the Guatemala air traffic control center.

Donovan unfastened his harness and got up out of the seat. "Here you go, Craig, you fly. I want to go back and see what's going on." Donovan patted Michael on the shoulder as he slipped from the cockpit and hurried back to the *Scimitar* control panel.

"The instruments are heating up," Lillian explained. "We made four passes right through the ash cloud. Professor Murakami thinks we're losing coolant."

"So far nothing has affected the controls," John said, without looking up from the small screen he was using to pilot the *Scimitar*. "We're hoping the liquid nitrogen is venting overboard—and not into the airframe itself. Once I maneuver it back into visual range, we can look for ourselves."

Donovan glanced at Malcolm. He had removed himself from the others and was sitting in a vacant seat, poring over computer printouts. Donovan walked closer and stood over the lead USGS scientist. "Did you get some information you can use?"

Malcolm looked up and nodded. "Based on the amount of sulfur dioxide being ejected, I'd say the chance of a volcanic eruption on Mt. Atitlán is increasing. I can't make any exact measurements until we get back and compare today's images with the satellite images, but I think we're seeing even more significant ground deformation than before. The bulge continues to develop on the south flank. With the degassing of the lava and the bulge—I'd say we have the potential for an eruption at least within the next thirty to sixty days."

"Anything else?" Donovan asked. He heard the Gulfstream's engines spool down as Michael put the *Galileo* into a slow descent toward Guatemala City.

Malcolm looked up from his paperwork. "We need to focus our energy on hoping that the damage to the *Scimitar* is minor and that we can get it back up in the air. Otherwise, we'll have no idea what's going on with the mountain. My worst fear is that there will be a lull in the volcanic activity, which is very likely. Something like that tends to draw all the evacuated people back to their homes. We need to keep feeding real-time information to the population, keep them out of the area—or we'll have a full-scale tragedy on our hands."

Once the Gulfstream was nearing touchdown, Donovan moved up to the jump seat in the cockpit to watch the *Scimitar* land. As they neared the approach end of the runway, Donovan could see the whitish vapor from the suspected liquid nitrogen leak streaming back from the small black craft. John did a magnificent job, and once the *Scimitar* was off the runway, the *Galileo* touched down. With the *Scimitar* leading the way, both aircraft taxied toward the USGS hangar.

Donovan leaned forward, his forearms resting on the backs of the pilots' seats. Michael was quietly relaying instructions to Craig. Donovan felt relieved that their flight had been cut short. What he wanted was to do was get back to the hotel and find

Buck. Hopefully, information about the gunman, as well as the people in the photographs, had been discovered.

Michael swung the Gulfstream onto the inner ramp, and off to the right Donovan noticed an older model Learjet on the ramp. It was white with orange stripes and bore a Mexican registration. A Learjet was no big deal—there were thousands of them built, and most of the older ones ended up in the third world. Donovan was about to look away when a white Mercedes sedan pulled up next to the Lear. He watched for a moment, mildly curious. A man jumped out of the vehicle. He was dressed in blue jeans, baseball cap, and a windbreaker. He scanned the row of hangars as if to see if there was anyone watching, but ignored the passing Gulfstream. Another man climbed from the passenger's side. He was larger, wore slacks and a white shirt, and had a beard. He rounded the vehicle, yanked open the rear door, and leaned into the back. An instant later, Donovan caught sight of a slender woman with long black hair being pulled from the van. Her hands were bound behind her back.

"Michael!" Donovan pointed over his friend's shoulder, directly at the van. "Do you see what I see?"

"It's her!" Michael said, leaning over to see. "I'm getting the impression she's not leaving because she wants to."

Donovan saw her being half-dragged out of the sedan and then yanked to her feet. "She's not leaving at all if I can help it. Michael, slow down a little bit. Whatever happens, don't let that Learjet leave!"

"What are you doing?" Michael called out as Donovan bolted from the cockpit.

Donovan ran as fast as he could all the way to the back of the Gulfstream. He kneeled next to the baggage door and threw the latch hard over, then slid the door up on its tracks until it remained open. Below him was the tarmac. Without stopping to think, Donovan dropped to the ground and rolled with the impact. He forced himself up and started toward the Learjet. Donovan calculated he'd have a momentary element of surprise. No one was expecting an intruder coming from the runway.

Donovan never slowed. He drew his weapon as he rounded the nose of the Learjet and began to yell, "Fuego, Fuego!" His cries of "fire" had the desired effect. Donovan saw a look of confusion and alarm form on the faces of the two men. Donovan used his Sig to hit the bearded man in the side of the head. There was a solid thud, and the man collapsed. The second man stepped back and tried to get to a gun that was tucked into the front of his jeans. The woman spun and delivered a vicious kick to the gunman's crotch. He let out a strangled whimper and went down on his knees, any thoughts about pulling his gun long forgotten as both hands went to protect his battered groin. Donovan clubbed him against the side of the head, and he crashed face first into the tarmac. He turned to the woman and leveled the Sig at her chest. There was no mistaking the rage that burned in her eyes.

"Turn around and get on your knees," Donovan ordered, then stepped back and pointed the gun at the startled Learjet pilot who had rushed from the plane. Donovan saw the ID badge dangling from the pilot's neck and yanked it free from its lanyard.

"What the hell?" The pilot sputtered in confusion as he took in the sight of guns and men lying on the ground.

"Where were you going to fly these people?"

"Toluca, Mexico. Just don't shoot!" The pilot stammered as he held up his hands. "We're a charter company—we're supposed to take four people to Toluca, Mexico, and then wait for further instructions."

Donovan glanced at the pilot's ID. He recognized the outfit, a legitimate operation based out of Toluca, just outside Mexico City. If they were supposed to take four passengers, there must be another car coming, and Donovan didn't want to be standing here when they arrived. "Close the door from the inside and stay there until the next car arrives. If I were you, I'd tell them you didn't see a thing."

The pilot nodded in furious agreement.

Donovan looked at the woman, who was still on her knees with her back to him, her wrists tightly bound with a plastic tie-wrap. "I'm going to help you to your feet. We need to get out of here. Can I trust you to not try to escape?"

"Hurry!" she urged. "The others will be here soon."

Donovan helped her to her feet, and as she stood there, she peered at him over her shoulder, a mix of relief and fear in her eyes. In the daylight he could see that she was older than he'd first thought. She was closer to thirty-five than twenty-five.

"Oh no," she said.

Donovan spotted the black Suburban coming fast. The headlights flashed on and off, sending some sort of prearranged signal. In the Mercedes, the keys were dangling from the ignition. "Get in the car." Without hesitation she dove into the rear seat. Donovan slammed the door behind her and then he slid behind the wheel. He knew the minute he pulled away from the Learjet the men in the Suburban would see their friends lying on the ramp. Donovan threw the Mercedes into gear, stepped on the gas, and the sedan lurched forward. He spun the car around one hundred eighty degrees, sending the woman crashing sideways into the door as he sped directly toward the black SUV. The front end of the Suburban dipped as the driver braked heavily. Donovan powered straight at them, swerving away at the last possible second, creating a moment's hesitation for the Suburban's driver as Donovan blew past them, accelerating through eighty miles per hour.

Donovan tried to picture the layout of the airport, to judge where there might be an access road that led from the ramp to the street. If he could make it into the city, he knew he could lose them. He glanced into the rearview mirror and was shocked at how fast the Suburban had turned around. He saw brief flashes from muzzle blasts, and the Mercedes' rear window exploded into thousands of tiny fragments. He heard the sound of more bullets striking metal. In the mirror, Donovan couldn't see the woman.

She was smart enough to stay down—or she'd been hit. Donovan weaved in and out of airplanes sitting on the ramp, searching in vain for a way off the airfield. The SUV was closing on them. Donovan noticed a faint smoke trail left by the Mercedes, and the smell of burning oil was unmistakable. Suddenly, the prospect of outrunning the Suburban seemed remote.

Donovan swerved back and forth, trying to throw off their aim, but in doing so the gap closed even further. The black SUV was now only thirty feet behind them, more smoke poured from beneath the Mercedes. Donovan desperately looked for a way to outmaneuver them. If he couldn't lose them, he and the woman would be easy targets when the Mercedes' engine finally seized.

Up ahead was the cargo ramp. The sound of a bullet pinging off the roof of the car brought a surge of adrenaline. They wouldn't last much longer out in the open. In the side mirror, all Donovan could see was the front grill of the Suburban, the powerful SUV towered high above them. Donovan winced and grit his teeth as another bullet thudded into the metal somewhere behind him. In an instant, Donovan calculated the distance to a Boeing 727 cargo jet parked to their left. The aging three-engine aircraft had seen better days, sitting faded and dirty on the oil-stained ramp, the name of some long-forgotten air cargo firm painted on the side. Donovan let off the gas pedal for a moment and allowed the Suburban to pull even with the Mercedes. The Suburban and the Mercedes were side by side, hurtling down the tarmac at seventy miles per hour. Donovan needed to time it just right. Only feet away, the gunman put three bullets into the hood of the Mercedes. Donovan gripped the steering wheel in both hands and swung the Mercedes hard to the left, smashing into the SUV with enough force to veer both vehicles to the left. The driver of the Suburban was momentarily caught off guard, and Donovan felt the SUV push back. Donovan held firm, and powered straight toward the forward fuselage of the 727. The accelerator floored, Donovan felt the SUV pull free as the driver of the Suburban tried in vain to stop. In a blur of aluminum, Donovan shrunk down in the seat as they flashed beneath the belly of the 727 only inches behind the nose gear. A brief shriek of metal on metal sent a shock wave through the Mercedes as they sped beneath the airliner. Glass cracked and spider webbed as the roof of the Mercedes barely scraped the aluminum belly of the Boeing. A second later the Mercedes shot out the other side of the 727.

Behind them, Donovan heard the sound of screeching tires, followed by the sound of crashing metal. The Suburban was a foot and a half taller than the Mercedes—everything above hood level was obliterated as the SUV slammed into the Boeing. The 727 bucked and groaned at the impact, lurching to the side as the remains of the Suburban's chassis careened into the undercarriage, came to a sudden violent stop, and began to burn. The Boeing's right main landing gear snapped sideways from the impact, collapsing the right wing down onto the Suburban.

Donovan accelerated the Mercedes. The 727, its wing tank ruptured, was pouring raw jet fuel onto the ramp near the burning Suburban. Moments later, both exploded into a massive fireball. The shock wave from the blast ripped past them, and Donovan felt his ears pop. The heat blew in through the hole where the rear window used to be and seared the hair on the back of his neck—then it was over. Behind him an orange cloud billowed up from the destroyed plane, the tail and wings jutted out from the black smoke as burning jet fuel gutted the 727.

"Are you okay?" Donovan called out, as he slowed and cruised through an open gate onto the small road that ran along the outside of the perimeter fence.

His passenger peered out the rear window at the carnage and then found Donovan's eyes in the mirror. "Did you drive under that plane? How did you...?"

"I've spent some time around the 727. I know a few things," Donovan replied, as he slowed dramatically and tried to understand where he was on the perimeter road. They needed to hide. A bullet-riddled car speeding from a crime scene would draw immediate attention.

"Where are you taking me?" she asked, as she struggled to prop herself up in the seat.

"I should drive you straight to the American Embassy and turn you over to them," Donovan replied with his eyes fixed on hers in the mirror.

"No, not the embassy," she shook her head vehemently. "Or the police—they are corrupt. They are involved in this."

He spotted a place next to an old abandoned hangar. In the tall weeds next to the building were two derelict cars. Donovan stopped and then backed the Mercedes in between them and shut off the engine. In between the *tick tick* sounds coming from the overheated motor, he could hear the wails of fire trucks.

Donovan forced open his door and got out of the car. The paint on the roof of the Mercedes was gone from grazing the belly of the 727. The rear door was partially wedged closed from the impact, but Donovan opened it and slid in beside her. It was a move she wasn't expecting—he held his gun low and close to her rib cage. He knew with her hands tied and her legs pressed against his, she was far less likely to try to beat the crap out of him again. "I want you to tell me everything. If you don't—I'm going to give you back to them."

She nodded and lowered her head. A moment later she put her chin up, shook her hair free from her face, and took a deep breath, steeling herself for a confession. "My name is Eva Rios. I live in the highlands on the western shore of Lake Atitlán. I saw the men who kidnapped the American woman. I know them—they are the ones trying to kill me."

CHAPTER THIRTEEN

The constant hum from the jet's engines made a perfect backdrop as Lauren read. The flight from Dulles International to Tri-Cities Regional Airport in Tennessee was only an hour. Montero was sitting across the aisle working on her laptop.

Montero handed Lauren the FBI file on Meredith Barnes' kidnapping and subsequent murder. The file represented the death of a woman that would have been Robert Huntington's wife—Meredith Barnes was the single lightning strike that had altered him forever. Had she not been killed, Lauren probably would not have met Donovan, let alone married him and had Abigail.

Montero possessed the entire file. There were dozens of photographs taken of the scene of the abduction. Pictures of the dead driver, their bullet-riddled town car, as well as dozens of empty shell casings. There were pictures of Robert Huntington, his eye bruised and nearly swollen shut from the beating he'd taken. Lauren knew what he had looked like back then, of course, but she'd not seen these—right after Meredith's abduction, the pain and loss plainly evident on his battered face.

Lauren examined each one. She could feel the urgency emanating from Robert. She knew his impatience well. The stark helplessness in his eyes back then was palpable. She went to the next group of photographs. They were of Meredith. Lauren only gave a cursory glance at the first several pictures, well aware of what Meredith looked like, how beautiful she was. The next one made Lauren's stomach churn. She averted her eyes, unprepared.

She gathered herself, and began once again. Meredith's naked body was crumpled faceup in a dirt field. Her long red hair partially covered her face, but the single bullet wound was clearly visible. Lauren skipped the next few pictures; they were close-ups of her and her injuries. She instead jumped to the autopsy report, which listed the cause of death as a single gunshot to the head.

It took Lauren another half hour to sift through the entire file. Meredith had arranged an historic ecological summit meeting in San José, Costa Rica. Meredith, with her passion for the earth and environment, had achieved the global recognition to assemble the summit. Leaders from almost every western hemisphere government were in attendance. Her dream was to sponsor an accord that would lead to meaningful laws that would severely limit logging in the world's rain forests and the overharvesting of severely depleted populations of fish and reckless oil drilling in Alaska, Canada, Central and South America. She'd convinced the World Bank to provide billions in zero-interest financing to support such actions in the third-world countries, the end result to help build alternative industries that would provide jobs and economic growth for the next thirty years. Her plan was brilliant, but quickly fell apart upon her death.

She became an instant martyr, but there was no one to fill the vacuum she'd left behind. Instead, her public latched on to the nearest object to vent their feeling of loss—Robert Huntington. Lauren slumped as she read the report stating that, without a doubt, Robert Huntington was the prime suspect in a scheme to murder Meredith Barnes.

Lauren paused, as she knew he'd been the target of speculation the instant Meredith's death was made public. While a shocked and mournful world held candlelight vigils, photos were released of Robert on a remote beach with a slender young blonde. Even though the photos were faked, it was all the evidence an angry public needed for the murder of Meredith to become a conspiracy by Robert Huntington and Big Oil to silence her voice. From there it became the fabric of public belief. Lauren scrolled through the pages until she found the reference to a lone person of interest, a petty criminal named Antonio Romero, a man who had been drunk when apprehended, who later died in custody. The last page in the file was a memo from the FBI, stating that the murder of Meredith Barnes had been closed upon the death of Robert Huntington.

Scrolling backward, Lauren found the interrogation and the affidavit that Romero had died from natural causes. She glanced down at the page numbers—there was an eleven-page gap. The entire interrogation report was missing. She noted the name of the FBI agent in charge: Special Agent Gordon Butterfield.

"Why is the interrogation missing from Meredith's file?"

"That's always been a big question mark. It's assumed that someone inside the Costa Rican police destroyed the report when Romero died. There's speculation that the interrogation methods were too severe and the transcript subsequently destroyed. The cause of death was listed as natural causes by a local medical examiner and the body promptly cremated at the request of the family. One of the highest profile kidnappings since the Lindbergh baby, and the FBI walked away with very little solid information. I heard that heads rolled afterwards."

"Was Butterfield implicated?" Lauren asked.

"His career took a hit, but he dodged the worst of it," Montero replied. "You've been going over that for a while—any insights?"

"It's not easy reading. I didn't expect the photographs," Lauren answered. "You're right though, there's a great deal of leeway in how this report was prepared and what it really says. The investigation was botched by either the FBI, or the Costa Rican authorities, or even by this unnamed group. It looks to me that someone took the path of least resistance and placed the blame on Robert Huntington, an easy task once he was already declared dead."

"When I discovered he was still alive, and then spent some time with him, I could easily see why he did what he did," Montero said. "Based on everything I know, I'd have done the same thing."

"It was a horrible time for him," Lauren replied. "William told me some things that broke my heart. How lost Robert was, the serious death threats, pills and alcohol. He hid in his Monterey house he'd shared with Meredith and nearly unraveled completely. If William hadn't stepped in and orchestrated what he did, I don't know if Robert would have survived."

"Hearing you speak about William the way you do, makes it all the more impossible to believe that he could have a hand in any of the manipulations the FBI is pursuing."

Lauren was about to reply when the chartered jet began to slow and make a descending turn. She peered out the window, and in the distance, spotted the Tri-Cities Airport tucked into the picturesque hills of Eastern Tennessee.

"That was a quick trip," Montero remarked as she collected her work and put everything into her briefcase. "I reserved us a rental car. Once we land, there should be an e-mail from Deputy Director Graham as to Butterfield's exact whereabouts."

"What if Butterfield doesn't want to talk?"

"Oh, he'll talk." Montero smiled knowingly as the jet's landing gear was lowered and the seat belt sign came on.

Lauren had no doubt that Montero could be a formidable interrogator, though neither one of them possessed any official capacity. Butterfield was a retired FBI agent, and Lauren doubted that Montero would scare him all that much. The wheels touched down and they taxied to the executive terminal. Montero's e-mail was waiting and she quickly typed their destination into her phone's GPS. As they deplaned, Lauren issued instructions to the crew to remain on standby. She assured them she'd call when they were on their way back to the airport.

Once in the car, Montero sped toward Deer Creek Country Club.

"What do we do if he's somewhere out on the course?" Lauren asked.

"We go find him," Montero said. "He's pushing seventy, how hard can he be to catch?"

"I'm not sure *catch* is the right word," Lauren said.

"Here we are." Montero braked and turned into the tree-lined lane that led to the parking lot. She double-checked her Glock and turned toward Lauren. "Ready?"

They hurried through the doors into the air-conditioned building and made their way down a hallway filled with framed pictures of famous golfers. Lauren heard people talking, and Montero continued toward the rear of the building and ultimately found the pro shop.

"Excuse me?" Montero said to a young man behind a counter. "I'm looking for Gordon Butterfield."

"Yes, ma'am," he replied politely as he glanced at a large clock on the wall. "Go out those doors, down the stairs. He's not scheduled to tee off for another fifteen minutes so he'll be on the putting green. You can't miss the orange slacks."

Lauren fell in behind Montero and easily spotted Butterfield. From Montero, Lauren knew that Butterfield was in his late sixties and severely overweight. He wasn't an inch over five-foot seven, wearing a beat-up floppy hat and dark glasses. He was all upper body, a white shirt stretched over an enormous stomach and large rounded shoulders. He was leaning over a putt, and Lauren wondered briefly how he could even see the ball, let alone stroke the tiny putter that looked like a toothpick compared to his massive arms. She walked closer and watched as the golf ball traveled across ten feet of green, curved toward the cup, and dropped into the hole. He turned around as if sensing their arrival, then returned to practicing.

"You both have FBI written all over you." His gruff voice came out as almost a bellow. He slapped another ball into position and took aim. "What do you want?"

"For starters, how about your undivided attention?" Montero said.

Lauren hadn't expected this to be easy. From everything

she'd read, and from what Montero had explained, Butterfield could be a difficult man.

"Are you the good cop or the bad cop?" Butterfield asked without looking up.

"Actually," Montero said, stepping closer, "we're both bad, and unless you want your ass kicked by a girl here in front of all of your golf buddies, I suggest you listen to us."

Butterfield looked up and removed his glasses, sizing them both up. He fixed on Montero then slipped his glasses back on his face. "I know who you are. The dark hair is a bit deceptive, but you're Special Agent Veronica Montero, the FBI's poster girl for freedom and patriotism. To what do I owe the pleasure of such an esteemed visitor?"

"We're looking into an old case," Montero said. "One that involved you."

"I read that you're not FBI anymore, you're in charge of some women's shelters in Florida," Butterfield said to Montero, then shifted his gaze to Lauren. "What's your story?"

"This case involves a friend of mine," Lauren said.

"I'm retired," Butterfield said. "Go back to DC and leave me alone."

"I'm not afraid of much, Mr. Butterfield," Lauren chose her words carefully. "Not even you. But one of the few things that *does* scare me are the people who killed Meredith Barnes."

"I'll be damned," Butterfield said, this time far quieter than before. "Is someone finally going after that bastard William VanGelder?"

Lauren felt her knees start to buckle. She stood motionless, keeping her composure. Her expression remained steady as he stared at her. She tried to remain passive, not to give away the fact that she felt like he'd just punched her in the stomach.

"Let's go talk." Butterfield tossed his putter against his golf bag lying next to the green. "This way."

Lauren and Montero didn't say a word as they moved toward a bench situated well away from the other golfers. Lauren was still reeling by what Butterfield had just said.

Butterfield sat directly in the middle of the bench, forcing Lauren and Montero to stand as if he were holding court. "Before I tell you a thing, what's in it for me?"

Lauren watched Montero, who never flinched. Butterfield was a bully and used to getting his way. He was also highly intelligent. "Romero's missing interrogation report as a witness in the Barnes case. You got your ass handed to you over that, right? It's the one cloud on a solid career. Help us connect some dots, and I'll personally tell the director you were a critical part of our investigation."

"That works for me," Butterfield nodded. "It was always my theory that VanGelder had the pages destroyed," Butterfield said without emotion.

"Romero told you about VanGelder?" Lauren's stomach felt empty as she said the name of the man who was Donovan's closest friend, and a man she herself had grown to love.

Butterfield shook his head. "Romero was several steps removed from whoever had orchestrated the plan to assassinate Meredith Barnes. He'd heard some names, and, frankly, he wasn't afraid of the Americans, but he was terrified of someone in Central America. He died before we could find out who this person was—all we had was a nickname, or a code name: *la Serpiente.* Hell, I don't know if there's any truth to what Romero told us, everything could be a lie, or a misdirection. I do, however, believe Meredith Barnes, as well as others, were assassinated, not kidnapped, by a group that reached far into the boardrooms of corporate America. I heard whispers once that they called themselves the conclave. I think Meredith Barnes was killed to keep her from strengthening an already growing public resolve to keep them from drilling oil wherever and whenever they wanted. This collection of oilmen placed the blame squarely at Robert Huntington's feet and let him take the fall. To be honest, I wouldn't be surprised if they killed him to tie up loose ends. VanGelder is the one constant in this entire process. He could have easily killed Huntington."

"So, you don't think Robert Huntington killed Meredith Barnes?" Montero asked. "This unidentified group did?"

"Robert Huntington," Butterfield paused. "No way Huntington pulled the trigger, though he was certainly meant to take the fall, to swing the focus from those who did. You won't find that in any report, hell, none of my questions were ever formally acknowledged. But the mention of *la Serpiente* seemed to scare the crap out of the locals. I think it was part of the mythology created by the conspirators. I do know that to engineer a conspiracy as bold and complex as the murder of Meredith Barnes, doesn't happen without a great deal of money and influence—VanGelder's type of clout. William VanGelder is one of the most dangerous men I've ever come across. Meredith Barnes never stood a chance."

It was painful for Lauren to hear someone speak ill of William. She needed to move this conversation along.

"What about a man by the name of Hector Vargas?" Montero asked.

"Vargas is another turd in the punch bowl. He's a Mexican national who has just enough legitimate dealings to mask all of his criminal enterprises behind the smoke screen. Vargas has been in the background for years, but he's not the mastermind of anything significant. If the two of you want some answers, you need to start digging as far away from Bureau files as you can. In fact, there are two cases you should look into. They won't show up on any Bureau database because they were outside our purview, but I always thought they had VanGelder written all over them."

"What cases?" Montero asked.

"There were the Rochas, a Brazilian family. A mother and daughter were kidnapped in Costa Rica a few days before Meredith Barnes was abducted. I always thought it was a diversion to weaken an already shaky Costa Rican police force. The investigation was between the Costa Rican and Brazilian authorities. I don't remember all that transpired, but I think the mother and daughter were killed in a fire despite the ransom being paid. Afterwards, the father committed suicide and the family's holdings in Brazil were sold to an oil company."

"What company?" Lauren asked.

"Knight Oil, they were big back in the day, until they were bought out."

"Bought by Huntington Oil?" Lauren asked.

"That's right, and there was one other case, technically it wasn't a kidnapping, just good old-fashioned extortion," Butterfield said. "In Belize. A guy by the name of Franklin Lange—the CEO of a financial company that dealt in venture capital, and he dealt almost exclusively with the energy sector. His wife was with him in Belize, and she seemingly vanished, but no kidnapping was ever reported, no foul play suspected. According to Lange, she'd gone back to Texas. I could never prove anything, and when we found her at home in Dallas, it was obvious she'd been beaten, and she wouldn't talk. A day later, Lange packed up and went home as well, deciding at the last minute to cancel the financing of a huge oil exploration deal in Belize. A few weeks after that, the oil and gas rights were sold to Knight Oil. Their chairman and founder, Elijah Knight, was one of the men I suspected was connected to VanGelder."

"What happened to him?"

"My guess is there was a falling out, or a reorganization of some kind. VanGelder was brutal, he destroy—"

Lauren heard the bullet whiz past her ear and hit Butterfield square in the chest, the gun's report followed an instant later. Montero slammed into her from the side and pushed her to the ground. As Montero, her gun drawn, searched in the direction the shot had come from, other golfers were shouting, pointing toward what looked like a maintenance shed. Lauren looked at Butterfield. The bullet had hit him center mass, a red stain expanding on his white shirt, his chin rested on his chest, his eyes open and unblinking.

"We need to get out of here," Montero said. "We're going to the left and work our way around to the parking lot."

Lauren was up on her feet and running, knowing she'd never hear the gunshot if a bullet found her. Montero followed. They reached the rental car and moments later Montero squealed the tires as they raced out of the parking lot.

"How many people knew we were looking for Butterfield?" Lauren kept an eye on the road behind them.

"We've got big problems," Montero said, as she too checked to see if they were followed. "I have no idea, but the only people I told work at the Bureau."

"Do you think the FBI just assassinated a former agent?"

"Someone did. And yeah, it could have been the FBI, or the CIA, or this shadowy group Butterfield just told us about. Hell, it could have been anyone."

"Is there anyone we do trust?" Lauren asked.

"Why?"

"We have two names," Lauren said. "Franklin Lange, the guy in Dallas, and Elijah Knight. If either man is still alive, we need to talk to them before they end up like Butterfield. I especially want to know what William did to this Elijah Knight and why."

"There's a guy in Miami, he's a private investigator, good at what he does and very discreet. He has connections and he owes me. Let me give him a call and put him to work on this. He's not cheap, but if it's out there, he'll find it."

"If you trust this guy, do it. Make sure he knows we're in a bind, timewise. Money's not an issue." A frown crossed Lauren's face. "When you talk to this guy and set everything up, make sure that if something happens to you and me, Donovan has access to the information."

"Donovan doesn't know what you're doing, does he?" Montero asked.

"No, and considering the gravity of what we may have uncovered, he's not going to hear a word from me until we have concrete proof that William VanGelder is either guilty, or innocent. This isn't the time for guesswork or hearsay. William is a part of this family and as far as I'm concerned, he's innocent until proven guilty."

"I hope we stay alive long enough to know which," Montero said. "I need to call Deputy Director Graham and let him know what's happened. Can you call the airport and tell the pilots to be ready—I want out of here before local law enforcement figures out we're witnesses to a murder."

"Where shall I tell them we're going?"

"For now, we regroup and go back to DC. Someone is one step ahead of us—and that pisses me off."

CHAPTER FOURTEEN

"I don't believe you." Donovan was still trying to judge if Eva was telling the truth. "Why would they try to kill you last night—but today they want to take you prisoner? It doesn't add up."

She swallowed hard. "Yesterday, I was only a witness, someone easy to kill. Last night, after my friend picked me up, we drove around, and I tried to think. I decided to call the hotel, and that's when we spoke. My friend then took me back to his house, and they were waiting for us. They went through my phone, recognized the number for the hotel, and kept asking me about that particular call, and who I'd spoken with. I refused to talk, and, finally, this morning they took me to the airport."

"Where's your friend?" Donovan asked.

Tears flooded Eva's eyes as she shook her head. "I don't know. They may have killed him."

"Where did you see Stephanie? When did you last see her alive?"

"The day before yesterday. When we were evacuating Santiago because of the volcano, I saw them in a boat leaving from a private pier. They saw me, and I have been running ever since."

"Do you have any idea where they took her? Was there a little girl with them?"

"All I saw was the woman," Eva replied wide-eyed. "I know nothing about a little girl."

"How do you know it was Stephanie?" Donovan continued. "How do you know it was the woman who was kidnapped?"

"I know these men. They are very bad, some of them are with the police. They travel, no one really knows where they live, but they rob and steal from the tourists. I hear rumors that women are raped and killed. The people in my town are afraid of them. When I saw them, the blonde woman was tied up, I know everyone in the area and she's not from around here. My friends spoke of the murders up on the mountain, the woman who was taken."

Donovan closed his eyes, his mind reeling from the reality that Stephanie was in the hands of murderers and rapists.

"I am sorry," Eva said. "I apologize for the people in my country that would do these things."

Donovan heard the muted sound of a ringing cell phone. He leaned over and began feeling underneath the seat in front of her until he found a purse. He opened the leather bag and took out a cell phone. The incoming number was blocked. "In English," he said, then pushed the answer button and held the phone up to Eva's ear.

"Hello," she said.

Donovan was ready to snatch the phone from her hand if he didn't like what she said. She was mostly listening, her only replies were a series of "yes's."

"He wants to talk to you." Eva leaned away from the phone.

"Hello," Donovan said.

"If you want to see Ms. VanGelder alive, you will have the money ready by tonight. We will call you on this phone. Keep track of the woman. We want the money *and* her."

Donovan bristled at the man's voice. A hundred things ran through his mind, but he knew he needed to remain calm. "I need proof Stephanie is still alive."

"Have the money and the woman ready by ten o'clock tonight."

Donovan looked at Eva, then at the phone. The call had been terminated. "Do you have any idea who he was? What did he say to you?"

"That they are going to kill me." Eva looked away. "He said they would do very ugly things to me—and then I would die."

"Turn around." Donovan looked at her—she was obviously frightened—she'd been shot at, kidnapped, and right this moment, she was probably just as scared as he was.

"No," she said defiantly. "If you're going to shoot me, you do it face-to-face."

"I'm going to free your hands on one condition. Don't hit me again, or I *will* shoot you."

"I promise. I'm sorry about last night." She turned so he could free her. "I didn't know who you were, and I was afraid if my friend saw you he would be scared for me and want to kill you. He is very protective."

"Where did you learn to fight?" Donovan asked, as he used the knife he found in her purse to slice the tie-wrap.

"You don't survive very long in my world if you can't defend yourself. I learned how to disable a man when I was a young girl. It was the only way to remain pure."

Donovan looked at her phone and began to scroll through the numbers Eva had dialed recently. "Is this the number for the hotel?" Donovan asked, and held up the screen for her to see. She nodded.

"Mr. VanGelder's room, please," Donovan said. He waited as the operator put his call through. It was picked up after the first ring. "Buck, it's me."

"Michael just called. I'm on my way out the door. Where are you? Are you all right?"

"I'm fine," Donovan replied. "We're about three hundred yards south of the USGS hangar."

"We?" Buck questioned.

"I have the woman," Donovan replied. "We're in a parked Mercedes next to a bright blue hangar."

"Stay put, I'm on my way."

Donovan ended the call. He studied the phone in his hand, then looked at Eva. "You won't mind if I keep this for now? They're going to call back."

Eva shrugged as if it made no difference to her. "Your friend is named Stephanie, no? When you asked them if she was still alive—did they answer?"

"No." Donovan didn't want to talk about Stephanie. "What about your family?"

"I'm alone," Eva said. "My mother died a long time ago, my father was killed by the military during the civil war."

"What do you do?" Donovan continued. "You said you live in the highlands, near the volcano?"

"Yes, for years my family has owned a small hotel in Santiago. I run it, but now that we have been forced to evacuate, I fear I have lost everything. The Mayan elders have warned that the volcano would finally come to life—they were right. And if the volcano doesn't destroy the village, the looters will."

Donovan was sorry he'd asked. This woman's hardships seemed all-encompassing. She'd lost her home, her parents, her business, and had very nearly lost her life. Human suffering was what Donovan hated most in the world. Despite his immense fortune, there wasn't nearly enough money to help her or the millions like her in the world. He'd seen firsthand that for every dollar given to third-world countries, it was a miracle if ten cents reached the people it was intended to help. Donovan thought of Meredith, her passion to save the world from itself, and he felt the familiar heaviness grow inside—a weight that was always just below the surface.

"Do not be sad," Eva said, her hand reaching out to take Donovan's. "You will find her."

"I hope you're right," Donovan replied, feeling uncomfortable that he'd drifted off. He couldn't afford to be careless. The growing clouds cast a shadow on the car, and in the subdued light, for just the briefest of moments, Eva reminded him of Meredith. The large eyes and untamed hair, the full lips and unlined face, the resemblance was unsettling. Even after the shadow passed, Donovan couldn't take his eyes from her and he was assaulted with a barrage of images. He thought of Costa Rica, the ransom demands, the unyielding government officials who refused to deal with the kidnappers. He remembered the cloudless morning they came and got him from the hotel, the Costa Rican chief of police, as well as FBI agents and officials from the State Department. None of them had made eye contact with him as they silently drove to the outskirts of San José.

Donovan knew where he was being taken, but nothing could have prepared him for what he'd found when he arrived. Hundreds of people had gathered, restrained by the police called to the scene. As they spotted him, the mood changed from curious to angry. The onlookers grew vocal, yelling obscenities at him, some throwing rocks and bottles. Donovan had trudged through the muddy field, a path already worn in the soil. He remembered thinking that at least they'd had the decency to cover her with a sheet of plastic. No one asked him if he was ready, or gave him a chance to collect himself first. Someone had simply yanked the plastic free and exposed her. Meredith lay in the mud, her flawless skin covered with bruises and cuts. She was on her side, her face turned slightly upwards. Donovan could see the bullet hole in her forehead. Her sightless eyes seemed to look right through him. Donovan's knees gave way as if every single one of his muscles had failed in unison. His world was spinning—threatening to either topple him or cause him to be sick. Strong arms supported him as he tried to walk; they were forced to half-carry him back to the road. The entire crowd of onlookers seemed to be yelling at him, blaming him, their cries of anger and retribution seemed as if hurtled at him through a long tunnel. The rage of Meredith's death had penetrated to his very core, where it had remained, Donovan realized, since that day, and fed on him like the unwilling host he was.

"Is Meredith your wife?" Eva pointed at his wedding ring.

Startled, Donovan looked at her, questioning how she could know the name.

"You just said her name." Eva shrugged. "Are you married?"

"Yes," was all he said, feeling trapped, unable to explain. He looked at Eva. He'd saved her from these men, but in order to save Stephanie, he'd have to turn her over to the same men who would no doubt kill her. Donovan felt compelled to protect her. There was no way he could subject any woman to the brutality Meredith had suffered. But, deep down, he had no idea how he was going to save Stephanie without condemning Eva.

CHAPTER FIFTEEN

"Stop," Montero said, as Lauren reached to start her Range Rover.

"Why?" Lauren turned toward Montero.

"We need to talk," Montero replied. "You've hardly spoken since we took off from Johnson City. I mean, you just sat there for the entire flight back here. I know that watching Butterfield die was a shock, but I need to know exactly where you are, what you're thinking."

On the flight back to Dulles, Montero had been a whirlwind of phone calls and e-mails.

Instead of doing the same, Lauren had been deep in thought, troubled by everything she'd seen and heard since Montero had arrived. The FBI has a task force investigating William, followed by all the terrible accusations leveled at him by Butterfield. Then there was the horrible reality of the former FBI agent being murdered in front of them. Montero was right; someone was one step ahead of them, and the game had turned lethal. All the rules had changed, and Lauren had needed time to process.

"Let me ask you something," Montero said. "I understand why you might be upset, it's been a messed-up day. All the phone calls I made on the flight, I've learned some things. If we're a team, if the two of us are going to keep going, you need to know what I know. Or do you want to quit?"

"I hope you know me well enough to understand I'd never walk away," Lauren said. "I started with this idea that I could help find Stephanie. Donovan was in so much pain. I'd grown tired of lying to everyone to maintain my husband's charade, so I called you, the only person on the planet who knows his secret, and is also a trained investigator. In my mind, there was an outside chance we'd uncover something that would lead to Stephanie—but not the possibility of William being a murderer. What we're doing could destroy everyone I love."

"You're right," Montero replied softly. "You may be too close to this—maybe this is the one to sit out."

"It's far too late for that," Lauren said. "I can't undo what I've already seen and done. Though, at some point, I have to explain all of this to Donovan, or even worse, I have to confront William."

"We go where the evidence takes us," Montero shrugged. "We're also not responsible for the truth we find. You would do well to keep that in mind, because the truth will affect William, Donovan, you, even Abigail. If it turns out that William had a hand in Meredith's death, the repercussions will be catastrophic. By the time the FBI gets through with their investigation, I have no doubt they'll uncover the fact that Donovan is Robert Huntington. Can you imagine the headlines? William VanGelder and Robert Huntington kidnap and kill Meredith Barnes—then together they conspire to fake Huntington's death to avoid prosecution. Never mind that none of it's true, but the public is still angry, and there aren't any statutes of limitations for murder."

"Those were some of the particulars I was processing on the plane."

"Can I tell you something Donovan told me once? I think at the time, I was about where you are right now. I hated where the facts of a case were taking me, and I wanted it to stop. He told me to quit overthinking, to get pissed off that someone was trying to do me harm, and to fight back. It worked."

"He's angry all the time, of course he'd say that," Lauren replied. "I'm just a little staggered by everything we've learned. Typically, the information I analyze doesn't affect me emotionally. I'm not sitting this one out. We need to keep going, regardless of what we find, but what we're doing is having an effect on me."

"As it should. In fact, I'd be worried if it didn't," Montero replied.

"Let's head back to the house," Lauren said as she started the engine. "I need to make sure my daughter's safe. Now, what did you find out on the plane?"

"I talked at length with Deputy Director Graham. The preliminary report on Butterfield from the local police in Tennessee, is that he was killed with a single, high-velocity rifle round. All signs point to a professional hit. Due to Butterfield being former FBI, Graham is moving assets to take over the investigation."

"Did you tell Graham what Butterfield told us?" Lauren asked, as she merged into traffic.

"Of course not, but I did tell my private detective friend in Florida. Butterfield gave us three names. The Rocha family and the Franklin Lange family have been dead for years. But Elijah Knight died two nights ago in Miami. He was shot. The police are calling it a home invasion gone wrong. I have a contact at Miami homicide, and my friend says her gut feeling is it was a murder, made to look like a robbery."

"So, Elijah Knight is killed and then Gordon Butterfield?" Lauren asked, as she changed lanes and accelerated around a slow-moving truck. "That's no coincidence."

"I agree. My PI did some quick digging. Knight was once the CEO of the oil company that bore his name. He was a successful guy, had a building in Houston with his name on the roof, private jets, all the usual trappings of success. But he died poor, in a rented house in a not-so-nice part of Miami."

"So, he lost all his money, happens all the time," Lauren replied.

"He didn't lose his, it was stripped from him," Montero said. "Sixteen years ago, Huntington Oil began a hostile takeover of Knight Oil. It was a bitter fight, but Huntington won. At the time, analysts were quoted as saying Knight Oil was overvalued, and that Huntington overpaid for their assets."

"If it was sixteen years ago, then William was on the board of directors."

"Better yet, he was acting chairman due to an illness of the sitting CEO," Montero said. "William was running the show and initiated the takeover bid. When it was over, he's also the one that refused any kind of severance or bonus for Elijah Knight. In fact, William managed to negate Knight's stock options, and cancel millions in deferred pay. William did whatever he could to ruin the man."

"That's incredible," Lauren replied. "I've seen William operate in business mode, he's the kindest, gentlest man I know. You're describing someone I've never seen."

"Elijah Knight would disagree, as would two other former CEOs who were treated in the same manner."

"So it was personal? William, or others within Huntington Oil, wanted to ruin these guys? Are any of them still alive?"

"No, both deceased, but not one of them from natural causes. One died in a car accident, the other was ruled a suicide—possible murders made to look like accidents. My PI didn't have to dig into *la Serpiente*. In Latin American circles this guy is no myth—he's a legend. He's regarded as a brutal killer. He's a ghost, no one seems to know his actual identity." Montero snapped her head to the side as they sped through an intersection. "What's going on? Don't you live down that way?"

"I don't think we should go to the house quite yet," Lauren said.

"Uh oh," Montero said as she looked over at Lauren, whose eyes were fixed on the rearview mirror. "Which one?"

"The silver Chrysler sedan," Lauren said. "I'm pretty sure it's been with us since we left the airport."

"Can you think of any place close where we can stop and interview these guys without attracting any attention?"

"What about calling for help? The police, or the FBI?"

"No way, if we bring them in, then these guys have far too many civil rights. This could be our break, and I want to deal with them personally." Montero glanced into the side mirror. "I'm looking at two men in the front seat, is that what you're seeing?"

"As far as I can tell there are only two of them."

"That makes it a fair fight," Montero said. "Ideally, I'd like an enclosed parking garage, at least three floors high, without a lot of people coming and going. I'd prefer an office building over a shopping center."

"I can think of any number of places, except they're probably filled with security cameras."

"That's good. We want cameras. I just want to talk to these guys, but if this thing turns ugly, I want it to be on tape."

As Lauren moved to the outside lane, she glanced over and noticed that Montero's Glock was at the ready. She thought back to Montero's profile, how quick she was to resort to violence—and how adept she was at being the victor. Lauren found comfort in that fact.

"Are you up for this?" Montero asked.

"Yes." Lauren caught a red light and slowed. She watched in the mirror as the Chrysler stopped three cars behind. Both occupants wore dark glasses and they didn't appear to be talking to each other, just sitting and waiting. It felt dangerous to be stopped—she felt like a sitting target.

"You have a place in mind?" Montero asked.

"Yes, it's just ahead. An office building, we'll be there in five minutes."

"Okay, I'll explain exactly what's going to happen. We can orchestrate events up to a point, at which time it's going to become a fluid situation. When that happens, I need you to do exactly what I tell you to do, without hesitation. Is your gun loaded and ready to go? Can I count on you to react accordingly?"

"I'm good to go," Lauren said, as she glanced down between the bucket seats where she always wedged her purse. Exactly like Buck had shown her, the butt of her pistol was in the perfect position for quick action.

CHAPTER SIXTEEN

"Someone's coming," Eva whispered.

Donovan looked to his left; rounding the corner at high speed was Buck's Suburban. Donovan and Eva had just finished wiping down the Mercedes, hoping to remove any incriminating fingerprints. The Suburban rumbled to a stop in front of their car, and Buck flew out of the driver's seat and motioned for them to hurry.

Donovan took Eva's hand and helped her out of the car. Buck was holding the rear door open. They piled in the Suburban, Buck slammed the door, and moments later they were through the perimeter fence and racing down the main road away from the airport.

As Donovan glanced back at the oily plume of thick black smoke rising from the airport, he wondered how long it would take them to discover the bodies at the center of the inferno.

"What the hell happened?" Buck asked as soon as they were clear of the airport. "Do I even want to know how you managed to end up in a car full of bullet holes? And, am I wrong to assume you had a hand in blowing up an airliner?"

"The 727 blew up when the guys in an SUV that were shooting at us made a wrong turn. The two men trying to force Eva into a Learjet probably escaped though. By the way, this is Eva. Eva, this is Buck."

"We'll get to all of that later. But for the moment, let me see if I have this right." Buck glanced up, caught Donovan's eye in the mirror. "Michael told me you saw two men trying to drag her into a Learjet. You jumped out of the *Galileo*, rescued her, then got away—but not before getting shot at, and creating what I'm sure will become front-page news. I thought we'd agreed that we're supposed to be keeping a low profile."

Donovan paused, waiting to see if Buck was finished with his tirade. "I talked to the kidnappers."

"What!" Buck snapped his head around.

"The kidnappers called Eva on her cell phone," Donovan replied. "Two days ago, Eva saw the men who have Stephanie. We have to get back to the hotel—they told us to have everything ready by tonight. This whole thing could still go down today."

Buck nodded and whipped the Suburban hard to the left, crossed over the median, and accelerated back the way they'd just come. He studied his mirror to see if anyone copied the move he'd just made. After a minute when no one did, he nodded at Donovan that he thought they were clear, that no one was following. After making a series of turns to detect a tail, Buck pulled up to the front door of the hotel.

Donovan took Eva's hand and helped her out of the vehicle. He had seen her eyelids drift closed only moments before. He wondered how long it had been since she'd slept. He battled his own fatigue, but knew he'd never be able to sleep—not until this was over. They boarded the elevator and shot up to their floor without a word.

"Get her settled in your room," Buck said. "Then come down to William's suite so we can all talk."

Donovan urged Eva to follow him as Buck brought up the rear. Eva never strayed far from his side as Donovan used his key to open his room. He couldn't imagine what must be running through her mind. She'd been shot at, abducted, and now she was in a hotel with men she didn't know. She stood close, uncertainty in her eyes.

"I'm going to go talk to Buck. Why don't you take a hot shower, order yourself something to eat? There are some shops close by, call down to the front desk and see if someone can buy you some clothes. Charge everything to the room, but whatever you do, don't leave."

"I want to stay with you," she said quietly.

"I'm right down the hall. As you can see, there are guards stationed outside. You'll be safe. I promise."

She nodded, but with reluctance.

Donovan closed the drapes and switched on a table lamp. He picked up his briefcase and turned to her. She looked so fragile and scared standing in the near-darkness. Where had the tough-chick act gone? Was it all just an act? Or had her fear finally burned itself out and given way to exhaustion? He wondered how she'd react when it came time to tell her that the kidnappers wanted her as well as the money.

"You won't leave me?" Eva stepped in front of him before he could reach the door. "You promise?"

"You'll be fine." Donovan was forced to stop as she reached up and put her arms around him. "I won't leave the hotel without telling you. Okay?"

Donovan let himself out of the room, stopped for a moment to give the guards a heads-up about the food and clothes that would probably be arriving, and firm instructions not to let Eva leave under any circumstances.

Donovan knocked gently on William's door.

"Sit down," William said as he stepped aside to allow Donovan into the suite.

Donovan found a chair. "Okay, she's taken care of for the moment. What do we have?"

"We have a mess, is what we have," William said without ceremony. "Buck was just bringing me up-to-date on the afternoon's activities."

"What we need to talk about is Stephanie." Donovan wasn't in the mood to be chastised for his impulsive actions. "When I talked to the kidnappers, they said to have the money ready by tonight. This could happen in the next few hours, but they want the money—and Eva. They'll more than likely kill her if we hand her over, that's *if* we can convince her to play along. If she won't, and I don't think we can force her—then, according to them, Stephanie will be killed."

"I'm open to suggestions, gentlemen." William said.

Buck rubbed his forehead as he processed the latest development.

"We have to find a way to protect her, " Donovan said, "then convince her to join us."

"She seems rather attached to you," Buck offered. "Use it."

"The only way I'd do that is if I could assure her she'd be safe," Donovan said, his attention still fixed on Buck. "How do you envision all this going down? Is there any safe way to do this? Anything we can use to convince Eva to help?"

"It could happen several different ways. I've spent all morning seeing how much help we can expect. It'll be myself and four other men. I'll be the one making the drop; the best we can hope for is that they aren't as professional or as prepared as we are. We also have one card up our sleeve that they don't know about."

"What's that?" William asked.

"The *Scimitar*," Buck replied with a small smile. "It was born out of a military drone used in combat. We launch it, and we'll be able to use its surveillance capabilities to monitor wherever I go with the money. Once the drop is made, we'll be able to track them. We'll have the men I've recruited stationed throughout the city. That way, everyone should be able to stay close without being spotted. When the time comes, we'll know, and help will only be minutes away."

"This could work," Donovan said as he nodded his approval. "If we explain all this to Eva, maybe she'll help."

"We can't explain anything to her beyond that we need her help," Buck said quietly. "In fact, I won't do it if she knows what's coming. Nothing can destroy an operation faster than an amateur. She's scared, and if she becomes even more terrified, she'll start looking around for the help she's expecting. It's human nature, and there's nothing worse than tipping off the enemy to a surprise attack. I guarantee she'll get everyone killed."

"That makes sense," Donovan agreed. "I just don't know how we'll be able to convince her that we need her for bait. They've already tried to kill her, and, to be honest, I'm not sure what her frame of mind is right now."

"We have an extra million dollars," William said. "The kidnappers asked for three million—I brought four. Offer her a million dollars to do this. I'd even go so far as to offer her the million cash *and* we'll bring her back to the States with us. I can guarantee her entry. That might represent a deal she'd be willing to risk her life for."

Donovan thought about it for a moment, about what she'd said about losing everything, that her family was gone as well as her business. She'd already said she couldn't stay in Guatemala. "Fear is a powerful motivator, it might work. Except, last I heard the *Scimitar* was out of commission. That's why we came back early."

"What happened?" Buck asked. Clearly he hadn't heard the news.

"It had a coolant leak—the liquid nitrogen that's used to keep the systems working in the heat of a volcano leaked. I have no idea if it's flyable."

"We don't need it to fly in a volcano," Buck explained. "Just to orbit the city and watch what goes down. Would the *Galileo* need to be airborne, or could we control the *Scimitar* from the ground?"

"The *Scimitar* can be controlled from the ground as long as it's within line-of-sight range of the *Galileo*," Donovan answered. "Maybe a thirty-mile radius."

"Either way, we need the *Scimitar* in the air before ten o'clock."

"I think the two of you should go out to the airport and assess the situation firsthand." William put his fingertips together and lowered his head as he thought. "I'm also concerned about this business with the Learjet. Who are these people? Is there a way we can find out?"

"Yeah, maybe." Donovan pulled out the pilot's ID badge.

"You two go." William took a deep breath and stood. "But be back here as quickly as you can. We'll have to convince the woman and get everyone into position before the kidnappers call back. Donovan, it might be a good idea if your crew understands what's at stake, and let them know that once we have Stephanie, we may need to leave the country in a hurry."

"I'll take care of it," Donovan nodded as he and Buck headed toward the door. He turned toward Buck. "Let me tell Eva where I'm going, and I'll join you at the elevator."

Donovan slid his key into his lock, knocked lightly, and went inside. The bathroom door was wide open and Donovan could hear the shower running. He called her name and Eva opened the shower curtain and smiled. She shut off the water and reached for a towel. He turned away as she stepped out of the tub. "I wanted to tell you I'm going to the airport. I'll be back in a little while. Stay in the room—don't leave."

"Are you sure it is safe for you to go back there?"

"It's fine," Donovan replied. She breezed out of the bathroom wrapped in a towel and stood in front of him. Her freshly scrubbed skin glowed a soft bronze, her wet hair pulled straight back from her face. For the first time he saw the small tattoo at the base of her neck. Usually, he disliked tattoos, but the expertly crafted angel somehow seemed appropriate.

"Are you sure you can't stay?" Eva asked, the look in her eyes made it clear there was an implied invitation.

"I'm sure," Donovan leaned down and kissed her on the forehead. "Right now, we need to focus on keeping you alive."

CHAPTER SEVENTEEN

Lauren squealed the tires on the Range Rover as she rounded the corner that led to the parking garage. There was no ticket to collect, so she stepped on the gas and they raced up to the top of the first incline. The silver Chrysler closed the distance once Lauren turned into the garage. Tires squealed as she made the turn and roared between two rows of parked cars. As she reached the end, she braked heavily, and made the sharp turn up the next incline, then stepped on the gas. Just before they reached the second level, Lauren stood on the brakes and stopped. Montero jumped out, slamming the door as she exited. Lauren sped up the rest of the ramp, turned, and brought the Range Rover to a sudden stop.

Moments later, the silver Chrysler rounded the corner and hit the brakes but was going too fast to stop in time. Lauren felt the impact, thankful it wasn't enough to deploy the airbags. She held her pistol out of view behind her and stepped out into the garage. Lauren watched as the driver started to open his door.

As predicted, Lauren had their full attention and they never saw Montero racing up to the driver's side window. Montero yanked open the door, reached in, grabbed him by the hair on the back of his head, and bounced his forehead off the steering wheel twice, then leveled her gun at the passenger.

Lauren moved closer, and in the relative quiet of the garage, she could hear Montero.

"Toss your weapons outside and put both hands behind your head."

It wasn't until Montero said the words that Lauren saw the passenger's pistol.

In a blur, the man in the passenger seat pointed the pistol at Montero and fired. From where Lauren stood it sounded as if there were a single gunshot, but there were two muzzle flashes. The man slumped backward and Montero staggered sideways, her gun still up and ready.

"Ronnie, are you hit?" Lauren ran forward, pistol up, ready to fire. The amount of blood splatter inside the car and on Montero was shocking, and Lauren feared the worst.

"It's not my blood."

The man in the passenger seat was dead. Montero's shot had hit him just above the left eye. The driver was slumped sideways in the car, the side of his head matted with blood.

"Damn it!" Montero snapped. "What a goddamned mess! That idiot shot at me and hit the driver instead—amateur." Montero went to the driver and used the barrel of her gun to lift his chin enough to look at the man's face. "Oh, Jesus!"

"What?"

"It's Curtis Nelson, the guy from the Bureau." Montero let his head drop back to his chest. "Maybe shooting his partner wasn't an accident. If you have a mole inside the FBI and you're about to get arrested, maybe you make sure your mole will never talk. Either way, we need to go."

Lauren drove quickly but cautiously. They wound their way out of the garage into the sunshine. "How did everything back there go sideways so quickly?"

"Good question. We obviously surprised them, and they panicked and pulled weapons. I never saw Curtis' face until after the shooting was over."

"How bad is all of this?"

"Not good." Montero fished in her pocket for her phone.

"Who are you calling?" Lauren asked.

"Director Graham. He needs to know what happened back there, and you and I need to get clear of this as fast as we can. Where are we, exactly?"

Lauren gave her the information, checking the mirror for cars that might be following them.

"Director Graham, it's Montero. The parking garage of the Erickson-Lewis Building in Chantilly, Virginia, there's a silver Chrysler sedan, two bodies. One of them is Curtis Nelson. They followed us, and when I went to have a chat, guns were pulled. It'll all be in the security camera footage."

Lauren could only imagine how Graham was taking the news.

"No, we left the scene for our own safety. I believe there may be others, and, due to the fact that part of this threat came from inside the Bureau, we're going dark. We'll provide our own security until we're convinced you've eliminated the threat."

Lauren was impressed with how Montero was handling the situation.

"We're fine, thank you, Norman. I'll be checking my e-mail, but no open phone lines." Montero ended the call, turned off her phone, and slid the battery out, stuffing both into her pocket. "Hand me your phone, we need to shut it down, and then the next order of business is to find a place where I can clean up."

"We're headed back to my house. Your suitcase is there. I'll pull into the garage, there's a half-bath in that hallway. I'll bring you your things. You can clean up and change. No one will see you."

"We can't stay at your house."

"I know. Those people were following us with guns drawn, ready to shoot. I'm grabbing Abigail, and we're going to a place that very few people know about. We'll be safe there."

CHAPTER EIGHTEEN

Donovan ended his phone call with a small amount of frustration mixed with disappointment. He'd wanted to talk to Lauren, but his call had gone straight to voice mail. He quickly informed her that Stephanie was still alive, and that hopefully he'd have good news by tomorrow.

He hurried through the lobby and joined Buck in the Suburban to head to the airport. His next call was to tell Michael they were on their way. He also asked Michael if the Learjet was still parked on the ramp. Michael said no, they'd just reopened the airport, and he'd seen it take off only moments ago.

"We lost them," Donovan said to Buck. "Michael says the Learjet just took off."

"Can we find out where they went?" Buck asked. "Or more importantly—who chartered it in the first place?"

"Remember the handler who met us when we arrived? Those guys usually take care of all the private aircraft. I'm guessing he might be persuaded to talk."

Buck swung the black SUV up to the USGS hangar. He left the motor running. "Give me the ID badge you took from the Learjet pilot. I'm going to go have a little chat with the handling agent. You go in and brief everyone, get things started. I shouldn't be gone long."

Donovan didn't argue, extracting information from the handler was probably a job best left to Buck. He stepped out and went to find Michael. It didn't take him long to find the entire crew. They were huddled around the *Scimitar*, as if their entire purpose hinged directly on the experimental black aircraft. As he walked up, Donovan knew he was about to add another dimension to that concern.

"Donovan," Michael said. "You're just in time to hear the verdict on the *Scimitar*."

"We'll get to the *Scimitar* in a minute," Donovan said, as all eyes turned toward him. "I want to bring everyone up to date. Stephanie's kidnappers have made contact. The exchange could happen as early as this evening, and, if it does, we'll need to shift our airborne mission priorities away from the volcano."

"What is it you need us to do?" Janie asked.

Donovan turned toward Professor Murakami and frowned as he saw what looked like water dripping furiously from the *Scimitar*. "How bad is it?"

"What you're looking at, is the water from the last of the ice that formed when the liquid nitrogen line ruptured. It's a small leak, but, unfortunately, I'll have to purge the entire system. Once I do that, I can run a diagnostic and make sure nothing else is damaged. It'll take me the rest of the night. But, hopefully, I can recharge the liquid nitrogen, and we'll be able to fly again in the morning."

"Here's what I know right now," Donovan repeated. "Buck thinks that the exchange will take place here in the city. We'll be stretched pretty thin in terms of personnel, so the *Scimitar* is key. We need it airborne as soon as possible. It doesn't need to fly through volcanoes—it just needs to fly."

"You need the electronics, don't you?" John asked. "If the *Scimitar* is orbiting overhead, we can track cars, people, whatever we want."

"Exactly," Donovan replied. "We need to get it in the air before they call us back. Things will probably start moving quickly once we begin."

"If I seal off the liquid nitrogen system, I can run a quick diagnostic to make sure everything else is working," Murakami said with a shrug. "If there aren't any other problems, I can probably have it ready to go in two hours."

"Get to work, then." Donovan said, then turned to Michael. "Have the *Galileo* ready to go. We may want to get out of here in a hurry once we have her."

"What else can we do?" Malcolm asked, his arm wrapped protectively around his wife's shoulders. "Do you know for sure that Stephanie is still alive?"

"The kidnappers know we're going to want proof of life before we make any kind of exchange. Once we know for sure—everything will start."

"Mr. Nash," John asked, "do we know if Guatemalan air traffic control is going to let us orbit the city? I mean, to really do this right, I'll need to be able to maneuver the *Scimitar* wherever I want. I'm going to have to work on specific angles to keep the target in sight. I did this in the Air Force. The trick is not to allow any buildings or structures to obscure the view of the target. Depending on what happens, we can't be restricted, or we could lose sight of our subject."

"Let me take care of that part," Michael said. "I'll tell them it's a test flight. They already know we came in with a problem earlier. There's also very little traffic in the area due to the volcano. It'll be fine. Besides, what are they going to do? Shoot it down?"

"John, given the type of flying you just described, how long can you stay airborne?" Donovan asked.

"We don't have the endurance of the military model due to all the modifications, but I'd say we have a solid ten hours."

Donovan tried to picture the mission in his mind. "If we're simply flying over the city, waiting, you can control it without the Gulfstream being airborne, right?"

"Sure," John nodded. "All I need is line of sight. Without the satellite interface, it's the best I can do. To be on the safe side, I'm probably good for a twenty-mile radius around the airport. If we need to go farther than that, it'd be better if we launched *Galileo*."

"I understand," Donovan replied. "If Buck is right, then the kidnappers will want to do all this in the city. It makes sense—they're locals, familiar with the town. We're the outsiders."

"Where is Buck?" Michael asked.

"He'll be along shortly."

"We better start to work," Murakami said, as he turned to his toolbox.

"It sounds like we might be in for a long evening," Lillian said. "Maybe Malcolm and I should order food for everyone."

"Good idea." Donovan felt encouraged by everyone's willingness to do what they could. His thoughts circled back to Eva, and he wondered how willing she'd be? "Lillian, before you do that, what's happening with the volcano? I know that borrowing the *Scimitar* has left you in the dark. Do you think another day will make much of a difference?"

"Mr. Nash, for all I care, the volcano can erupt to hell and back right now," Lillian replied, her grim tone leaving no doubt she was serious. "The area has been cleared as much as possible. There's not anything we can really do beyond that—I think we've already helped minimize the loss of life, which is the main thing. My only concern is for you to get Stephanie back. The volcano can wait."

"As soon as this is over, I promise Eco-Watch's full support for your research," Donovan said.

Buck let himself into the office. "Did I miss anything?"

"That was quick," Donovan replied. "How did it go?"

"Our handler isn't the most discreet person I ever met, plus he's greedy, and can be bribed. The Learjet was chartered by a company out of Mexico City—*MSX Comunicaciones*—they own a dozen or more radio stations and newspapers in Mexico. He says they come in twice a month or so. I passed this along to William, so he can initiate a search and find out who's actually chartering the jet, and maybe even why."

"You think it's a real company, or just a shell for something or someone else?" Donovan asked.

"Hard to say, and we won't know until we track it down. What's the status of the *Scimitar*?"

"They're going to put it back together, run a few tests, and, if we're lucky, it'll be ready in two hours."

"Have the helicopter fueled up and ready to fly as well," Buck said. "I'd rather have the *Scimitar*, but a helicopter is a good second choice. Also, I want to know where the nearest hospitals are outside of Guatemala. Just in case."

"Both the helicopter and the Gulfstream will be ready to go once everything begins." Donovan opened the door to the hangar, spotted Michael, and motioned for him to join him and Buck.

"What's up?" Michael asked as he entered the room.

"Buck just brought up the fact that we may need an exit strategy that involves a first-rate hospital," Donovan said. "Can you identify the destinations in the US if we have medical considerations?"

"I already looked into that," Michael replied. "It depends on the ash cloud. Right now, we could go straight to Miami, but if the wind shifts the cloud to the northeast, then our best bet is either New Orleans or Houston. They're about the same distance."

"Let's make Miami primary, with Houston being secondary," Buck said. "I know people in both those cities that could be of help."

"Is there anything else going on out here that needs my attention? If not, I'm going back to the hotel," Donovan said.

"Excuse us for a moment." Michael grabbed Donovan by the arm and led him into the hangar out of earshot of the others. "You've got that look in your eye. What's happening that I don't know about?"

"What look?" Donovan replied.

"You're on a mission, one I don't know about. It's like you're in some other world. I've said it once, and I'll say it again. Something doesn't feel right. I think you need to step away, completely. We're pilots, we deal with weather and airplanes, not kidnappings and guns. Other people are far better equipped to do this than you and me. We're both out of our element, and you're being pulled in directions I can't predict."

"I'm fine," Donovan said.

"I know you care about Stephanie, but she's William's niece, and *he's* holding up better than you are. Why are you carrying a gun? Is this something you plan to do all the time?"

"I was shot at today."

"I rest my case," Michael said. "Someday you're going to put yourself in a position where I can't help you. I worry about that more than you know. Right now, I don't think I can protect you, because you don't seem to want to protect yourself."

"You're not responsible," Donovan said. "Don't put yourself in danger to help me."

"That's the problem—because I always will."

CHAPTER NINETEEN

"What is this place?" Montero asked, as the three of them pulled up to a simple but rugged iron gate.

Lauren punched in a code and the gate swung open, revealing a long, curved driveway that rose up a gentle hill and ended at a massive stone house situated well back from the road.

"Grandma's house!" Abigail cried out from her car seat, her enthusiasm clearly evident.

"It was handed down from Donovan's mother's side of the family. We call it Grandma's house. It's been in the family for over a hundred fifty years."

"Mommy, I want to go to the pond and catch frogs," Abigail said loudly. "Can you see the horses? I want a pony all my own."

"I don't see the neighbor's horses today, but we'll keep an eye out for them, okay? We'll go to the pond after dinner, and maybe Ms. Montero will help you catch a frog."

Montero turned and spoke to Abigail. "What do we do if we catch one?"

"My dad and I have a special bucket."

"Then what do you do with them?" Montero asked.

"They're my pets, I keep them, but they always get away when I'm sleeping. My dad says they're smart, so we just catch more."

Lauren pulled around back to the four-car garage and stopped. She left the engine running, stepped out, and went to a metal box obscured by bushes and disabled the second of three alarm systems. The garage could now be opened. Lauren eased the Range Rover inside and shut off the engine. Abigail hit the ground running and made straight for the tire swing that Donovan had hung from a sprawling oak tree.

"This place is amazing," Montero said, as she gathered up some of the groceries they'd brought from the house.

"It's almost two hundred acres. It's where Donovan is the most relaxed. Abigail loves it out here as much as he does."

"I can see why."

Lauren opened the door and deactivated the last of the alarms, but reset the perimeter alarm so they'd know if anyone else came onto the property. "The kitchen is through there. I'll get the air conditioning going. It won't take long to cool down the place, and then I'll get Abigail down for a short nap."

Montero glanced at her watch. "I need to check in with my guy in Miami. Is there a landline I can use? I don't want to risk using my cell phone."

"There's a small office through there, make yourself at home," Lauren said, then turned back to Montero. "You know, if you don't mind, I'd like to check in with Donovan first. Let him know we're out here."

"No problem," Montero replied, as she went out to retrieve the rest of their things from the SUV.

Lauren sat down at the desk. From the window she could see Abigail. She stopped for a moment at the sight of her daughter in the tire swing, pumping her legs and swinging back and forth, happily giggling as she spun around in great climbing circles. Behind her was the small lake that Donovan called the pond. She caught herself wishing he were here, that the three of them were here, and that none of the last year had happened. She shook off her wistful thinking and focused on the hard reality of the situation.

Three people had died today, and, as far as Lauren knew, their only connection was Central America and William Van-Gelder. Lauren looked at Abigail—could the man her daughter knew and loved as Grandpa be a killer? Had William orchestrated the death of Meredith Barnes and others? Her heart said "no," but everything she'd heard today pointed toward a potentially different verdict.

Lauren reached for the phone. She needed to hear Donovan's voice, see how everyone was holding up, find out if there were new developments. She started to call his cell and then decided that if he were with a group of people he wouldn't be able to talk. Instead, she retrieved the piece of paper with the number for his hotel and dialed. He probably wouldn't be there, but if he was, he'd be able to talk. If not, she'd simply leave a message. The hotel operator put her call through to his room.

It rang and rang. Lauren was about to hang up when someone picked up the phone.

"Hola," a groggy voice said.

Lauren froze, uncertain what to do or say. It was a woman's voice, and Lauren had woken her. Had they connected her to the wrong room? Should she just hang up and redial?

"Hola?"

"Yes, I'm sorry," Lauren said, finally. "I was looking for Donovan Nash."

"He's not here," the woman replied.

"Who is this?" Lauren asked, finding a woman asleep in her husband's hotel room troubling in ways she couldn't begin to calculate.

"My name is Eva. Who is this?"

"This is Donovan's wife. Do you know where he is?"

"Meredith?" The woman asked, her voice still thick with sleep.

"What did you say?" Lauren said, stunned. What had Donovan told this woman?

"Donovan said his wife was Meredith. Is that not right?"

"It's a long story. Where is he?" Lauren felt her fear beginning to win out over her other emotions.

"He and Buck went to the airport. They'll be back later. Can I give him a message?"

"No, no message. I'll call him later," Lauren replied and hung up. This Eva woman's relaxed demeanor was beyond irritating. Did Donovan feel free to jump into bed with random women he met on the road? Was he finished with her and their marriage? Lauren didn't know what to think, and decided that at the moment she didn't have the luxury to dwell on the possibilities. Later, she told herself, she'd talk to him later.

"Abigail, come on, honey." Lauren stepped out on the patio and called to her daughter. "It's time for a nap. Mommy will read you a story."

"That was quick," Montero said.

"Voice mail." Lauren shrugged.

Abigail slid from the tire and ran toward her mother. Lauren watched as her daughter stopped; something had caught her eye. She bent over to try to catch something, but the grasshopper buzzed out of reach. In the blink of an eye, the chase was on. Both her husband and daughter were impulsive free spirits, and in that moment, still burned by the phone call, Lauren wondered if her husband had ever been faithful.

"Are you okay?" Montero asked.

Lauren dabbed at the tears that had formed, then turned and smiled at Montero. "I will be, some things just caught up with me is all."

"It's been a day," Montero nodded. "You enjoy your daughter. I'm going to call Miami, then I'd love a shower. Once Abigail is asleep, we'll talk if you want?"

"Thank you," Lauren said. "I'm glad you're here. I can't bring anyone out here who doesn't know the secret. Beneath that big sycamore tree out near the next hill is an old family cemetery. Donovan's mother is buried there along with some other ancestors. The Huntington family ghosts are everywhere around here."

"I know," Montero said. "The pictures in the kitchen alone gave me chills. Robert as a boy, his parents, it's like a museum."

"Down the hallway to the right is one of the guest bathrooms. You should find everything you need." Lauren turned toward Abigail, who was still after her quarry. "Come on, sweetie."

Lauren led her daughter to her room. As always, Abigail grabbed a country version of her beloved stuffed animal, Shadow. The golden retriever was identical to the one at the house, designed to watch over Abigail's room between visits. Abigail pulled a book from the basket, kicked off her shoes, and climbed up onto the bed. Lauren covered her with a blanket.

"Is Ms. Montero really going to take me frog hunting?" Abigail asked.

"It sure sounded like she was," Lauren replied. "I'm going to go too. I'll take pictures and we'll send them to Daddy."

Abigail nodded her approval and then handed her mom the book she'd chosen.

Lauren was reading, and Abigail was making animal sounds along with each different barnyard creature illustrated in the book, though she was fading with each turn of the page and quickly dozed. Lauren pulled the cover up, tucked it under Abigail's chin, and quietly left the room. She found Montero had showered and dressed, her dark hair still wet.

Montero was writing furiously and looked up as Lauren entered.

"She was tired." Lauren sat down in a leather chair in the corner. "Feel better?"

"Much, thank you."

"Okay, what did your guy in Miami tell you?"

"Before we get to that, can I ask you a question?"

"Sure," Lauren said, aware that her instinct to withdraw was probably unnecessary, but she felt her defense mechanisms switch on anyway.

"Your tears today, they weren't about today, were they? Butterfield died, but we didn't kill him, we didn't even know him. The two people in the car, they made their choice. As one of a handful of people on earth with whom you can speak freely, I'm here to listen."

"Thank you, but I'm fine, really," Lauren said.

"You're one of the most intelligent, pragmatic people I've ever met. To see you emotional was...unexpected. I can't just shrug it off as if it never happened. If we're going to be partners, I need to know you're with me in mind and spirit. What would you think if you saw *me* tear up?"

"I'd be thinking what you're thinking, that something must be wrong. You and I aren't exactly the overly emotional types." It had been a long time since Lauren had another woman she could talk to that wasn't family. "Business first, tell me what the guy in Miami found."

"Okay," Montero said. "*La Serpiente* is a hired gun for whatever crime you want committed. He earned the name by being not only elusive, but also lethal, like some sort of venomous viper. To the best of his knowledge, *la Serpiente* disappeared fifteen years ago and is thought to either be dead or in prison."

"That doesn't give us much," Lauren said.

"Someone is cleaning house. As of today, not a single victim, or suspect, connected to *la Serpiente* is still alive. Whoever killed Butterfield and Knight may be a member of the conclave Butterfield talked about before he died."

"Do we think this *la Serpiente* kidnapped Vargas' granddaughter to make some fast money? Maybe he's been in prison. The girl escaped, and in a completely random set of circumstances, Stephanie gets taken."

"It's possible. But if it is *la Serpiente*, then he knows Stephanie is William VanGelder's niece, a man he's possibly worked for in the past. How does that play out?"

"One of two ways, as a business deal," Lauren said. "This is what Donovan told me William was working toward. Or the kidnapper, if it is *la Serpiente*, is panicked, and trying to eliminate all his ties with the past."

"What are you thinking?" Montero asked.

"I'm thinking about Hector Vargas. We have no idea if he's

been in touch with the kidnappers since his granddaughter was abducted."

"I say that's far too dangerous," Montero offered. "We can't let anyone outside our camp know what we know. Vargas could do anything, including panic, and that in turn could put Stephanie in even more danger."

"I know," Lauren nodded in agreement. "It's just that I'm afraid Donovan is unraveling in Guatemala over Stephanie's kidnapping, and that the man he reveres as a father might be the cause of a great many things, including the death of Meredith Barnes."

"If William's behind this, then Donovan is perfectly safe. William has kept the State Department, as well as the FBI, out of this investigation from the beginning. You're right, to him, it's a business deal, and according to what we've learned, there's no one better at wheeling and dealing than William VanGelder."

Lauren listened to Montero's words, but her thought process was leading her somewhere completely different. "Earlier, when I was upset, it was because I called Donovan's hotel room in Guatemala. I wanted to talk to him, but I knew if I called on his cell phone, chances were he'd be with William, or Buck, or Michael, and unable to really talk."

"Makes sense, go on."

"A woman answered. She spoke English with a thick Spanish accent. I woke her up. She said Donovan wasn't there. When I identified myself as his wife, she asked me if I was Meredith."

"Oh, Jesus," Montero whispered. "What else did she say?"

"Nothing, I was caught off guard. I was upset, so I hung up." Lauren shook her head at the memory. "I think he's in trouble, and I also don't think there's anyone with him who's in a position to understand, let alone help. The only person down there with any knowledge of the complexities of Donovan's state of mind is William, and, as of right now, I don't know if William has his back."

"Has there ever been a time when William didn't have Donovan's best interests at heart? I mean, you know them better than

I do, but Donovan values loyalty above all else, and if he ever thought William wasn't one hundred percent behind him, I think you'd have heard about it."

"I have no reason to believe that William is any less compartmentalized, damaged, and secretive than Donovan. That's the frustrating part. William, hell, Donovan, could each be a cold-blooded killer, and I don't think I'd have a clue."

"Oddly enough, the two known killers are you and I," Montero said.

"That's different. You're a former FBI agent and I was—"

"Protecting your husband," Montero finished Lauren's sentence. "And I was doing it for God and Country. It doesn't make either one of us right or wrong. What we did have though, was the unwavering belief that the lethal course we took was the only way to solve the problem."

"What are you trying to say?"

"We don't have enough information to do anything about William, or this conclave, or the woman in Donovan's room. What we do know is they're using their formidable skills to get Stephanie returned unharmed. Any direct confrontations between you and William compromises that mission, and I don't think that's what we're after. If you continue down this path toward confronting William, then you'd better make sure that you're right, or I promise you you'll lose any option you might harbor of being a family again. How do you think Donovan would react if William had a part in killing Meredith Barnes?"

"I can't imagine," Lauren said, her voice nearly a whisper.

"How do you think they'd both react if you accused William, and he was innocent?"

Lauren hung her head as she played out the implications. "I'd never have the trust of either one of them again."

"That's the price each of you may pay if we continue. I don't know what truth we're headed for, but it might not be what anyone wants. You may have to step out of your science and reason safety zone and contemplate the human cost." Montero reached across the table and took Lauren's hand. "All I'm saying is that rational thought will only take you so far when the family you've known implodes. Relationships are about emotions, and yours is on the brink of tearing itself apart. You and Donovan are both used to winning. If we continue, I can promise you, no one gets out of this one unscathed."

"Thank you for that," Lauren said as a sad smile came to her lips. "You're right, I'm a scientist. I use logic to arrive at facts that can then be used to provide tangible results. It's how I grew up, it's how I operate."

"Throw all of that out for one moment. You love your husband, and he's in trouble. Imagine this. There's no data to help him, just your woman's intuition coupled with a gut feeling. What's your move?"

"I'm not sure," Lauren felt out of her comfort level and more than a little outmaneuvered by Montero, though she knew the former FBI agent was trying to help.

"Feel, then think," Montero urged. "We need to leave William, Donovan, and Eco-Watch alone until Stephanie is home safe. That's a given. We'll let the FBI grind on those issues. The moment we need to shut down the FBI, we'll show them the pictures Stephanie took of the kidnapping, and make the case that there is no retribution being leveled toward William. If you can, once Donovan's home, work *with* him on the William question. It's what you've asked of him, to be let into his world, to allow you to help, *before* he's overwhelmed. Show him the same respect."

Lauren felt the sting of truth as Montero's words hit home. In a single instant she flew through a flurry of emotions—from anger, to denial, to gratitude—that Montero had not only the insight, but the ability and guts to explain the situation.

"Which leaves us with what part of our investigation we haven't looked into?" Montero asked. "The information only we hold?"

"Marie Vargas was kidnapped eighteen months ago, and then again six days ago," Lauren said as she jumped to her feet and began to pace. "What's happened between then and now? Who are the players and who has the most to gain? I have an idea. This may sound crazy, but please, hear me out."

"I'm listening," Montero said as she displayed a rare smile.

CHAPTER TWENTY

Donovan let himself into his room. The lights were out, and it took a moment for his eyes to adjust. The curtains allowed in enough light for Donovan to see a room service tray, as well as an empty shopping bag next to a stack of new clothes. He could see the pile of tags on the table. She must have tried them on and then removed the tags before folding them up again. He looked at the bed. All he could see was her hair spilled out over a pillow, her slender body outlined by the sheet. She was curled up, her arm wrapped around a pillow. It struck Donovan once again how much she resembled Meredith. Donovan shook off those thoughts. He didn't want to go there—couldn't go there right now. Instead, he clicked on a light and called her name.

"Eva," Donovan said gently, not wanting to startle her. "Eva, wake up."

She moved under the covers but didn't respond. Donovan went to the side of the bed and switched on another light. He reached over and put his hand on her shoulder. She immediately awoke—terror in her eyes as she struck out at him, twisting to escape his touch. He stepped back, surprised. Her facial expression was filled with raw fear, her chest heaving like a trapped animal.

"You're okay," Donovan said. "It's me. It's time to get up."

She focused on him, as if trying to understand. Finally, she brought the sheet up to her neck with one hand and brushed her hair away from her face with the other. "What time is it? Did they call?" she asked, looking for the clock that would help her reorient herself.

"Not yet," Donovan said as he walked to where she'd left her newly purchased clothes. He picked up the stack and placed them on the bed. "Get dressed. I'll come back in a few minutes—we need to talk."

"No," she said. "Don't leave me. It won't take me long."

Donovan turned away and heard Eva throw back the sheet, then she went to the bathroom and closed the door. Minutes later she emerged, pulling her hair out from underneath the collar of a simple black long-sleeved shirt. She'd tucked the shirt into a pair of equally dark slacks, then rolled up her sleeves. She looked at herself in the mirror, using one hand to arrange her thick hair. "I'm a mess."

"You look fine," Donovan said. "Let's go."

Moments later they were in William's room. She curled her legs underneath her in a chair and sipped on a bottle of water. Donovan thought she looked frightened and fragile. He didn't know what scared him most, that she would be too afraid to go—or that she'd place too much trust in them and be killed.

"Eva," William started. "May I call you Eva?"

She nodded, her questioning eyes jumped from William to Buck to Donovan, as if she were somehow in trouble but didn't understand why.

"We have a situation, as well as an offer we'd like to discuss with you." William tried his best to disarm her with a smile. "It's a rather delicate matter, but I want to assure you that we will be as concerned for your safety as we possibly can. I want you to listen very carefully as we explain, and I hope you can find it somewhere in your heart to trust us."

"What has happened?" Eva asked, looking close to tears.

"When I talked to the kidnappers earlier today," Donovan knelt down to be eye level with her, "they told us to have the money ready by ten o'clock tonight."

"Yes, I remember," Eva nodded.

"They also want you." Donovan held her eyes with his, trying to keep her calm. "We want them to believe that you're part of the exchange. I can assure you, you'll be protected at all times."

"How can you protect me from them?" Eva wrapped her arms around her legs and pulled them even closer into her body. Her eyes were beginning to fill with tears. "They want to kill me."

"They also want three million dollars," William said quietly, his tone designed to pacify her. "As I said before, we can protect you, we just need you to cooperate."

"How will you protect me?" Eva sniffed and wiped the tears from her eyes. She stared at the ceiling, her lips trembled.

"How is not important," Buck said with quiet confidence. "I used to be a US Navy SEAL. I'll be with you the entire time. I won't let anything happen to you."

"If you help us," William added. "I'll make sure you can have a new life anywhere in the world you want. Europe, the United States, anywhere you feel safe."

Eva closed her eyes at the enormity of William's words. She lowered her head into her knees, her hair tumbled over her face, small tremors shook her body as she cried.

"I'll also give you one million dollars," William added at exactly the right moment. "But if you won't help us—I'm afraid we can't help you at all."

Donovan knew he'd just seen William do what he did best—mix diplomacy with shrewd manipulation. He'd done it with the silky smooth tone of someone who seemed to care a great deal about the outcome—making Eva believe that there was only one way out of her particular hell. They were all waiting for her to react when the cell phone on the table rang. Donovan and Buck glanced at their watches and thought the exact same thing—it was too early.

William answered the call, put the phone on speaker, and set it down on the table. "This is William VanGelder."

"It is time," a muffled and heavily accented voice spoke. "Is the money ready?"

"Yes," William replied. "I need to speak with my niece."

"In a moment. Let me tell you what I want. You put the money, Eva, and the man who took her from us, into a non-embassy vehicle."

Donovan was helpless, there was nothing he could do but listen. Eva raised her head at the sound of her name. Her cheeks were damp with tears. Donovan saw the defeat in her eyes, the pallor of resignation on her face.

"No!" William said forcefully. "That's not part of the deal! We have the money and Eva. We'll meet you wherever you want. The man you speak of is not part of the deal. Is that understood?"

"Then we have no deal."

Donovan felt his anger burn. He'd always assumed that Buck would be the one delivering the money. He had the utmost faith in Buck's skills to even the playing field. He had far fewer skills, giving the advantage to the kidnappers.

"You have until dawn to change your mind," the voice said before terminating the call.

"It's a classic tactic," Buck explained. "They're stalling. They want us to worry, to argue, to get no sleep. They want to wear us down with ever-changing demands—until we're either too tired, or too anxious, to respond, hoping that we'll make a mistake."

"What's your suggestion?" William asked.

"We tell them no," Buck replied without hesitation. "I don't want Donovan in the line of fire. I'm the one they're going to have to deal with."

"I'm going to throw this out there." Donovan stood as he thought. "Buck, wouldn't it be better on several levels, if you were the one who was mobile? They think they'll be able to separate us, and have to deal only with me. I'm assuming they aren't all that happy with what I did today at the airport. If I'm the delivery person, then you're free to do all your Navy SEAL stuff and keep me out of trouble."

"I don't like it," William said, shaking his head.

"If Donovan goes—then I will agree to go as well," Eva said, her voice strained, a little uncertain.

Donovan turned to her. Her hands shook as she looked up at him. The silence in the room told him everyone was thinking—recalculating the equation. "It could work. With Eva's help, this could work. If we retool our plan, and I go instead of Buck, they'll think they have the upper hand. They, in turn, might make the mistake of underestimating us."

Buck rubbed his eyes. "You make a good point—except that now you put two amateurs into the loop and take out the professional."

"But that adds you to the surveillance and response team. Personally, I'm willing to take that risk, especially if it ensures that Eva will go too." Donovan glanced at her, and she nodded her head in agreement.

"Now wait just a minute!" William said angrily, holding up his hands. "We're not agreeing to anything. Let's think this through. Buck, exactly how do you see this whole thing going down? I want to make sure we all understand what to expect."

"I'm convinced more than ever that the drop will be here in the city," Buck said with authority. "Everyone who has tried to get to Eva has done so here in Guatemala City. I don't know how big this group is, but they're at least three men short right now, and an urban setting is probably more manageable for them. My best guess is that we'll get a call early in the morning—don't be surprised if they try another delay tactic—I don't think these guys are top-notch professionals. They could be doing what we're doing, trying to decide the best way to handle the exchange."

"Do you think it will be a drop?" William asked. "Or do you think there will be an actual face-to-face?"

"They want Donovan and Eva. They'll also want to see the money for themselves. It has to be a face-to-face. In fact, we'll insist upon it, which puts us in direct contact with the kidnappers."

"What do you have in mind?" Donovan interrupted. "How do you protect us?"

"I'll be following you as best I can without being detected. My guess is they'll run you around the city, drive you past their own lookouts to see if you're being tailed. I assume you'll be talking with the kidnappers on Eva's phone—but we'll be in contact as well. At some point there's an ultimate destination. I'll be in position when you arrive and deal with them however the situation dictates."

"Eva," William asked, "how do you feel about this? How do you think these men might react?"

Eva had been sitting quietly, seemingly trying to follow the conversation. She seemed startled at the sound of her name and responded. "I know they are bad men. They have been criminals for a long time. One of them used to be in the police, but I think he is not doing that anymore. They are dangerous because they hold no value for a person's life. Which is why they want to kill me, and now I think maybe they want to kill Donovan too."

"You'll each be wearing a Kevlar vest," Buck said. "Just as a precaution."

"What is Kevlar?" Eva asked, her face clouded with confusion.

"A bullet-proof vest," Buck explained. "You wear it and it protects you. If someone shoots you the bullet is stopped."

There was no escaping Eva's drawn expression, and the look of deep fatigue in her red-tinged eyes. Eva held little resemblance to the confident woman he'd seen stride into the hotel bar. He wondered if she would hold up until morning.

"Buck," William broke the silence. "Give it to us straight up. What are the odds of pulling this off without any of our people getting hurt?"

"Hard to put it into numbers," Buck replied without hesitation. "All the plans in the world shift the moment someone goes off script. The side that reacts quickest in a fluid situation usually prevails. In this case, I have to think the advantage is ours."

"Donovan." William pressed the tips of his fingers together, contemplating his next words. "Obviously, I don't want you involved. I believe I've made myself clear on this issue. I'd feel better had they requested that I deliver the money rather than you, but right now we are not in charge, they are. I need to make certain you're sure about this. If not, I fully understand, and we'll try to force the issue in another direction."

"I appreciate what you're saying." Donovan knew that William's speech was more for Buck and Eva. William knew he wasn't going to back away from this. He looked at his long-time friend and gave him a gentle nod to show he understood. "We have Eva on board, and I think that the sooner we get this resolved—the better it'll be for everyone. So, to answer your question, yes, I'm in."

CHAPTER TWENTY-ONE

Donovan glanced at the luminous dial on his watch: four-thirty in the morning. He hated waiting, it left him with far too much time to think. He wasn't sure, but he thought maybe he'd closed his eyes for a little while, but the dream of Meredith had awoken him with a start. One moment they were together, happy, then moments later, she was gone forever.

He'd been anointed in the rituals of death since he was a boy. He'd watched both of his parents die when their yacht had sunk during a storm in the Pacific Ocean. He'd clung desperately to a piece of wreckage. The image of his mother slipping beneath the waves had forever imprinted on his fourteen-year-old brain. Death changes life, alters everything it touches. Donovan knew he'd been changed violently and permanently by death's cold hand.

He found himself not caring what happened to him this coming day, only that he succeed. The only feelings he allowed himself were anger and determination, the two essentials to the mission. If he failed, if Stephanie were murdered, he knew it would change him yet again. He wondered how many times a man could be changed by death, until all that was left was a shell waiting for death's final embrace.

A hand touched his shoulder and Donovan, startled, looked up to see William standing over his chair, dressed in a suit.

"It's time to wake up," William whispered.

Donovan nodded and looked over at Eva, curled up on the

small sofa, her shoulders rising and falling with each breath. Earlier he'd covered her with a blanket, and she'd given him a small smile, a hopeful smile, but one filled with apprehension. Donovan had no idea where Buck was. He'd left earlier, advising Donovan to try and get some sleep. When Donovan had told him the same thing, Buck had shrugged and told him SEALs didn't need sleep.

Eva raised her head and found Donovan. "What time is it?"

"Almost five," he said as he walked to the window and opened the drapes. Raindrops streaked the window and clouds hung low, brushing the tops of the buildings. "Time to get up."

Eva nodded and headed to the coffee pot on the bar.

As she ran the water, Donovan went to the door that led out to the hallway and peered out the peephole. Instead of the embassy guards, he saw Buck standing outside the door. The former SEAL was dressed and ready for combat. Donovan opened the door.

"I was just going to wake you," Buck said. "Let me get the rest of my gear and I'll be there in a second."

Donovan waited as Buck went into his room, moments later returning, carrying a duffel bag and two weapons. He held the door open as Buck strode through and placed everything on the sofa. Buck extended his hand toward Donovan. "Hand me that Sig you've been carrying around."

Donovan pulled it out from under the cushion of the chair he'd slept in and gave it to Buck. The former SEAL popped the clip and extracted the round from the chamber. He ran his practiced eye over the weapon, and then in a blur of motion reloaded it and handed it back to Donovan.

"If you're comfortable using this, it looks like it's in pretty good shape," Buck said as he leaned over and unzipped the black duffel bag. He pulled out two bulletproof vests, handed one to Donovan and the other he laid out for Eva. "Put these on under your shirts. They're pretty thin, I don't want it obvious that you're wearing them."

Donovan stripped down to his undershirt and pulled the small but surprisingly heavy garment over his head. Buck helped pull the Velcro straps tight, and Donovan rotated his arms until it felt comfortable. He slid into his shirt and buttoned it up to the next to last button.

Buck stood back and checked it out. "Perfect." He turned to Eva, instructed her to turn around and remove her shirt. Buck repeated the procedure, making sure her long hair wasn't trapped beneath the vest. She buttoned up her shirt and turned to face them.

"It's a little more obvious on her." Donovan saw that the outline of her breasts were muted by the shape of the vest.

"This isn't a beauty contest," Buck said, then turned to William. "We need to get the money ready."

"It's in the bedroom," William replied.

"Do you need help with the money?" Donovan asked.

"I've got this. We still need to divide the cash." Buck allowed William to lead him to retrieve the cases of money.

Donovan took a steaming mug of coffee from Eva. "Thanks," he said and tried to offer her an encouraging smile. She looked a little less frayed than last night. He hoped she would be able to hold it together once they started.

"Did you get some sleep?" Eva asked.

"I'm fine, though I'm ready to get this underway. I hate the waiting," Donovan replied. "How are you feeling?"

"I don't know." She shrugged and wrapped two hands around her own cup of coffee. "I trust you, but I also feel that I have no choice. I don't understand why all of this is happening to me, and I feel out of control."

"Hopefully, that'll go away once we start. I think the waiting is the worst part."

"I feel that you are not a patient man," Eva said, bluntly. "I mean, you seem like someone who is used to getting what you want. Will that go away once we start?"

"You're not exactly seeing me at my best." Donovan ran his hand back through his hair.

A small look of surprise came over Eva's face, as if she'd just remembered something. "I forgot to tell you. Meredith called yesterday when you were at the airport. I'm sorry."

"You spoke to my wife?" Donovan's eyes darted toward the nearest phone. "Yes, her name is Meredith, yes?"

"No." Donovan felt his stomach knot up. "You misunderstood. My wife is Lauren. What did she say?"

"She said she would call back." Eva shrugged. "I'm sorry, I was asleep when she called and I forgot."

"It's okay." Donovan thought of Lauren calling his room and finding a sleeping woman. He only hoped that with William and Buck's help, he'd be able to explain.

"She is a very lucky woman," Eva said.

"I'm not so sure she feels that way right now," Donovan said, as Buck and William came into the main room carrying the two suitcases of money. Buck snatched a black duffel bag from the sofa and went back into William's room. He emerged moments later and the bag looked heavy.

"It's all here," William said. "Three million dollars."

Buck hoisted the duffel bag. "Here's the other million. We'll hold onto this until we get back." He looked at Eva. "Then we can figure out what you want to do with this much money."

"Where did the guards go?" Donovan remembered the empty hallway.

"I've given them their assignments," Buck said. "We have four men, two from the Diplomatic Security Service, and two from the Canadian embassy. William has a single driver from the embassy in the event he needs to travel. Everyone should be in strategic positions shortly. I'll be in radio contact with them at all times."

"What about us?" Donovan asked.

"You'll have your phone." Buck said. "Dial my number and leave the connection open. The key is to let me know where you are at all times. I don't know how many gyrations these guys are going to put you through, but I'll be able to stay on top of everything without being seen."

Donovan nodded that he understood.

"Courtesy of the Canadians, I'll be in a car the kidnappers won't recognize as being from the US embassy. I have enough firepower to do pretty much whatever I need to do. But you have to keep me informed of everything that is happening."

Donovan was about to ask about the assortment of weapons when Eva's cell phone rang. Donovan felt his adrenaline begin to pump as Buck handed it to him. "Remember to ask Stephanie a question only she can answer."

Donovan looked at William, who nodded, and then he answered and put the phone on speaker.

"We're ready," Donovan said.

"Who am I speaking with?"

"My name is Donovan. I want to talk to Stephanie."

"I recognize your voice. You have the money?"

"I told you we're ready. Now I want to talk to Stephanie." Donovan's entire world was focused on the thought of hearing her voice, letting her know he was coming.

"Donovan?"

At the sound of her voice Donovan felt his throat constrict, Stephanie sounded so alone and frightened. He thought of the last words Meredith had said to him. She'd told him she loved him, and not to pay the ransom—for twenty-two years her words had plagued him, haunted him, for she must have already known she was going to be killed.

"It's me." Donovan said in a hushed voice, trying to control his emotions. "Are you okay?"

"Yes," Stephanie replied.

"Do you remember what I swore I wouldn't do while I was in Montana?"

"You haven't shaved?"

"Hang on a little longer," Donovan said, his voice stronger this time, it was definitely her.

"Listen carefully." The hard-edged male voice had the phone

again. "Take the money, and the girl, and drive north out of the hotel on the Avenue *La Reforma*. Keep this phone—you are being watched. You have ten minutes."

"I understand." Donovan severed the connection, and then slid the phone into his jacket pocket and glanced at his watch. "I spoke to Stephanie, she's alive. We've got ten minutes to get on the road."

CHAPTER TWENTY-TWO

Lauren jolted awake with a start. For a moment she couldn't place her surroundings, and she felt her apprehension escalate as she struggled to understand. In the darkness, the dull hum of engines helped her pull it all together. She was on a chartered Gulfstream headed to Guatemala City. Her eyes went to the display mounted on the forward bulkhead. The moving map showed they were at 44,000 feet over the Gulf of Mexico.

With mixed feelings, she'd left Abigail with Montero. They'd gotten along wonderfully, and Abigail loved staying at the country house. Lauren had briefed Montero on the house, its security systems, the armory and safe room in the basement, as well as the means to escape if need be.

They discussed different plans of action, including getting Abigail to Lauren's mother if Montero needed to vanish. Lauren also left enough cash for Montero to cover any contingency. Without having all the answers as to who might want to hurt them, having a highly trained former FBI agent watch over her daughter brought Lauren some measure of comfort.

Despite their history, she'd grown to like and trust Montero. The woman was capable, smart, and not afraid to act. These qualities Lauren had known about; she was surprised to find that Montero possessed such an insightful spirit. The other not-so-surprising aspect of Montero was her investigative mind. Once they'd decided to focus on Marie Vargas, Montero flew into high gear, and the two of them began to pull together information from Montero's friend in Miami and Lauren's government sources. When Lauren had left for the airport, Montero was still digging, connecting seemingly unimportant details. Now, somewhere out in front of her in Guatemala was her husband. With all the information that she and Montero had gathered, Lauren couldn't ignore the fact that her husband might be in very real trouble.

Each minute, the Gulfstream put her six miles closer to Donovan, and as Lauren ran each scenario, she kept coming back to the one set of events that scared her the most. What if her husband was finished with their marriage? She'd left him almost a year ago, and while the underlying causes of their split were still firmly in place, they seemed committed to working on their issues. Donovan's self-imposed exile to Montana was designed to give him some perspective, to try to put his ghosts behind him, and live his life focused on the future instead of the past. What if he found his answers and they didn't involve her? Could he walk away from her? Her husband was one of the most complex men she'd ever met and, as she'd learned over the years, complex worked great when it was functioning, but an upheaval created nothing but chaos. For Donovan, the loss of Stephanie would go far beyond an upheaval. Her death would be catastrophic.

She threw off the blanket and stretched, then smoothed her hair away from her face and pushed the button that would open the louvered window shade. She found the sun was just coming up in the distance.

"Dr. McKenna," the flight attendant stood beside her, "can I get you anything? Coffee, some juice? We have omelets for breakfast, if you'd like. I could start heating everything up."

"I'd just like some coffee for now, thank you." Lauren sat up straight in her seat and pressed her hands into her face, trying to pull herself together. It was a miracle she'd slept at all. Last night, after she'd made the decision to go to Guatemala, she'd talked to Abigail and then put her daughter to bed. In between helping Montero, she'd arranged the details of the flight, thrown together a few things, and then driven herself to the private terminal at Dulles airport. It was a four-hour flight, and Lauren calculated she'd slept for about an hour—which was all the sleep she was going to get for now. She grabbed her purse and headed for the lavatory in the rear of the plane.

Lauren leaned into the soft lighting around the mirror and could see the red spider webs surrounding her pupils, the result of not enough sleep and the dehydration of being in the airplane. She dug in her purse until she found some eye drops and relished their soothing effect. She combed her hair and straightened her blouse. As she returned to her seat she was delighted to find a cup of coffee waiting for her. Lauren took a sip and began to methodically run through what she was going to do when she arrived.

If she went straight to the hotel, she might catch Donovan before he left for the day. She had no idea if he was flying or not. If she missed him, then her second choice was to find William, though at the moment she didn't want to put herself in a position that would lead to a confrontation. Lauren processed the third and least pleasant option, what she would do if she found Donovan with Eva. Would she confront him, or just quietly go home and wait it out?

"More coffee?" The flight attendant asked as she walked from the galley with a pot in her hand.

"Yes, please," Lauren said. "Can I check my e-mail from here?"

"Of course," the flight attendant replied. "We have global satellite capability. There's a small compartment by your elbow with connections and a card with instructions."

Lauren had her laptop resting on the foldout table in front of her, and within a minute she'd established a connection and the *Washington Post* filled the screen. She scanned each page until she found the article she wanted.

FBI involved in Chantilly Double Murder
Fairfax County police are being assisted by the FBI in

yesterday's double homicide in a parking garage in a Chantilly office park. Shortly after 1:00 p.m. reports of gunfire inside the structure were reported. According to the FBI, the security footage has so far discovered nothing of interest. An unnamed source revealed that there were no witnesses and no immediate suspects. The Fairfax police and FBI are asking the public for any help in identifying the perpetrators. The victims' identities have yet to be released. This brings to twelve the number of homicides in Fairfax County for the year.

Lauren gathered from the article that, thanks to Montero's call to Deputy Graham, there wasn't going to be any blowback from their confrontation in the garage. The FBI was in charge, and since no suspects would be arrested, the shooting would quietly become unsolved.

Quickly, she scanned the international section for any news out of Guatemala. The only snippet she found was an increase in volcanic activity connected with the recent awakening of Mt. Atitlán. Lauren clicked to open her e-mail and seconds later her inbox popped up on the screen. She quickly scanned the list. Most could wait, but there was one from Montero.

Lauren,

Abigail is asleep and all is quiet at this end. I'm still waiting for my West Coast contacts to report back on our earlier requests. I'm interested in what they'll turn up after eighteen months.

I couldn't sleep, so I went back through the photographs Buck sent us, the ones Stephanie took on the mountain. I began to analyze each one looking for anything we may have missed. I may have found something. I pulled in some help from a computer guy I know. I only sent him partial screen

grabs, so he has no idea what the full images actually represent. I've attached four isolated sections I
think you'll want to see.

Regards,
Montero

Lauren double-clicked on the file and drummed her fingers
on the table, impatiently waiting while the images downloaded.
She adjusted the angle of her screen as the first picture material-
ized. It took her a moment to understand she was seeing a section of the foliage extracted from the original photo. Just above
the shoulder of one of the men in the foreground was a shape. It
was somewhat obscured, but when she squinted at it, she knew
Montero had found something they'd initially missed. There
was a figure in the trees, a fourth man going into the woods instead of coming up the path. She scrolled down and found the
second frame and found a far better image. The fourth person
was dressed in camouflage, gun in hand, hat pulled down low, a
branch obscuring the face. Lauren searched the details and then
scrolled down to the next image. Montero had blown it up until it filled the entire screen. It was a tattoo. Lauren studied the
ink, it was delicate and high quality, the artwork she was looking at was most certainly an angel. She clicked on the final image
and it put everything into context. Lauren could see dark hair
pulled up under a hat, telltale strands had found their way down
the neck—a neck that could only be described as sleek and feminine—the fourth kidnapper was a woman.

CHAPTER TWENTY-THREE

Despite the early hour, the traffic was chaotic. Motorcycles shot by on either side, and the lumbering buses created small strangle-holds in the traffic each time they stopped. The windshield wipers stroked back and forth, and Donovan settled down and tried to focus on driving the Suburban. The initial instructions were to turn out of the hotel and travel north. He matched their speed with the traffic and tried to spot Buck in the rearview mirror, but had no idea where the former SEAL might be. His cell phone was on the console, the open line would transmit everything he said to Buck.

"How far does this road go?" Donovan asked Eva. She'd been silent since they'd started. Her mood somber, as if she expected the worst, and had resigned herself to whatever fate had decreed.

"I don't know." Eva pulled her hair back from her face and turned around to look out the rear window. "I am not very famil-iar with the city."

"Don't look back," Donovan said, remembering what Buck had said about telegraphing their moves to the enemy. "They're probably following us as well as Buck. We need to convince them we're alone."

Eva snapped around as if she'd been slapped and faced for-ward. She sat rigid in her seat. "I am sorry."

"It's okay. Try to relax," Donovan tried to reassure her. "We just do what we're told and pretend we're alone. Let Buck and his men do the rest. We'll be fine."

"Are you afraid?" Eva asked, slowly turning her head to look at him.

"Yes," Donovan replied truthfully. "But I'm even more afraid for Stephanie."

"I hope the people who did this to us die a painful death."

Donovan was a little taken aback by the force of Eva's words, the hatred in her voice. He looked over at her and could see her small hands balled up into fierce little fists. A vein pulsed in her slender neck. "Keep that thought and stay focused."

Eva turned to him and lightly rested her hand on his shoulder. "I have trust in you. You are one of my guardian angels. You've already saved me once."

Donovan was about to reply when Eva's phone rang. Without taking his eyes off the road, he swept it up and answered. He listened intently as the kidnappers issued the next set of instructions.

"As you go north you will to come to a traffic circle. Veer to the left, then go north on Seventh Avenue."

Donovan could see the circle. The traffic slowed, and he wasn't sure which lane he should use. With no obvious markings, the street signs were hard to see in the rain. "The circle is straight ahead. Which way do I go?"

"West, and then north."

A horn blared behind them. Donovan ignored it as he swung the Suburban hard to the left. He saw Eva brace herself as he called out to her. "Look for Seventh Avenue." Another horn, this one much louder sounded next to them. Donovan didn't care. He concentrated on finding a street sign, anything that would tell him which way he was supposed to go.

"I see it!" Eva pointed at a street sign. "Which way?"

"North." Donovan braked heavily, the tires skidded on the wet pavement. He yanked the wheel to the right, cut off a taxicab, and then nearly ran down a bicyclist. Once he'd negotiated the turn, Donovan merged into traffic. He was still holding the phone. "We're on Seventh now."

"Good. Now travel on that road until you see a bank on the left side of the road. It will be Calle Twenty-Eight, turn left."

Donovan understood, avenues ran north and south and calles, or streets, ran east and west. "Look for a bank on the left," he said to Eva, trying to talk and drive at the same time. He braked and swerved wildly as a brightly colored bus pulled away from the curb and nearly broadsided them. Donovan knew that a fraction of a second slower and he'd have wrecked the Suburban. A quick glance down told him that his phone wasn't on the console, it had slipped off. Donovan handed the cell phone connected to the kidnappers to Eva. "You talk to them."

Eva took the phone, her hands nervously pulling back her hair. "Hola, are you there?"

Donovan reached down and tried to locate his phone by feel. Finally, he felt the soft rubber of the case between his seat and the console. Using two fingers, he slid the phone upward until it was free, but one quick look told him he'd lost the connection with Buck. He fumbled with the device, turning it in his hand until it was right side up, and then thumbed the redial button. Once he was reconnected, he reached up and slid the edge of the phone under the sun visor, careful to make sure the microphone port was exposed.

"The turn is coming," Eva said.

Donovan put both hands on the wheel, grateful to devote his full attention to driving. He changed lanes to the inside, wanting to spot the upcoming turn before the last moment. His eyes darted back and forth trying to watch the traffic and the buildings and everything else in between. A traffic light ahead turned red and Donovan slowly stopped. He used the opportunity to glance at Eva. She sat looking at him, wide-eyed, listening to the kidnappers.

"He says to drop the other cell phones out of the car now." Eva frantically gestured for him to lower his window and toss it out. "He says hurry, before the light changes."

Donovan didn't have time to think. Furious with himself

for allowing the phone to be spotted, he quickly did as instructed and dropped his phone on the pavement. Ahead of him the light turned green and horns immediately began honking as he hesitated. "It's gone! What now?"

"It's gone!" Eva said. "I promise, it is laying in the street. Please don't hurt anyone." Eva was nearly pleading into the phone. "I can't do this, I am going to give the phone back to Donovan."

Donovan held out his hand for the phone. Eva slumped, shook her head in dejection, and spoke into the phone. "I understand. I will do as you wish. I can relay the instructions."

Eva looked at him and swallowed hard. "They do not want to talk to you. Only me."

"Fine." Donovan checked the traffic behind him, hoping Buck was still following them.

"He says the bank is one more block," Eva relayed. "It will be a left turn, followed by a right turn at the intersection after that." Eva paused as she listened. "We will then be going north on Sixth Avenue."

Donovan maneuvered around a truck and swerved to shoot the gap in a small group of pedestrians. A few were holding colorful umbrellas against the rain and paying little attention to the traffic. He nearly overshot the next turn and had come to a complete stop. He jammed on his horn to try and move the car that was blocking his path. The driver flipped him off as Donovan inched forward and then whipped the Suburban between two cars, missing each by inches.

As they shot forward, he looked in the mirror. As the intersection fell away behind them he didn't see any vehicles make the same turn. He slammed his hand on the wheel in frustration. He tried to even out his breathing, Buck still had the advantage. He wondered what everyone aboard the *Galileo* could actually see from the *Scimitar*? Donovan eased into the lighter traffic and looked over at Eva, waiting for her to relay the next instructions.

Reading his intentions, she spoke to the kidnappers. "We are on Sixth Avenue now. Where do you want us to go?"

"What are they saying?" Donovan pressed, impatient for the relay.

"They say to go straight for now." Eva pointed, then listened to the voice on the phone. "Yes, I see it."

"What are we looking for?" Donovan asked.

"Turn here." Eva pointed in the direction she intended. "They said to loop around the park."

As Donovan did as instructed, he noticed that despite the low clouds and rain, it was getting lighter outside. He felt as if the kidnappers were sending them on a prearranged route, that nothing about this was random. With the improving weather the traffic seemed to be getting heavier, harder to negotiate. Off to his left he could see one of the most modern buildings in Guatemala City, an abstract silver-and-white construction with a sloping roof and large oval windows. He had a vague idea where they were.

"The road splits. Which way?" Donovan let up off the gas as they approached an intersection.

"They say go to the left," Eva relayed. "Drive underneath the theatre."

As they went into the tunnel, the road curved, and Donovan had no idea how long they'd be invisible to the *Scimitar*. He hoped they'd be able to pick them up when they came out the other side.

"They say they know about the car following us." Eva shot a worried look behind them and then turned to face Donovan. "He says once we exit the tunnel, jump the median and go back the way we came. They're going to have us switch cars, and if we don't do exactly what they say, they will shoot the hostage."

CHAPTER TWENTY-FOUR

Lauren couldn't take her eyes from the volcanoes that jutted up to the west. They were descending, but the Gulfstream was still above the clouds. She could see three distinct peaks; the closest had a darkish-gray plume coming from the top of the cone that spread out far above them in the atmosphere.

The Gulfstream plunged into the clouds with a definitive bump, and the outside world turned into an opaque gray nothing. She could hear the familiar sounds of the flaps and gear moving into position, followed by an increase in the noise from the engines. Below her she began to see the ground, not the orderly buildings one saw in the States, but a seemingly random array of buildings, roads, and shacks, some perched precariously on the sides of hills. What little color there was seemed to jump up from the maze of billboards that lined the traffic-filled streets. As they flew lower, Lauren could finally see the airport. She was startled to see the remains of a burned-out airliner off to the side, followed by other derelict planes crammed together next to hangars in various states of disrepair. She knew it was nothing that didn't exist in the US; Americans were just better at hauling everything out of sight.

The Gulfstream roared over the end of the runway and touched down. Lauren held her computer in her lap as they decelerated. Out the window, just ahead of them, she spotted the Eco-Watch jet. The door was open and she could see the column of superheated exhaust from the auxiliary power unit distort the air around the tail of the jet. They were getting ready to leave on a mission. If she could get over there in time, she'd at least find Michael and maybe even Donovan as well. She reviewed her story as to why Montero's photo discovery was so important that she'd chartered a jet and flown to Guatemala. It was a little flimsy, but it would have to do.

To her relief, the pilots taxied over and pulled into a parking spot not fifty yards from the *Galileo*. Lauren gathered her things and waited with her passport as the handler and a customs agent came up the stairs. The inspection was cursory, the unsmiling official glanced at her paperwork, then at her, then spoke to the handler. Whatever was discussed was brief, and as soon as the customs officer deplaned, the flight attendant motioned to Lauren that it was okay for her to get up from her seat.

The crew said their good-byes, repeating that they would wait to hear from her as to when they would return to DC, and reminding her that the volcano could change at any moment. Lauren thanked them and quickly made her way down the steps into the damp morning air. She shook her head at the handler who offered her an umbrella and a ride in his van. She declined. Without waiting for permission to be granted or denied, she set out and hurried across the ramp toward the *Galileo*. When she was halfway, she saw Michael emerge from the airplane. He went down the steps two at a time and started toward her. Lauren had quit trying to guess what type of reception she thought she'd get from Donovan and William and was happy that Michael was the first person she'd be able to question. As he approached, she couldn't miss the troubled frown on his face.

"What are you doing here?" Michael said as soon as he was within earshot. He reached out and took her shoulder bag and then stopped in front of her—waiting for an answer.

"Where's Donovan?"

"You chartered a jet?" Michael replied, his eyes swung from Lauren to the gleaming Gulfstream and then back to her. "I don't understand?"

"Where's Donovan?" Lauren repeated.

Michael lowered his head and followed. "William is aboard the *Galileo*, as for Donovan, I think William should be the one to explain."

Lauren turned and was about to say something, but the apprehension in Michael's eyes stopped her. What had happened to Donovan? Michael was usually upbeat and positive. She'd seen him under great stress before, and even then he'd never lost his sense of humor. But right at this moment, looking at Michael, she was more concerned for Donovan than she'd ever been in her life. As she reached the stairs that led up into the *Galileo*, she could feel the tiny hairs on her neck begin to tingle with fear.

"Lauren!" William called out the second she stepped into the cabin.

She took a quick look up into the cockpit, hoping she'd find Donovan sitting there. Instead, she found Craig, who nodded a solemn greeting. As she turned, she saw two people seated at one of the forward science stations. She was familiar with the inner workings of the Eco-Watch jets—it was on a series of hurricane hunter missions that she'd first met Donovan—but it struck her as unusual to have so much interest focused on the instrumentation when the airplane was sitting on the ground. She stepped toward William and discovered the same look of trepidation that she'd found on Michael's face—a similar expression that seemed to be shared by the other two people in the cabin. "William, what's going on—where's Donovan?"

"Please, sit down." William stepped away from the computer screens and motioned for Lauren to join him in the rear of the plane.

Lauren walked past the monitors and slowed, searching for anything familiar that might help her understand what was happening. She could see a grainy, false-color image that she knew was being transmitted by an infrared camera. The lens was focused on a traffic-choked street; next to it was another screen showing the same angle, but this view was being generated by synthetic aperture radar. She glanced at the strangers; the only person that was talking was the young man seated at the console. His voice was low and controlled, but she heard the words Buck and Suburban. None of this made any sense to her. She shook her head in confusion and joined William.

"What's going on?" She refused to sit, instead, she met William eye-to-eye and studied his face for clues. "Where's Donovan and who's he with?"

"We're making the exchange. If everything goes as planned, we'll have Stephanie back soon."

"Donovan's making the transfer?" Lauren said as she glared at him, questioning.

"Mr. VanGelder! Buck just confirmed that the Suburban has been abandoned. They've changed vehicles or they're on foot. We've lost them."

Lauren turned and went to the console. William was right behind her as she struggled to fill in the missing pieces of the puzzle.

"John, what happened?" William put his hand on the young man's shoulder and leaned in to get a better view of the screen.

"They went through an underpass and then doubled back. I never found them when they came out the other side. I'm tracking three potential vehicles they could be in, but they're all going in different directions now. If they're on foot they're doing it carrying the cases of cash. If they step outside, I'll be able to spot them."

"Can you track all three vehicles?" William shot back.

"For a little while. I'll have to climb the *Scimitar* to keep all of them within my field of view. I should be able to track them until our ground units can verify which car they're in."

"Do it," William ordered, and then turned to Lauren. His tone softened as he started to explain. "We're making the swap. Donovan has the money, and he's in phone contact with the kidnappers. We're using the *Scimitar* to track them. Buck and his handpicked team are on the ground, ready to move in when it's time."

"But you just lost him!" Lauren felt overwhelmed by what William had just said. She knew all about the *Scimitar* project, but struggled to grasp the implications that even with all the technology in play, Donovan was somewhere on the streets of Guatemala City. She thought of the brutality of the kidnappings she'd been immersed in for the last three days. She felt her stomach churn as she thought of Donovan's mental state. How since he'd been pulled back to Central America, he'd been fixated on Meredith and the mistakes he'd made.

"We're doing everything we can," William said.

"Get him out of there!" Lauren said to William.

"We can't." William shook his head. "It's too late for that. I'm sorry you had to show up in the middle of this, but you'll have to trust us—trust me."

"Is he alone?" Lauren asked.

"What is Buck telling us?" William said, as if to avoid Lauren's question.

"Buck and his men have narrowed it down to two vehicles," John replied. "One car is heading north, out of the city. One of his men is trying to get a visual right now. Buck sent two of his team to search where they abandoned the Suburban. The other likely target is coming this way—toward the airport. Buck is trying to get close enough to spot them, but the traffic is getting heavy and he's ten minutes behind."

"Damn it to hell!" William slammed a fist into his open hand.

"John," Lauren said, "you just said where *they* abandoned the Suburban. Who's with my husband?"

"She's a local, she's also a witness," William sighed. "The kidnappers demanded she be part of the swap."

"And you offered her whatever she wanted and promised to keep her safe?" Lauren replied, and her words caused William to look away.

"John, how sure are you that you picked up the correct vehicles after they dumped the Suburban?" William asked.

"Ninety-five percent," John said with confidence.

"What if you're wrong?" Lauren asked. "What if he's in that five percent and you've lost him completely? What do we do then?"

John looked at William, then turned around and silently faced the console.

Lauren spun as Michael came up the stairs into the *Galileo*. He was short of breath from running. Lauren searched out his eyes—more than anything she needed Michael's strength.

"I just spoke to Malcolm and Lillian," Michael said in a rush of words. "They said the seismic activity on Atitlán just went through the roof and that we should stay on the ground."

"What does that mean for us—for Donovan?" Lauren demanded.

"Nothing," William shot back. "The volcano is one hundred miles away. We're well out of the range of any immediate threat."

Lauren looked into Michael's face and found a distressed expression that exactly mirrored what she was feeling. Michael seemed to understand and moved to her side.

"You've still got him, right?" Michael floated the question to the others.

Lauren shook her head solemnly.

"You lost him? What in the hell happened?" Michael looked at the faces around him for answers and found only silence.

"I think I might have him!" John maneuvered the *Scimitar* somewhere above them in the cloudy skies. "Buck just relayed that the car headed north isn't them. I'm bringing the *Scimitar* in for a closer look at the final target—the one coming our way. Just give me a second."

Lauren squeezed Michael's arm and stepped closer to the console. The picture on the screen jumped as John rapidly zoomed in on a white car. Lauren wasn't sure which view would give them the best perspective, and her eyes darted from one monitor to the other. The infrared view zoomed in close, and she could see the ghostly image of the car in question. Heat radiated from its engine and drivetrain. The car rounded a corner and shot past slower vehicles. She let out a silent prayer that it was Donovan they were looking at, that he'd been found and was again under their watchful eye. Lauren focused on the screens, but couldn't correlate the two together. She didn't know where the car was in relation to the city—or to her.

"I think they're coming to a stop," John said, as the vehicle made two quick turns and then pulled up next to a building.

"Where are they?" Lauren asked excitedly, as she watched the car maneuver into a narrow parking spot between two other vehicles. A figure jumped out from behind the wheel, went to the trunk, and pulled out two hard-sided cases. Lauren would recognize his shape and movement anywhere. Donovan.

"They're here!" John backed off the zoom and on the screen were the obvious view of a hangar and an assortment of small planes on a ramp. John snapped his head around toward the others. "They're here at the airport. It's a hangar up at the north end of the field!"

"Damn it to hell!" Michael said. "Where's Buck?"

"He'll be here in ten minutes," John answered, getting immediate confirmation in his headset.

"That could be ten minutes too late," Michael said.

Lauren stared transfixed at the white image she knew was her husband. He'd pulled the cases out of the trunk and was now at the passenger side—helping someone out of the car. In comparison to him, the person was much shorter, more slender, and obviously female. She watched as Donovan and the woman disappeared into the hangar. Moments later, they came out of the building onto the ramp and ran headlong for a small airplane parked nearby.

"Switch the view from the infrared camera to the high-resolution, real-time optics and zoom in," Lauren said it as an order, not a request. Moments later, the view showed a raven-haired woman at Donovan's side as they climbed into the Cessna. "John, grab that image!"

"Got it," John replied.

"Is the *Scimitar* linked with the *Galileo's* server?"

"Uh, yeah," John said, "we use it as backup for all the data we collect.

"Tag that image so I can find it. Now, where's Buck? How far out is he?" Lauren spoke evenly, though inside she felt as if the life was being sucked out of her. Was this the woman she'd spoken to—the woman who'd been sleeping in Donovan's hotel room? She looked into the faces of the others for some clue, were they going to stop her husband from getting into the small plane? Was she ever going to see Donovan again—or would her last memory of him be with another woman?

"Buck's not going to get here in time," John said, without turning from the console. "He says to get Janie airborne in the chopper and continue to track the plane. He'll be here in five minutes."

"It's an amphibian, a Cessna 185," Michael said. "Once they leave, they'll be able to land anywhere, a dirt strip somewhere, a lake, even the ocean. If we ever had the upper hand, we just lost it."

Lauren watched in distress as the Cessna with Donovan aboard began its takeoff roll. The sound of a propeller plane could be heard from outside the *Galileo*. She could see Michael's face contort in frustration. She could also hear the sound of rotor blades spinning up, and she leaned down to look outside. Parked out at the edge of the ramp was a white helicopter that Lauren didn't recognize, as well as a jumpsuited man in a helmet standing outside.

"Janie's flying?" Lauren asked.

"Yeah," Michael replied. "She's with Eric, the pilot from the *Atlantic Titan*, and Cesar, a flight mechanic on loan to us from the Guatemalan army."

"Buck's pulling up now," John said.

"Which way is the Cessna headed?" Michael said through a tightly clenched jaw.

"South," John answered. "Due south, toward the ocean. We need to get airborne or I'm going to lose them altogether."

"Track them as far as you can," Michael said as he stepped away. "We're five times faster than they are. We'll be able to make up the ground quickly."

Michael hurried to the cockpit and slid into the captain's seat.

"Michael!" Buck called out as he rushed up the stairs of the *Galileo*. "Get ready to depart, but don't start the engines until I tell you." Without waiting for a reply, Buck dashed to the *Scimitar* console.

"Where are they?" Buck asked as he studied the screens.

"He's headed south in a Cessna," Lauren said. She watched as Buck did a double take, and then stood to face her.

"What are you doing here?" he asked.

"Waiting for you, or someone, to tell me what the hell is going on—and what you're going to do about it! Why are we waiting?"

"Our military friends are bringing over something I need," Buck replied coolly, in stark contrast to Lauren's urgent demands. "Lauren, please trust me, this isn't as hopeless as it looks."

"I have no idea *what* it looks like," Lauren answered. "Donovan is with a woman in a small plane with two suitcases full of money. Do we know if Donovan is flying the plane—is she? Or is there someone else onboard?"

"I picked up three distinct heat sources," John replied. "There are three people aboard the Cessna."

"Lauren," Buck exhaled heavily. "The woman is harmless, she's a local named Eva Rios. She knows who took Stephanie. We've been protecting her, but when the ransom demands came, they wanted her and the money—she agreed to help. My guess is that the pilot is part of the kidnapping crew. They don't know we have the ability to follow them, so the advantage is still ours. We've got time to react."

"Why is Donovan with her—instead of you?"

"They demanded that he be the courier," William jumped into the conversation. "We felt that the situation was controllable—that the risks were acceptable."

"Is there any chance that this Eva—is the woman from the photos you sent me?" Lauren leveled her gaze at Buck. She felt her nerves crackling in anticipation. The instant she saw the cloud of confusion spread across Buck's face, she knew that he had no idea what she was talking about.

"What woman?"

"I've lost them," John called out as he looked away from the console. "I don't dare push the *Scimitar* any farther or we run the risk of losing the link."

"Keep it on station," Buck replied without taking his eyes from Lauren. "What woman?"

"We enhanced the photos." Lauren eyed her briefcase. "Hell, it's faster to *show* you what I've discovered."

"A military jeep just pulled up," William said.

"Hold that thought," Buck said to Lauren, and then rushed to meet the soldier who was coming up the stairs of the Gulfstream.

Lauren snatched her computer from its case and quickly powered it up. She sat, silently urging her computer to cycle through its start-up protocols. She watched as Buck stowed the heavy satchel he'd gotten from the soldier and pushed the button that retracted the stairs into the fuselage of the *Galileo*.

"Michael, let's go!" Buck called over his shoulder as the heavy door locked into place.

Lauren typed in her passwords and found the file that Montero had sent her. She could hear the sound of the Gulfstream's first engine begin to spool up. She clicked the mouse and the first picture appeared on the screen. She looked up as both William and Buck leaned in over her shoulder. She didn't say a word as she clicked through the sequence. When she pulled up the final image, the one showing the computer-enhanced tattoo, she saw

Buck's jaw harden and his eyes threatened to burn through the screen.

"Look familiar?" Lauren sat back and studied Buck's face.

Buck nodded. "I saw it this morning—when I was helping Eva put on her bulletproof vest."

"She's one of them," Lauren said as she heard Michael start the second engine.

"Son-of-a-bitch!" Buck shook his head in frustration. "She played us the entire time."

"She took the Navy SEAL out of the equation, and now she has Donovan, *and* the money."

"Michael!" Buck spun and called toward the cockpit. "Get us in the air—now!"

Lauren began typing, accessed the *Galileo's* hard drive from memory, and quickly found Eva's picture. She attached it to an e-mail, typed "urgent" in the subject line, and then pounded out a short message:

> Ronnie, this is the woman with the angel tattoo. She goes by the name Eva Rios.
>
> —Lauren

She finished by including the number of the *Galileo's* satellite phone, hit "send," then reached for her phone. Montero picked up almost immediately.

"I just sent you an e-mail with a picture," Lauren said without introduction or pleasantries. "It's her, Eva Rios."

"I'm looking at the photo as we speak," Montero said. "I'm on it."

"As fast as you can. She has Donovan and Stephanie."

"Oh no," Montero whispered.

Lauren disconnected the call as the Gulfstream moved away from the hangar toward the runway. She sat down and strapped herself in tightly. Never, in her years aboard Eco-Watch's Gulfstream, had she seen the pilots taxi as fast as they were this moment. Michael only slowed as he made a turn, and swung the big jet onto the runway and pushed up the throttles. The *Galileo* swayed gently from side to side as it hurdled forward and accelerated rapidly before lifting free from the concrete. Michael pointed the *Galileo* skyward and they were immediately swallowed by the low-hanging clouds.

CHAPTER TWENTY-FIVE

Donovan was strapped into the front seat of the noisy Cessna. To his left sat the pilot, a young man with a grim expression and a serious demeanor who knew what he was doing in the cockpit. His practiced hands flew around and he quickly had the engine started and wasted no time in taxiing toward the runway.

There was no other traffic, and Donovan watched as the pilot smoothly added power to the three hundred-horsepower engine, and the lightly loaded Cessna surged forward. As they lifted off, Donovan saw the *Galileo* sitting outside the USGS hangar, and next to it sat another Gulfstream. The registration number told him it was from the US, but he had no idea who it might have brought down, or if it had anything to do with William or Eco-Watch. The last thing he saw before they left the airport behind them was the main rotor blades on the helicopter begin to turn.

They'd started flying south, but after ten minutes or so, the pilot had abruptly banked the Cessna to the west. Donovan had been watching—the pilot had been very casual about how he flew until the last few minutes. The ceiling kept dropping, as rain splattered and vaporized against the plastic windshield. Now the young man was sitting up straight, straining to keep them over the narrow ribbon of road directly beneath the airplane. It was their only defense against flying into the cloud-obscured hills.

The money was secured in the baggage compartment behind Eva. As they'd boarded, she'd whispered to him that she was
afraid of heights. She sat rock-still, her arms wrapped defensively
across her chest, her face a mask of anxiety.

Donovan hadn't been offered a headset, so he had no idea
who the pilot was talking with. The frequency he'd set in the
radio could be anyone—air traffic control, another airplane, or
the kidnappers themselves. Donovan had hundreds of hours in
small single-engine airplanes like this one—though he'd never
actually flown an amphibian. The pilot in him had soaked up
everything that was going on around them. The floats beneath
them had wheels that could be used on land or retract so they
could land on water. If the airplane was headed anywhere other
than Lake Atitlán, he'd be surprised. It was also the last place he
wanted to go.

Now that they were airborne, he forced himself to try to
relax. The lake was a good twenty minutes away. He knew it
would all start in earnest once they landed, but at least he had
a small breather, a time-out to try to mentally prepare for what
was about to happen. He'd tried to keep Eva relaxed, but as they'd
climbed into the Cessna, he'd seen the unmistakable signs of
the nonstop fear she'd endured. She moved slowly and without
emotion. He had no idea what was running through her mind—
he turned and glanced back at her again and was met with the
vacant eyes of someone who looked past the point of caring. It
crossed his mind that perhaps she'd never been in an airplane
before. If she'd grown up in a small village, that possibility wasn't
out of the question.

Donovan had faith that Buck and John had managed to
follow them after the car swap, and that the *Scimitar* was poised
overhead, still tracking them. The kidnappers had played their
hand well, leading them through the city, and then ending up
guiding them back to the airport. The other scenario, the one
that Donovan understood was just as real, was that they'd lost

him—that none of his friends had any idea he was in a small plane flying to what must finally be the rendezvous at Lake Atitlán. If that were the case, then he and Eva were in trouble. Donovan thought about the .40 caliber Sig tucked into the waistband of his pants and wondered if it would be enough.

The rain started hitting the windshield harder and the sudden onset of turbulence jolted Donovan's attention outside the Cessna. The forward visibility had dropped to less than a mile, and they were gradually descending to maintain contact with the ground, now less than three hundred feet above the rain-slicked road. The pilot inched them closer to the lush green hillsides and began a series of well-choreographed turns that kept them centered directly over the highway. Donovan couldn't do anything but watch as their wingtips seemed to reach out for the treetops as the pilot flew them through the valley.

Turbulence shook the small Cessna, and a rivulet of water leaked from above and dropped onto Donovan's pant leg.

He raised his voice above the roar of the engine and the slipstream. "Can we still get there?"

The pilot simply nodded and turned his attention back to the delicate flying that now required his full concentration. Donovan looked back at Eva and saw that she looked pale and more than a little queasy. The visibility ahead was getting even worse. Donovan eyed the ragged bases of the clouds. Flying in this terrain without local knowledge would be nothing more than an accident waiting to happen. It was like walking through your own house in the dark, you could make it to the bathroom, but try it in a strange house, and you were going to run into something.

The small Cessna sliced through the hanging wisps of gray clouds, and Donovan felt the G-force from the steep bank push him down in the seat. As they sped westward, he looked down as the ground rushed past in a blur, then out front, where the rising terrain marked the narrow mountain pass they needed to navigate. The weather dead ahead looked worse than what they'd been flying through. Donovan remembered when he and Buck had flown out to the volcano in the helicopter. If they could get past the next ridge, they'd be at the eastern shore of Lake Atitlán. Donovan had no idea what would happen after that.

CHAPTER TWENTY-SIX

"Have you found them yet?" Lauren was out of her seat and next to John the moment the *Galileo* burst out of the tops of the clouds.

"Not yet," John replied. "Now that we're airborne, I can widen the search parameters."

Lauren looked back at William who was still seated, staring out the window. Up front, Buck was in the cockpit with Michael and Craig. A glance toward them and she could tell that something unusual must be happening out the left side of the Gulfstream—the attention of all three of them were fixed in that direction. She crossed the aisle, bending down to see for herself.

The morning sun, now reduced to an orange ball, cast an eerie, subdued light across the horizon. In the distance, she could see the volcano throwing ash and debris high into the sky. The dangerous cloud rose and spread out high above them. Lauren headed to the cockpit. On her way, she felt the airplane stop climbing.

"I'll have to level off at 10,000 feet," she heard Michael say, as he flattened out their climb and adjusted both throttles. "I need to keep us beneath the ash cloud. If the engines suck up too much ash they'll eventually fail."

When Lauren touched Buck on the arm, he immediately stepped aside so she could move in for a closer look. What she saw out the windshield seemed to be right out of an artist's conception of a prehistoric past. Low clouds stretched to the horizon, the peaks of at least five volcanoes thrusting their way up into the thin air, Atitlán spewing a boiling plume of volcanic steam and ash far into the sky.

The shrill ring of the satellite phone pealed in the cabin. Lauren raced to the science station and snatched it from its holder.

"This is Lauren."

"Lauren, it's Ronnie. I've got something. I went straight to Deputy Graham at the FBI with this photo, and he in turn sent it priority one to the National Security Agency for facial recognition. This Eva woman lit up the board. She's been issued driver's licenses under different names in Arizona, California, and Oregon. All the addresses she's ever used are bogus. The only constant is she always uses the name Eva, either as a first or middle name. Other than that, she's a ghost, a fabrication."

"What else? Give me something I can use," Lauren said.

"Listen to this, I have a friend at the NSA. He ran Eva's image. Initially, they got hundreds of possible hits, but were able to quickly pinpoint which one was her. My friend saw my name attached to the case, and contacted me because some of the hits originated from the missing or exploited children domain. It's not a hundred percent certain, but the girl flagged because of similar facial structure to a missing child years ago. She was fifteen at the time and kidnapped in Costa Rica. The name of the child is Daniela Angela Rocha."

It only took Lauren a second to recognize the name. "Are you telling me this could be the girl who was kidnapped and missing the same time as Meredith?"

"Yeah, and her mother's name was Angela Eva Rocha. Seems like the name Eva and angels are a serious theme within the family."

"Who else knows about this?" Lauren asked.

"For now, just you and I," Montero replied. "Though, when the FBI analysts sift through the data, they'll find it sooner or later."

"Okay. We need to capitalize on our head start." Lauren's thoughts raced through the possibilities and implications. "What about the missing girl, Marie? Have you been able to find her mother in California?"

"Yes, she's in the Bay Area. I have a friend, a former FBI agent who's now a private investigator, making contact with her this morning."

"You need to be there," Lauren said. "You need to ask this woman everything you can about Eva, and about Hector Vargas."

"I'm glad you agree. We were just about to leave for the airport," Montero replied.

"We, as in you and Abigail?" Lauren was caught off guard by the news and wasn't sure how she felt.

"At this point, I'd rather Abigail be in the hands of a professional, rather than babysat by your mother," Montero explained. "I promise, I'll protect her with my life. Besides, she thinks it's a great adventure."

"She would," Lauren sighed. "Let me talk to her."

"Hi, Mommy," Abigail said. "I'm going for an airplane ride to California. I'm going to see the ocean and maybe a whale."

"Are you going to have fun and be a good girl?"

"Uh huh," Abigail replied.

"I think I have something!" John called out. "It's a small plane. It might be them."

"Where?" Buck was instantly at John's side.

"Mommy has to go now," Lauren said. "I love you, sweetie, have fun. Can you hand the phone back to Ms. Montero?"

"She's all smiles," Montero said as she came back on the line.

"Okay. Keep me posted. I have to go, and please, be safe."

"I promise."

Lauren slid the phone back into its cradle and joined William as they crowded close to the *Scimitar* console.

"It's them! I can just make out the floats." John pointed first to the infrared screen, then at a map of Guatemala. "They've turned west—toward the volcano."

"I knew it!" Buck rubbed his hands together in anticipation.

"Relay the information to Janie. Find out how long until she arrives at the lake."

"I just talked with her. She can't fly direct to the lake due to the poor visibility. She's going to try to work her way around and try to approach from the south."

"Does she know about the latest USGS information regarding the volcano?" Buck asked.

"Yes, sir, she does."

"Tell her to keep us updated," Buck said. "Now, how long until Eva and Donovan arrive at the lake?"

John did the calculations. "The Cessna will be at the eastern edge of the lake in four minutes."

Buck leaned over and shouted toward the cockpit. "Michael! We have them! They're headed for the lake at the base of Atitlán. How fast can you get us there?"

"Ten minutes," Michael called out over his shoulder.

Lauren felt the Gulfstream surge beneath her feet as Michael pushed up the throttles. They were now thundering through the morning sky toward the distant lake.

Buck clenched his jaw and his eyes darted around the interior of the *Galileo*. "Lauren, I'm going to need your help."

She nodded. Though she had no idea what he was going to do, she held on dearly to the slender thread of confidence he'd shown.

CHAPTER TWENTY-SEVEN

Donovan could finally pick out the glimmer of the lake. They'd barely made it through the mountain pass. The clouds had lifted enough for their pilot to make a brief radio call. Donovan couldn't figure out why, despite the improved weather conditions, the sky had grown darker. He wondered if there were thunderstorms building—that the billowing moisture had obscured the sun.

They were still flying over the narrow road that ran from Guatemala City to the lake. If Donovan remembered correctly, this route would take them directly over the small village of Panajachel, which sat on the north shore of Lake Atitlán. Once over the water, they could land anywhere along the rugged shore, or perhaps the transfer might take place out on the water in a boat, far from any prying eyes. Whatever the case, he was on his own. He wondered at what point they might think to frisk him for a weapon. Would he have a window to kill the kidnappers before they could harm Stephanie?

Donovan watched the pilot, trying to get a feel for where he was looking, hoping for a clue as to where they were going to land and how soon. Between the hills to the south, Donovan could now clearly see the lake. The wind was out of the north— the calm, unruffled water gave way to a light chop several hundred yards from the shore. The pilot, too, was looking at the water, and with one hand, reduced the power and started a wide descending turn toward the lake.

Donovan knew the closer they came with the money, the

more anxious the kidnappers would become. The proximity of the three million dollars was the most dangerous part of the equation. Donovan looked at the pilot as they descended closer to the water. They sailed over the rock-strewn shoreline and banked again. They were now parallel to the shore only a hundred feet above the calm water. The pilot reached out and pulled the lever that lowered the flaps. As he did so, his cotton jacket opened just enough to reveal a gun. Donovan spotted the varnished wooden handle of a pistol tucked up under the pilot's left arm and felt the muscles in his legs tense. If he was putting down flaps, they were about to land.

Donovan scanned the lake. There weren't any boats for at least a mile in any direction. Structures haphazardly dotted the hillsides, ranging from shacks to larger buildings that might be houses, or even small hotels. Donovan spotted a few wooden docks that stretched out into the lake. He also saw some places without docks, where boats were simply pulled ashore.

Up ahead, just off the nose of the plane, Donovan caught a flash of light. When it winked again, the pilot reacted. He pulled back on the throttle and lowered the remaining flaps. They eased down the last fifty feet, and with a rumble that filled the small cabin, the floats kissed the water and they were down. Donovan took a measured breath as they turned and drifted toward the wooden dock where the signal originated.

When the pilot reached across his body to pop open his window, Donovan thought for a moment that the gun was going to appear in the pilot's hand. He glanced back at Eva. She was staring out at the shore, her eyes searching. He wondered if she recognized where they were.

Using the wind and the momentum from the plane, the pilot cut the engine, and they drifted on a line to intersect the long wooden dock. Donovan could only see one man waiting for them. He had a bandana covering his face, an automatic rifle in his hands. Beyond the uneven dock there were stairs that led up the hill to a concrete building. The grass and shrubs were overgrown, and the once-white paint was faded and peeling. The glass in the windows had been broken, and part of the roof had collapsed. The place looked like it had been abandoned a long time ago.

The pilot pushed hard on the rudder and slowly the plane pivoted to the right. He opened his door and slipped out onto the aluminum float. Moments before they would have hit the dock, the pilot jumped onto the pier and put both hands on the wing strut of the Cessna, using all his weight to slow the plane. They bumped the pilings gently, and the pilot quickly went to work tying off the plane. Donovan could see that the other man had stood back, watching. He used the barrel of his gun to motion them out of the plane.

As Donovan unfastened his seat belt, he could hear Eva doing the same thing. He scooted across the pilot's seat toward the open door. He tried to control his breathing. Stephanie must be in the dilapidated building up the hill. They'd only sent one guard down to meet the plane, one who didn't seem particularly alert. Donovan calculated the angles. If he could get close to the man with the machine gun, he could take him out with a silent blow to the head with the Sig. He could then draw down on the pilot and disarm him. With these two incapacitated, he and Eva could make their way up the hill unopposed. His senses took in every detail around him as he waited for the moment to attack.

The plane was rocking back and forth from the waves they'd created upon landing. He needed to be firmly on the dock before he made his move. In the distance he could hear a dull roar that seemed to be coming from the clouds themselves; it sounded like distant thunder, but didn't have the rolling ebbs and flows that came from a storm. The rumble was nearly continuous. As Donovan stepped down to the dock, he felt a strange vibration rise up from the wood. The air smelled of gasoline and rotted fish, as well as the unmistakable odor of sulfur. Now he understood. The low reverberation was coming from the volcano—no doubt spewing ash and gas unseen above the clouds.

Donovan turned to help Eva from the plane. Once she was planted on the wooden planks, he was going to make his move. With his eyes, he motioned for her to be ready. She was within easy striking distance to incapacitate the pilot who was unloading the cases of money. The man with the machine gun had momentarily diverted his attention from them, his eyes following the cases filled with cash.

Donovan separated himself from Eva at the same time he reached behind his back for his Sig. The guard was still fixated on the money as Donovan felt the full weight of the weapon in his hand and he raised it like a club. A roar filled his ears, and he felt as if he'd been slammed in the back. Another roar and he dropped his gun and watched as it clattered away. He went down hard, his face hitting the rough planks of the dock. He couldn't draw a breath as two more gunshots rang out. Darkness began to inch in from the edges of his vision. Footsteps rushed past, but nothing really mattered as he closed his eyes and gave in to the nothingness.

CHAPTER TWENTY-EIGHT

"Oh, dear God," Lauren's anguished cry echoed through the cabin of the *Galileo*. She slumped against Buck and felt as if all her energy had just been sucked out of her. "We're too late."

"No!" William said and turned away, the color rushing from his face.

Lauren's eyes filled with tears. The ghostly off-white infrared image had shown with perfect clarity the two white flashes of heat that came from Eva's outstretched arm. She'd shot Donovan twice in the back, and he'd crumpled face down on the dock. Without any hesitation, Eva then smoothly turned and shot the other two men, their lifeless bodies falling into the water.

"Michael!" Buck shouted toward the cockpit. "Flash the cabin lights thirty seconds before we're over the coordinates. Make sure we're depressurized, and slow down as much as possible."

"He's dead." Lauren felt her whole body shudder as Buck guided her to a seat. He lowered her gently.

"No, he's not," Buck answered softly, yet with conviction. "She shot him, but I think she shot him to save his life. In a firefight, no one is going to shoot someone who's already been shot and appears dead. Donovan's wearing a bulletproof vest—she knew that. She's got something else in mind."

Lauren nodded her understanding as Buck hurriedly unzipped the satchel the military had delivered. He pulled out a parachute, gloves, and a set of goggles. In less than a minute he'd strapped on the chute, secured his automatic weapon, and was ready to jump from the Gulfstream.

"I'll be down there shortly," Buck said to reassure her. "Just keep watching through the *Scimitar*."

Her ears popped from a sudden pressure change.

Buck pulled out a small radio and brought it to his mouth. "Michael, can you hear me?" Buck hesitated, and then nodded as his transmission was returned. "I'm moving into position."

Lauren followed as Buck rechecked his gear and knelt in the baggage compartment. The fact that her ears had already popped told her that Michael had fully depressurized the plane.

"It's going to get loud. When Michael flashes the lights, I want you to slap me on the shoulder."

"Can you do me a favor?" Lauren asked. "I think you're right. Eva has an agenda, and we need to know what it is—keep her alive."

"That's up to her." Buck adjusted his goggles.

"Her biggest enemy is going to be Donovan. Don't let him kill her, please."

Buck nodded, then swung the lever and slid the baggage door upward on its tracks.

Lauren winced at both the noise and the swirling wind that poured into the opening. Racing past below them were the waves from the lake. Buck crouched like an athlete. As Michael flashed the lights, Lauren slapped Buck's shoulder, and he was gone.

Lauren pushed the door down and locked it, before rushing forward to watch events unfold over John's shoulder. On the screen, all she could see was a small dot, then a part of the image seemed to separate and pull apart—becoming two distinct sections until silently, a canopy formed before her eyes. Buck's chute had opened and he was hanging from the nearly invisible lines, swaying gently back and forth. John banked the *Scimitar* to give them a different perspective. He zoomed in until they could see Buck's arms and legs. He adjusted the image, and it took Lauren a moment to understand what she was seeing. Buck was spiraling down in a tight arc, collapsing part of the chute to lose altitude in a hurry. His maneuvering looked as if he was out of control, until he flared and gently touched down on the narrow wooden dock.

Lauren put one hand over her mouth and waited—praying that Donovan wasn't dead. William's face was etched with equal parts concern and worry as they watched Buck slip from the parachute harness and gather in the billowing silk. He discarded the spent canopy in the water, brought his machine gun to his shoulder, and hurried to Donovan. Fresh tears filled Lauren's eyes, and she held her breath as Buck rolled Donovan over onto his back and leaned in, the two white images blended into one.

She tried to focus on the screen, the infrared lens didn't give a true three-dimensional view of what was happening, and the wing of the Cessna tied to the dock momentarily blocked her view. John swung the *Scimitar* into a tight turn to reposition the cameras. With the new angle, she could see that Donovan was sitting up. When Buck held his thumb in the air to signal that Donovan was alive, Lauren couldn't see much more through the tears that filled her eyes. Everything she'd learned from Montero came flooding past the shock of seeing her husband gunned down. She had no idea what was going to happen in the next few minutes. Somewhere up the hill were Stephanie and Marie. As well as Eva—whoever she was.

CHAPTER TWENTY-NINE

Donovan gasped against the pain, trying to pull air into his lungs. He hadn't opened his eyes, but he recognized Buck's calm voice urging him to breathe. Strong arms had pulled him into a sitting position, and Donovan used his hands to steady himself. His lungs shrieked, and he coughed as the cool air made it all the way down. He blinked wordlessly at the pain that radiated across his back. When he opened his eyes, he could see the lake and the two bodies floating face down in the water. He groaned, managed to twist the other way, and found Buck leaning over him.

"You're all right," Buck said, more command than statement.

Donovan nodded, still uncertain what had happened, or how long he'd been out. "What happened?" he managed, fighting a wave of dizziness, trying to rise to his knees. The pain in his back nearly doubled him over.

"Shake it off. The vest stopped the bullets." Buck hooked an arm under Donovan's and pulled him to his feet. "Eva shot you. She's one of the bad guys."

"What?" Donovan wobbled slightly back and forth. The cobwebs were starting to clear, but each breath radiated a sharp jab from between his shoulder blades.

"She's been playing us the whole time," Buck explained. "Lauren figured it out."

"Lauren? How did...?" Donovan tried to understand. He managed to grab another breath, and the pain was less this time.

"I have to get up to the house," Buck said, letting go of Donovan to see if he could stand on his own.

Donovan read the urgency on Buck's face and began to feel it himself. Buck held a machine gun equipped with a silencer. He saw the collapsed parachute in the water and understood at least on some level how Buck had arrived.

"You need to come with me. They might circle back down," Buck explained. "How do you feel? You just took the equivalent of two ninety-mile-per-hour fastballs right in the back. You're going to live, but you took a beating."

Donovan reached down, picked up the Sig where he'd dropped it, and fell in step behind the former SEAL. Buck put the radio to his mouth and spoke quietly. The volume was turned down so Donovan could only hear a muffled reply.

"All I want you to do is stay close to me. Understand? Let me do the shooting," Buck whispered. "John says Eva went this way; he also says there's someone up beyond those trees."

Each step radiated pain down Donovan's spine, but he forced himself to keep pace with Buck. He scanned both the path and the foliage around the house. He listened carefully for anything above the soft sounds of their footsteps in the dirt. All he heard was the faint roar from the volcano, and he could feel the subtle, unnerving vibrations in the ground.

Buck hesitated for a fraction of a second and then swept his gun around the trees that John had described. On the ground lay the third body Donovan had seen since they'd landed. This one had two bullet wounds in his chest and a look of surprise etched on his lifeless face.

"She's making quick work of her friends," Buck whispered, then spoke into the radio. "John says it's clear from here to the west side of the house. Follow me and stay low."

Donovan nodded and though his back ached, he did as he was told, his fear and adrenaline propelling him forward. They reached the house and pressed themselves against the cool wall of concrete. With his gun out in front of him, Buck threw himself through the open door, and Donovan followed. They were in what was left of the kitchen. The odor of gunpowder, burnt food, and the buzzing of flies greeted their sudden arrival. Donovan's eyes jumped from the familiar cases of money sitting on the floor—to the body sprawled by the table. Buck kept the body in his sights as he went to the downed man, a pool of thick blood spreading out from beneath him. Donovan saw the knife in the dead man's hand, and the trail of blood that led away from the kitchen.

"I think Eva wants the money for herself," Buck whispered. "I also think this guy may have cut her."

"Do you really think she did all this?" Donovan asked, matching Buck's whisper.

Buck nodded and put his finger to his lips as they picked their way across the littered floor toward the next room. To their left, up a narrow stairwell, Donovan could hear the sound of voices. The trail of blood told them that they needed to go upstairs. Buck gingerly put his weight on the first step, then placed his foot near the side, closest to the banister; it creaked ever so slightly.

Donovan mimicked each move Buck made as they climbed. Three steps from the top, Buck stopped and crouched down as he peeked over the top—scanning the space above them before motioning for Donovan to follow. They both heard the murmur of voices coming from their left. Donovan tightened his grip on his pistol and waited for Buck to round the corner at the top of the metal banister. The voices came from just beyond the door at the end of the hall.

Buck gestured Donovan off to the side, then reached down and gripped the doorknob. The telltale crimson drops on the floor told them what they needed to know—Eva had gone into this room. Every nerve ending in Donovan's body was crackling with energy, his mouth was dry, he swallowed hard and waited.

In one fluid motion, Buck put his shoulder to the door and pushed into the room, going low and left. Donovan followed him and stayed high and right. The room was darker than the hallway, a piece of burlap tacked up over the single window. The air was heavy from the smell of a recently fired weapon. To his left, just within his peripheral vision, Donovan saw a man seated in a steel chair with his head bowed, his hands hanging limply at his side. The wall behind him was splattered with his blood. He knew the man was dead.

Donovan swung right, looking down the barrel of the Sig, and found Stephanie sitting upright on a filthy cot. Her blonde hair fell in tangles to her shoulders. Her eyes were covered with black fabric, her hands bound in front of her with a plastic tie-wrap. Kneeling over her was a woman. Eva snapped her head at the intrusion as her eyes flew wide in astonishment.

Donovan saw the knife in Eva's hand—and the blood. Donovan tightened the pressure on the smooth metal of the trigger; he knew Eva wore a bulletproof vest and he leveled his aim on the flesh above her collar, confident that at this range he couldn't miss. He heard a scream, but tuned everything out, the words didn't register. All he wanted was to save Stephanie. He squeezed the trigger until the gun bucked in his hand.

CHAPTER THIRTY

Lauren stood transfixed, her attention torn between the building that Donovan and Buck had entered and the billowing cloud from Atitlán that now filled the window of the Gulfstream. She was tuned into everything around her, and she watched as John maneuvered the *Scimitar*, keeping the infrared pinpointed on Donovan, and the synthetic aperture radar trained on the volcano. The mountain was spewing volumes of black ash into the air; the bright sunlight had nearly turned to dusk as the sun was obscured by tons of volcanic debris. She, along with William and Michael, were waiting for word from Buck. Lauren's fists were clinched tight, her fingernails digging into her palms.

The instant that Buck had leaped from the plane, Michael had banked the *Galileo* away from the volcano, and they'd accelerated away from the dangerous ash. Once they were a safe distance from the plume, Michael turned the airplane over to Craig, coming out of the cockpit to stand behind her. They were all waiting.

"Call them," Michael said, breaking the nearly unbearable silence.

"Buck ordered me not to," John stated. "He told me before they went into the house not to transmit under any circumstances. Normally, Special Forces guys are 'wired up' as they call it. All of the communications are silent, using earpieces and microphones. We didn't have that kind of time. He only has the handheld radio; any transmission I make will be heard through the speaker and could give away their position, so all we can do is wait."

Michael leaned closer. "Do we have any idea what's going on in there?"

John shook his head. "Only through the windows. The concrete is blocking any heat signatures from inside the building."

"What about Janie and the helicopter?" Lauren asked, as she felt her eyes start to burn from staring at the screen.

"I just spoke to her," Michael said. "She's forced to go the long way around. She thinks she can be here inside half an hour—maybe."

"What was that?" Lauren pointed at the screen.

"I missed it," John said. "What did it look like?"

"Some sort of whitish something?" Michael hesitated as he spoke. "It came from left to right. There it is again. Is it just a glitch in the transmission?"

"Uh oh," Lauren said under her breath. She immediately went to one of the large oval windows and looked south. The objects on the screen were white-hot debris raining down from the volcano. A fresh wave of boiling ash mushroomed skyward.

"Oh God," William said in a hushed tone as Michael bolted for the cockpit.

Lauren gripped the back of John's chair as Michael threw the Gulfstream into a steep bank and brought the engines up to full power, climbing to a point above the debris.

Lauren absorbed every shred of data on the *Scimitar* control panel. Her eyes jumped from one screen to the other—the volcano was starting to expel huge chunks of thick orange lava. Each mass was flung free of the cone as it fell away into the cauldron of ash. On the infrared screen, Lauren watched the house. Tied up at the dock, she could see the Cessna's wings rocking back and forth in a wide arc from the waves created by the initial shock wave. She glanced at William and discovered that his face had gone slack, as if he couldn't quite grasp what he was seeing.

"Call them!" Lauren urged again. "Buck's radio can't be any noisier than a volcano!"

"We have to be patient," John replied. "Give them a little more time. When he's clear, he'll call. He knows we're up here waiting."

"It's just one woman," William said to no one in particular. "How hard could it be for Buck to take down one woman?"

"William, I think I know what Eva's doing," Lauren's brain was churning at a hundred miles per hour. "We watched as she shot Donovan in the back and then killed the two men on the dock. Eva doesn't know we're watching. She killed another man as she made her way up to the house with the money. She's eliminating all the kidnappers."

"But why?" William replied. "For the money?"

"Perhaps, but that's not her endgame. If all she wanted was the money, she could have taken it in Guatemala City when she was with Donovan."

"Did she come back to the lake to release Stephanie?" William asked, a tiny vestige of hope in his voice.

"The girl," Lauren said, as it all made sense to her. "I think Eva's plan is to take the money, the girl, *and* free Stephanie. To do that, she needed to eliminate her foot soldiers, and, if I'm right, Eva didn't kidnap Marie Vargas. She rescued her. Now all she has to do is survive Buck and Donovan."

CHAPTER THIRTY-ONE

Donovan's ears rang from the gunshot. The recoil had forced the gun upward. He tried to bring it down, to level the pistol for a second shot if necessary—but it wouldn't move. Only then did he realize that Buck had an iron grip around his wrist, keeping him from aiming his weapon. His shot had missed Eva by only inches.

Buck snatched the pistol out his hand. "Donovan, it's under control!"

"Donovan?" Stephanie had curled up defensively at the sound of the gunshot. She slowly turned her head at the sound of Buck's voice, her blindfold still firmly in place. "Donovan—are you there?"

Frantically, through the bluish smoke that lingered in the air, Donovan searched for Eva's body. He found her next to the cot, her eyes were wide open and staring at him with a mixture of anger and disbelief. Buck had the silencer of his gun pointed at her temple, her knife-wielding hand pinned to the floorboard by his boot.

Donovan stepped past Eva and went to Stephanie's side. He sat and carefully pulled off the blindfold. As her eyes fluttered open, she buried her face in his shoulder. He could feel her tears of relief.

"Stephanie?" A small, tentative voice sounded from across the room.

"Marie! It's okay. We're safe!" Stephanie sobbed the words over Donovan's shoulder.

Donovan turned and saw the curled-up form of a young girl huddled under one of the empty cots. A blindfolded face was barely visible in the shadows.

"Get her," Buck called out to Donovan, as he picked up Eva's knife and sliced Stephanie's bonds, all the while keeping a careful watch on Eva.

As Donovan gently helped the little girl out from under the cot, he could feel her tremble. Stephanie joined him and pulled the girl close. Donovan took the knife from Buck, and with great care, freed the little girl's hands, which instantly shot around Stephanie's neck in a fierce hug. Both of them sobbed quietly as days and days of stress flowed from them.

"Stephanie said you'd come," the little girl said, as she looked up adoringly at Donovan. "She promised me you'd save us, and you did."

Donovan embraced the raw emotion he felt at finding Stephanie alive—that Stephanie had promised the young girl he'd come was overwhelming.

"What's your name?" Donovan cupped her face in his hand and brushed her long black hair away from her eyes.

"Marie Vargas," she said, as she peered between Donovan and Stephanie at the scene beyond.

Donovan turned and glared at Eva, then he shifted his gaze to Buck. "Why did you stop me from killing her?"

"Just a hunch," Buck said as he looked down at Eva, the pain on her face clearly evident. "Are the others dead?"

"Yeah, every one of them," Eva said without a hint of a Spanish accent. "How in the hell did *you* get here?"

"There are a few things you didn't know about," Buck replied, and then furrowed his brow as he glanced at her injured arm. "How bad are you hurt?"

"I'll live," Eva said as she studied the knife wound in her forearm.

"What is she talking about?" Donovan asked, confused, then turned to Eva. "What happened to your accent?"

"Eva saved us," Stephanie explained softly, as though she couldn't quite trust her voice or emotions. "She made sure we weren't harmed."

A muffled explosion rocked the house. Dirt and plaster seemed to pour from the ceiling and fell around them.

"Are we under attack?" Eva asked.

"I don't think so," Buck said, as it grew even darker outside.

Donovan yanked away the burlap that covered the window. In the hazy air across the lake he saw a curtain of ash descending from the overcast. A series of waves were spreading out across the lake from the epicenter of the blast. Donovan turned toward Buck. "The volcano!"

Buck helped Eva up from the floor and then pulled a tie-wrap from a pocket in his fatigues. "Until I can properly interrogate you."

Eva turned around obediently, placing her hands behind her back as Buck secured her wrists. He picked up her knife and gun and secured them in his pockets, then propelled her toward the door.

Donovan led the way down the steps, and Buck called out for everyone to stop in the kitchen. Buck pulled the radio from his jacket and transmitted to the *Galileo*.

"John, this is Buck. We're all clear in the house. We have Stephanie and Marie. Everything clear outside?"

"Affirmative," John's voice crackled from the radio. "I have no other observed people in your vicinity. The helicopter is still trying to get to you, but no firm ETA yet."

"Roger," Buck replied, telling the others. "We'll be safer staying inside for now."

"Marie and I need some water," Stephanie said, holding the young girl in her arms. "Is my camera equipment here?"

Eva motioned to a cooler against the far wall, and Donovan lifted the lid and pulled two large bottles of water from inside. Eva then nodded down the hallway. "Your camera bag is in a closet in the front room."

Relieved, Stephanie tried to put Marie down, but the terrified girl only gripped her harder.

"I'll go with you," Buck said as he led Stephanie and Marie from the room. As he left, Buck handed the radio to Donovan. "I think someone up there would like to hear from you."

"Lauren?"

Buck nodded.

Donovan wasn't sure what to say. His wife was circling high above him in the *Galileo,* and he had no idea how she'd gotten there or why. He pressed the transmit key. "Lauren, are you there?"

"I'm here. Are you safe? Is everyone okay?"

Donovan crumbled a little at the sound of her voice—it seemed like ages since he'd spoken to her. "We're all good. Stephanie and Marie are doing fine. How did you...when did you...?"

"Did Eva survive?"

"So far," Donovan replied, as he glared at Eva.

"Get us out of here, and I'll tell you everything," Eva said defiantly.

"Start talking now."

Eva's eyes softened as she lowered her voice to a barely a whisper. "Don't kill me. I protected the hostages. I shot you on the dock to take you out of the equation, to protect you from those animals. I recruited those men, and then I killed them when I was finished. They're criminals, and they deserved exactly what they got."

"Why?"

"Revenge," Eva whispered.

"Donovan," Lauren transmitted. "Ask her if her last name is Rocha."

Donovan didn't have to ask, the shocked expression on Eva's face at hearing her name spoke volumes.

Donovan keyed the microphone. "That's her name. Who is she?"

"Ask her if Hector Vargas is *la Serpiente*," Lauren said.

"Yes, he's the snake. When I was fifteen, I was kidnapped along with my mother. He killed her, but I escaped and went into hiding. Afterwards, they ruined my father and took away my family's home. It took me a lifetime to discover who was responsible, and now I've made them all pay."

"We can help you," Lauren said. "Donovan, you need to protect her at all costs."

"The kidnapping was all a setup?" Donovan struggled to rearrange all the events of the last two days. "Everything you said and did was a carefully orchestrated lie. The shooter at the hotel, he was one of your guys? Then the demand that I be the one that delivers the money instead of Buck. This morning, as we were driving around, you were making it all up as you went, weren't you? Everything you did was intended to manipulate me into bringing you here with the money?"

Eva nodded. "I couldn't have Buck deliver the money—he's far too dangerous. You, I could handle. My plan was to take the money, and Marie, and vanish—but I needed to leave Stephanie in the hands of people who would care for her. If you hadn't stopped me, Marie and I would be miles away from here by now."

"How were you going to get out of here?"

"The pilot was supposed to fly the three of us to Mexico." Eva shrugged. "His services were easily bought. What I didn't expect was for him to try to kill me and take the money for himself. When I saw in your eyes that you were going to go for your gun, I knew there was going to be a firefight on the dock. I had to shoot you first, so no one else would, and then I killed the other two men. In fact, I killed them all."

"Where did you get the gun?" Donovan asked, attempting to piece together everything Eva had done.

"It was taped under my seat in the plane," Eva explained. "I put it there several days ago. That's all I'm telling you until we're safely out of this place."

Donovan's jaw hardened as the ramifications of her actions came into focus. He didn't know if he wanted to kill her or hug her. She'd protected Stephanie, but she'd also kidnapped her to begin with, which left a hundred unanswered questions.

"I hear a helicopter." Eva tilted her head as she listened.

Above the rumble of the distant volcano, Donovan, too, thought he heard the distinctive thumping of rotor blades.

"Everyone, heads up," Lauren's urgent voice came over the radio. "You've got a helicopter coming in fast, hugging the shoreline to the east, and it's not ours."

Donovan pulled Eva to her feet, just as the aging, military-green Huey flashed over the house, pulled up, and then came around and hovered briefly over the open area between the dock and the house. A dirty cloud of ash and debris blew outwards and upwards from the rotor wash as the helicopter settled firmly onto the ground.

"They'll focus on the house," Eva said. "We need to be outside."

Without a word, Donovan herded Eva out the door and eased them both, unseen, down a path into the thick overgrowth. He turned his attention to the first man out of the chopper. He could clearly see the white tape across the bridge of his nose. To his right, he recognized the next man as the one Eva had kicked when they'd escaped the Learjet. Mounted near the door was a heavy machine gun, the gunner had it trained on the house. Donovan drew the Sig from his belt.

"They won't shoot into the house for fear of hitting Marie," Eva whispered.

"Who are they? How did they find us?"

"They're Vargas' men," Eva said. "I'm thinking our pilot must have been bought all along. He probably radioed our destination to Vargas."

Donovan stayed low as the two men approached. Behind them, the blades of the helicopter were still turning, the pilot planning on a quick departure. Donovan couldn't shoot from where he stood; the sound of his gun would no doubt bring a hail of bullets from the helicopter. In the doorway of the house, unseen by the approaching men, Donovan spotted Buck. Using hand signals, he gestured for Donovan to stay put and that he'd handle the intruders.

Donovan gripped and re-gripped the pistol—his palms had grown wet with perspiration. He could hear each individual footfall as the first man approached. It was the guy with the broken nose. Eva crouched down to make herself as small as possible. Donovan expected Buck to kill both men without making a sound. Instead, from the far side of the house, came a barrage of gunshots, followed by the muffled report from Buck's automatic weapon.

The guy with the taped nose was now running for the door of the house. Without hesitation, Donovan raised the Sig and fired twice in succession, then once more as the intruder staggered. All three rounds hit their target, the impact from the heavy bullets spun the man into a crumpled heap on the stairs.

"Follow me!" Donovan pulled Eva to her feet to make a dash for the house when the heavy machine gun from the helicopter began to fire. The noise was deafening as large-caliber rounds exploded the ground in front of them. Donovan pushed Eva backward and shielded her from the incoming fire. At the same time, the helicopter's engines spooled up, and the chopper lifted off.

"Donovan," Lauren's voice sounded from the radio. "They've got you and Eva cut off. Turn around and run west. If you keep going there's a path you can use to work your way back to the house."

Donovan stayed low and moved as quickly as he could through the underbrush as the helicopter returned. Hovering over the shore, its machine gun ripped up the ground all around the concrete structure.

"We need to get closer to the helicopter. We can't do anything with a pistol," Eva said.

Donovan found the path that Lauren had described, but instead of turning right, which would lead him to the safety of the house, they went left, toward the lake. Branches slapped at his face as they pushed down the hill. Donovan calculated the distance. It wasn't far now. As they reached the edge of the foliage, they stopped and crouched in the brush, hidden from the helicopter. The dock was only twenty yards away. In the shallow water, where Eva had sent the body of one of her men, was an automatic weapon.

"We need a diversion," Donovan said, pulling the radio from his pocket. "Michael, can you hear me?"

"We hear you," Michael's voice crackled through the speaker. "You're down by the lake, close to the dock, right?"

"Yeah," Donovan replied, understanding that they'd been watching via the *Scimitar*. Eva looked at him, perplexed at how they'd been observed by an airplane she couldn't even see. "How about a little diversion?"

"The *Scimitar* is going to arrive in thirty seconds, which should distract them for a moment."

A small grin came over Donovan's face. "Perfect."

"Roger," Michael replied. "Get ready."

"What's happening?" Eva asked, as Donovan balanced on the balls of his feet, getting ready to sprint to the dock.

"That diversion we were looking for? It's about to arrive in the shape of a jet-black Predator drone."

"You've had a goddamned drone all along?" Eva rolled her eyes and pursed her lips as if a great many things suddenly now made sense.

Donovan nodded as he recognized the high-pitched whine from the *Scimitar*'s turboprop engine, closing fast.

"There it is! I see it," Eva said.

The *Scimitar* flew directly toward the cockpit of the helicopter. When the pilot saw the threat, he hesitated, caught off guard, then he overcontrolled. The helicopter swung abruptly left, banked and climbed away. At the last possible second, the *Scimitar* peeled off, narrowly missing the helicopter. With all eyes on the *Scimitar*, Donovan took off running downhill, the uneven ground treacherous; he clenched his teeth at the pain in his back.

Low over the lake, the helicopter gathered speed, recovered from the evasive maneuver, and banked toward Donovan as he reached the water. He waded in waist deep, and then dove under, swimming to where he thought the gun would be. Forced to surface and take a breath, the sound of the approaching chopper told him he was running out of time. Ten feet more and he spotted the weapon lying on the bottom. He grabbed it by the barrel, surfaced, and swam close to the dock. He ducked under the wooden structure as the helicopter roared overhead.

Donovan fixed the front sight on the cockpit. Through the Plexiglas, he could see the pilot, both of his hands on the controls. Donovan leaned into the stock, pulled the trigger, and held it down. The rifle jumped in his hands as a stream of bullets ripped into the target. He saw a dozen holes splinter and then demolish the Plexiglas. The helicopter staggered hard right and spun away from the shore, its blades sending loud shock waves across the water.

Donovan held his breath as the helicopter flew low as if it were going to hit the water, but it righted and continued a wide turn until it was once again headed in his direction. As he aimed to fire again, he saw the orange flash from the barrel of the machine gun. The bullets hammered into the water twenty feet left of him and shredded parts of the dock. The helicopter continued to bear down on Donovan. The gunner had the range and there was nowhere for him to hide.

CHAPTER THIRTY-TWO

Even though she knew it was coming, Lauren felt her stomach drop as the *Galileo* plummeted from the sky. She'd raced to the cockpit the second the *Scimitar* had flashed past the helicopter. Michael had put them into a steep dive. She braced herself between Michael and Craig, the roar from the slipstream making conversation impossible as she strained to see out the windshield. They broke out of the overcast directly over the lake with Michael's eyes fixed on the shore. He banked the Gulfstream hard and pointed it directly at the circling helicopter.

Lauren could see the helicopter make a wide arc, the disk from the spinning rotor blades visible ahead of them. "Go faster!"

Michael fine-tuned the thrust from the big Rolls-Royce engines and ignored the pings from the falling debris slamming into the *Galileo*. He allowed the Gulfstream to descend until they were only ten feet above the water.

Lauren watched helplessly as the helicopter completed its turn, slid into position, and once again approached the dock. As the *Galileo* thundered closer, just above the waves, Lauren could see muzzle flashes from the dock. The helicopter returned fire, its heavy-caliber weapon throwing up explosions of water and pieces of the wooden dock.

Michael inched the throttles forward. As the hills grew closer, the helicopter and house seemed to fill the windscreen. Lauren held her breath, terrified that Michael had somehow misjudged. Every muscle in her body was wire taut. She wanted to cry out for Michael to climb. She held on to the seat back as hard as she could. She bit her lip as she saw the machine-gun bullets make a wide arc headed toward Donovan. Geysers of water flashed into the air from each heavy slug. They were close enough now that Lauren could spot the pilot turn and see the Gulfstream. In an instant, she saw two bodies in the water, and she caught a glimpse of another figure surfacing yards away from the dock. Donovan was pointing his rifle up at the helicopter.

In a blur of motion, Michael slammed the throttles forward and cranked the Gulfstream up and away from the scene. Lauren was forced painfully into the side of Craig's seat as Michael banked the jet into a punishing turn and pointed the nose nearly straight up. The Gulfstream's wings bit heavily into the air and they rocketed upward, just clearing the trees and rocky hills. An instant later they were enveloped in the low clouds. Lauren couldn't move, pinned into place by the G-force from their massive climb. Behind them, she had no idea what was happening.

***

Donovan surfaced. The moment he'd seen Michael racing across the lake, he'd ducked below the waves and swum away from the dock until his lungs felt as if they'd burst. As the Gulfstream thundered past only scant feet above the helicopter, the jet blast and disturbed air made it impossible for the gunner to get off an accurate burst. As the unexpected turbulence rocked the helicopter, Donovan saw all heads aboard the helicopter turn toward the house as Buck's bullets tore into the helicopter. Donovan squeezed the trigger and saw the pilot slump as he concentrated the burst directly on the man flying. The nose of the helicopter came up and the tail began to rotate to the right. The helicopter climbed into an even steeper angle and began to rotate wildly as it banked past the point of return and slid sideways into the ground below. Donovan turned his head as it slammed to earth between the dock and the house, exploding into a red-and-orange fireball. The shock wave punished his ears, and debris from the shattered sections of the wildly spinning rotors peppered the water around him.

Donovan heard Eva call his name as she ran toward him. Moments later, Buck, with Marie in one arm, his weapon in the other, pounded down the hill. Stephanie was close behind. Donovan waded ashore and surveyed what was left of the helicopter. The tail boom had ripped away and the fuselage was lying on its side. Buck handed Marie to Stephanie, and then ran toward the helicopter and inspected the burning wreckage.

"They're all dead," Buck called out. "We need to get out of here. Donovan, did the Cessna take any hits from the helicopter?"

"No, I don't think so." Donovan thought back to the firefight. All the gunfire had been directed away from the floatplane.

"Can you fly us out of here?" Buck asked.

"Sure," Donovan nodded. "But I don't know how far we're going to get. When we came in, the weather between here and Guatemala City was terrible. I'm not going to try to thread our way through those hills, it's too dangerous. What about Janie? Is there a chance she could still come get us?"

"I don't think we can afford to wait. We need to get out of here before anyone else arrives, and the farther away from that volcano we can get wouldn't be a bad thing, either."

Donovan looked out across the dark water of the lake. Buck was right, they didn't want to be here if another helicopter arrived, or a boat full of armed men. Studying the sky, he could see the ash and debris as it rained down from above, almost like snow. Bigger chunks glowed and fluttered, streaming smoke. The entire horizon to the south was pitch black from Atitlán's eruption.

"The money?" Eva asked, as she looked up toward the house.

Donovan quickly did the math, four adults and a child in the thin air nearly a mile above sea level. They could already be overloaded. "Leave it."

Eva lowered her head, then took one more wistful look up at the house and the three million dollars.

Donovan pulled the radio from his pocket. He keyed the transmit button as he followed Eva down to the plane. "Good job, Michael. We've had a change in plans. We're going to get airborne in the Cessna, but I'm going to need your help to get out of here."

"What do you want us to do?" Michael replied.

"Once I get this thing in the air, I'm going to need some-place to go. The weather east isn't any good. Is there another way out of here?"

"Straight west is really all you have. You'll have to climb above the hills, but we can use the *Scimitar* to guide you through the mountains. Once you clear them, the terrain falls off quickly, and you'll be well away from the fallout from the eruption. It'll be a nice downhill trip all the way to the ocean."

The two men Eva had killed had washed near the shore, their blood a crimson-stained halo in the clear water. Donovan swung under the Cessna's wing strut and yanked the door open. The keys were still dangling from the ignition. Donovan knelt and untied the first of the two lines that held the plane to the dock.

"You do know how to fly this, right?" Eva asked.

"Of course," Donovan said without looking at her.

"Buck, you're up front with me," Donovan said, as he slid the pilot's seat forward and motioned for Stephanie to get in first, followed by Marie, then Eva.

As Eva waited her turn to board, Buck sliced the tie-wrap from her wrists. "Behave."

Eva nodded and climbed into the cramped back seat of the Cessna. Donovan made sure everyone found a seat belt, then slid the pilot's seat aft so Buck could swing himself onboard and get situated into the front seat on the right side of the plane. Dono-van untied the last rope and pushed off. The light breeze floated them out from the dock. He switched on the red master switch, confident that everything about flying a Cessna would come back to him. It was the other part that worried him—he'd never actu-ally flown a floatplane.

Donovan slid the seat up and slammed the door. He found

his seat belt and jammed it into place. He pushed on the rudder pedals and felt the sharp pain arc up his spine. Donovan pushed in the mixture, put his hand on the throttle, and turned the key. The propeller lurched into motion. Moments later the engine caught and started. The entire airframe vibrated as Donovan studied the engine gauges, relieved to see that they had oil pressure. He set the flaps and stepped hard on the right rudder, then the left, to get a feel for how the amphibian handled.

"*Galileo*, you ready?" Donovan keyed the radio.

"I'm here," John responded. "The *Scimitar* is circling overhead, I'm going to keep it above and behind you, just do what I say."

"Is there a VHF backup?" Donovan suddenly didn't trust the little battery-operated radio in his hand very much.

"131.85," John replied.

Donovan switched the Cessna's primary radio to the new frequency. He looked at Buck, then back at the women, all strapped in tightly. Eva had her eyes closed, and he saw her cross herself. Without another word, Donovan pulled the controls as far back as they would go as he simultaneously pushed in the throttle. The engine and propeller made a tremendous noise and the entire airframe shook and shuddered. Slowly, the Cessna's nose rose up and blotted out the view forward. Donovan worked the rudders and watched out the side window. As their speed built, the Cessna bounced and skittered over the waves. Donovan watched with concern as their speed crept up ever so slowly. The green shoreline that looked so far away when he'd started now loomed much closer.

Donovan kept his right hand on the throttle, and eased up on the back pressure, trying to will the Cessna up on the step. A floatplane, just like a boat, has a speed where the hull accelerates up onto the surface of the lake instead of plowing through it. They needed to reach that velocity before the plane would fly. The roar from the straining engine, mixed with the water pounding on the aluminum floats, was deafening. Donovan could feel the Cessna picking up precious speed, but it seemed too slow.

The rocky face of the rapidly rising terrain began to fill the windshield. He jockeyed the yoke in his hands and then rocked the wings, hoping that he could pop the floats free of the suction created by the water. Donovan could almost feel the tension from the others, as they, too, saw the hill dead ahead. Through the seat of his pants, he felt a different vibration, more staccato, as almost begrudgingly, the Cessna climbed up on top of the waves. They were picking up speed, and Donovan's eyes darted back and forth between the airspeed indicator and the shore.

Donovan eased back on the yoke, and the sound of the water banging against the floats vanished for two seconds as they lifted free, then just as quickly they settled and kissed the water once again. Trying desperately to get a feel for the airplane, Donovan gently pulled back once more and the floats pulled free from the water. They were airborne, but just barely, staggering through the air just inches above the lake.

Donovan felt the controls jerk in his hands, a horrendous noise filled the cabin, and the airplane shuddered, the left wingtip nearly touching the waves. Reflexes honed by thousands of hours flying allowed Donovan to level the wings before they cartwheeled to their deaths. The Cessna vibrated and shook, and it took almost full-right rudder for Donovan to keep the plane flying straight. He fought to keep the Cessna from dipping back into the water and began to turn the airplane away from the shoreline. Gingerly, he guided them into a careful turn to the left, away from the shore, but as they turned, the Cessna wouldn't climb—they were still skimming just feet above the dark water.

A shrill horn began sounding in the cramped cabin, telling him he was on the verge of stalling the airplane. Donovan leveled the wings, urging the airplane to keep flying, amazed that somehow it did as he asked. He took a deep breath. Never taking his eyes off the lake, he reached down and put his hand on the flap handle. Carefully, he milked them up, each small change helped increase their speed. With the flaps all the way up, the stall horn silenced, and the Cessna slowly climbed away from the water.

"What in the hell happened?" Buck yelled above the noise.

"We hit something." Donovan didn't dare let go of the controls. "The airplane's really messed up. We're at maximum power, but we're not climbing."

They were struggling through the sky; Donovan had to keep the Cessna between the clouds overhead and the water below. Ahead of them, the mountains jutted up well into the overcast. The sharp odor of sulfur was starting to fill the cabin. In a few minutes he'd have to start a turn back the way they came. They were trapped.

Donovan turned around until he could see Stephanie; she held Marie tightly, the young girl's face buried in Stephanie's shoulder. Stephanie's grim expression told him her relief at being rescued was short lived. Donovan inched further around and could see Eva looking out the window, her face shock-white.

He turned his attention back to flying the Cessna. To the south, clouds of ash blotted out the horizon. All around the lake, the hilltops were obscured by either clouds or ash. At this altitude there was nowhere to go. He looked out the window at the left float. As he studied the damage, he could see shards of torn aluminum peeking out from underneath. The entire float was canted outward at an odd angle, no doubt creating a tremendous amount of drag. He keyed the microphone. "Guys, we have a problem. Can you get the *Scimitar* down here to take a look at my left float?"

"Yeah, sure, hang on," John said. "What am I looking for?"

"Tell me if there's enough of it left to set the airplane back down on the lake."

CHAPTER THIRTY-THREE

Lauren was helpless to do anything but watch as John maneuvered the *Scimitar* below and behind the Cessna. She could easily see that the float was bent to the left, but it wasn't until John zoomed in that she saw the full extent of the damage. Whatever they'd hit had ripped the entire bottom off the forward section. Where there should have been smooth metal, similar to the curved hull of a canoe, there was a jagged rip at least six feet long.

Michael burst from the cockpit and hurried down the aisle to get a look at the damage. He studied the image, shook his head, and then picked up a microphone. "Donovan, we're looking at the damage to your plane, and it's not good. Whatever you hit took out the bottom six or seven feet of the left float. It's also canted about ten degrees outboard."

"Is there any chance I can safely set this thing back down on the water?"

"No way. The second the left float touches the surface you'll cartwheel the thing. We just got a message from Malcolm and Lillian. They're monitoring the eruption on the *Scimitar's* synthetic aperture radar. They say they can see a lava dome beginning to build on the south side; it coincides with the earthquake swarms they're seeing."

"Michael, this airplane is barely climbing."

Lauren could hear Donovan's stress and fatigue; it matched her own. She leaned over William to get a better look outside the

Galileo. She could see Atitlán, and far to the south, through the ash and clouds and beyond the mountains, she could also see the blue Pacific Ocean.

"What's your altitude now?" Michael asked.

"Five thousand four hundred."

"Keep climbing, buddy, we'll find you a way out of here," Michael said.

"Michael," Donovan said. "When I look south, I can see a sliver of clear air between the mountains. There's actually blue sky to be seen. If I can clear the ridge, what's on the other side?"

"There is a saddle between Atitlán and San Pedro that's lower than anyplace around the lake," Michael replied. "It also puts you at the foot of the erupting volcano. If you could get over the ridge, there'd be a sloping valley all the way to the ocean. The terrain goes from six thousand feet down to sea level in about thirty miles. It's also where Janie is right now. She didn't have any luck negotiating the terrain to the west."

"What about poison gas?" Donovan asked. "If we have another encounter like before, I won't be able to fly the plane."

"Malcolm told us that most of gas is being released and sent far up into the atmosphere with the steam and ash."

"South it is, then," Donovan replied. "Use the *Scimitar* and find the absolute lowest altitude we can fly and still get over that ridge."

"I'm hesitant to fly the *Scimitar* that close to the volcano," John said as he glanced up at Michael. "We're flying without the main coolant system. We could lose the entire ship."

"So be it," Michael shrugged. "If the conditions are that bad through there, I'd rather find out with the *Scimitar* than the Cessna."

"Of course, you're right." John snapped his head back to the screen.

"Don't worry about it," Michael replied. "If we break it, we'll buy another one."

Lauren had listened to what Donovan was thinking about

doing. She looked into Michael's eyes as he processed the task at hand. William nudged her and gestured out the window. To the south, from out of the thick gray ash spewing from Atitlán, chunks of orange-and-red lava were being hurtled hundreds of feet in the air.

CHAPTER THIRTY-FOUR

Donovan held the Cessna steady as they flew in wide circles over the water. The visibility through the valley on the southern horizon kept shifting and changing. Donovan worried that their window might close permanently and they'd be trapped over the lake until they ran out of fuel.

"I found the first-aid kit," Stephanie called out from the back seat. She held up the plastic case.

Donovan turned toward Buck. "Hurry! Help her find the gauze. Everyone needs to cover their mouth and nose before we start. We also need to close all the vents and openings in the airplane."

Buck nodded and turned in his seat to help Stephanie. Donovan searched the instrument panel and shut down all the outside air coming into the cabin. There was nothing he could do about the ash being sucked up into the engine through the air intake. Though a piston engine wasn't quite as temperamental as a jet engine, the ash would eventually start clogging the valves.

The pinging of hot cinders bouncing off the metal skin of the plane sounded like rain. He tried to not think about that as he stretched against the tightness in his back, the dull pain shooting up and down his entire spine. His arms felt heavy on the controls. Donovan's eyes shot to the outside temperature gauge mounted up where the right wing joined the fuselage. Almost a hundred degrees. Donovan knew the closer they flew toward the volcano, the higher it would climb.

"Here!" Buck had a large gauze pad in his hands. "Hold this over your mouth."

Donovan did as instructed, and Buck quickly used a length of elastic bandage to hold it in place. Donovan adjusted the improvised surgical mask so that it rested just below his eyes. It would have to do. He took a quick glance at the others and found they all had a similar setup to ward off the ash.

"Donovan. It's John. The *Scimitar* just made it through to the other side."

"How was it through there?" Donovan replied, his voice muffled by the gauze.

"Not great." John paused. "The lava being hurtled out of the cone is sporadic, unpredictable. The temperature spiked at nearly two hundred degrees, and there was at least thirty or forty seconds of heavy ash and turbulence. After that, you'll break out into the clear. If you can reach five thousand, nine hundred, fifty feet, you won't fly into a mountain. I promise."

Donovan looked down at the altimeter. They were three hundred feet short.

"Your heading looks good," John said smoothly. "I'm bringing the *Scimitar* back around to monitor your progress. Then you're good to go whenever you're ready."

"We need to lighten the plane," Donovan yelled over his shoulder. "Find everything that can be tossed out and hand it up to Buck."

Donovan removed his bulletproof vest; the twists and gyrations were painful. Then he handed over his Sig. From the back, Donovan saw Stephanie's camera bag, Eva's vest, the first-aid kit, as well as a bag of tools being passed forward. Buck added his machine gun, ammo, knife, and a pistol. The former SEAL cracked the door and, careful not to hit any part of the plane, tossed each item into the lake. The Cessna slowly clawed upward until the altimeter finally showed that they'd reached the five thousand nine hundred fifty feet required.

"We made it," Donovan transmitted. "But it won't climb another foot higher. We have no margin for error."

"Donovan, as you run up the valley toward the pass," Lauren's voice came over the speaker, "fly over the lava flow coming down from the cone. The heat from the lava will be rising, it'll be just like what sailplanes use to gain lift. The thermal effect of the rising air should help lift you above the top of the ridgeline."

"And if it doesn't?"

"Be a glider pilot, circle inside the thermal until you have what you need, though I have no idea what the temperature increase does to your engine."

Donovan thought back to a trip he and Lauren had taken to the Swiss Alps. They'd both been transfixed by the glider pilots as they wheeled silently in their long, slender-winged machines in the rarified air high above them. He doubted he had enough room to turn the Cessna but kept the thought to himself. He looked down at his engine instruments. At full power, the cylinder head and oil temperature gauges were already uncomfortably high. If it ingested superheated air, the engine would quickly start breaking down. The fleeting glimpse of blue sky in the distance was enticing, but the lava, ash and debris, intermittently splashing into the water, told him there was the equivalent of an aerial minefield between them and safety.

"Let's do this," Donovan transmitted and banked the Cessna to the south. "The ash is swirling in the pass. I might not always be able to see the ground. John, it's your job to keep me over the lava flow and out of the rocks."

"We going?" Buck asked.

Donovan nodded, and then looked back into the expectant faces of his passengers. "Strap in tight. This is going to get rough."

Stephanie put her hand on his shoulder and squeezed.

Donovan tightened his seat belt, the lake below had turned dark and gray. He could feel the heat and a rivulet of sweat trickled down from his temple. He squinted through the ash that came rushing past the windshield like snow in a blizzard. A quick glance told him the temperature had already climbed another forty degrees. He wondered if they would all slowly cook in the small aluminum oven that was the Cessna.

The first jolt of turbulence surprised him with its fury. The Cessna rose gently then shuddered as it slammed into the unseen air currents. Marie cried out in fear from behind him, but Donovan couldn't look back to reassure her. He couldn't even reassure himself as the Cessna bucked in his hands. He shot a furtive glance at the thermometer—the heat had increased dramatically as they hurtled into the curtain of ash. Donovan's eyes burned as if he were standing too close to an open oven. The air in the cabin became dry and hot. It was painful breathing, and there were particles of ash floating freely around him.

The controls lurched in his hands as the Cessna rode the turbulence and climbed. Donovan kept his eyes glued to the altimeter. He couldn't afford to lose any altitude or they would careen into the rocks below. Debris being thrown from the volcano started pounding the Cessna. Donovan tensed as dime-sized nicks were left in the plastic windscreen. A crack in the Plexiglas arced out from one impact site. The terrain rose up on both sides. Turning back was no longer an option. He pressed on, wiping the sweat that was now stinging his eyes. They rode out another wave of turbulence that slammed them up and down in the gray nothingness. A momentary break in the ash let Donovan see straight down into a river of fire. The airplane shuddered as the rising heat pushed the struggling Cessna upward.

"Turn left, ten degrees," John's voice came through the speaker.

Donovan knew that somewhere behind them, the *Scimitar* had a clear view inside the maelstrom. He corrected his heading just as a larger rock hit the metal above his head. The sharp reverberation made his ears ring. He urged the Cessna to hold together, his body drenched in sweat as he fought to hold his heading and altitude—the two things that would get them through safely. A glance at the engine instruments told Donovan time was running out. Each needle had climbed into the red.

A vivid flash of lightning lit up the darkness. Donovan winced as he tried to blink away the spots that danced before his eyes. He knew that the discharge had come *from* them, that they were generating tremendous amounts of static electricity as they flew through the ash. The tips of the propeller blades glowed brightly in the darkness that surrounded them. More debris pelted the thin aluminum skin, and Donovan had no idea if the Cessna would hold together.

"How much further?" Buck called out.

Donovan didn't reply—the heat burned his throat as he inhaled, his eyes were tiny tear-filled slits. He could hardly see the instruments, his vision blurry in the heat. In an instant the engine missed a beat, then another. Quickly, and with fatal certainty, the engine began to tear itself apart, and the propeller ground to a halt.

Donovan felt the Cessna begin to settle. Forward visibility briefly improved to a quarter of a mile, and he could now see the top of the ridge. They weren't going to clear the burning trees. The Cessna wallowed through the air, the stall warning horn blared, filling the cabin. The airspeed was bleeding off, and Donovan couldn't stop the process. He lowered one notch of flaps in a desperate attempt to increase the lift, but nothing changed. There was no room to turn, no place to crash land. All their options were gone.

"Are we going to clear the trees?" Buck shouted and pointed out the front of the plane. "Donovan, talk to me! Are we going to make it?"

Donovan glanced at Buck and solemnly shook his head. "No. We're going down."

"Fly this thing out of here!" Buck yelled, then, in one swift motion released his seat belt, opened the door, and pushed himself free of the plane.

Donovan had no time to react, no time to reach out and stop his friend. Buck's words echoed in his head as he felt the airplane respond. In shock, Donovan eased back on the controls. Two hundred pounds lighter, the Cessna's performance improved enough to give Donovan a fragment of hope.

Donovan put the Cessna over the center of the lava flow in hopes of gaining whatever lift he could. Straight ahead was the tree-lined ridge top, the vegetation engulfed in flames. He aimed the Cessna at the lowest spot, holding the controls tightly as branches beat the bottom of the floats. Every muscle in his body strained against the coming impact when the battered Cessna burst free into the clear air on the south side of the volcano.

The temperature dropped rapidly, and Donovan wiped the tears from his eyes. Spread out below them were sloping hills filled with the terraced fields of coffee growers. Donovan pegged the Cessna at its best glide speed and did everything he could to put as much distance between them and the volcano.

The empty seat next to him burned in his chest. Sorrow welled up inside and tears ran from his eyes. Donovan had to fight through his grief and begin the search for a place to land the Cessna. From his left side, the *Scimitar* raced past. Donovan understood, wiped the tears from his eyes, then banked the Cessna to follow.

CHAPTER THIRTY-FIVE

Lauren had watched in horrifying real time as Donovan had flown up the lava flow, losing altitude. As the Cessna descended, she'd seen Michael begin to shake his head in denial, his fingers turning white as he gripped the back of John's chair. In one terrible instant, an object had fallen away from the Cessna and landed in the lava. Moments later, the Cessna clipped the burning limbs at the top of the ridge and somehow kept going.

"What did we just see?" John said. "Hang on, I'm going to re-play it."

"Don't! Don't ever play that again—for anyone," Lauren snapped. The tears came slowly, as if her subconscious wouldn't allow the full impact of Buck's death to reach her. The optics aboard the *Scimitar* had allowed her to recognize him before he'd dropped from the field of view. The image was burned into her psyche and, with each passing moment, the magnitude of the loss seeped deeper as a solitary tear trickled down her cheek. A wounded sob erupted from somewhere deep, and she began to shake from the intensity of her tears. She covered her face, leaned over, and cried. She wept for Buck, for his family, for all the people he'd touched, and all the lives he'd saved. Lauren couldn't shut off the kaleidoscope of images that played in her mind.

She remembered the first time she met him, the lethality that he kept just under the surface, yet the kind and considerate manner in which he always conducted himself. How he'd protect-ed Abigail, always thoughtful as to the effect his presence might have on the toddler. Abigail loved him. They all loved him. Buck had meant so much to her and Abigail over the years, his calm demeanor, and his quiet confidence. He'd always seemed to know when to talk and when she'd needed solitude. He'd always been there for her. A phone call and he'd come to her rescue. Now all of that was lost forever. In a final act of selfless bravery, he'd saved the lives of four more people, including Donovan and Stephanie, and she'd never be able to thank him. She cried for her husband, she had no idea what he would be feeling. The empty seat next to him would be heart wrenching. He'd lost so many people. How would he cope with losing Buck?

Wracking sobs pummeled her as she felt arms reach around her and pull her close. She looked up and found Michael, tears streaked down from his pain-filled eyes. Beyond him stood William, his face etched with shock and disbelief.

"I can't raise them on the radio, so I maneuvered the *Scimitar* past the Cessna's left wing. I think the abrasion from the ash took out the Cessna's antenna. I'll use the *Scimitar* and start searching for a clearing, a road, anywhere Donovan can set the airplane down."

Lauren watched as John focused the synthetic aperture radar image on the ground. At each possible spot, he'd zoom in and wait for Michael to make a determination. On the third try, John zoomed in on a road. It ran uphill slightly, with some kind of crop planted on both sides that would give the wings plenty of clearance. At the end, the road made a sharp turn as it reached a grove of trees.

"That's perfect!" Michael slapped John on the back. "Now fly back to the Cessna and do whatever it takes to get Donovan to follow the *Scimitar* back to that spot. He'll know what to do when he sees what I see."

"How can he land a floatplane on a road?" John asked.

"Because he's flying an amphibian, he has wheels. Remember when they took off from the runway in Guatemala City?"

"He's right behind us," John called out, as he found the Cessna and zoomed in on Donovan. Lauren could see her husband's long hair and beard streaked white with ash. Tears ran from his eyes, and Lauren felt her heart break a little more at the sight. She caught sight of Stephanie in the back, a young girl's arms wrapped around her neck. Hidden in the shadows sat Eva. Lauren turned to William who stood next to her. Whatever he'd done over the years, what she saw this instant was an elderly man getting a glimpse of the niece he'd thought he'd lost. He tried to force a smile, but couldn't.

As John banked the *Scimitar* toward the section of road that Michael had selected for the emergency landing, Donovan followed.

"Where's Janie?" Michael asked.

"She's headed this way. She should be on the scene within minutes of them touching down."

"Thank you, John," Michael said, and then turned to Lauren. "We'll get through this."

Lauren loved Michael for his encouragement. He was trying to hold everyone together until the Cessna was safely on the ground.

Michael turned back to the screen. "How far to the road?"

"Two miles," John replied.

"How high is he above the ground?" Michael asked, a new sense of urgency in his voice.

"They're twelve hundred feet above the section of road," John said.

Michael squinted and cocked his head as he did the calculations. "That's enough. It'll be close. John, as fast as you can, use the *Scimitar* to circle the spot we found. The sooner Donovan can see what we have in mind, the better off he'll be."

Lauren clutched onto the reassurance that Donovan had Michael looking out for him.

"I'm there," John said, as the *Scimitar* reached the road and then climbed away from the opening in the trees. He leveled off and then threw the *Scimitar* into a tight-banked turn only a hundred feet off the ground. John zoomed in on the Cessna, and they all watched as Donovan rocked the wings in acknowledgment.

"He sees it," Michael said. "Where's Janie?"

"She's coming in fast from the west," John replied. "Her ETA is five minutes."

"Is she going to be able to land on the road?" William asked.

"Yeah, I think so," Michael replied. "Either way, the new helicopter has a rescue hoist. They'll get them all out safely. John, position the *Scimitar* to the east so we can see what's happening without getting in anyone's way."

"Will do," John nodded, and with a gentle flick of his wrist he climbed the *Scimitar* and set up a holding pattern, keeping all the cameras focused on the gliding Cessna.

Lauren took in the motionless prop, the damaged float, and the blackened, dented skin of the airplane Donovan was trying to land, and had no idea how any of this could turn out well.

CHAPTER THIRTY-SIX

Donovan spotted the *Scimitar* climb away from the road, effectively marking his spot. He was thankful that John had been so quick to find him a place to land. The interior of the plane was remarkably quiet, the air rushing only a whisper. He judged his descent rate and distance. Everything had to be just right; there wouldn't be a second chance.

The road snaked up from a series of buildings, leveled out for perhaps eight hundred feet, and then turned up another hill. If he landed short they'd be in the trees; landing long would produce the same result. The drag from the float was the wildcard, forcing Donovan to do it all by feel the first time.

He tried to picture Michael's description of the damage to the float. The Cessna's heavy main wheels were housed inside each pontoon. If Donovan had to guess, they were located farther aft than the damage. The main wheels were stressed for the impact of landing. Hopefully, they would extend, but he wouldn't know until they touched down.

Donovan turned toward the women, forcing himself to look past the empty seat next to him. "Is everyone buckled in as tight as possible?"

"Yes," Stephanie replied.

"There's a section of road that should work like a runway, but we're going to treat it as a crash landing," Donovan said. "When I tell you to, I want everyone to assume the position, heads down, and hands over your head. Once we come to a stop, unbuckle, and we'll get out of the plane as quickly as possible."

"Donovan," Eva leaned forward and whispered so that only he could hear. "Whatever happens, don't return Marie to her grandfather. She belongs with her mother in California. I have a feeling your wife knows what I'm talking about."

Donovan nodded his understanding. He eyed the slender ribbon of dirt carved out of the forest and lowered the first notch of flaps. Seconds later he moved the lever on the console that lowered the gear. He heard noises from below, which told him that something had happened, but the light on the panel indicated the gear was unsafe. He wouldn't know if the gear was down until they landed.

He lowered the next segment of flaps and allowed the Cessna to slow to seventy knots. He'd wait as long as possible to make sure he'd reach the road before he selected full flaps. Off the left wing, Mt. Atitlán loomed large. The rising plume drifted east, obscuring the entire sky. Donovan gave his own seat belt one last pull, then set the flaps to full, and the airplane slowed dramatically.

He cleared the trees, and the instant before they hit the road, Donovan eased back on the elevator and flared. The stall warning horn sounded and they touched. The vibration from the uneven surface shook the airplane violently and instantly the Cessna tried to veer left, off the road.

Donovan was helpless to do anything as the Cessna plunged into a shallow ditch that lined the road. In a painful shriek of tortured metal, the impact tore the already damaged floats from the airframe and spun the airplane sideways as they ripped through the field of thigh-high coffee plants. Acting like a net, the plants served to slow the Cessna quickly. In a roiling cloud of plants and soil, the airplane spun to an abrupt stop.

From the back of the plane, Donovan could hear Marie's sobs. Stephanie let out a slow groan of pain that galvanized Donovan into action. He released his seat belt, popped open the door. With the floats gone, the fuselage rested on the soft ground. Donovan crawled out of the cockpit into the dirt, turned, and peered into the rear of the cabin.

"I may have broken my ankle," Stephanie said through clenched teeth.

Eva untied the elastic bandage holding the gauze patch to her face. She pointed to a piece of aluminum laying in the dirt and Donovan quickly retrieved it, then bent it slightly and handed it to Eva, who gently fashioned a crude but effective splint for Stephanie's ankle.

"Sit tight," Donovan said to Stephanie, as Eva, who was closest to the door, began to crawl from the plane. Marie, hesitant to leave Stephanie, finally inched toward Donovan, taking his offered hand. With Eva and Marie free of the plane, Donovan eased in and sat next to Stephanie.

"I can't move my foot at all," Stephanie said.

"Okay, this might hurt a little, but I need to get you out of here."

Stephanie nodded and unfastened her seat belt. Donovan backed out of the cramped space and inched her toward the door. He slid his arms beneath her and lifted her free from the Cessna. He ignored his pain and carefully set her on the ground beneath the wing.

"Help me up," Stephanie said.

As Donovan lifted, she put her weight on her good leg, and together they hobbled away from the plane. He stopped and stood as the distant sound of a helicopter's beating rotor filtered through the trees. To the west he spotted a white dot flying in their direction. He had no idea where the *Scimitar* or the *Galileo* were, but he knew he was being watched. He briefly raised both thumbs into the air to indicate that everyone aboard had survived, and then fought an overwhelming sense of loss at the fact that he hadn't arrived with everyone.

He surveyed the destroyed Cessna, startled by the amount of damage to the top of the wings. Dents ranged from dime-sized dings to divots the size of a saucer. The antennas were all sheared off. Scorch marks from the destroyed engine streaked from underneath the engine cowling. Cessna's sturdy little airplane had taken a pounding, yet still did all that was asked.

"I hope that's ours," Stephanie said, swiveling her head at the sound.

"That should be Janie." Donovan turned to see if he could spot the helicopter.

"I can't believe he's gone." Stephanie laid her head on his shoulder.

"I can't even think about it," Donovan said, knowing that at some level Buck's death was beyond comprehension, and also aware that if he let it, his grief would be all-consuming.

"Please don't," Stephanie whispered. "If you do nothing else with the rest of your life, hold the loss of Buck up to the light of day. Don't bury it as you've done with the others. You need to deal with the past, and the present, or the pain is going to destroy you."

"I'm not having that discussion now," Donovan replied.

"It's coming right toward us," Eva said with an element of concern in her voice.

Donovan looked up and spotted the helicopter. It was close enough for him to confirm Eco-Watch's brand new Bell 412. Janie was no doubt being vectored to their position by the *Galileo*. He waved his arm.

Janie brought the 412 in fast, raised the nose, and slowed dramatically. She then delicately eased the big machine down until the skids kissed the dirt. The side door was open, and Cesar jumped to the ground, keeping his head down he ran toward them.

"We must hurry," Cesar called out. "The volcano is very unpredictable."

Once again, Donovan lifted Stephanie; she looped her arms around his neck for support.

Cesar ran back to the chopper, climbed in, and readied himself for Donovan to set Stephanie in the cabin. The moment Stephanie was inside, Cesar secured her in a row of seats that allowed her to lie down. Cesar pulled a first-aid kit from its rack and Donovan helped Marie and Eva up into the cabin. Once they were aboard, he jumped up and went to the cockpit where Janie and Eric sat.

"Are we good to go?" Janie asked as she turned to him. "Where's Buck?"

Donovan lowered his head. The sound of Janie using his name felt like a physical blow. He shook his head. "Buck didn't make it."

Janie looked up, closed her eyes, and let her head drop. She started to shake her head back and forth, as if trying to escape the information.

"He went quickly," Donovan put his hand on Janie's shoulder. He knew that she and Buck were close, that he had once saved her life, pulling her out of a burning helicopter. "Are you going to be okay?"

Janie nodded, swallowed hard, and then turned back to the business of getting the helicopter ready to fly.

"I'll make sure everyone is settled," Donovan said and then returned to the cabin. Cesar was attending to Stephanie, and Marie, already strapped in, sat close. Donovan looked around. "Where's Eva?"

Cesar looked up, clearly surprised. "She was right there a minute ago. She helped the girl with her seat belt."

Donovan looked at Marie. "Did you see where she went?"

Marie pointed in the opposite direction from the crashed Cessna.

Donovan inwardly cursed and went back to the cockpit. "Are there any guns onboard?"

"Yeah." Eric removed a Glock from a holster tucked under his arm and handed it to Donovan, butt first. "Buck gave it to me this morning. Said we might need some firepower."

"Thanks." Donovan took the weapon. "How about a hand-held radio?"

"On the bulkhead behind you," Eric pointed.

"Eva bolted. I'm going after her." Donovan turned on the radio, finding the battery fully charged. "Get Stephanie to a doctor. I'm going to instruct the *Galileo* to meet you when you land in Guatemala City. It's essential that Marie, the young girl onboard, is delivered to Lauren. No one else. Understand?"

"Understood," Janie nodded.

"Now go, and as soon as you can, come back and get me. I'll be monitoring 131.85."

"Will do, skipper," Janie replied.

Donovan returned to the cabin, still clutching the Glock. He leaned down and squeezed Stephanie's hand. "I'll see you later."

Stephanie nodded. Donovan placed his hand on Marie's head. "You don't have to be afraid anymore. There's someone waiting for you. Her name is Dr. Lauren McKenna. You'll be safe with her."

Marie looked up, and the expression in her young eyes was a familiar one to Donovan. In one form or another, he'd seen the same look of fear and doubt in the mirror since he was fourteen years old. He turned away, jumped to the ground, and moved to a position where Janie could see him. Janie spooled up the engines and the blades spun against the air. She adjusted the pitch of the main rotor, and Donovan could feel the power of the blades resonate in his chest. The helicopter lifted off and climbed away. Within moments the chopper vanished behind the trees, and the thudding rotors faded in the morning sky.

Donovan heard another sound, more of a roar than the staccato beating of a helicopter. He turned and looked north. Mt. Atitlán, with renewed energy, expelled tons of ash and lava high into the atmosphere. He was far enough away to be beyond the range of the falling debris, but he knew all of that could change in an instant.

CHAPTER THIRTY-SEVEN

"Track her!" Lauren said to John, the instant it became evident that Eva was on the run. She watched as Eva's ghostly infrared image ran down the hill toward what appeared to be a small collection of buildings, an agricultural station of some kind. Another figure jumped from the helicopter and quickly moved away from the machine. Dust began blowing outward, and crops near the helicopter were flattened outward, as the chopper lifted off and accelerated down the hill.

"I've got her," John replied. "I've also got a radio transmission from Mr. Nash. I'm going to put him on speaker."

"*Galileo,* this is Donovan. How do you read?"

"Donovan, it's John. We have you on speaker in the back of the *Galileo.* Is everything okay?"

"Several things I need to pass on. Lauren, are you there?"

"I'm here."

"Tell William that Stephanie will need medical treatment upon her arrival for what appears to be a broken ankle. Otherwise she's fine. There's also the matter of Marie. She's fairly traumatized, doesn't want to be very far from Stephanie. Eva gave me a message: Marie's mother is in California. She said under no circumstances were we to allow Marie to be returned to her grandfather. She said you'd understand."

"I'm not sure it's our job to get in the middle of an international custody battle," Michael said.

"No, Eva's right," Lauren said to Donovan. "We'll meet the helicopter in Guatemala so William can be with Stephanie. I'll look after Marie, but you need to catch Eva."

"That's my plan," Donovan said. "Which way did she go?"

"She fled downhill toward a collection of buildings." Lauren studied the infrared image from the *Scimitar*. "The place is empty, hers is the only heat signature. I think everyone within fifty miles of you has been evacuated."

"Get to Guatemala City and then come back here. I told Janie the same thing. Hopefully I'll have Eva, and the helicopter can pick us up."

"You're going to be on your own for a little while," John said. "I'll have to take the *Scimitar* with us when we leave so I don't lose the link."

"I understand," Donovan replied. "She's not getting far. Call me when you're back in range."

Lauren watched as Donovan began running down the road. She could tell from his gait he was hurting.

"What did Eva mean when she said you'd understand about Marie?" Michael asked.

"I need to make some calls before I can fully answer that question. For now, let's get back to Guatemala City."

"We're headed there now," Michael said. "John, I'm headed up to the cockpit. I'll fly slowly so we don't lose the *Scimitar*. How are you doing on fuel? Can we keep the *Scimitar* aloft while we're on the ground?"

"That was my plan," John replied. "It'll make for a quicker turnaround so we can get back on station to assist Donovan."

Lauren had heard enough. They all had jobs to do. She slid into a vacant science station, removed the satellite phone, and punched in a number from memory. She entered her code and skipped through her voice mails until she heard Montero's voice. She listened to the message, disconnected, and then dialed the phone number Montero gave her.

"Hello," Montero said.

"It's Lauren. I'm calling from the back of the *Galileo*. Where are you? How are you doing? How's Abigail?"

"We're good. We're airborne on the charter headed to San

Jose, California. Abigail just dozed off, but she's great. We're having a blast."

"We have Stephanie and Marie."

"Oh, thank God," Montero replied. "Is everyone okay?"

"No, not really. Buck didn't make it, he's..." Lauren felt her tears threaten to push through at the thought of him. "I can't even talk about that right now. But I needed to tell you some things. Eva confirmed that her last name is, in fact, Rocha. She also told me that Hector Vargas is *la Serpiente*."

"Do we know anything else yet?"

"No, it's too soon. Did you turn up anything more on Marie's mother?"

"I did. A contact from the Los Angeles Police Department pulled a file for me. It looks like after Marie's father was killed, Hector abducted his own granddaughter and took her to Mexico. There's evidence to suggest that Marie's mother may have initially reached out to child recovery services, then abruptly stopped."

"As in she changed her mind?" Lauren asked. "Or she found someone."

"I managed to get her phone records. Her call pattern suggests she was communicating with someone in Los Angeles, someone using a phone registered to one Eva Rios. I'd say she found someone. Also, I spoke with Director Graham again. He's seen the security tape from the garage and it corroborated our story. He told me the dead FBI analyst was holding a burner phone. There were five calls made to the Mexican Consulate in Guatemala."

"Hector Vargas?"

"No proof, but the FBI is going back through all the international phone intercepts for that time period to see what they can find. We may get lucky and hear a conversation."

"Is there anything else?"

"I don't think so."

"Thank you for everything. Tell Abigail that Donovan and I love her, and we'll see her very soon. Keep me updated and give some thought about what it might take for me to bring Marie straight to California, for her own safety."

"I'll look into it. You be careful."

Lauren hung up and discovered William standing directly behind her.

"I overheard you," William said. "Rocha, Hector Vargas—how do you know those names?"

"I don't want to have this conversation with you right now." Lauren rubbed her temples with her fingers as she collected her thoughts.

"You've been digging, and I need to know what you've found."

"I'm not the only one digging. The FBI has a task force looking into you and Huntington Oil for any connection to Stephanie's kidnapping."

"To what end?" William asked. "What do they think I may have done?"

"The gist of what I know is that there's speculation that Stephanie's kidnapping may have been payback for your past dealings in Central and South America."

"Precisely what dealings?" William said softly, almost a whisper. "I'm serious. We're not playing games here."

"Are you part of the conclave?" Lauren matched his tone. "Are you a part of the organization that eliminated people so their assets could end up as part of Huntington Oil?"

"It sounds like you've already decided I'm guilty."

Lauren refused to back down despite the piercing stare from the depths of William's considerable intellect. The color had returned to his face, a bright crimson flush that left her no doubt that he was way past being angry. She'd infuriated him, and with the way she felt at the moment, she didn't really care. "The evidence is damning. Explain it to me."

"You're no doubt referring to the FBI report on Meredith Barnes. And I assume you know about Elijah Knight and the others I ruined. Be warned, the risk of asking questions is that you may hear answers you don't like."

"I'm listening."

"Donovan's father was a member of the conclave. His grandfather was a founding member," William said quietly. "It was a loose gathering of like-minded oilmen. There was never any price fixing or crimes of any kind committed. Their worst transgression was the occasional bought politician who would help further the business. Much of the same thing happens today, legally, through lobbyists and political action committees. After the death of Donovan's father, the conclave began to decay, lacking focus and leadership at a time when greed was viewed as good. Once Meredith was gone, and Donovan had left his previous life behind, I was on the outside. I sat on the board of Huntington Oil, the day-to-day operations out of my hands, but I became aware of certain events. I took a keen interest in a set of seemingly unrelated crimes."

"I spoke with former FBI agent Gordon Butterfield, and he pointed his finger at you as the man behind the scenes. In the last two days, Butterfield was murdered, and Elijah Knight is dead as well, probably murdered."

"Butterfield was a pompous ass and a bully. Knight wasn't much different, he just wore better suits. Knight was part of the conclave; he did unspeakable things. I admit I did use my influence on the board of Huntington Oil to arrange the purchase of companies I suspected of using kidnapping and coercion, even murder to gain assets. Then I personally destroyed those men financially. Once under the Huntington banner, I dismantled their wealth and power and left them broken men."

"You dismantled the conclave?"

"I ground it under the heel of my shoe," William said, his voice not much more than an angry whisper. "Each one of those bastards deserved worse than they got."

"For ordering the death of Meredith Barnes?" Lauren found it difficult to draw a breath as William nodded his head in confirmation. "Does Donovan know?"

"Of course. I told him years after the fact. At the time, Donovan was in no shape to retaliate with a measured response. I destroyed those responsible, but I never found the actual killers."

Lauren looked into William's eyes. The rage had ebbed, and what she found she might describe as hope. Hope that she believed what he'd just told her. Hope that they could survive this conversation, if not for themselves, then for Donovan. Lauren stood and went to him. She wrapped her arms around him and held him tight as if she could help support the burden he'd been carrying. Then she whispered. "I think I know who killed Meredith."

William pulled away and looked at her expectantly.

"Hector Vargas is *la Serpiente*." Lauren said. "Eva tracked him down."

"Why?"

"Her last name is Rocha. Vargas kidnapped her and her mother days before Meredith was taken. Her mother was murdered, but somehow Eva escaped."

"I remember it well. Her father eventually killed himself, and the family property went to Knight Oil. Do you think Eva's exacting her revenge?"

"Yes, it's my belief Eva has no intention of returning Marie to her grandfather, in fact, instead of demanding a ransom, Eva's been blackmailing Vargas into killing all the men responsible for the death of her family."

"Except right now she's running from Donovan. How desperate is she?" William asked. "Will she hurt him if she's cornered?"

"I don't think so. She saved him once already. She also made sure Stephanie and Marie were safe and treated well the entire time they were being held. But I think there's a bigger issue at stake here than getting Vargas."

"What could be bigger than Meredith's murderer?"

"Twenty-two years ago, a fifteen-year-old Eva was kidnapped by Hector Vargas, who I also believe kidnapped Meredith. It's possible that Eva and Meredith may have been held prisoner together."

CHAPTER THIRTY-EIGHT

Donovan, Glock up and ready, entered the small house, rounded the corner, and found Eva sitting at the kitchen table. Thanks to the *Scimitar* he knew that the cluster of dwellings were empty except for Eva, who hadn't run very far. She appeared to be trying to reapply a bandage to her arm. In the instant before she turned to face him, Donovan could see that she'd bled through her previous dressing.

"Why didn't you leave me out here?" Eva said as she looked up into the barrel of the pistol.

"I couldn't."

"I'm not worth the trouble." Eva lowered her head as tears rolled from her eyes and dropped to the table. "I kidnapped Stephanie, I shot you. I'm the reason your friend, Buck, is dead. You should have left me behind, or are you here to take me to the authorities?"

"No authorities." Donovan put the pistol on the table out of Eva's reach and gestured to her wounded arm. "Let me see."

Eva leaned back as Donovan pulled another chair around and placed it next to hers. She'd obviously searched the house and found some isopropyl alcohol, scissors, tape, and a roll of gauze. "You don't ever do anything the easy way, do you? This is going to hurt."

"Just get it over with," Eva said as she turned her head and looked away.

Donovan gently positioned her arm and then unwrapped the saturated dressing and placed it under her arm to absorb the alcohol. Then he began cutting small sections of the tape. "I admire your courage. I'm not sure I'd be as patient, or go to such lengths, to punish the man who kidnapped you twenty-two years ago."

"I'll never stop."

"Which is why I came back for you. I think we're after the same person," Donovan said, as he clutched her wrist firmly and then quickly poured the alcohol into the wound. Eva's entire body tensed from the pain. She tried without success to pull her arm free as a low moan escaped her throat.

Donovan dabbed her arm dry and began applying the sections of tape as makeshift butterfly stitches. Eva watched as he closed the wound and then gently wrapped her arm in gauze. When he was done, she sat back and tested her fingers.

"You're a very good medic."

"I've spent my whole life trying to heal certain wounds."

"That's not what I meant."

"I know what you meant," Donovan replied. "It took me a while, but I recognize the name Rocha. Tell me about Costa Rica. I'd like to hear your story."

"I've never talked about that time with anyone."

"I was there as well," Donovan said.

Eva's eyes narrowed. "You weren't one of them. I'd have remembered."

"Someone I know was kidnapped at the same time. I never saw her again."

"I *won't* talk about her. I never have." Eva's eyes flooded with tears.

"Why not?"

"If I had, Vargas would have known that I am alive. He would have come after me before I could get to him. Hector Vargas is the man who killed my mother, the man who—"

"Killed Meredith?" Donovan finished her sentence.

Eva nodded, the memory triggering more tears as she impatiently wiped them away with the back of her hand.

"Marie's grandfather, Hector Vargas, killed your mother and Meredith Barnes?"

Eva nodded. "And I'm going to kill him."

"Before we crashed, you told me that Marie's mother was in California. Were you hired to recover Marie for her mother?"

"No, not hired. I read about the death of Hector's son in the newspaper. He was every bit the animal his father is; a drug deal went sideways, and he was shot and killed. I thought Hector might come to the United States for the funeral and I would have my chance to kill him. Instead, he sent his men to grab his grand-daughter. I sought out Marie's mother, Alicia, who was in hiding, terrified that Hector would have her killed. I liked her, felt a kin-ship. She's a victim, as is Marie, so I offered to return her daughter."

"Whatever gave you the idea that you could take on a man like Vargas?"

"When I escaped from Vargas in Costa Rica, I knew I couldn't ever go home again. I moved north, trying to get to someone in California. Along the way, I did what I needed to do to survive, until one day I met up with a guy named Tyler. He wasn't much older than me, a runaway with a motorcycle. I spent the next few years in Los Angeles with Tyler, until he went to prison for grand theft. After that, I spent time with a skip tracer. We'd find and bring in people who'd jumped bail. During that time, I honed my investigative skills, and started looking into Costa Rica."

"What happened to the person in California you were trying to get to when you left Costa Rica?"

"He died in a plane crash before I could get there." Eva swal-lowed hard and wiped at her eyes. "There was so much sadness. He was a very rich and powerful man with no real friends. After he died, I had nowhere to go."

"We are talking about Robert Huntington, aren't we?"

"How did you know?" Eva eyed him suspiciously.

"It makes sense. Meredith Barnes, Robert Huntington. Did Meredith tell you to find him?"

Eva nodded. "She and I spoke a great deal. We both figured we were going to be killed. She always told me that if I ever made it out alive to find Robert. She gave me something to give him. Not that it matters now."

"May I ask what that was?"

"Proof that I wasn't some crazy. You figure that all kinds of messed-up people try to get to someone like Robert Huntington, for any number of reasons."

"Yeah, I suppose. What did she give you?"

"A locket she wore on a chain around her neck. When you open it, there's this tiny gold planet Earth and a beautiful inscription."

"To Meredith from Robert, one love, one eternity." Donovan recited the words he'd had engraved on the locket.

Eva opened her mouth to say something, then hesitated, cocked her head, and the truth seemed to come over her slowly. Her expression went from disbelief to shock, until there was finally a knowing look in her eyes. "You're him."

Donovan nodded without fear. "You finally found me."

"You bastard!" Eva jumped to her feet and swung at him with her good arm.

Donovan caught her wrist inches from his face, shot to his feet, and stood toe to toe with the enraged woman. All he could feel was guilt. He wrapped her in his arms and held her close until her fury burnt itself out and she was quietly sobbing in his arms. He had it coming, he'd been her beacon of hope, and he'd selfishly dropped out, and in the process destroyed her chance of deliverance. In a life filled with regrets, Eva moved near the top. Had she reached him, he would have known who Meredith's kidnappers were. He could have killed Hector Vargas twenty-two years ago. How many ways their lives would have been different had she gotten to him before Robert Huntington ceased to exist.

"I'm sorry I wasn't there for you," Donovan whispered. "It seems that Costa Rica changed, damaged, both of us."

Eva pulled away and looked up at him. "Do you know how

many nights I thought about her, the things she told me, and when I escaped, all I wanted to do was find you."

"You did find me. And Meredith was right, you're safe now."

"Do you ever think about her?"

"Every day."

"But you married someone else?"

"I did, and you'll meet her. She saved your life. I was ready to kill you at the house today."

"I remember. Does your new wife know about Meredith, your past?"

"Yes. My past is the source of our ongoing conflict," Donovan said and lowered his head at the thought. "We're separated because I can't seem to let go of the past, of Meredith."

"I understand, but I can promise you Meredith wouldn't be happy," Eva said. "The most important message she wanted me to give you was to move on. That life was short, and you of all people could accomplish remarkable things if you had the right partner to help keep you focused."

"She told you that?" Donovan remembered Meredith laughingly saying those very words one day as they walked on the beach in Malibu.

"She said that her work was finished, and that her death would help further her message. She was right. She also said that your work was about to begin."

Donovan found his own eyes beginning to fill with tears. "Did she blame me for what happened?"

"No, she didn't blame you at all. In fact, she said it was her idea to leave the conference and go somewhere so the two of you could be alone. She confessed that there'd been threats she'd not told you about. She worried terribly that you'd blame yourself, like you did about your mother's death. Meredith was brave. She accepted full responsibility for what happened to her."

"Were you there when she died?"

"I was there when he came for her. She knew. She'd been taken from the cell once already that day. It was when she spoke to you on the telephone, when she told you not to pay the ransom. She wasn't sad." Eva sniffed and wiped at her fresh tears. "I can't tell you how happy I am that she still matters to you. She'd told me she'd never been happier than when she was with you."

Donovan could only nod, his vision clouded by tears. He leaned over the table and supported himself with his arms. He felt stripped of all of his defenses. He stood, exposed, years of rage and guilt seemed to slough away in huge chunks.

"She loved you very much."

Unable to talk, Donovan nodded his head as a show of thanks. For years he'd pleaded with the heavens for the truth of what had happened to Meredith, and now that it was being handed to him by a woman he'd nearly killed it was almost too much to comprehend. That Meredith spoke to a fifteen-year-old Eva, who was now standing before him, impacted him in ways he couldn't fully fathom. There was the sadness of imagining Meredith as she neared the end of her life. Followed by the immeasurable relief that she didn't blame him, she loved him, and was at peace with her fate. Then there was a mountain of regret that Meredith had been insightful enough to send him this angel of mercy, and he'd bailed before Eva found him. The fact that he could actually act on this regret in a positive way was a miracle, and, for that, he was thankful. Even in death, Meredith had done what she always did, which was reach out to him and try to heal him. In her last hours on earth, she took a long shot to send a message he may never hear, and tried to soothe him, get him to move on and finish the life he was supposed to live. The same message he heard from Lauren. Despite how badly he'd failed at that mission, he felt warmth. Strength from Meredith's memory that he'd never experienced before.

"Is that why you faked your death? It was too painful for you to be without her?"

"It was a horrible time in my life. I probably wouldn't have survived as Robert Huntington."

"I understand. I wasn't sure I was going to survive that time in my life, either."

"How did you escape Vargas?" Donovan asked.

"It was the day after they killed Meredith. I think they underestimated the police response and the general chaos and rioting in the city. One of the other men, not Vargas, came to get me. He wouldn't make eye contact, so I figured he was going to kill me. There was shooting upstairs that distracted him. I broke free and ran as more shots were fired. I found a storage room with a small window and I escaped into an alley. I've been running ever since."

"We've both been running." Donovan held his hand out to her and she moved in close and clutched him as if she were never going to let go. They stood that way for a long time before Donovan finally spoke. "What would you have wanted me to do, had you found me all those years ago?

"Make me feel safe. Meredith said she always felt safest when she was with you. She said with you she felt like she could do anything in the world. My family was gone, I had no one, and I wanted to feel like that."

The floor beneath their feet swayed, dishes tumbled from the open shelves. With Eva still in his arms, he pulled them both under the sturdy table and closed his eyes as dust from the ceiling came down in miniature avalanches. The tremor finally subsided and Donovan stood, found his Glock and the radio in the dust-choked room, took Eva by the hand, and ran for the door.

Once outside, Donovan stopped at the sight of the volcano. Mt. Atitlán was boiling over with lava and ash. Two successive explosions erupted from the cone. Earth and lava flung into the sky, moments later, both thunderous reports reached their ears. Donovan winced at the fury. Without warning, another blast ripped the entire top of the mountain outward. Donovan pulled Eva to the ground and shielded her as best he could as the shock wave ripped into them. The cracking and splintering of trees, along with the sound of shredded buildings, filled the air. As the roar from the destruction of an entire mountain reached his ears, the oxygen was pushed from his lungs. Donovan fought for a breath.

He held Eva tightly as they were whipped by sand and dirt. When he risked opening his eyes, he saw trees snapped in half, buildings destroyed.

Donovan rolled over and squinted though through the dust at what was left of the volcano. Instead of a cone spewing ash into the sky, only part of the mountain remained. The entire southeastern section was gone. A half-mile-wide river of lava was pouring down the steep slope.

"Eva, come on! We've got to go!"

Her eyes grew wide when she saw the threat. "Oh, dear God!"

Donovan put the radio to his mouth as they began to run toward the road. "Michael, Janie! Where are you?"

CHAPTER THIRTY-NINE

The instant the Gulfstream's door was fully opened, Lauren hit the ground running. Janie and Eric had already landed. Lauren reached the open door of the helicopter and found the expectant faces of Stephanie and Marie. Lauren climbed aboard and hugged Stephanie, thankful she was alive. Her friend's ankle was covered with an inflatable cast, but Lauren could still see the pain etched in her eyes.

"Marie, this is my friend Lauren. I told you about her, remember?" Stephanie said. "She's going to keep you safe while I go to the hospital."

"I want to stay with you," Marie said.

"I know, and I'll see you soon, but they don't let kids in hospitals. Remember when I said I'd keep you safe?"

Marie nodded.

"It's still the promise I'm making to you, and Lauren can protect you even better than I can right now."

On the other side of the helicopter, a fuel truck pulled up to top off the tanks. Lauren reached out to Marie, and the eight-year-old tentatively took her hand. She pulled the child closer and was about to step out of the helicopter when William arrived. He pulled himself into the cabin and fiercely hugged his niece. They held on to each other for long moments.

"I'm fine," Stephanie finally said. "Thank you for coming to get me."

"I'll always be there for you," William said, and then turned to Lauren. "Thank you. I'm glad you did what you did."

"I'm sorry I doubted you." Lauren hugged him. "Now that Stephanie is safe, I'll make sure the photographs of her capture end up at the FBI. With some help, I'm sure we can get them to stop their investigation."

"I have faith," William said.

Lauren and Marie hopped out of the chopper and retreated to a safe distance. Stephanie blew Marie a kiss just as Cesar closed the door. Lauren knelt to be at eye level with Marie. "You must be hungry and thirsty. See that jet over there? How would you like a sandwich and some juice? There's also a bathroom."

Marie nodded.

Lauren took her hand and they walked toward the *Galileo*. She followed Marie up the stairs, but the girl abruptly stopped as she reached the top and found Michael standing there. "Marie, this is one of my closest friends, Michael Ross. He's the captain of this airplane.

"Michael, this is Marie. She's our newest passenger."

"Hello, Marie," Michael said.

"Are we going flying?" Marie asked.

Behind Lauren, the fuel truck pulled away from the helicopter, and its main rotor began to accelerate. Moments later, it lifted clear of the ground and accelerated across the field to the south. They were going to drop William and Stephanie at a hospital and then go get Donovan and Eva.

"Are we getting fuel?" Lauren asked.

"No, we're good," Michael replied. "We're three times faster than the helicopter. We'll give them a head start, and then we'll go. You two get settled."

Lauren put her hands on Marie's shoulders and walked her down the aisle, past John, until they were at the rear of the plane. Lauren opened the lavatory door and switched on the light. "There's a sink, soap, and towels in there. Make yourself at home. I'll be right outside the door if you need me."

Marie slipped into the small lavatory and latched the door. Lauren exhaled and leaned against the door. The moment the adrenaline stopped she was going to crash under the weight of Buck's death. They'd lost Eco-Watch members before, but Lauren felt a special connection with Buck. They all did. He was the man who'd come to the rescue on so many occasions. It wasn't as if they'd just lost a friend—they'd lost their guardian angel—and she felt exposed, vulnerable. She crossed her arms across her chest and fought the tears.

Through the window, Lauren caught sight of Michael inspecting the plane. She saw him react to something unseen, as if he'd lost his balance. Confused, she moved toward the window as the floor of the *Galileo* jumped and shuddered beneath her feet. She managed to steady herself and sit heavily in one of the chairs. Even though Mt. Atitlán was a hundred miles away, she could see a monstrous curtain of ash boil up above the haze level, followed by what sounded like a massive sonic boom.

Marie bolted out of the lavatory, terror in her young eyes. In the front of the plane, Michael rushed up the stairs.

"Craig, start the engines, we're going now!" Michael began closing the *Galileo's* door and turned toward Lauren. "Buckle up, this is going to be fast and dirty!"

"John, is the *Scimitar* okay?"

"We're fine, but I can't fly any farther west until we get in the air."

Lauren situated Marie into one of the seats and made sure she was buckled in tight. She could hear the big Rolls-Royce engines light off and quickly settle into an idle. She took a seat across from Marie as Michael added power, and the *Galileo* barreled down the taxiway toward the end of the runway. Michael lined up on the centerline of the runway and pushed the throttles forward. As the *Galileo* lifted free of the runway, the gear retracted with a resounding thump, and they accelerated and climbed steeply.

The Gulfstream burst from the low-hanging smog and haze into the clearer air above. High above, Lauren could see that the ash reached well into the stratosphere, propelled by strong upper winds. As the Gulfstream banked, her eyes followed the ash to its source. In the distance she saw that the entire southeastern quadrant of Atitlán had blown out. In a wedge that fanned out from the epicenter of what used to be the cone, she could see the destruction of the landscape. Trees lay flat, and fires had been ignited by a torrential flow of expelled lava. From where she sat, she had no idea where Donovan and Eva were in relation to the volcano, but if they had been directly in the blast zone, they never had a chance.

Lauren threw off her seat belt and went forward to where John sat. She lightly touched his shoulder so he'd know she was behind him. She studied the screens and found nothing recognizable—blotches of heat mixed with what looked like trees.

"Where are they?" Lauren asked quietly.

"The *Scimitar* is just now arriving overhead. The fires are going to make their infrared signatures hard to find."

"Call them on the radio!" Lauren felt helpless, her anxiety climbing, her thoughts turned to the source of strength she'd grown to rely on, and she realized once again that Buck was gone.

"Michael's been calling since we broke ground."

Lauren lowered her head. Of course he was. "Where are Janie and Eric?"

"We're considerably faster than they are, we just passed over them a minute or so ago. Once we find Mr. Nash, we'll vector the helicopter in for the pickup."

Lauren glanced down the aisle at Marie, who was looking at her, uncertainty reflected in her young face. Lauren forced a smile; her heart went out to the young girl. Marie was caught in the middle of a firestorm that was not of her making, they all were, and there was nothing any of them could do but wait.

CHAPTER FORTY

Towering far above, shooting up into the atmosphere, the ash generated its own lightning—electrical spider webs exploding within the cloud, the thunder booming above the omnipresent roar of the volcano. In the distance, Donovan could see trees igniting from falling embers.

"Michael! Where are you?" he said into the radio. There was no answer.

"Where are they?" Eva asked.

"I don't know," Donovan replied, as he scanned the destroyed buildings. In the rubble, he spotted something he hadn't expected, the shattered remains of a wooden boat paddle. He grabbed Eva by the hand, and they navigated the fallen trees, working their way away from the road. The terrain sloped away from the buildings, and Donovan found a well-worn path. Fifty yards later they came to a small stream. The gorge was steep; at the bottom, surrounded by sand, the water was moving, tumbling from one pool into another as it surged downhill. There was no sign of a boat.

"With all the burning trees, I think using the river will move us downhill faster than the road. Ready?" Donovan asked as he started down the embankment, still holding Eva's hand.

She let out a small scream as they slid down into the water. This part of the river was only waist deep, and Donovan held the radio over his head to keep it dry. Together, using a combination of wading, treading water, and floating, they allowed the river to move them away from Atitlán.

"*Galileo* calling Donovan."

The transmission was scratchy, but Donovan splashed his way to the rocky shore and stopped. He keyed the microphone. "Michael, you're weak, but I read you."

"Donovan! The *Scimitar* can't find you. Say your position!"

"We're south from the Cessna, in a valley following a stream."

"I copy. John is repositioning the *Scimitar* as we speak. How far south from the crash site do you think you've traveled?"

"Maybe a third of a mile. Right now we're in a pretty narrow gorge. How far out is Janie?"

"Ten minutes, fifteen at most." Michael said. "Can you hear the *Scimitar*? John says he's following a river."

"The river's too loud. We have to keep moving, I don't think Janie can extract us from here anyway."

Donovan and Eva pushed back into the river and once again began wading downstream. He kept looking upward, hoping to see either the *Scimitar* or the helicopter.

"The water is getting warmer," Eva said. They negotiated a waterfall by staying to one side and gripping the rocks as they carefully stepped down to the next pool.

Donovan hadn't noticed until she'd brought it up, but it was warmer. He looked out ahead of them. The rocks were wet, but the water level was a good foot lower. The water was not only growing warmer, it was also dropping.

"Eva, we need to move faster." Donovan looked upstream. "I think we may have a problem."

Overhead, the high-pitched scream of the *Scimitar* echoed through the forest canopy, faded, and then circled back around.

"Donovan," Michael's urgent transmission sounded over the radio. "You need to climb—get out of the gorge, now! A river of lava is flowing down the ravine."

Donovan looked up at the nearly vertical rock walls that surrounded them. Climbing wasn't an option. Upstream, the surging lava had choked off the river at its source. The water level continued to drop dramatically, until all that remained of the river was a smattering of pools. Panicked fish flopped in the sand and mud.

"It's too steep to climb," Donovan said as he and Eva began to run. "Michael, how far do we have to go until there's a place for Janie to lift us out of here?"

"John says that just around the next bend you're going to come to a cliff. Janie might be able to hoist you out there."

"Will she get there before the lava does?"

"John says 'yes,'" Michael replied. "But it's going to be close."

The wet mud and sand made it slow going as they moved downhill. Donovan kept looking behind them, expecting to see the torrent of lava that would envelope them. He kept studying the shore, trying to visualize a way they could climb free. All he found was sheer rock and scrub brush growing in the cracks. They'd be lucky if they could get ten feet up the wet rocks.

Up ahead, as they ran, Donovan could see an oval of open sky. The smell of smoke grew stronger and the heavy odor of sulfur filled the air. The sand and mud gave way to rocks, slick with moss and mud. As they neared the cliff, they slowed, walking carefully as they approached the precipice. Donovan grasped Eva by the hand, and with each step, she resisted. He glanced back to see terror filling her eyes.

"We need to get close to the edge," Donovan said.

"I can't," Eva said as her knees started to buckle. She closed her eyes as if to blot out the sight of the drop-off.

Donovan put his arm around her waist and eased her forward. He could feel her entire body tremble, and he remembered her fear of being up in the plane. Being out in the open must be far worse for her, he thought. She was nearly paralyzed when he could finally see over the edge. Donovan gently picked her up and stepped up onto a rock that split the river; now they were higher than the surrounding riverbed, and its surface was dry. The drop was easily a hundred feet. At the bottom were huge boulders amid a shallow pool of still water. If they had to jump, they wouldn't survive.

"Eva, we're on a flat, dry rock. I need to set you down," Donovan said as he carefully lowered her to her feet. She held on tightly as he pulled the radio out of his pocket. "Janie, this is Donovan. We're as far as we can go."

"Roger that, I'm five minutes away. We'll plan to hoist you out."

"We'll be ready," Donovan said.

"John, how far away is the lava?"

"You'll see it shortly—it's almost to the last bend in the river."

Donovan snapped his head around as the first red-hot edge of the molten rock surged, expanding as it coursed down the gorge. As the lava relentlessly moved toward them, they were helpless. They were trapped. He pulled Eva close. They didn't have much time. He decided at some point he'd jump, taking Eva with him, rather than burn to death.

Eva heard it first and opened her eyes, looking skyward. As Donovan turned, the helicopter came low and fast over the trees, swung steeply out into the valley, then pulled into a hover. Hanging nearly motionless in the sky, Janie guided the helicopter toward the face of the cliff, the hoist line already being lowered.

Donovan watched as the padded sling, looking impossibly small, swung back and forth from the cable. Janie moved sideways, inching the ring closer to where they stood. Donovan positioned himself as near to the edge as he dared. Rotor wash buffeted them both, making conversation impossible, and the ring hung out in space, ten feet away.

Behind him, instead of pulling away, Eva screamed and pressed herself up against his back. He turned and saw that the lava had picked up speed, now only thirty feet away. Vegetation along the banks of the gorge burst into flames. Looking at the molten rock seared his eyes; the heat was beginning to envelop them as if they were standing too close to a roaring bonfire.

Donovan turned and looked up as Janie banked the helicopter. The leverage she created swung the rescue harness even farther away, and then, just as Janie had planned, the harness reversed course and swung toward him.

"Eva, don't move!" Donovan yelled as he freed himself from her grip, calculated the arc of the harness, then launched himself over the cliff out into space. His right arm threaded the sling, and his entire body jerked to a stop, swinging high above the valley floor. Instantly, he pumped his legs and used his weight to keep his inertia going, just like Abigail in her tire swing. He spun to face Eva as he was propelled back toward the cliff.

Eva, eyes wide and unblinking, was standing alone, bouncing up and down as the lava reached the rock. Donovan braced himself, swung in, reached around her waist, and plucked her from the ledge. Eva screamed as she was yanked from the rock and swung away from the lava, spinning outward into midair. Clutching him desperately, she buried her face into Donovan's chest. He could feel her gasping as he locked his hands firmly around her and looked up at the helicopter.

Janie immediately banked the helicopter away to keep them from swinging back into the lava. Donovan breathed in the cool air as they gently spun above the valley. The river of lava was now a bright red-and-orange waterfall plunging over the edge of the cliff. He relished the rush of euphoria at still being alive.

Above him, Cesar began to winch them up toward the helicopter. As they reached the door, Cesar reached out, clutched the cable, and pulled them both into the cabin. He unhooked the hoist line and slammed the door shut.

Donovan lay on his back, spent. His breath came in huge gulps. Eva held him tightly. She sobbed tears of joy, and he pulled her close.

CHAPTER FORTY-ONE

"Donovan!" Janie called out. "I've got Lauren on the radio. She needs to talk to you. She says it's urgent."

Donovan finished his second bottle of water and secured the empty container. Below them was Guatemala City. The airport was only ten minutes away, the *Galileo* was already on the ground. He'd spoken to Lauren shortly after Janie had rescued them. He wondered what could be so important. Cesar handed him a headset. He slid it on and found the transmit button. "Donovan here."

"Hey, we just landed at Guatemala City. Vargas and his men have been here. He was demanding to know where his granddaughter was being held. He threatened Malcolm and Lillian at gunpoint. They had no choice but to tell Vargas where Stephanie had been taken. I think William and Stephanie are in danger, and you can get there faster than any of us."

"What happened when you called William?" Donovan asked, as Eva began to look concerned and motioned to Cesar for a headset of her own.

"Straight to voice mail," Lauren replied.

"We're on our way. Don't call the hospital. I want our arrival to be a surprise. I'll keep you posted and have Michael get the *Galileo* ready to fly us out of Guatemala," Donovan said, then pushed the button that would allow him to speak with Janie and Eric.

"Janie, did you copy all that?"

"Yes, sir. I've already changed course. When I landed earlier, the Centro Medico Hospital, being private, didn't want to admit Stephanie until William flashed his State Department credentials."

"Janie, how far out are we?" Donovan asked.

"Eight minutes."

Donovan watched as Eva began to peel away the gauze covering her wound.

"What are you doing?" Donovan said as he reached out to stop her.

"If we land with a bleeding woman, I promise you they'll take us straight to where they took Stephanie."

Donovan nodded and, while Eva made a fist, he ripped off each of his makeshift butterfly stitches until her knife wound was once again bleeding profusely. She pressed it to her chest, to the already blood soaked material of her blouse.

"Hospital in sight," Janie said over the intercom.

Donovan double-checked the Glock and once again slid it next to the skin in the small of his back, making sure his shirt and jacket hid the weapon. He looked over Janie's shoulder and found a modern white building. On the roof was a white circle with a red *H* painted in the center. Janie expertly set the 412 down in the exact center of the vacant roof. As she powered down the helicopter, a door along the perimeter burst open, and three people in orange vests ran to meet them.

Cesar opened the door and motioned for the medical staff to hurry. Donovan was easing Eva toward the door as a quick exchange in Spanish took place outside, and then Cesar turned, nodded that he'd been successful, and helped lift Eva to the gurney.

"Stay here as long as you can," Donovan said to Janie. "If they make you leave, circle and be ready for anything."

Donovan jumped to the concrete and hurried after Eva. A short elevator ride down and the doors opened. They pushed the gurney down the polished floor, and as they rounded a corner, they saw two men in suits standing outside the sliding glass door that led to the emergency department. Donovan recognized them from the hotel—they were Hector Vargas' men.

The emergency room consisted of at least seven individual cubicles. They were fully enclosed, making the job of finding Stephanie and William more difficult. Eva was whisked into an empty room and the door closed behind them. One nurse began opening cabinets and pulling out supplies the doctor would need to suture the wound closed. The other nurse took Eva's vitals and placed a compress over her forearm. They both excused themselves and left the room, assuring Eva that the doctor would be with her shortly.

As soon as the nurses left, Donovan stepped out of the room and began reading the charts hanging outside the occupied rooms. He located Stephanie's cubicle, and Eva followed as he pushed through the door. A woman dressed in scrubs was lying face up on the floor, a pool of blood spreading from her slit throat. Stephanie was on the bed, a cast on her ankle, and to Donovan's left was Hector Vargas, a knife pressed to William's throat.

"Stand down, Mr. Nash." Vargas smiled and increased the pressure of the blade on William's flesh for emphasis.

Donovan was caught by surprise, furious with himself for not having drawn his own weapon. Eva huddled close behind, and he felt her gently begin to slide his Glock from his waistband.

"Keep your hands where I can see them, Mr. Nash. I see you brought Eva to me. Thank you. Now, tell me where my granddaughter is, or I'll kill this old man."

"We didn't find her," Donovan replied.

"Bullshit!" Vargas hissed. "Eva, tell me where Marie is!"

"I have no idea what you're talking about," Eva replied as she gripped the pistol.

"Eva, I've done what you asked. I eliminated everyone you wanted. Now tell me where my granddaughter is being held."

Donovan felt her reach all the way around his waist with her left arm; the firing angle took William out of the equation. Donovan flinched as Eva fired, the bullet ripping into the wall next to Hector's ear. He ducked as Eva fired a second shot that found flesh, and Hector doubled over, holding his ribs. Donovan kicked the knife away as Eva planted a foot, then kicked Hector as hard as she could in the jaw. Hector's head snapped backward and he hit the floor.

Eva aimed the Glock at Hector's temple and steadied herself, as if she wanted to relish the moment.

"Vargas' men will have heard the shots." Donovan was the first to reach Stephanie, and he pulled her from the bed. "Eva, we'll deal with him later. Get the door. We need to get out of here, now!"

Eva led the way with the Glock. She burst from the treatment room and the hospital staff backed away. Vargas' men had just pushed through the outer doors, then stopped at the sight of Eva.

"Fire escape to the roof," William said as he led them toward a stairwell marked "*salida*."

Donovan ignored the pain radiating down his back as he took the stairs, carrying Stephanie. He heard two sharp reports as Eva fired the Glock, then slammed the door behind her.

William flung open a door, and daylight flooded the gloomy stairwell. As they burst out onto the roof, Donovan heard the welcome sound of Janie spooling up the turbine engines. Behind him, Eva fired off two more rounds down the stairs, telling him that their pursuers were coming fast. Gasping in the thin air, Donovan handed Stephanie to Cesar, then turned around to help William into the helicopter. He waved to Eva to hurry as she ran headlong for the chopper and leaped into the open door.

The engines reached full power, and Donovan could feel the skids getting light just as the door swung open and three men, automatic weapons at the ready, rushed out and fired at the helicopter. As he ducked, Donovan saw that the man in the middle was Vargas.

Slugs ripped through the aluminum skin of the helicopter, and Janie spun the machine in midair to try to make a smaller target. Donovan silently urged her to fly them away from the deadly barrage of bullets. They seemingly hung in space, not moving, when a shadow flashed across the cabin. Donovan snapped his head up just in time to see an object coming in high and fast from above. The *Scimitar* impacted at a steep angle directly between the helicopter and the gunman; black debris peppered the doorway, followed by a brief fireball that enveloped what was left of the drone, and then quickly burned itself out.

"Janie! Set us back down!" Donovan yelled forward, grabbing his Glock from Eva. The moment the skids touched, he jumped from the helicopter and picked his way through the debris as fast as he could. Two charred bodies marked what was left of the gunmen. Donovan slowed as he reached the heavy fire door that opened into the stairwell. He took a deep breath and flung it open, Glock at the ready. Splayed on the steps below him was Hector Vargas, wounded but still alive. Hector's eyes narrowed into hate-filled slits as he recognized Donovan.

"*La Serpiente*," Donovan said, stepping forward until he towered over Hector. "You and I have some unfinished business."

"Who are you?"

Behind him the door opened, and Donovan felt someone at his side. William.

"To answer your question, I'm Robert Huntington. I've come back from the grave to kill you."

Hector's eyes flew wide open as he searched Donovan's face for any truth to the words.

"I'm William VanGelder—the last surviving member of the conclave." William reached out and slid the Glock from Donovan's grasp. The pistol bucked twice in William's hand. Donovan's ears rang as Vargas' corpse relaxed and slid down the steps until it rested on the first landing.

William handed the gun back to Donovan.

"Why did you take that from me?"

"It was a murder, plain and simple. I have diplomatic immunity, and you don't. I'll deal with this." William drew out his cell phone and punched in a number as they headed back to the helicopter. "Oh, and talk to your wife. She found out far more about me than anyone was ever supposed to know. I think she and I are good, but the FBI is involved. We may have to do a little maneuvering to make all the problems go away. She'll explain it to you."

Donovan was about to ask questions when William put a finger to one ear to drown out the rotor noise and began speaking into the phone.

"Can you get us to the airport?" Donovan called out to Janie as they climbed aboard.

"You betcha." Janie replied, and moments later the Bell 412 lifted free from the roof, pivoted smartly, and headed north.

CHAPTER FORTY-TWO

The moment the helicopter touched down at the Guatemala City airport, Donovan jumped to the ground, turned, and helped everyone to the tarmac. He gave Cesar a heartfelt handshake and then made his way to the cockpit.

"Thank you both for everything," Donovan said. "I'll see you soon."

Donovan caught up with the others as William finally disconnected the phone call he'd made the moment they'd lifted off from the roof of the hospital.

"That was the ambassador," William said. "My diplomatic immunity has been stretched pretty thin. We all need to go as quickly as possible."

They all hurried toward the *Galileo.* Michael was waiting at the foot of the stairs. Donovan knew that no one but Michael would have flown the *Scimitar* into a kamikaze dive to save them.

"Good to see you," Michael said as the two old friends hugged.

"Thank you," Donovan replied, unexpected gratitude flooding his senses. "I don't know what to say. You saved us all."

"I told you I'd always try."

Over Michael's shoulder, Donovan saw three official cars come screeching to a halt. Armed men set up a perimeter.

"They're ours," William said. "Courtesy of the embassy, but we all need to go, now!"

"What about Janie and Eric?" Donovan asked.

"They're coming with William and Stephanie on the *Galileo*," Michael said. "You, and Lauren, Marie, and Eva are going on the other Gulfstream. We'll come back later for the helicopter, if we still have one."

Donovan, Eva following, hurried toward Lauren. Behind him, the first of the *Galileo*'s engines began to spool up. He climbed the stairs and wrapped his arms around his wife, hugged her tightly, and then kissed her. "I don't know how you put it all together. But thank you."

"You're welcome," Lauren said.

"Eva, this is my wife, Lauren. I'm pretty sure the two of you have a few things to discuss." Donovan heard and then felt the right engine being started. He spotted Marie, then turned to Lauren.

"Is Marie doing okay?"

"I think she'll be fine," Lauren replied. "She knows that Eva is a friend of her mother. In fact, I just got off the phone with some people who've been helping us. We're taking Marie to San Jose, California, to be with her mother."

Donovan's eyes narrowed as he looked at an equally confused Eva. "We're going to California?"

"I can't go with you," Eva said. "I have no passport. I'll use the chaos of the volcano to go into hiding. I'll get home, eventually."

"You're fine," Lauren said. "The immigration details have been taken care of. You're coming with us."

"How is that possible?" Eva asked.

"Apparently, nothing is impossible," Donovan said.

Donovan placed his hand in the small of Lauren's back as the flight attendant closed the main cabin door. They walked down the aisle toward the twin, facing club seats near the rear of the cabin. Lauren sat in the aisle seat, and Marie slid next to her in the window seat. Eva took the seat across from Marie, which left one seat for Donovan. Lauren helped Marie fasten her seat belt as the door closed and the left engine was started.

"You should have seen Michael when the four of you burst out onto the roof of the hospital," Lauren said to Donovan. "He's the one who immediately understood what was happening, that you might not get airborne in time. He never hesitated, he never even blinked, he just took control of the *Scimitar*, told Janie to hover over the roof in case she lost power, then dove the *Scimitar* straight between you and the shooters. Then he picked up the microphone and told Guatemalan air traffic control that the *Scimitar* had suffered a malfunction and that we'd lost contact with the drone."

"He's one of a kind." Donovan tilted his head. "How *are* we going to enter the country without Eva or Marie having passports?"

"Taken care of," Lauren said.

"Who's meeting the plane?" Donovan asked.

"Marie's mother, for one, and most likely some FBI agents. They and the US Marshals Service are going to help Marie and her mother with a new place to live."

Donovan nodded his approval. "Witness protection—nice work."

"I don't want to talk to the FBI," Eva said.

"I've arranged for you to receive immunity, in return for your testimony involving events related to repatriating Marie with her mother. We have it in writing. You'll be going with us to Washington, DC. Donovan and I will take care of everything, and, after you're finished with the FBI, I understand William has something for you."

"Money?" Eva's eyes grew wide.

"A deal is a deal, is what I was told." Lauren shrugged.

"Then I'd like to give half of it to Marie and her mother."

"That's incredibly generous, but there's no need," Lauren replied. "Donovan and I have already made arrangements for Marie and her mother."

The Gulfstream swung out on the runway and powered down the pavement, until the nose lifted and they pulled free from the earth and climbed skyward. Donovan looked to the west; the towering plume of ash rose from the distant volcano. He said a silent good-bye to Buck as they banked toward the northwest.

Once they leveled off, Donovan got up, found his suitcase,

and ducked into the lavatory. He looked in the mirror, at the eyes that reflected back. They were all that remained of Robert Huntington, and he also found something he didn't recognize. With the thinnest of smiles, he understood that for the first time in nearly a quarter of a century, he was seeing something besides guilt and anger.

CHAPTER FORTY-THREE

Lauren closed her eyes. She hadn't had any sleep for what seemed like days. When she opened them, Donovan was standing in the aisle. His long hair was still damp, but his clothes were fresh and his beard was gone.

Donovan ran his hands over his freshly shaved face. "That part's taken care of, the haircut will have to wait until tomorrow."

She smiled—her old husband had emerged from a hairy, dust-covered cocoon ready to face a different world.

Eva did a double take, then nodded her approval as she slipped past him to take her turn in the lavatory.

Lauren yawned and stretched. The flight attendant brought several blankets and used one of them to cover Marie, who was sound asleep. She took drink orders, and when she returned, she brought a tray of small sandwiches. Donovan put several on his plate and leaned back to eat.

"How long since you've eaten anything?" Lauren asked.

"It must have been yesterday," Donovan replied between mouthfuls.

"We won't have much time to talk in private until we get back to Virginia," Lauren said. "You do want to go to Virginia, right? I guess I shouldn't jump to conclusions. I suppose we could make arrangements to get you back to Montana."

"I'm going to Virginia. I want to see Abigail." Donovan looked at his watch. "It'll be really late when we land. Do you want me to get a hotel room?"

"No," Lauren said, as she took a sip from her bottle of water and helped herself to a sandwich. She'd put a great many wheels into motion, and she wasn't going to tell Donovan until the very last minute. What he needed now was rest, and, if she explained her actions ahead of time, he'd never be able to sleep.

"William said he'd talk to General Porter, Buck's uncle," Donovan said. "Tell him what happened."

Lauren nodded as her husband's eyes grew moist at the thought of the former Navy SEAL. The two men had forged a friendship out of a work environment, and Buck was a member of the inner circle of a tight-knit, Eco-Watch family. "Did William say anything else to you?"

"He mentioned that the two of you had a little dustup," Donovan replied. "He also said he thought you both were good."

"Yes." Lauren was relieved that Donovan seemed in no mood to hear all the details. "The FBI put some things in motion, but we have the proof that should shut down their investigation of William."

"It's not the first time he's caught their interest," Donovan replied. "You'd think they'd learn by now."

"Was I right about Eva? Was she there?"

"Yes." Donovan set down his water and looked at Lauren. "She told me some things."

Lauren nodded. It was obvious that Donovan wasn't yet in a place where he could talk about what he'd learned. She, herself, needed to understand that he'd talk about it when he was ready.

"So, we're taking Eva all the way back to Washington with us? What's the play? I don't want her to spend any time in jail."

"The deal brokered with the FBI was immunity for Eva, in exchange for everything she knows about Vargas and his cronies."

"Who are all mostly dead at this point. Does the FBI know about her connection to Meredith? Is her knowledge of that part of the deal?"

"I think that's between you and Eva. Did you tell her what your relationship was to Meredith?"

"I did. I had to, or she would never have told me what she

knew. For twenty-two years she carried a message for me from Meredith. She never told a soul until today."

"Then you need to talk to her. I'd say you both need each other right now. I think she could easily make the FBI happy with a detailed account of Vargas' activities, beginning with Marie's abduction."

"I do need her right now," Donovan said. "I can't just thank her and send her on her way with a suitcase full of cash. That's a recipe for disaster."

"Not that you need it, but you have my full blessing to help her in any way you can."

"That's important to me. In fact, I'm going to need your help and advice with several other things I've been thinking about."

Lauren heard the words she'd longed to hear. Donovan needed her and was reaching out to her first, instead of telling her after the fact. Perhaps it was a start?

Eva opened the lavatory door and stepped into the cabin. She was wearing the same clothes, but she looked remarkably fresh and clean, the dust and ash were gone. At the sight of the food, she grabbed a plate and helped herself, then sat down next to Donovan. "What are you two talking about?"

"You," Donovan said, then stood as he pointed toward the couch that ran along the wall. "Now, I need to grab a nap."

In the quiet hum from the engines, it didn't take long for Donovan to drift off to sleep. Lauren unbuckled her seat belt and motioned for Eva to follow her to the front of the plane. Lauren took a seat and offered Eva the seat across from her.

"I'm glad you and I finally have a chance to talk," Lauren said.

"How did you figure out who I was?"

"It started with some photographs, and ended with the FBI, the NSA, and your angel tattoo. I have a friend—in fact, she's the one who worked out your deal with the FBI—she's a brilliant detective. We know you didn't kidnap Stephanie on purpose. Then, when we figured out you were the one who grabbed Marie, but never asked for a ransom, we knew that you had no intention of returning her. You were working for Marie's mother, and black-mailing Vargas into eliminating everyone who had anything to do with the death of your family."

Eva nodded.

"It worked, because you'd figured out who they all were."

"I always knew who my kidnapper had been, but he was un-touchable, or at least in the eyes of a young girl. I was willing to kill him, but I wasn't willing to go to prison. So, for years, I watched and waited. I discovered he had a son living in Los Angeles and I began to dig into his life. That was when I found his wife and daughter."

"Did you kill Hector's son?"

"No. He was violent like his father, but without the brains. His stupidity got him killed."

"And then Hector came and took Marie away from her mother."

"At the time, Marie's mother was having problems. She had gotten into trouble with prescription painkillers. Hector viewed it as a weakness and decided that Marie would be better off with him, so he had her abducted. I came into the picture after Marie's mother had cleaned up and was actively trying to find her daughter."

"So you offered to help."

"Yes, I thought I could exact my revenge and return a young girl to her mother," Eva lowered her head. "Something I never had."

"So it was you that demanded the death of Gordon Butter-field and Elijah Knight?"

Eva nodded. "There is also a man who currently works with the FBI. His name is Curtis Nelson—he's Butterfield's inside man at the Bureau."

"He's dead," Lauren said.

"Good," Eva replied.

"Why not go after William VanGelder?" Lauren voiced the question just to hear the answer from a completely different point of view.

"At first, the evidence pointed toward him. But, as I dug deeper, he seemed to be destroying the men who'd hired Hector to do their bidding. I finally ruled him out."

Lauren felt a wave of relief wash over her. Eva had just confirmed what William had said, and this from the perspective of a woman who had been digging for years.

"You still haven't answered my question. When did you know I was part of the Rocha family?"

"I didn't for sure, until you told me. I had a hunch. Your age was about right. Your motivation fit. Then there's the fact that you shot my husband in the back to keep him from being killed."

"So, based on a hunch, you kept him from killing me?"

"If I was wrong, I suppose he could have shot you later." Lauren shrugged.

Eva's expression softened, and she reached out for Lauren's hand. "I know your secret. I know who he used to be, and I think what I was able to tell him was...helpful."

"In what way?" Lauren asked, desperately wanting to know more.

"From the moment I met your husband, I knew he was a troubled man. You could see it in his eyes. I've watched as he drifts off into deep thought, it's as if he goes to a different place or time. He once said Meredith's name aloud. Which is why when you called his room and identified yourself as his wife, I thought your name was Meredith. I didn't make the connection to *that* Meredith until he told me."

"Exactly why were you in his room?"

"Hector's men had found me. It was my own fault. I'd trusted the wrong man. They were going to remove me from Guatemala so Hector's men could break me and find Marie. I was a dead woman, but Donovan stopped them. Donovan took me back to the hotel, where he kept me safe while they figured out what to do next."

"Is that when you dreamed up your plan to run the ransom drop from the inside?"

"No, that was always the play. The first night I met Donovan was at the hotel bar. There was a plan for one of my men to make it look like someone was trying to kill me. I was going to play the victim to gain attention and sympathy, but Hector walked in, and everything went wrong."

"That was a pretty gutsy move," Lauren said, impressed.

"It was actually Stephanie who helped me fine-tune everything. I needed a way to get Marie out of the country, but I wanted Stephanie to be safe. She knew what would get Donovan's attention and allow me to control events from the inside. The outcome depended on me being long gone before Donovan and Stephanie were rescued at the lake. I had no idea a drone was being used to follow my every move."

"We're clever like that," Lauren replied. "I know it's none of my business, but, for my husband's sake, do you think you were able to pass anything along from Meredith that might make it easier for him in the future?"

"I think it already has."

"So, is my husband's secret safe?"

"Yes," Eva said, without hesitation. "Robert Huntington and I have a shared past, an event that forever changed who and what we were. It's why I had to hide. If it was known I was alive, I believe a great many people would have wanted to silence me. I vanished, and, in a way, so did he. If anyone understands what that's like, it's me. Our continued safety and freedom depends on keeping that secret."

"I can't thank you enough," Lauren said. "I do have a favor to ask."

"Name it."

"We're not landing in San Jose."

"I don't understand," Eva said, as she pointed up to the moving map display on the bulkhead. "It shows San Jose."

"The crew is in on the deception," Lauren said. "I don't want Donovan to know until we arrive."

Eva leaned closer. "What do you need me to do?"

CHAPTER FORTY-FOUR

The sound of the Gulfstream's landing gear locking down into place woke Donovan from a sound sleep. He sat up, groggy, and tried to orient himself. Lauren and Eva were talking. Marie was awake, sitting next to Lauren. He peered out the window and guessed there was another two hours of daylight remaining.

Tree-covered hills flashed below them. He was confused, where were the nonstop buildings and crammed freeways of the Bay area? He turned and looked at the flight display on the bulkhead. Instead of San Jose, the screen showed them on final approach for Monterey, California. Had they diverted?

"He's awake," Eva said.

"What are we doing?" Donovan asked, his mouth dry from sleep. "Why are we landing here?"

Lauren unfastened her seat belt and joined him on the couch. "I lied about San Jose. Everything is taking place in Monterey. Just be patient. We're about to be met by the FBI. Once Marie is reunited with her mom, and they're on their way, I'll explain."

Donovan felt the Gulfstream flare and the main gear kiss the pavement. The airplane slowed and turned off the runway. Moments later, they came to a stop in front of Monterey Jet Center. For Donovan, it was a strange sensation to once again be in Monterey. He thought of his former house on 17-Mile Drive, bordering the back nine at Pebble Beach. The peninsula was also where Meredith had spent the majority of her childhood.

The engines were shut down and the cabin door lowered. Heavy footfalls told Donovan they were about to have company.

"Mr. Nash."

Donovan turned at the sound of his name and found FBI Special Agent Christopher Hudson standing in the aisle. Lauren was the first to react. She and Hudson shook hands. Donovan stood and shook Hudson's hand as well. It had been almost four months since he'd met Special Agent Hudson, first in Hawaii, then in Laguna Beach, California. He remembered the man as being smart and capable. "What brings you to Monterey?"

"I'm still on the West Coast, and, since I know you, as well as former FBI Agent Montero, I was invited to assist with the transition. I wanted to come aboard and say 'hello.'" Hudson went to where Eva was standing and reached out a hand. "Ms. Rocha, nice work. It's a pleasure to finally meet you."

"Nice to meet you too," Eva stammered, hesitating before returning the handshake.

"And you must be Marie." Hudson knelt and took the young girl's hand in his own. "My name is Christopher, but you can call me Chris. I'm one of the people who helped find your mother. She's waiting inside. Would you like to go to her?"

Marie nodded.

Hudson stood as Marie slid out of her seat. Lauren gave her a hug and wished her good luck, as did Donovan. Marie waved goodbye to Eva as she turned and followed the FBI agent off the plane.

Donovan was fully awake now and turned to his wife. "Montero? Did Hudson really just say her name? What have you been doing?"

"Investigative things."

"She's your FBI insider, isn't she?" Donovan asked. "You called her! You called her the moment I left for Guatemala."

"When I made the call isn't really important."

"So, this is over? No Customs, Immigration, anything?" Donovan asked, still unsure of all the wheeling and dealing his wife and Montero must have engineered.

"Not quite," Lauren said.

"Hello," a familiar voice called out from the open door. "I have someone here who's pretty excited to see you two guys."

Donovan spun at the sound of Montero's voice, just in time to see the former FBI agent set Abigail down. His daughter let out a squeal of delight, ran down the aisle and jumped into Donovan's arms. She gave him a big hug and a kiss, then touched his face where his beard had been.

"We missed you!" Lauren moved in and Abigail slid from her father's arms into her mother's.

Donovan stood and gave Montero a brief hug, then watched in bewilderment as Lauren did the same. The last he knew, the two women weren't friends, they didn't even know or like each other.

"It's so good to see the both of you," Montero said. "And I'm so sorry about Buck. I know everyone was close."

Donovan inwardly winced at hearing Buck's name, then recovered. "Eva, this is former FBI Agent Ronnie Montero, an old family friend."

"It's nice to finally meet you in person," Montero said. "We have a great deal to discuss."

"You're *the* Ronnie Montero?" Eva asked, as she looked from Montero to Lauren to Donovan.

"We'll have plenty of time to talk on the flight to Washington," Montero said. "Think of me as a new friend, and as your liaison with the FBI."

"Aunt Veronica and I had fun!" Abigail announced. "I have a new pet. It's a humpback whale!"

"A stuffed one," Montero added.

"Aunt Veronica?" Donovan questioned.

"Abigail's the only one who gets to call me by that name," Montero said with force.

"It looks like they're pulling up the car now," Lauren said, then addressed Abigail. "We'll be back in an hour or so. Can you be a good girl and let Daddy and me go somewhere that's just for grown-ups? When we come back, all of us are going to fly home to Virginia."

"Can you bring me back something?"

"It sounds like you've been getting plenty of new things."

"We'll get situated and wait for you here," Montero said.

Donovan followed Lauren and Eva down the steps and out into the cool evening air of Northern California. The smell of the ocean and the trees reminded him of his long-ago home. As he thought of his past in Monterey, it suddenly occurred to him that Lauren was taking him to the one place he'd never been.

The drive to the cemetery was brief, and as they wheeled in through the ornate gate, Donovan felt his throat tighten. The driver followed Eva's directions until she instructed him to pull over and stop. Cypress and pine trees grew tall among the marble grave markers. In the distance, Donovan could see the ocean.

"It's beautiful," Lauren said.

"I used to come here and visit her grave," Eva said. "But I haven't been here for years."

"I can stay here if you'd like," Lauren said.

"No, I need you," Donovan said, and they all got out of the car as Eva led the way. Donovan clutched Lauren's hand as they wound their way to the base of a Cypress tree overlooking the rolling hills that ended at the sea.

Quiet tears rolled freely down Donovan's face as he saw her grave marker. Meredith Helen Barnes. The stone was simple marble—her birth and death dates carved in the polished face—a life that had ended far too young. Her parents had added a simple inscription: "One earth, one voice—forever." Lauren squeezed Donovan's hand to let him know she was there for him. He was aware that Eva was standing slightly apart from them, her face wet from tears. She looked at him, and when Donovan held out a hand to her, she took it and moved in close.

As Donovan drifted through his sadness, he understood that so many things had changed. Aftershocks from his past seemed to ripple the air around him. With Eva, he held the hand of the brave fifteen-year-old who was the conduit to Meredith's last days. Eva represented a miracle that Donovan had sought for twenty-two years. Lauren represented the future that Meredith had wished for him, and Lauren the only woman he could imagine spending it with. Standing there, he realized his weren't the tears of rage, or even regret, they were the tears of absolution and the hope for a better future. Meredith, through Eva, had set him free.

EPILOGUE

A week had passed since Howard "Buck" Buckley had been memo-
rialized at Arlington National Cemetery. Hundreds of people had
attended—both military and civilian. Donovan had met Buck's
family, his girlfriend Shannon, his extended family, and so many
other people whose lives Buck had touched. He heard over and
over how much Buck had loved working for Eco-Watch, and Donovan was pleased to announce that the new Eco-Watch ship under
construction would be christened the *Howard Buckley*.

The day had been an emotional one, yet in the end, Buck
had lived well, and, as his close friends had eulogized, Buck had
died well—unselfishly saving the lives of those counting on him.
Donovan spent some time with Buck's former SEAL team members. Each one of them explained that they would throw themselves on a grenade if it meant saving the others. It was how they
operated, and Buck had exemplified that dedication to duty.

Now, a week later, Donovan could let his thoughts of Buck
sit quietly in the background. He inhaled and took in the perfect Northern Virginia evening. For the first time in twenty-two
years, friends gathered at Donovan's country house. They were a
collection of special people, and they all had come, no questions
asked.

Abigail was having a day. At the moment, she was sitting on
Aunt Veronica's lap, with William on one side, and Stephanie, her

foot now out of the cast, on the other. Abigail was hamming it up as Stephanie shot pictures.

To William's left sat Eva, who was talking with Erin Walker, a reporter for the *Washington Post*. Between Lauren and Montero, William's issues with the FBI task force had evaporated. The mess they'd left behind in Guatemala City was a little more difficult to solve, but Eva's deposition and William's political clout went a long way in absolving William, or anyone at Eco-Watch, of any wrong-doing. Donovan then issued sizable hazardous-duty checks to every Eco-Watch employee who was involved, including Cesar. The success of the *Scimitar*, though limited, was impressive enough for the Eco-Watch board to authorize the construction of two more. The Bell 412 had been seized by the Guatemalan government, and Donovan had finally shrugged off the loss as the cost of doing business. They were working with Bell for a replacement.

"Donovan, look who I found," Lauren said, as she came out of the house with Henry Parrish in tow.

Donovan stood and the two old friends shook hands. It had been years since they'd last seen each other in Chicago, at Leo Singer's funeral. Leo had been a longtime mutual friend who knew both Donovan and his father, as well as Donovan's secret. Donovan wished Leo had lived long enough to be at this gathering. Despite the never-ending stress of being the CEO of Wayfarer Airlines, Donovan thought Henry looked well. "Thank you for coming. It's been too long."

"How could I say no to your lovely wife's invitation to attend a family get-together?"

"She's tough to say 'no' to," Donovan replied.

"I can't believe how big Abigail is getting," Henry said. "She's as beautiful as her mother."

"Thank you," Lauren said, then turned to Donovan. "I think we're all here."

"I guess it's time then," Donovan took his cue. The seven people in the entire world who knew his real identity were finally in one place.

"Abigail, honey, can you please come inside for a minute?" Lauren called to her daughter.

Montero lowered Abigail to the ground and she ran toward her mother.

"I'd like to introduce my good friend, Henry Parrish," Donovan addressed everyone seated on the patio. "I've known Henry since our days flying together at Huntington Oil. Henry, I believe you know William and Stephanie. That's Erin Walker, and next to her is Eva Rocha, the newest member of this little group. And last, but not least, is Ronnie Montero. You may have read about her in the newspaper a while back."

"Or on television, or on the cover of magazines," Henry added. "She's more famous than you are."

"As it should be," Donovan laughed. "The bar is over there, help yourself. Mingle and chat, I need to go help Lauren and Abigail."

"Anything I can do to help?" Henry asked.

"Relax and enjoy yourself," Donovan said, as he left his guests on the patio and went to find his wife. He found her and Abigail in the kitchen, putting the final touches on the refreshments. Several bottles of very expensive champagne had been opened and placed on ice. Donovan took the bottles out to the patio, Lauren followed with the glasses, and Abigail carried the napkins.

Once everyone was seated and the champagne poured, Donovan stood and cleared his throat. "I'll be brief, but I would like to say a few things. Thank you all for being here. It's been too long since a group of friends gathered at this home. You've made today one of the best days I've had in a very long time. As you all know, at times, my situation seems to make things complicated, for me, and for my family as well. A fact that has caused me to withdraw from the people I need the most. What I ended up doing was making things worse, for me and for them. Recent events have allowed me to take a long, hard look at the important aspects of my life, which leads back to all of you."

"My solution to this situation is to say 'hello.' I've missed you. Of all the souls in this world, the seven of you are the individuals I feel most comfortable with. It's my wish that we all be friends, or perhaps more than that—a family of sorts. I want you in my life, my family's life, and I want us to be a part of your life. In the past, I let the knowledge you had about me keep us apart, when I should have welcomed the fact that you respected what you knew, and continued to keep it a secret. For that I am forever grateful, and it's why you are the most important people in the world to me."

Donovan held up his glass. "To William and Stephanie, you inherited me, and from that moment to this one, I've been in good hands. To Erin Walker, if memory serves me correctly, you and I met right here at this house. You were trespassing, and a police officer introduced us. Thank you for keeping your promise.

"To Ronnie Montero, former FBI agent, and apparently my daughter's second-favorite aunt, we met in an interrogation room in Florida. We got to know each other as we chased down a terrorist, and you too, kept your promise. To Henry Parrish, we met on the job more years ago than I care to remember. You formed the foundation for me to become not just a privileged pilot, but also a serious professional. Thank you for that gift.

"To Eva Rocha, a remarkable young woman, who for twenty-two years carried a final message to me from Meredith. Eva, you humble me with your strength and perseverance.

"And finally, to my wife Lauren, and our daughter Abigail, I can't imagine a world where we're not together. Cheers."

Everyone raised their glasses and sipped their champagne.

"There is one more thing," Donovan said as he drew Abigail closer. "As a way to say 'thank you' for allowing me to live the life I've chosen, I wanted to share a little something to help each of you live the life of your choosing."

Abigail took five envelopes from her dad, and, with Lauren's help, hand-delivered an envelope to Montero, Erin, Stephanie, Henry, and Eva.

"Please, open them." Donovan watched the expressions as five people opened envelopes and discovered five-million-dollar checks made out to each of them; the funds drawn from an account William oversaw, money that could in no way be traced to Donovan's Huntington Oil fortune. Lauren hugged him as he took in the sight of this small gathering of people who had changed his life for the better. Now he'd returned the favor, and, for the first time in a very long time, Donovan felt whole.